Praise for
Angus Macallan and *Gates of Stone*

"With tense political drama and rip-roaring action in a fresh and believable Asian-inspired setting, *Gates of Stone* reads like a collaboration between Joe Abercrombie and James Clavell. Add ancient feuding sorcerers and a queen who would eat Cersei Lannister for breakfast, and you have the makings of an excellent fantasy debut. Angus Macallan is a compelling new voice in epic fantasy."　　　　—Peter McLean, author of *Priest of Bones*

"I meant to give *Gates of Stone* a quick look before I started reading it—and couldn't put it down. Angus Macallan is a brilliant storyteller!"

—Taylor Anderson, *New York Times* bestselling author of the Destroyermen series

GATES OF STONE

❧

A Lord of the Islands Novel

Angus Macallan

ACE
New York

ACE
Published by Berkley
An imprint of Penguin Random House LLC
1745 Broadway, New York, NY 10019

Library of Congress Cataloging-in-Publication Data

Names: Macallan, Angus, 1965– author.
Title: Gates of stone / Angus Macallan.
Description: First edition. | New York: ACE, 2019. | Series: A Lord of the Islands Novel; book 1
Identifiers: LCCN 2018010875 | ISBN 9780451490278 (trade pbk.) | ISBN 9780451490285 (ebook)
Subjects: | GSAFD: Fantasy fiction.
Classification: LCC PR6104.O535 G38 2019 | DDC 823/.92—dc23
LC record available at https://lccn.loc.gov/2018010875

First Edition: February 2019

Printed in the United States of America
1 3 5 7 9 10 8 6 4 2

Cover illustration by Greg Ruth
Cover design by Katie Anderson
Book design by Laura K. Corless
Interior art: key silhouette © VectorWeb/Shutterstock.com;
cracked cement wall texture © Abstractor/Shutterstock.com
Map by David Lindroth Inc.

ONE

CHAPTER 1

———— ❈ ————

Extract from *Ethnographic Travels* by
Professor Tolmund K. Parehki of the University of Dhilika

*Of the Seven Principalities of the Khevan Empire, Ashjavat least
resembles any of the others. It is the most southerly province, many
weeks' ride from the harsh snowfields of the Khevan heartland; it
is the most temperate and fertile region, the most recently acquired
in conquest, and the territory most profoundly affected by influ-
ences from beyond the Ice-Bear Throne's domain. Centuries of trade
between Ashjavat and the lush tropical islands of the Laut Besar,
the great ocean a thousand watery leagues to the south, have mellowed the inhabitants, one might even say civilized them, and created a race apart from the warlike barbarians of the north. Art and
music flourish here and Ashjavati poetry is rightly admired across
the world. Sweet red wine, rather than harsh marak spirit, is drunk
at the feasts for which the princes of Ashjavat are famous, and the
soaring beauty of the Basilica, the architectural jewel at the heart
of their glittering city, is the envy of the whole Empire.*

Katerina stared at the skeletal body of the Holy Martyr.
The long, carved hands at the end of the jointed wooden
arms were nailed to the fork of the Holy Tree above the
Martyr's head. The unnaturally stretched limbs and correspond-
ing angle of the torso meant that the ribs were absurdly prominent. Indeed, the emaciated body on this Martyr gave the rack of
bones a bladelike sharpness that Katerina had never seen on a

statue before, and certainly never on any living person. *You could slice gherkins on them,* she thought, stifling an impious giggle. *You could cut a loaf of black bread.*

This was the Southron style, she knew. She had seen these Martyrs at home in Khev in her governess's picture-books, and once in a dusty chapel window made of broken pieces of colored crystal that was tucked away behind the Imperial Palace. However, now that she was down here in this strange little backwater, now that an actual Holy Martyr statue was within spitting distance, she found the image grotesque—indeed, almost comical.

Her family, which was as old as the ice-bears, had always given fealty to the ancient Khevan Gods: brutish giants who strode about the heavens wielding hammer and lightning bolt and smiting humans whenever they grew bored of quarreling with each other. But the Emperor had not forbidden the new faith, despite its oddity, and the worship of the Martyr was spreading fast throughout the Seven Principalities. Accordingly, her farsighted governess had made sure that she had a firm grasp of the tenets of this bizarre new religion.

The archbishop of this same faith, standing before the High Altar of the Basilica of Ashjavat, was mumbling on interminably about the sacred duties of a wife and mother. Katerina let the words wash over her, only sampling a phrase now and then to relish its absurdity, and continued staring at the extraordinary statue on the wall behind him. She scarcely believed in her own Gods, and nothing, nothing on this wide Earth could induce her to give any credence to this ridiculous, skinny, half-naked wretch. It occurred to her that if the red-and-orange-painted Flames of the Unbelievers had not been consuming the Holy Martyr's stick-like white legs—and here she smothered another bubble of merriment—this malnourished fellow would certainly have expired from hunger in a day or so anyway.

The same could hardly be said of the bridegroom looming at

her side—Prince Khazeki might have embodied the very meaning of well fed. Not that he was overly fat. Indeed, thought Katerina, stealing a sideways glance at him, he was passably handsome in an exotic Southron way: long, muscular limbs, broad shoulders and a barrel-like torso. His blue-black hair, high cheekbones and dark brown eyes—inherited, she assumed, from his mother, a Han Venerable from the vast rice-lands of the Celestial Republic to the east of the Empire—gave his looks a pleasing quality. His considerable weight, too, gave him a physical presence that was appealing. It was a shame really, she thought, that all this prime Southron manhood would soon be wasted.

Prince Khazeki's strong right hand was grasping hers, and she could feel the greasy mingling of their palm-sweat as the archbishop moved on to the part of the ceremony in which he sternly informed the newly joined couple before him that the fleshly side of marriage must only be undertaken for the purposes of reproduction. This archbishop was a ludicrous fellow with an enormous white beard, a stiff golden cape, and a baggy red hat embroidered with silver thread. Katerina could not look at him without wanting to laugh.

A pair of massive, solid-gold urns stood at either side of the altar, one filled with the Holy Wine, the other with the Holy Oil and each tended by a junior priest in shining silver robes. Almost everything in the Basilica seemed to be fashioned from gold or silver—it was a dazzling place, no denying it, and Katerina had been rather impressed at first. Her young tastes had been forged by the austere sensibilities of the frozen north—dark pinewoods, thick black furs, white-plastered walls or plain gray stone, a discreet crystal vase here or there. Gold was scarce and used sparingly—one might catch the gleam of broach or belt buckle, perhaps see a single golden goblet set at table for the Emperor himself, but no lesser man. Here in the south, gold seemed as common as wood. From her governess's geography lessons, she knew that this was because Ashjavat was the nearest of the Empire's Seven Principalities to the Laut Besar, that legendary warm southern ocean studded with tropical islands. Gold flowed north from the Laut Besar, along with slaves and spices, timber and obat and wonderful tales about pirates, sorcerers, monsters and demons.

Katerina stared at one of the massive golden urns, as tall as she was. That quantity of precious metal, she reckoned, could keep an Imperial Cossack regiment in black bread and gherkins for about two years. Her efficient governess had taught her about the logistics of warfare, the cost of supply, the quantities of *materiel* needed, along with everything else. She studied the distorted image of the pair of them, bride and groom, prince and princess, reflected in the curved side of the golden vessel. She looked well that day, she thought: in the traditional wedding colors of white and red. Her long, almost-white fair hair had been gathered into a single fat plait that hung down her back and threaded with ruby rosebuds; her lips had been given just the lightest touch of cochineal; her large eyes, the pale blue of the summer sky over the Khevan steppe, had been skillfully lined with kohl; a crown of white roses adorned her pale brow; and the wedding dress—glossy Han silk the color of poppies—fit her like a second skin. A long train flowed out behind her like a trail of blood down the steps from the altar, where two of her bridegroom's owl-eyed nieces clutched the silver-embroidered hem. At her narrow waist was a silver chain from which hung the five golden keys of the gates of Ashjavat—a symbol that she would hold the Principality securely for her new lord and master until death should part them. That was the bargain she had made today with this marriage of two strangers: and she would keep it. She always kept her bargains. Next to the keys hung a short, slim ceremonial dagger, the golden scabbard encrusted with rubies and diamonds, the symbol of her duty to use all and every means, even including deadly force, in defense of her husband's rightful property.

Yes, she thought, she looked well—as she should. It was her wedding day, after all. And the sixteenth anniversary of her birth, to boot. Katerina smiled up at her big, handsome Southron husband. Today was the day that her life could truly begin.

The wedding feast had been interminable, a numbing succession of courses—one of the Ashjavat ladies had whispered to her that ninety-nine was the traditional number—served on magnificent golden plates but cool as contempt by the time they had made the long journey from the kitchens at the rear of the palace to the high table in the echoing Hall of the Ancients. Katerina had stopped eating after the twelfth course, and thereafter merely waved away the giant platters. The food would not be wasted, she knew, even when the two hundred or so noble guests who filled the lesser tables with their noise and stink were sated. The uneaten platters would feed the army of servants who had prepared the gargantuan meal and the scraps would be given to the poor who gathered at the gates of the palace in their thousands, awaiting their share of the wedding bounty. Instead of eating, she watched her husband, and dutifully filled his goblet with rich Rhonos wine, whenever it dipped below the half-full mark. She had only a single glass herself—savoring the sweet unfamiliar flavor as much as the knowledge that it had been transported two thousand miles from the Frankish lands at the western edge of the Empire to reach this table for her wedding feast.

When the slave-dancers came out and began their swaying, sashaying routine, she caught the eye of the Captain of the Palace Guard on the far side of the hall, leaning nonchalantly on his long spear by the door and watching the graceful girls with an openly lustful eye. He was a notorious gambler and rake named Jan Artur, extraordinarily vain of his cheekbones and long black mustaches, but with a reputation of excessive, even reckless physical courage. He was handsome, yes. His brown, muscular chest was bare and he wore the local loose silk trousers and a pair of pistols stuffed into a black sash around his waist. Artur stopped ogling the dancers and now stared directly at her, smiling broadly. The soldier wanted her, as she well knew; in fact she thought he was about three parts in love with her. That was good. She had deliberately set out to win his affection and loyalty by asking his advice as a newcomer to Ashjavat and flirting a little with him. Katerina had once playfully laid her small white hand on his smooth, bare, brown chest. Now he was very nearly in her pocket, hers to use for her pleasure or to dispose of just as she wished.

Captain Artur grinned at her from across the crowded room; he even had the audacity to wink. Katerina stiffened. The man was indiscreet. He would never do as a long-term lover, she decided. Yet the captain seemed to have absolutely no fear of Prince Khazeki's famous jealousy. Perhaps then some other practical use could be made of him. The princess raised her eyebrows, lifted her glass fractionally to Artur and drank the last sip of wine.

After that single glass she drank only springwater for the rest of that endless meal yet she was, in spite of herself, deeply impressed by her new husband. For his capacity for drink, anyway. Goblet after brimming goblet was downed with no seeming effect but a slight reddening of his swarthy cheeks and a brighter glitter in his eye when he smiled over at her. She had attended a few of the boyars' feasts back at home in the dining halls of the Imperial city, on one occasion being given the honor of sitting next to her father, Emperor Kasimir, as he lolled in the Ice-Bear Throne and basked in the false praise and boorish wit of his drunken guests. The boyars could all drink, even the youngest of those Imperial lordlings. It was said that a true Khevan went from drinking mother's milk to throwing down the fiery marak-grain spirit without stopping at anything milder in between. And the Imperial feasts had always been cacophonous affairs, reasonably decorous for the first hour and then descending into a riot of red-faced, bawling, sometimes brawling men—and women—who gorged and puked and stumbled about like the ancestral Barbarian Fathers, the sons of the divine sky giants. Even Emperor Kasimir, when he had been in his full strength, had swilled and sworn and yelled and wrestled with the best of them. She had herself had one vision-blurring glass of marak too many before now. More than once.

But not tonight. Tonight she had a task to accomplish. This Khazeki, this burly, wine-swigging, Southron princeling, would have fitted in well in the north, Katerina thought as she leaned forward toward him, arching her back and pushing her small, silk-clad breasts out in front of her. Her father and his drunken boyars would certainly have warmed to his bombast and bottomless capacity for drink. But she could not afford to indulge him too much: time was a factor. She fixed his warm brown eyes with her cool blue ones, and said: "Is it not yet the hour for the bedding, my lord?"

He was swift and vigorous, and no more clumsy than some of the men she had straddled in the north, and once he had pumped his seed inside her and rolled over, they lay together naked, sweat cooling, legs entangled in the blankets and furs. He asked her if she was satisfied and she said that she was. In truth she was merely impatient, but she had played a part for as long as she could remember and it was not difficult for her to act the sated, sleepy lover. It had been a long and tiresome day.

"Would my lord perhaps enjoy a pipe before he sleeps?" she said shyly, and when Khazeki grunted in affirmation, she slipped from the bed, quite naked, her flesh goose-pimpling in the cold air, and went over to the pipe rack and the obat paraphernalia on the stand in the corner of the room. She opened the obat box and twisted off a lump of the waxy gum inside, rolling it between her palms to warm it and form it into two round balls. She selected a long cedarwood pipe from the rack and carried it and the obat balls, candle and taper over to the side of the bed, set them down on the table. Khazeki completely ignored them. He gave her a lascivious smile and ran his eyes down her naked body.

"Later," he said.

The second time took so much longer. He plowed away endlessly, from behind this time, his hairy belly slapping noisily against her small buttocks, and at one point Katerina despaired of him ever finishing his rutting before dawn came and the whole household awoke. And then it would be too late. But he did, eventually, with one enormous thrust and groan, then he flopped onto the bed, leaving her to stagger to the water closet on trembly legs, there to squat and piss and wipe herself fiercely with a wiry hank of sheep's wool.

She mastered herself and came back smiling to the bedside. She held the long pipe to his lips and put the lit taper to the first amber ball of obat in the bowl. Khazeki sucked greedily at the mouthpiece, drawing in the smoke, which he held as long as he could, then released in a long, blue, pungent plume. Katerina caught the sweet scents of wood oils, resin and the sharp, burned-citrus tang of the obat residue. The expelled smoke passed before her face and she could not help but sip in a little of the blue vapor before it dissipated into the air. Even at secondhand, it was a powerful dose and she felt a softening of the edges of her reality, tendrils of pleasure creeping down her spine and along her limbs. Khazeki's eyelids were already drooping as she pressed the second ball of obat into the bowl and offered the pipe up to his lips. Once again he sucked in the dense blue smoke and breathed it out like a sleepy dragon. He lay back on the pillows and smiled at her, the pupils of his eyes now vast black holes that almost entirely eclipsed the brown irises.

"You will make an excellent wife, Katerina," he murmured. She smiled back lovingly, took a corner of the linen sheet and wiped a fine thread of drool from his slack lips. Then she walked around to the other side of her broad marriage bed and climbed under the blankets beside him. She lay still for a while, feeling the effects of the tiny amount of obat in her own bloodstream, and listening to his deep, slow breathing.

Today was the day that her life could truly begin, she told herself. Today was the day. For a moment she pretended girlishly that she did not have the stomach for this enterprise. But she knew, deep in her core, that she did. It was a small thing. But the vital first step on the road she must take. His breathing had turned to snores. So, it was time. She slipped from the bed and walked quickly over to the pile of her clothes on the chest on the far side of the room. She slid the ceremonial dagger from its extravagantly jeweled sheath on the silver belt chain. She tested the edge on her thumb. It was quite blunt, of course, not being made for real combat but merely for display at the ceremony; but the blade was the length of her hand, the point was sharp enough for its purpose and the steel thin and strong.

She stepped back over to the bed and looked down at the cheek of her new husband, even now prickling with a fresh crop of stubble. A hank of blue-black hair had fallen over his nose and she tenderly brushed it back into place. Then she placed the tip of the slim dagger an inch forward of his ear and, using both of her small hands and all of the weight of her shoulders, she shoved the blade down hard. There was a tiny noise—pock—as the steel punched through the thinner skull-bone at the temple and sank deep into his sleeping brain. Khazeki's eyes flew open. His right leg kicked once. Katerina worked the slim blade, left and right, left and right, in its bony slot. And her new husband lay still.

CHAPTER 2

J un felt another slug of hot sweat slide down his bare, brown ribs and bury itself in the scarlet-and-gold sarong that was wrapped around his loins. It was his only garment, save for a scrap of gold ribbon that tied back his long black hair, and it was already uncomfortably moist. The night was absurdly hot. Even two hours after the sun had sunk behind the sacred mountain to the west, the sweat welled and trickled all over his skin. The fan-boys had all been dismissed for the night, that was the problem, and the huge Pavilion of War was hot as an oven and dim as a cave.

The Pavilion was lit only by four single palm-oil lamps, and one was hung from each of the four pillars that supported the thatched roof. It was ostensibly empty save for Jun himself, sitting cross-legged on a rice-straw mat in the center of that wide, square space, with a horn-and-bamboo recurved bow in his left hand, and a light bamboo shaft in his right. There was no breeze either. The night seemed bunched and tense, as if awaiting the coming of the rains with just the same quiet eagerness as the parched lands and people of the Island of Taman. Jun took a long breath in through his nose, sucking the hot air down into his lungs; then he released it slowly through his mouth. *Extend the senses,* he told himself, mimicking War-Master Hardan's precise, clipped diction. *Feel out into the darkness. Be at one with the night.*

It was no use; Jun's mind was wandering. He had been sitting here for the best part of an hour, holding the bow and arrow and waiting for one of four targets—man-sized rice bags stuffed with straw—on the four sides of the Pavilion to be released from the eves. They would swing down and he would nock, draw, loose the arrow, skewer the bag—and so call an end to this ridiculous so-called training session. He wanted a long, cold drink. He wanted to take a dip in the Moon Pool—his favorite of all the swimming places in the Watergarden—and then emerge dripping to lie naked on the silk cushions in his airy apartments while one of the servants fanned him dry.

Hardan was certainly taking his time—the cruel old bastard. Jun's orders from his trainer had been quite clear: sit and wait and shoot when a target drops. And Jun did not quite dare to disobey the War-Master's explicit orders—the Gods knew why—he was a ridiculous old fart, a buffoon in his bamboo armor and stiff cloth-of-gold headdress. Even his kris was absurd. The wavy-bladed sword was far too long, easily the length of Jun's outstretched arm, and when Hardan tucked its scabbarded bulk into his sarong-sash at the back it stuck out in a most awkward and vulgar manner. He didn't even try to be elegant, or so it seemed to Jun. No breeding, that was the issue.

Yet there was something terrible about him that commanded Jun's respect: a residual air of black menace, a whiff of the feral blood-stink of the battlefield—even if he had not swung that over-long kris in anger for twenty years or more.

A pair of sweat-beads began a long parallel journey down Jun's spine. Damn the man. Jun was not afraid of him. He was a prince of the blood, heir to the Gods-blessed Kingdom of Taman, beloved only child of the Son of Heaven. Hardan was peasant-born. A nobody. A prince should not be intimidated by a warmongering oaf with no sense of either style—or timing. Jun decided that he would wait a hundred heartbeats more and then simply get up and leave the Pavilion of War and go off and find something to drink. Perhaps later he might even step out of the Watergarden and make his way down to the village by the sea to watch the shadow-puppet play. There might be a cooling breeze off the ocean and there were often pretty village girls there who were only lightly guarded by their rapt mothers. No, too much effort for such a hot night. He would summon one of the palace maids to his chambers, encourage her to drink a little rice wine, offer her a few coins or a pretty necklace and . . .

Something white flashed in the corner of his eye. Jun snapped his head to the left, saw the big rice bag beginning to swing downward. With almost no conscious thought, in one smooth movement, he lifted the bow, nocked the bamboo arrow to the string, drew the cord back to his ear—and loosed. The shaft flew—smack!—and punched into the stuffed rice sack, dead center, before it had even begun the upswing.

Jun let out a small whoop of triumph. He put down the bow and began to get to his feet, his joints stiff after such a long stillness. Halfway up, Jun froze. He saw the second rice bag swinging, down from the eves to his right, on the opposite side of the Pavilion. He stared at it, unable to move, as it completed its slow arc, down and up into the gloom of the Pavilion's ceiling, and began the reverse journey. Belatedly he fumbled for his bow by his feet, his clumsy reaching hand knocking over the quiver of arrows to spill the shafts, the steel heads clattering across the polished-stone floor. He gathered the loose arrows, dropping some of them in his panic, then releasing all but one and finally getting it nocked on the string. He felt a touch of cool metal on the back of his neck and heard a clipped and horribly familiar voice say, "By now you would be a dead man, my prince."

Jun lay naked and spread-eagled on the huge pile of silk cushions. The drops of water from his swim had stained the expensive fabric, leaving it black and wrinkled—but he did not care. An ancient retainer, a fattish little fellow with long gray hair who seemed at least a thousand years old, was crouched beside him fanning his body with a huge leaf-shaped instrument woven from palm fronds. For the first time that enervating day, Jun felt deliciously cool. He rolled over onto his side and picked up a sheet of palm leaf and studied the dozen lines of spidery black scrawl the page contained. *The Last Dance of the Dragonfly.* He liked his title, but the rest of the poem seemed a little less brilliant than it had the night before when, after three pipes of prime-quality obat, it had come to him all of a piece, no doubt a gift from goose-winged Hureshi, God of Writing, Poetry and Wisdom and he had written it down in a feverish hurry lest the scintillating words fade from his mind. Had he really described the dying dragonfly as the color of a fresh scab? It seemed a rather ugly way of saying dark red. Did he want ugly? Perhaps he should say that its four wings were the color of a mortal wound—but that seemed a little off, too.

Jun decided he was too tired for poetry. He stretched out a languid hand to his right. The servant, with near-clairvoyant anticipation, pressed a tiny porcelain cup of chilled rice wine into his groping fingers. Jun knocked it back in one, belched politely and handed back the delicate cup without once glancing at the old man.

He rolled onto his belly and looked out through the open shutters of his private pavilion at the tranquil darkness of the Watergarden. The hot-weather home of the Son of Heaven and his family, the Watergarden was a series of interlinked square pools, brimming with fresh springwater. The pools were joined by statue-lined walkways, filled with lily pads and clumps of tall bamboo, and dotted with waterspouts that tinkled delightfully, driven by a complicated Han plumbing system beneath. The various pavilions that sheltered the people of the court from the fierce heat were arranged around the outside of the pools, so that each one was no more than a dozen feet from a cool, lapping surface.

The fat full moon was reflected from the nearest pond, making the garden almost as light as in daylight. The only sound was the gulp of the blue-and-white carp taking a night insect from the water's surface and the gentle rustle as the bamboo leaves caught the merest whisper of wind.

This was just how things should be, Jun thought to himself, calm and ordered. Everything in the place that the Gods had decreed for it—the insect eaten by the carp, the carp speared during the day by darting, jewel-bright kingfishers, and man engaged in contemplation on the banks of this charming watery universe. This Watergarden was a place of beauty, a place that ill-bred boors such as War-Master Hardan could never understand.

Jun cringed inside as he recalled the trainer's words to him after missing the second rice sack and allowing the veteran to sneak up behind him. The War-Master had wielded the phrases as efficiently as he wielded his weapons. Woefully incompetent. Sloppy. Weak-willed. Lacking in sufficient military discipline. Jun had no desire at all to be filled to the brim with military discipline—whatever *that* was. He wanted to lie here on these cushions and ponder the secrets of the universe. Maybe write another line or two about dragonflies. He was a soul-rich poet not a bloodlusting soldier, and what use anyway was all this training? The hours he spent with bow and sword. The endless repetitions of the strikes, blocks and throws of the Han unarmed-combat style that Hardan favored. He had no ambitions to go to war—and Taman was too insignificant, too poor to attract the ire of the great powers of the Laut Besar. It was a foolish waste of time. He'd make his protests about the War-Master's behavior tomorrow at the council before the Son of Heaven himself.

Yet Jun was not much looking forward to that meeting. Hardan had told him that he would be reporting his shortcomings to his father at the monthly council meeting the next day, and advised Jun to be there, sober and contrite, to listen to the charges against him. Insubordination. Insolence to a superior officer. Absence from a training session without prior consent (after one gargantuan obat party with two lovely and willing girls from the south, Jun had been too exhausted at noon to climb out of his bed). Punishment would no doubt be dire: confinement to his apartments for a day or two, loss of his allowance for a week, maybe two weeks, something of that draconian order.

The prince could well imagine his father's pained expression, the old man with his kindly, round face and halo of fine white hair, his stiff, embroidered jacket and gold-crusted sarong, a bony, brown finger tap-tapping on the hilt of the Kris of Wukarta Khodam. This was the ancestral sword of the Wukarta, the royal family of Taman, a long, thin, decrepit blade, notched and pitted, and said to be more than a thousand years old. It was drawn from its much-newer oiled-walnut scabbard and set in its stand at the Son of Heaven's right hand at every royal council meeting, as it had been for centuries. The sword, the Khodam as it was known, was a legendary blade: it was claimed that it had been forged by the divine Grandfather Pande himself, ancestor of the blacksmiths' clan, when the world was still young. Its magic could only be awoken by a drop of sacred blood from the true line of his family but, once roused, so the old legends went, the sword had an awesome power.

It was all nonsense, of course. Many of the old princely families scattered around the rim of the Laut Besar had treasured objects that they claimed were magical, cups that never emptied, carpets that could supposedly fly, arrows that never missed their marks—tales for children and ignorant peasants. Jun had never seen the Khodam wielded in anger but he was certain that the frail, ancient metal would fracture at the first clash.

But it did undeniably have some more prosaic power: whenever the Son of Heaven wished to shame Jun he gently laid his hand on the hilt of the Khodam and invoked the ancestors, asking his son what the venerable dead would have made of his childish actions. And, Gods curse it, it never failed to work: Jun always felt the weight of the disapproval of the ancestral spirits when the old man solemnly touched the old sword. He remembered then that his father had been a noted warrior in his youth, and in his heart he knew himself to be a disgrace to his illustrious family, to the generations of dead Wukarta warriors. It would be the same tomorrow. He would squirm; his father would lecture him sadly, patiently; War-Master Hardan would smirk from the ranks of the councillors at the Son of Heaven's left.

Well, that was tomorrow. Tonight was tonight. Jun reached out another languid hand, received another tiny cup of wine and sank the draft in one. His belly felt pleasingly warm. His limbs cool. His mind aglow. The shadow play at the village by the sea would be in full swing now; everyone would be there. There might be a plump suckling pig, stuffed with saffron rice and roasting on the coals. Perhaps he would indeed stir himself and go down there, catch himself a nice salty fisher girl . . .

The prince frowned. He was looking in the direction of the fishing village. Something was wrong. At the far edge of the Watergarden, beyond the wall of shaped volcanic stone, above the big ceremonial gates, the air was orange-red, flickering. The smell of smoke came to him, harsh in his nostrils. And sounds. Could those be screams? He turned to the servant—and saw that the old man was gone. Disappeared. The wine flask and the fan were placed neatly by the edge of his cushion pile, but the wrinkled gnome was nowhere to be seen. Jun made to call for him but realized that he did not know his name. He did not know any of their names. There was no need to know their names—it was not as if he was ever going to converse with them. He shouted: "Hey!" and clapped his hands loudly. No response.

Jun got slowly to his feet. He could not understand what was happening. Something was burning beyond the walls—could it be the huddle of filthy dwellings on either side of the gate, the line of shanties occupied by the sweepers, the Dewa, the lowest caste of servants who emptied the privies, slaughtered the pigs, gutted the fish and dealt with all the daily unpleasantness that no one else wanted to sully their hands with? Who would want to burn their homes? Who—frankly—would want to go anywhere near their stinking hovels?

He shouted "Hey!" again. And this time he could see the dark shapes of people coming out of the pavilions around the edges of the square pools. Lanterns were being lit. Torches sparked and flamed. He saw his father standing in front of the Royal Pavilion, half-dressed in a sleeping sarong but bare chested, with his body servant beside him and one or two of the palace women exclaiming and pointing over the wall at the smoke and flames. And there was Hardan, his bamboo armor strikingly yellow in the torch-light, his long kris sticking out awkwardly as usual. He had a score of men of the royal guard with bamboo pikes mustered behind him. He was issuing orders, gesturing at the gate. But Jun could not hear his words.

There was a tearing crash—shockingly loud. The wooden double doors of the Watergarden burst open. A wave of yelling strangers burst through the portal, hundreds of armed men, shattering the tranquility of the palace, tumbling down the steps like a breaker on the beach and almost falling into the first pond of the garden. One man dropped a brutal-looking chopper, and only prevented himself from falling into the Ghost Tiger Pool by catching hold of a stone statue of that noble animal, one of a pair that guarded the walkway to the Royal Pavilion. The tide of men, shouting, shoving, steel blades glinting—were now pouring down the central walkway between the pools toward War-Master Hardan, the tiny royal guard, his aged father and his terrified servants.

Jun was paralyzed by this sudden, appalling entrance. He

could see the intruders clearly now, backlit by the leaping flames in the gaping entrance. The Dewa shantytown was burning savagely, and beyond Jun could make out leaping flames in the fishing village beyond, only occasionally obscured by rolling banks of smoke. The Watergarden was filled with menacing strangers. And more were coming in behind them, spreading out left and right from the gates, waving their weapons. None was armed or dressed alike: Jun had only the impression of a herd of stampeding beasts in colored rags with flashing blades, screaming mouths and eyes rolling in skull-like faces. Missiles hissed out of the mass of attackers, arrows and javelins. A musket fired. Hardan was shouting at his guards, trying to get them into line at the end of the walkway between the enemy and the Son of Heaven. Getting the pikes lowered against the foe. The royal guard started forward in a double line, shouting: "Wukarta! Wukarta!" Their long spears wobbling up and down out in front.

They drew blood. The pikemen stabbed into the mass of intruders, and Jun could see men falling, screaming, and the pike points come back bloody. A few of the intruders got past the pike heads and crashed into the wall of guardsmen. And the War-Master in the center of the front rank met them, doing terrible execution with his overlong kris. The line held, the spears punching forward, skewering the foe, other guardsmen, face-to-face with their enemies, stabbing close quarter with their long knives. Hardan hacked the sword arm off one yelling fiend. But muskets barked from the crowd of enemy on the walkway, arrows flew and men of the royal guard stumbled and fell, leaving dangerous gaps in the line.

Then attackers gathered their courage, and suddenly surged forward. They brushed aside the inexpertly held pikes, leaped into their thin ranks and rolled over the lot of them in one swift, howling charge. The pitiful handful of royal guardsmen was entirely devoured. Dull blades made more terrible by the flashing firelight

chopped down and came up bloody, hacked bodies spilled sideways, splashing into the black water. Shrieks of pain and shouts of
crazed laughter filled the air.

Jun knew that he must not stand idle but he could not move his
legs. They seemed glued to the stones of the ground. His mouth
was wide open. His eyes wider. It did not seem real—perhaps
this was all just some terrible but very lifelike obat dream.

He saw Hardan erupt out of the huddle of writhing bodies at
the end of the central walkway by the Royal Pavilion, his long kris
swinging. He took the head clean off a bald fellow with a long
pigtail. He severed the shoulder and arm from another heavily
tattooed man—then a long spear stabbed him hard in the side, the
steel point crunching through the yellow-bamboo armor. Hardan's body jerked with the impact. He roared, fell to his knees; the
spear was retracted. But the War-Master lurched up again and
turned to face his foe, the kris lifted high. Hardan stepped forward. At the same moment, a long-handled ax looped out of the
mass of foemen and hacked into the side of his face and Hardan
fell back to one knee, the blood black on his cheek. The axman
pulled his blade free, swung again, and the top half of Hardan's
skull wheeled away and splashed into the Moon Pool.

The War-Master's death spurred Jun into movement: he darted
back into the pavilion, rushed through the first room and into the
second. In the darkness he scrabbled with the lock of the chest
that held his most precious possessions. He got the big lid open
and rummaged inside to find bow and quiver. Then he hurtled
back to the entrance to his apartments and looked out in absolute
horror.

The Watergarden was already burning. The enemy were all
over the paths, in and out of the pavilions—hundreds of unfamiliar faces, savage in the leaping flames, gleeful—some already
splashing playfully in the pools, a knot of men by the Pavilion of
War crouched over a screaming girl. He saw his father by the

steps of the Royal Pavilion, a lone pikeman at his back, two servants with long knives on either side.

His father, naked but for his sleeping sarong, had the Khodam in his right hand, its pitted steel glittering in the light from the fat moon. As Jun watched, the Son of Heaven lightly touched the palm of his left hand to the wavy blade, pulled it down, the metal slicing through the skin, and immediately a pulse of color seemed to leap from the touch of his blood and expand through the blade, surging up its entire length, changing its ancient silver to a deep and fiery red.

Jun could hardly believe his eyes.

The Khodam was now a tongue of flame in his father's hand. A pair of shaven-headed men, their faces painted with horizontal yellow stripes, rushed at the king, curved swords slashing down at his bare head. He ducked and swept the Khodam across his front and the two men parted at the middle, four sections tumbling, blood jetting high, as if they were made of no more than bean curd. Then a mass of men, a dozen at least, followed them in, hurling themselves at the slender old man with the blood-red flaming sword. His father whirled the blade in a complicated pattern, carving into the crowd, arms, legs spinning away, bodies falling, piling on the flagstones, slipping into the nearest pools. An arrow lanced out from the mass, missed his father and took the servant behind him in the throat. His father advanced, the sizzling Khodam held high and to the right. He slashed diagonally through an iron-armored fellow, slicing him through from shoulder to hip. A spearman ran in, jabbed at the half-naked figure, his long, probing shaft immediately hacked away; then his father leaped quickly in and separated the man from his head. A space opened up between the Son of Heaven with the terrible red blade and his horde of enemies.

Jun stood and stared, his bow and arrows forgotten in his hands. Forty paces away, the Son of Heaven was standing alone, the Khodam brandished high, the mob of a hundred jostling men on the walkway between two pools held at bay by its glowing, ruddy power. A spear arced out, and his father jumped nimbly out of its path.

A tall, slim figure in a long, gauzy gray cloak stepped forward out of the mass of enemies. He held out his arms wide, as if holding back the tide of men. His only weapon was a long black staff. At the head of the staff was a large green jewel, the size of a hen's egg, which was protected by a thin curve of sharp, shiny steel, like a miniature scimitar blade, which rose out of the wood of the staff to curl over the top of the jewel and end in a needle-point. The man's headdress was an elegant fan of starched, pure white peaks of decreasing size. Through the thin cloak, Jun could make out a black-and-white-checkered sarong and green silk jacket. His narrow, dark-skinned face was lit from beneath by a dropped and guttering torch on the causeway, and Jun could see it perfectly clearly: a broad, flattened nose, high cheekbones, a slash for a mouth and two large, dark, hooded eyes.

The tall man said something quietly to his father, and Jun heard his father laugh bitterly, and lift the Khodam higher. The Son of Heaven boldly stepped toward the gray-clad stranger, who grasped the bladed head of his staff and gripped. Jun could see the blood ooze from between the stranger's fingers as the flesh of his palm was forced onto the sharp steel and the green jewel suddenly seemed to throb with life. The man gave a high, harsh cry, like a word of command; then there was a sound like an axman splitting the trunk of a palm tree, a creak that grew into a deafening crack. The gauzy cloak fluttered down, a buzzing filled the air and a black amorphous mass boiled out of its folds.

A swarm.

There was no sign at all of the tall stranger. He had utterly vanished. Jun's father shouted in fear and stepped back, but the swarm, now spreading out and distinguishable as a mass of black flies glinting with flecks of iridescent green, the whole teardrop-shaped and the size of a house, rose in the air high above his head, hovered above the raised Khodam and descended. It swooped down onto the Son of Heaven, smothering him. The night was vibrating with the deafening saw of insects. Jun saw the flaming blade of the ancient kris sweep through the mass of flies, a few insects exploding, popping with flashes of brilliant green, their husks falling like thin rain wherever the sword touched, but thousands upon thousands of flies were all over his father, a shiny, heaving mass, tiny bodies crawling into every orifice, eyes, nose, mouth, ears, pulsing like a living black carpet over his entire body.

The hum took on a deeper, more urgent note. The Khodam swept once, twice through the empty air, and then dropped from fingers now dripping with black. The shapeless, writhing lump that had once been his father crumpled to its knees, and toppled over onto one side.

The thump as the body of his father hit the ground broke Jun out of his trance. The horde of men on the causeway gave a roar of approval and, as if released from some barrier, immediately rushed forward. A colossal wave of terror crashed down on Jun. He dropped bow and quiver, turned on his heel and, a world of nameless horror clamoring inside his head, he ran full pelt back into the darkness of his pavilion.

CHAPTER 3

Extract from *Ethnographic Travels* by
Professor Tolmund K. Parehki of the University of Dhilika

The sprawling city of Singarasam is the chief marketplace of the Laut Besar. More accurately, it is a bubbling stew of filth and iniquity, greed and vice where tens of thousands of people of all colors and creeds come together from across the world to trade "obat"—a powerful narcotic, which is cultivated on several islands in the Laut Besar but nowhere else on this Earth. Other rare and valuable cargoes—including spices, timber, slaves and gold—are exchanged here, too, but obat is the most lucrative and important commodity by far, and the city began life some hundreds of years ago as a place for the early Han merchants to safely store their harvests of the precious leaves and resin.

Today, when not engaged in trade, the teeming hordes of Singarasam enjoy nothing better than murdering their enemies in the dank back alleys of the city, except perhaps for lying to, scheming against and stealing from their dearest friends—but they are rather less enthusiastic about paying their annual tribute in silver to the Lord of the Islands. This is the traditional title of most powerful of the local sea raiders, the pirate chief who occupies the First House, as his gaudy palace is known, and who calls himself King of Singarasam . . .

They made him wait. To show their contempt for him personally and for his equally insignificant trading house, they made him wait for more than an hour. Nearly two. It was not the first time he had been made to kick his heels by a foreign ruler. But this was different. This was quite deliberate. This was humiliation Singarasam style.

Farhan Madani had heard the bells on the Exchange toll the twelfth hour, the last hour of business when the counters were slammed shut, and the clerks began to gather up their precious sheaves of palm leaf before tallying up their day's trade. He had heard a mad preacher howling endlessly on a street corner at passersby, begging them to give up their sinful love of money and follow the true way of the Holy Martyr. Now, outside the First House, in the narrow, crowded streets of Singarasam, the skinny, half-naked Dewa vendors would be pumping the oil stoves to start the seething fires, chopping vegetables, garlic, ginger, chilies and small, nameless chunks of offal and bone that would make the base of the delicious fiery soups they sold by the bowlful all through the long, warm night.

Farhan was hungry. He had not eaten since dawn. And at his age—nearly forty years—he liked to be fed regularly, and to savor his food in quiet comfort. After he had seen the Lord of the Islands—if he ever *was* granted an audience after this endless wait—he would order a bowl of the rich, fragrant soup from the Dewa street cooks to either celebrate his triumph or drown his sorrows. Celebrate! He would certainly be celebrating after this meeting! How could he not? How could the Lord of the Islands— the great Ongkara himself, fail to be delighted by his proposal. For Ongkara, there was no risk, no possibility of loss. He was being offered pure profit for something that would not cost him a copper kupang. Farhan would be celebrating after this audience. He knew it. The delay was merely a piece of the famous Singarasam shadow-puppet theater designed to make the Big Man feel even more powerful and remind the supplicant of his lowly place. It meant absolutely nothing.

Would they have made him wait this long for an audience with an important official at home in Dhilika? Probably not. The elite state functionaries in the capital of the Indujah Federation, a powerful trading conglomeration that occupied a vast peninsula two thousand leagues to the west of the Laut Besar, were of a brisker stamp. He would have been seen promptly at the given time or not at all. But he was not at home now. This was Singarasam, the greatest, indeed only proper city in the Laut Besar and, while it had been the base for his one-man trading company for the past year and more, he had never felt comfortable here.

The weight of the leather bag on his lap, however, was quietly reassuring. It was a fine-looking gift—and he was sure it would ease the way for him. The Lord of the Islands would be pleased, he would be sweetened, he would be made generous and malleable.

The alternative—that Ongkara might refuse him—was unthinkable. There were people, very serious people, who would be extremely angry if Farhan were to fail. And there were also his debts to consider, too. Farhan did not know the precise value of his debts, the exact number in silver-ringgu coin—how could he, when the interest was calculated on a daily basis?—but he knew it was a mountainous sum and that his chief creditor, Xi Gung, was growing impatient. When the head of the mighty House of Xi became impatient with one of his clients, terrible things happened. Xi Gung preferred to take his payment in cold, hard silver—but he would take it in dripping flesh, too, if necessary. Farhan shuddered, pushed the evil thought aside. Ongkara would see sense. The Lord of the Islands would provide. All would be well.

"Lord Madani?"

Farhan had been so enfolded in his thoughts that he had failed to notice the servant standing before him. If he truly *was* a servant—the quantity of bullion sewn into his jacket and sarong would have paid the interest on Farhan's loans for a week. And his manner was hardly subservient—by his expression he seemed to be smelling something foul, an odor that apparently only he was refined enough to detect.

"Yes, that's me, Farhan Madani," he said, standing up stiffly from the bamboo armchair, and brushing at the deep crease marks in his best blue-linen jacket.

"His Royal Highness has a few moments at his disposal and has graciously agreed to grant you a brief audience."

The servant turned and began to glide toward a vast pair of doors.

"About bloody time," muttered Farhan, hefting the leather bag in his arms.

The servant stopped, turned smoothly on the heel of his golden slipper, and said, "Did you say something, Lord Madani?"

"Nothing important," said Farhan, hoisting up a weak smile for the man.

"I thought I heard you say something about time. I thought that perhaps I heard you say that you did not have the time to see His Royal Highness at present—and if that were the case, then I would gladly show you back down to the street. There is a discreet trades-man's entrance not far from here that could also perfectly well be used as an exit."

"No, no, I'd be delighted to pay my respects to His Royal Highness right now. The sooner the better, in fact."

"Very good," said the servant, and he continued leading the way to the tall doors. Farhan followed after the man, head droop-ing, knowing himself bested.

◆ ◆ ◆

The Audience Hall was a shock to Farhan's sensibilities. It was big, to be sure—three times the height of a man and a bow-shot in length and width—but that was to be expected. What made his jaw drop was the extraordinary ugliness of the place. It was decorated in the high Han style—naturally, for the First House was the original trading warehouse of the Han adventurers who had founded the island haven of Singarasam all those centuries ago—but since then each occupant of the palace had added his or her own sense of pomp.

A double line of blood-red pillars, circled by golden dragons with yellow beards, purple spine crests and splayed green feet, made a kind of tunnel through the center of the hall leading to the Obat Bale where the Lord of the Islands was seated in his splendor. There were more golden dragons, silver eagles, jade fish and blue-lacquer bulls on the ceiling. The floor was speckled gray marble with purple-and-green lotus-flower mosaics. And the whole huge place was lit with a thousand candles hanging from half a hundred gold-chased crystal chandeliers. It was as bright as noon in there—brighter, as the golden scales of the many, many decorative dragons seemed to multiply the reflected light. Farhan blinked—he had a strong urge to cover his eyes. A vast gong beat three times. He stumbled slightly at the onslaught of clashing colors and sounds, recovered, raised his chin and strode manfully down the center of the hall toward the distant Obat Bale as the golden-clad servant sonorously intoned the names and titles of the Lord of the Islands—King of Singarasam, Lion of the Southern Lands, Dragon of the High Seas, Scourge of the Lawless, Shield of the Righteous, Font of All Harmony—Ongkara the Fearless.

Farhan reached the dais on which the Obat Bale was placed and fell to his knees on the white rice-straw mat, arms extended, prostrating himself in awe before the majesty of the Lord of the Islands in the time-honored fashion. The servant announced him inaccurately as Lord Farhan of the House of Madani—Farhan was no lord, and the House of Madani had but a single occupant, himself. Yet he was not going to complain at being made to sound grander than he was. He gently knocked his forehead on the mat, three times, then three times, and three more times, then held his position, waiting patiently for the Lord of the Islands to take notice of him.

He had been prepared for another long, undignified wait with his face pressed to the ground and his arse in the air and was surprised to hear Ongkara saying crossly, "Get up, man. Get up and say your piece—I haven't got all night."

Farhan cautiously raised his head and looked directly at the Lord of the Islands for the first time. The Lion of the Southern Lands was seated in a wooden throne, which was placed on a vast, square, white-canvas bag stuffed tight with dried obat leaves—the Obat Bale, which signified the first trade that had enriched the rulers of Singarasam. He was flanked on either side by two stern-faced Jath guards, dark, bearded men with black turbans, loose black robes and huge drawn scimitars. To Farhan's surprise he saw that Ongkara was a little frog of a man, short and thick in the body but with long, skinny brown limbs and an outsized head under a tall and heavy-looking jewel-encrusted golden crown. His eyes were small, black and angry; his small nose was flattened to his face; his mouth was as wide as the length of Farhan's hand. He was every bit as ugly as his Audience Hall, Farhan decided, before hurriedly thrusting that undiplomatic thought away lest it show on his face.

"Your Royal Highness, I come bearing a wondrous gift of enormous value, as a token of the high esteem that my House has for your person," said Farhan. And he reached inside the leather sack and pulled out a small, shiny yellow statue of a lion, its right forepaw lifted to strike some invisible enemy, mouth open in a roar of rage. It was a decent, lifelike piece, of some antiquity, or so the shopkeeper had told him when he purchased it that morning at a grubby little emporium by the docks for far more than he could afford.

"For you, my King," Farhan said, holding out the lion, "a memento of our first meeting. This exquisite solid-gold piece is more than a hundred years old, more valuable than a dozen real beasts of flesh and blood, and it was made for your illustrious ancestor Jinwa the Valiant, first of your line to call himself the Lion of the Southern Lands."

There was no possibility that Ongkara was in any way related to the notorious Jinwa—a brutal Han warlord who had died without issue, poisoned by his own Grand Vizier, a venal little sadist who had promptly ascended the throne and named himself Tang the Magnificent. But, as Farhan knew well, the etiquette of the court dictated that all the Kings of Singarasam must claim to be descended from each other in one impressively unbroken bloodline.

Farhan held out the golden statue with both hands toward Ongkara. Its weight was quite considerable—perhaps it really was made of solid gold.

One of the black-clad Jath guards stepped forward, grabbed the lion in one hairy paw and passed it up to the King without the slightest ceremony. Ongkara turned the little statue over in his hands, letting the candlelight play on the golden surface.

"You say this animal is more than a hundred years old?" he said.

"Yes, Highness, it was made by the legendary blacksmith Grandfather Pande who forged it in a fire made from the bones of a giant lizard monster . . ."

"Really? It seems very small for its age." Ongkara snickered at his own wit then tossed the lion casually onto the Obat Bale beside his knee, where it bounced once and lay still.

Ongkara looked down at Farhan.

The silence was appalling. One of the Jath guards gave a cough,

as explosive in the quiet as a firecracker. It sounded like a smothered laugh, to Farhan's ear.

"So, Master of the Silver Tongue, Lord of the Liars," said Ongkara, at last, "what is it that you wish from me?"

Farhan blinked. He was slightly shocked that Ongkara already
knew his hated nicknames. But, of course, the man had his spies.
Just like everyone else.

"Why, sire, I wish for nothing more than your continued good
health and a long, happy life—may your glorious reign last for a
thousand years."

"Thank you," said the King. "If you truly wish for nothing
more than my health and my thousand-year reign, Lord Liar, then
I shall bid you good night."

"I also wish to swell your royal coffers, sire," said Farhan
quickly. "For what is a long life without the necessary means to
enjoy it?"

"Quite. Well, then, get on with it, man, swell my coffers—
how?"

"With gold, sire, gold from the Konda Pali mine below the
Gray Mountain on the Island of Yawa."

"I'm listening . . ."

"The Konda Pali mine eats men, sire, as I'm sure you know—
the life of a slave in that deep hell is less than six turnings of the
moon. Half a year, sire, is all a mine-slave can expect to live before the heat, the ceaseless labor, the foul air beneath the earth, or
the cruelty of the guards makes an end of him. Half a year. The
mines of Yawa produce two things, sire—ingots of the purest gold
and the corpses of those who toil in them. So the Han engineers
who control the mines, the Gold Masters, are ever hungry for
fresh meat—they need slaves and more slaves, hundreds, even
thousands of men and women to be fed into the sunless earth to
wrest gold from the depths and bring it up into the light. They

will pay a hundred silver ringgu for a healthy male, or ten fingers of gold; fifty ringgu for a woman."

"Go on," said the King, leaning forward slightly. Farhan felt a glow in his belly. The fish was on the hook; he could feel it tugging on the line.

"If I may, sire, I would now direct your imagination east to the endless, impenetrable teak forests of Ziran Atar. The tribes who inhabit that unmapped land are sturdy, well muscled and for the most part untroubled by knowledge of the rest of the world. Some say that they are the direct ancestors of the Ebu people, the original inhabitants of the Laut Besar, driven into exile there when the New People arrived. They have almost no metal; they still use tools of wood, flint and obsidian. And they are not united in any sense, except in their dread of some foul witch goddess—the Queen of Fire, they call her—who they fear will burn up their souls. The Atari tribes are warriors, though, a vigorous and aggressive people who are constantly at odds with their neighbors. And when they vanquish an enemy tribe, they take them captive and either sacrifice them to the Queen of Fire in hideous, blood-washed rituals or make them their slaves, have them toiling in the fields, drawing their water . . ."

"And you plan to obtain these slaves from the Atari tribes, ship them across to Yawa and sell them to the Han engineers at the gold mines."

"Your Royal Highness is as perceptive as he is generous with his time," Farhan said, bowing low. Ongkara ignored his remark and frowned.

"And what will you use to pay for these slaves—what will you give the Atari in exchange for their captured neighbors?"

"Iron, sire. Iron swords and knives, forged spearpoints, axes and arrowheads. The beauty of this scheme, as I'm sure you will already have divined, sire, is that when one group of savages has armed itself and vanquished the next—they sell the captives to us. But the losers will also be keen to trade to equip themselves with iron weapons so that they can face their foes on an equal footing at their next encounter. Thus we create an endless supply of slaves."

Ongkara sat back in his throne. He seemed impressed.

"I am the fabled alchemist of the storybooks, sire: I shall transform base iron into pure gold!" Farhan had been preparing this line for days now but it had sounded far better in his head. Ongkara seemed not to notice its cleverness at all. He was frowning again.

"You could just go there with a force of well-armed men and capture the natives yourself. Pack them in the holds, ship them over to Yawa, get your gold without spending anything on iron goods. Wouldn't that be far cheaper? These savages have no real weapons; they can't be all that difficult to subdue."

This is going to be easier than I thought, Farhan reflected. *This froggy little pirate has not the slightest moral reservations about this venture. What people said of him was true: Ongkara would sell his sister to the whoremasters for a single finger of gold.*

What he actually said was, "Once again, sire, you have amply demonstrated your extraordinary sagacity. It would indeed be much cheaper to subdue them as you describe—but only the first time we did this. What would happen, sire, next time our sails were seen off the coast of Ziran Atar? The tribes would flee inland, running and hiding in fear of our slave catchers. Each time we came there it would become a little harder to collect the slaves, a little more dangerous. My earnest hope is that this should be an ongoing concern. A well from which we can draw water for years, perhaps decades, to come. If we pay them with a few cheap iron trinkets, the natives will fill the slave pens on the beach for us with their brothers and sisters. We arrive, we load the cargo into the holds, we pay the price in iron to the local headman and we

are off to Yawa to collect our gold. We can do this time and
again—and Ziran Atar is vast, sire; there will never be a shortage
of flesh for us to harvest."

Ongkara was nodding, smiling even now.

"You are ambitious, I'll give you that, Madani. And you seem
to have thought it all the way through. Tell me, then, what is it
that you want from me?"

"The journey to Ziran Atar will be long and arduous, sire, and
fraught with no little danger. We must pass by the deadly Kamput
Shore and avoid the terrible menace of the swooping fire-birds.
The waters there are thick with evil pirates and head-hunting
dyaks. We will put in at Banjarput on the Island of Kalima—in the
shadow of the vengeful Mountain of Fire. We will pass through
the Piri-Piri Isles, where the ghosts of the sea dead are said to
roam among the obat groves, singing their lethal . . ."

"I know the route, Madani. I've been sailing these waters for
forty years or more. And the fire-birds are not real—they are
merely children's kites dipped in oil and set ablaze. Just tell me
what it is that you require from me."

"Your flag, sire," said Farhan.

"What?"

"I wish to fly the Lion Standard of the King of Singarasam, the
mark of the Lord of the Islands himself, from my masthead below
my own humble pennant. I also wish for a letter of marque from
you stating that I am your captain, acting under your orders, with
the authority to punish your enemies, and that I and my crew are
under your personal protection at all times and in all waters. And
in exchange for that small token of your royal esteem, I shall give
you ten percent of the gold bullion when we return to Singarasam
in no more than three moons from today. I estimate that your
share will be worth in the region of two thousand silver ringgu."

If Farhan had hoped that the King of Singarasam would have
been impressed by this figure—it was a huge sum, equivalent to

a year's profit for a medium-sized Singarasam trading house—he was to be royally disappointed.

Ongkara sniffed and reached a long arm around himself to scratch at his backside. Farhan looked up at him in expectation. In case this preposterous oaf had not managed to grasp the size of the reward being offered, Farhan said, "It is the equivalent of two hundred fingers of pure gold, sire, a delightful sum, I'm sure you will agree. And all you have to do to gain it is give me a piece of cloth and a letter."

"That's all you think my name is worth?" said Ongkara. "You ask for my protection—the auspice of the Lord of the Islands—for a pittance. My writ runs from the setting to the rising sun, from the far frozen north to the empty southern ocean. A mere two thousand ringgu? I should have you flayed alive for your impertinence."

Farhan was drenched with shock. He knew that this was no idle threat.

"If you wish to go cruising around the islands under my flag, merrily enriching yourself, having all the sea folk of the Laut Besar bow and scrape to you," the Lord of the Islands was booming now, his squat torso swollen with rage, his spindly arms gesturing wildly above his head, "then I demand in return a far more suitable recompense. I want fifty percent and I don't want that to be an 'estimate' or 'in the region of.' I want ten thousand ringgu in cash on your return, and no quibbles about slaves who died on the passage, or wily Han merchants who cheated you out of this or that. Ten thousand. Cash. An hour after your ship touches the quay in Singarasam Harbor."

Farhan relaxed. His shoulders came down. The fish was as good as landed. Now it was really only about the negotiation.

"Sire, I am but a poor man," he began. "I have many debts. And I must hire and outfit a ship, bear the cost of purchasing the iron goods, shackles, chains, whips, brands and the like. There are the ships stores to consider, and dry rations for the slaves . . ."

"I know all about your debts. I think that my good friend Lord Gung of the House of Xi would be most interested to hear about your plans to depart from Singarasam. And I'm still quite seriously considering having you flayed alive for your impertinence." Ongkara glared down at the merchant but seemed a little calmer now.

"Fifteen percent," said Farhan quickly. "I think I could just manage fifteen."

"Forty, and not a penny less."

"Sire, it would be madness to embark on this most arduous and dare I say perilous of missions unless the subsequent reward is satisfactory for all parties. But perhaps I could go to seventeen, merely out of my immense personal regard for your Royal Highness."

"Thirty percent—and that's final. If the next words out of your slimy liar's mouth are not 'I agree, Your Royal Highness,' then I shall call for my torturers."

"I agree, Your Royal Highness . . . that seventeen is perhaps a little ungenerous. Shall we say twenty percent? How does four thousand shiny silver ringgu sound?"

"Damn you, Madani. Twenty-five. And my patience is at an end."

"Done," said Farhan, bowing low before the King. "Twenty-five it shall be. The Lion of the Southern Lands is as irresistible in matters of commerce as he is in the heat of battle."

"With any luck we'll never actually have to pay him," Farhan said to Captain Cyrus Lodi, who was pouring out two measures of marak spirit into a pair of small earthenware cups. "Ongkara will be swept away by events: killed, imprisoned or exiled—rendered impotent anyway. And then he can whistle for his money. That is, if everything goes to plan," he continued.

The merchant lifted the cup in salute to his old friend, slid the spirit down his throat and set the vessel down on the tabletop with a click.

Ah, yes, the plan, thought Farhan, feeling the marak burn savagely in his belly. The slave-trading tale he had sold the Lord of the Islands was pure, green-liquid buffalo shit, of course. The true plan, little did that froggy upstart know, was to change the face of the Laut Besar. The true scheme that he and Cyrus Lodi were about to embark on was an effort to alter the political balance of the whole region in the favor of the Indujah Federation.

They were going to start a war.

Farhan Madani was indeed the lord and master of a small trading house, through which he dabbled in the gum and spice trades, but he was also employed by the government of the Indujah Federation and paid a moderate stipend each month by a secret government organization called the Amrit Shakti in exchange for, among other things, providing reports on political, military and commercial matters throughout the whole of the Laut Besar.

The Amrit Shakti was the watchdog, guardian and iron fist of the Indujah Federation. Its thousands of members worked busily but quietly to root out spies at home and to further its commercial interests abroad. Shakti agents watched dissidents and loud-mouthed lawyers, quietly assassinated revolutionaries and rebels, threatened, bullied or bribed foreign potentates. It had been known to topple kings and change the course of conflicts with a word in the right ear. The Amrit Shakti was in fact the most powerful component of the government of the Indujah Federation: indeed, some whispered, the Amrit Shakti *was* the government of the Federation. And Farhan, sometimes reluctantly, did its bidding.

"When has everything *ever* gone exactly to plan?" said Captain Lodi, pouring himself another cup of marak. He was a thick-chested, square man with cropped gray hair, a year or two older than Farhan but looking far more ancient due to a face much battered by weather.

Darkness had fallen and the two old friends were alone in the master cabin of the *Mongoose*, which was tied up at a quay in the main harbor of Singarasam. The cabin was a decent-sized space, at least by the cramped standards of the trading ships of the Laut Besar, in which a tall man could stand without crouching, and a long table could be laid to seat a dozen hungry crew members. But then the *Mongoose* was no ordinary trading ship: she was well armed and deadly, like the snake-killing animal she was named for, but surprisingly capacious belowdecks. She was also fast. The ship was driven through the waves by three tall masts rigged with fan-shaped sails, and Captain Lodi swore she could outrun anything in these waters except, perhaps, for one of the new Han light battle cruisers.

"Well, pay him, don't pay him—a few thousand ringgu will make no difference here or there," said Farhan carelessly. "It's just a handful of copper *kupang* compared to the stakes we're playing for. A transport of the Celestial Republic, filled to the gunwales with pure gold ingots—has there ever been a bigger prize?" Farhan grinned. "It's going to be a grand payday for us, old friend. A reward more lavish than any we ever dreamed of."

The ship's captain scowled at Farhan's levity but said nothing.

"We're going to be rich, Cyrus. Very rich. And with the blessings of the Amrit Shakti to boot, we can write our own tickets in the future. Talking of money, have we any petty cash left in the strongbox? Anything at all to spare? I'm a little short just now as it happens."

"Nothing—just coppers . . . all right, maybe five ringgu, at most. But you can't have it. I'll need it. Apparently our credit is no longer good in this city." Cyrus Lodi gave Farhan a hard stare from beneath his thick, frost-colored brows. "Xi Gung's name was mentioned at the chandlers, along with yours. And I had to pay cash for almost everything we needed."

"How soon before we are ready to leave?" Farhan asked, sending his cup skidding toward the captain with a practiced flick of his finger. Lodi refilled it.

"I have the stores and water—my hold is stuffed full of old iron junk that is taking up far too much space. But my crew is ashore, drinking and smoking obat and whoring and, as they may not get a run on land for months, I would prefer to give them a little more time. Say in two days: the ebb tide. An hour before midnight. Does that suit?"

"It suits me well. I have a few private affairs that I must settle. But I don't want to leave it too long. Ongkara is not entirely stupid."

"I'm glad you recognize that," said Lodi. "He is easy to despise but he made it to the top of the dung pile here so he cannot be a complete imbecile. His wrath is to be feared."

"I agree. And our true objective is sure to leak out, too. But we should be good for two more days. He thinks he bested me in the negotiations. To be safe, I suggest we dump the iron when we're at sea. We'll need the room in the hold when we pick up the troops from Istana Kush—that is, if they don't mind sleeping in the slave decks. I hear these Dokra companies are rather touchy about their honor, in fact, extremely precious about it—for bought-and-paid-for mercenaries. Although they are reputedly the best on the market."

"They'll do as they are damned well told," said Lodi. "Or I'll dump them over the side, too. Soldiers—pah!—far too choosy these days about where they lay their lubberly heads."

"We need them, Cyrus. The plan comes to nothing without the Dokra. They should be well content, at least, with their pay. It is lavish by any standards. Who offers gold for swords these days? An hour ago I was discussing the opposite exchange."

Captain Lodi said nothing. He scowled at the teak deck between his broad boots.

"Two days, then," said Farhan.

"Two days," said Lodi. "But no more gambling. You cannot afford to make a mess of this mission. The Amrit Shakti will never forgive you if this goes all to cock. Neither will I."

CHAPTER 4

Katerina slid a linen shift over her head and shoulders, covering her naked body. She glanced once at the corpse of the big man lying in her marriage bed, and admired the blue-black of his glossy hair and the contrast with the trickle of scarlet upon the white silk pillow. It was a shameful waste of a handsome male, she thought, but it had to be done. And now it was. She walked over to the pair of big window shutters at the far end of the room. They were in the old Indujah style and reached from the floor almost to the ceiling. She threw them open and looked out onto the courtyard beyond. It was a dry, chilly night, with a quarter moon high above the palace wall on the far side and, as far as she could make out, the courtyard was empty. The palace was silent. The revels had continued for an hour or so after the happy couple had retired for the night and then, no doubt at the urging of the stewards, the guests had tiptoed away into the night or composed themselves for slumber.

She reached into the leather valise in the corner of the room where she kept her washing things and pulled out a coil of thin but very strong silk rope attached to an iron hook. Stepping over the low sill of the Indujah window, she walked calmly across the empty courtyard and across to the wall that marked the palace boundary. Beyond its twenty-foot height sprawled the dense network of filthy, narrow streets that made up the city of Ashjavat, the metropolis that gave its name to the whole of this wide Southron principality.

Her principality now.

She whirled the iron hook once, twice, and hurled it upward. It hit the top of the wall and clattered down again, landing with a thud at her feet. The noise alarmed her. She paused for a second, listening. But nothing broke the stillness of the courtyard. She tried again, giving herself more of the silken rope to swing, and this time the hook caught the lip of bricks at the top of the wall. She tugged once, and finding the hook secure, she left the rope hanging in the chill air and went back to her chamber, stepping back over the sill and making sure to only half close the pair of shutters behind her. She sat down on the bed, drawing an ice-bear fur around her shoulders—suddenly she felt very cold. Then, glancing again at the corpse, she hissed through her teeth with frustration.

A mistake, she thought. A bad one, too. But it could be rectified.

She shrugged off the white fur, and went over to the corpse. The jeweled handle of the ceremonial knife was still sticking out from the dead man's temple. She tugged the little weapon loose— with a surprising amount of difficulty. It was as if the prince's skull did not wish to give up its prize. Then she went to the water closet, where she washed the gore from its shiny length. She dried the blade, replaced the dagger in its sheath on the silver belt, and sat back down again on the bed, drawing the bearskin up over her shoulders once more.

It was, she judged, about an hour or two before dawn. There was no reason to wake the palace this early—the servants had all worked very hard to give her a perfect wedding; they surely de-served a little more time in their cozy beds. Gods knew there would be mayhem enough for everyone when the world did fi-nally awaken.

It was, she realized, the first time she had been totally alone in weeks—she did not count the cooling corpse of her husband as company—in months, actually, and she relished the feeling of freedom. She settled the white bearskin more comfortably around her shoulders and gave herself to her thoughts. What would Papa be doing now? she wondered. Was he still alive, even? The Emperor had still been living, just, though clearly sinking fast, when he had summoned her to the Imperial Palace and told her that she must marry this large, rich, Southron princeling. But that had not been the worst shock she had received that short snowy November day, exactly two weeks and two days ago . . .

The runners of the sleigh hissed in the snow, and Katerina looked out of the fogged-glass window and glowered at the indistinct shapes of the peasants who lined the road to pay their respects as a Princess of the Blood passed them by. It was her time of the month and she felt clammy and puffy and her temper was short. Indeed, she had ordered her maid, Ilana, to be whipped for being clumsy while fixing her hair that very morning. The Cossack guards had tied her up to the post in the parade ground and flogged her until the blood puddled in the snow, and Katerina had watched every stroke of the long, leather knouts from her bedroom window. After that savage punishment, Ilana would be no good for work for a month, Katerina knew, and that cack-handed slut Sara would have to do her duties. She must learn to control herself, Katerina thought. Her maid's incapacity would be most inconvenient.

The princess wiped the glass with her scarf end and waved languidly with a silk-gloved hand at the vacant, doughy peasant faces that flashed past her window. And when they had passed through whatever one-mule town that had been, and were back in the clean white expanse of the snowfield, she rummaged in her furs for a slim flask of marak and took a frugal sip. Not too much; it would not do to greet Papa drunk. No, just a sip to make the cramps in her belly more bearable. An hour later they stopped the sleigh to change the horses and Katerina stepped down from the stale but warm interior and into the frigid blast of winter. She raised an eyebrow at the Niho knight who was seated on the roof of the sleigh, muffled in furs and black-lacquered armor with only his flat black eyes showing below his helmet rim. The man immediately understood her query and lifted an arm and pointed to a building constructed of pine logs, which was gently steaming in the frosted air.

As Katerina relieved herself in the fetid stink of the latrine hut, lifting her skirts and straddling the log-lined pit to piss into its mist-wreathed depths, she thought about the meeting with the Emperor that would come at the end of her journey. The summons had been unexpected, unusually brusque in its tone and delivered by a captain of the 5th Imperial Cossack Regiment, who had arrived with a troop of twenty riders, delivered the crisp note with the Imperial seal and departed within the hour. There had been no need to wait for a reply. When the Emperor of Khev himself summoned you, you could not refuse.

The summons was unusual, too, in that, at this time of year, when the ground was ice-locked, few people were put to the inconvenience of travel, even by the Emperor. He had adopted one of the customs of the new religion some years ago and would summon his extended family to the palace for the Feast of the Martyr's Nativity, on the day that had once been celebrated as the midwinter solstice, and all twenty-odd cousins, uncles and aunts—none holding a rank below Grand Duke or Duchess—would roost there in gloomy, drink-sodden splendor for all twelve days of the celebration, gossiping, complaining, arguing, plotting, playing the tedious and never-ending games of power. For the rest of the long, snowbound winter, the Imperial family lived in happy seclusion in their own lavish private palaces, scattered in a hundred-mile arc around the Imperial city of Khev.

That city seemed utterly deserted as Katerina's sleigh rushed up the grand boulevard toward the Imperial Palace and slewed to a halt outside the vast, ironbound gates. The air had grown colder still and driven all the inhabitants of Khev indoors. And it was indeed a shock as Katerina stepped down, out of the brazier-heated interior of the sleigh, and her boots crunched into the snow. She stumbled slightly and, in that instant, a black-clad form had leaped down from the roof of the sleigh, landed like a cat beside her and was offering a steel-bar arm for her to clutch.

The Niho knight—his name was Yoritomo, Katerina recalled, and he was captain of her twelve-strong detachment of bodyguards—did not seem to notice the cold, despite having sat on the roof of the sleigh for the past four hours as it sped through the snowscape. She had read somewhere that because of their harsh, mountainous homeland the Niho knights' blood was different from ordinary men's—a thicker, more viscous, purplish fluid—and that they could deal with extremes of temperature far better as a result. Whether this was true or not, Katerina did not know. But the middle-aged man in black-lacquered armor beside her, now offering her his arm, seemed entirely unperturbed by the frigid air that was now, after only a few moments outside, making her own uncovered nose tingle painfully. His near-black eyes looked at her impassively from under the broad rim of his black helmet. And while Katerina's breath was pluming like dragon's smoke before her face, Captain Yoritomo seemed not to be breathing at all.

The Niho knight marched beside her, by her right elbow, like an equal, as Katerina entered the palace and made her way through a massive hall and toward the audience chamber. The knight's right hand was tightly gripped around the hilt of a long, slightly curved sword, which was stuffed through the sash bound around the armor at his waist, and Katerina knew that he could draw and strike down an enemy faster than the blink of an eye, if she were threatened. She had seen him do it. Two years ago, a raggedy Martyrite madman had once shouted obscenities about fire and death and lunged at her in the marketplace and Yoritomo had cut the wretched fellow almost in half before she knew what was happening. That knowledge gave her courage as she swept through the opening double doors and marched into the audience chamber toward the high dais, where a figure in Imperial blue and gold sat beneath a vast canopy.

"Princess Katerina Kasimirovitch Astrokova," intoned a servant beside the huge double doors, and Katerina dipped her knee and bowed her head before the Imperial throne.

"Daughter," said a rich, slow, well-modulated voice, a voice like the slide of warm honey, "come closer. Come nearer to me."

Katerina was aware that the Niho knight had melted away to her right and that she was moving, almost unconsciously, toward the dais. From the corner of her eye she could see the massed ranks of Khevan courtiers and the envoys from a dozen lands: strapping bearded boyars, huge-bellied in leather and fur; tall, pale, flame-haired Franks from the western lands; neat Han lords with their smooth, round faces; merchants from the Indujah Federation, all flashing dark eyes and easy smiles, with an outrageous compliment ever on their lips.

She took a step up toward the Emperor, and for the first time risked a direct glance at her father's face. The shock of it nearly made her falter, but she forced herself to put one foot before the next and sank to her knees at the top of the steps. She gazed at her father, wrapped in a thick, blue, cotton-stuffed silk gown embroidered with golden eagles, and wearing a capacious blue-velvet cap pulled down over his ears, with a golden lightning-bolt pin stabbed into the front of the cloth above his speckled eyebrows. It was the face beneath the cap that made Katerina draw a sharp breath. It was gaunt, the big square jaw and sharp cheekbones pushing through the tight white skin, and had sunk in on itself. The teeth were splayed and prominent. The eyes, softly brown as old leather, seemed huge, bulging even, and the irises were ringed with the gray bands of age.

The Emperor pushed forward a wrinkled, liver-spotted hand, and Katerina seized it quickly in both of hers and bestowed a dry kiss on the papery skin.

She had not seen her father since the summer and the change in him, his palpable weakness now, the obvious proximity of death, was a reproach. He had been full of life then, dominant, virile, laughing—now his very stare was a self-pitying complaint about the inevitable mortality of all mankind, even the most high of that doomed race.

"Are you well, my dear?" the Emperor said quietly.

"I am, Father," she said. And did not dare to ask the same of him.

He smiled at her then. "I worry about you, Katerina. I hope you know that," he said. "And I only want—all I have ever wanted is—is what is best for you."

"I know it, Father. I worry about you, too."

"There is no need to worry about me—my future is plainly written," he said with a smile. "There are no surprises in store for me. But your life lies ahead of you—a long and happy one, I hope and pray. But I must think not only of you but also of the fate of the Empire when I am gone. It is the burden of our rank, my dear: we do not have the luxury of thinking only of ourselves, of our own comfort and happiness. There are duties that come with our privileges. You understand that, I think."

Katerina felt her heart sink. Whatever was to come next—it would be bad. Her father was trying in his own clumsy way to soften the blow. She was his only daughter; there were no longer any sons to carry on his name. And she thought, with a hollow stomach, that she might have an inkling of what the old man had in his mind . . .

The Emperor made a beckoning gesture with his right hand. And Katerina half turned and saw a tall young man, a year older than her, with very long yellow hair, broad-shouldered, slim, straight as a lance, walking toward the throne. She knew him

well. She had grown up with him, in fact: it was her cousin Vladimir, her aunt Oksana's eldest son. A prick. An arrogant prick who
made a great show of his devotion to the Holy Martyr. He had
tried to kiss her the summer before last, when she had visited her
father, and the boy had been astounded, then angry, when she had
slapped his face. He'd tried to grab her then, using his superior
strength. And she'd dipped her shoulder, as she had been taught
by her retired Cossack defense instructor, and punched him in the
groin to teach him some better manners.

They had not spoken since.

"You know Archduke Vladimir Barezhnikov, of course, my
sister's boy."

Katerina allowed that she did. She was staring at his face, and
he was smiling horribly at her. *He knows,* she thought. *He knows
what fate the Emperor has in store for me.* She knew it, too, then. But
the white noise buzzing in her head made it impossible to think
or even hear. Her father was talking but she could only see his lips
moving. She shook her head to clear it.

". . . and there is the Imperial Army to think of, my dear. The
Emperor is commander in chief of all the regiments, as you know.
Even the wildest, hairiest Cossack trooper must swear a personal
oath of loyalty to him. The Emperor must command the respect
not just of the boyars— and they can prove troublesome enough—
but also of the whole Army and its entire officer corps; otherwise,
he wouldn't survive a month. That is where the true power lies,
with the Cossacks and Army; so you see, my dear, it really must
be a man on the Ice-Bear Throne if the Empire is to survive into
the new age. But you will be well provided for, have no fear. The
Ministry has found a splendid match for you, a handsome young
Southron fellow, very rich . . ." He gestured to a flunky, who
leaned forward and whispered in his ear. "Yes, yes, of course, he
is the Prince Khazeki of Ashjavat. And you will take all your people with you, of course, maids, servants, guards and so on. You

will lack for nothing, my dear, I promise you, for the rest of your life. I only want for you to be happy . . ."

Seated on the bed, with the cooling corpse of her very rich Southron husband by her side, Katerina still felt the embers of rage in her heart glow and pulse as she recalled the satisfied look Vladimir had given her when she had been dismissed by her father. Had that long-haired turd yet placed his skinny arse on the Ice-Bear Throne? Surely not. She would have heard, even down here, more than a thousand miles from the Imperial city. The news of the death of one Khevan Emperor and the accession of another would certainly have flown to the four corners of the world in a matter of days.

She told herself that the succession was entirely within the gift of the Emperor—he might choose anyone of royal blood, even the meanest, raggedy-cloaked count, if such was his whim. There were no fixed laws about the transmission of power. The Emperor was perfectly entitled to choose Vladimir. Indeed, perhaps it was a wise choice . . .

But another voice in her head drowned out these sensible words. *He is my father and I should inherit his mantle. I am his closest living blood. There is no good reason to overlook me. None, save my sex. None, save the absence of a prick between my legs. If he thinks I am weak, he is wrong. I will show him differently. I will show my father, I will show Vladimir the Usurper, I will show the whole world that I am a true daughter of the Ice-Bear.*

Katerina looked out of the partially opened shutters, and saw that the first pink light of dawn was suffusing the courtyard outside. It was time.

She slipped off the heavy bearskin, glanced quickly at the corpse, threw back her chin, opened her mouth and screamed, and screamed, and screamed.

CHAPTER 5

The crawl space beneath the Pavilion of War had only just been wide enough to allow Jun to squeeze inside. It was a long corridor an arm's length high and wide that stretched under the full span of the Pavilion. He had worked his way into the space backward—there was no room to turn around—and pulled a rice-straw basket in front of him to block the entrance. He shoved a hank of his sarong into his mouth to stifle his sobbing, and closed his eyes tight against the darkness.

Behind him somewhere he could hear the scurry of rats. In other circumstances their rustling might have made him nervous but, when compared with the sounds he could hear from outside the crawl space . . . Screams, awful gurgling screams, the sounds of men and women dying hard. The crackle of flames; the thump and crash of the stone statues being knocked from pedestals, the ripping of fabric and paper screens, the tinkling smash of crystal, the angry shouts of warriors. He heard the voice of the tall, gray-cloaked demon—for what else could he be?—issuing orders to the men. He knew it was his voice because it was like chilled flint and seemed drenched in evil. He could barely make out the words over the tumult but one name was repeated several times and when he finally allowed himself to understand it, his soul shriveled up as tight as his ball sack: Arjun Wukarta—his own name, and the demon was urging his brutal men to seek him out.

He knew he should not be in there, hiding like a mouse, as the invaders ransacked his father's house, and pillaged his family's most treasured possessions, but he could not see the point of emerging into the bloody chaos, where he would immediately be seized and slaughtered—or worse. The image of the Son of Heaven being smothered by the swarm was in the forefront of his mind. The topless head of War-Master Hardan, too: what would that veteran have to say about Jun's cowering in a rathole? He did not care: Hardan was dead. If Jun emerged from his rathole, he too would die. It was true—it meant certain death for Jun to leave that cramped space. He knew it as well as he knew anything but it did not make him feel any better.

Eventually, after what seemed an eternity, the noise began to abate; the screaming stopped, the voices faded. Even the rats had departed. Jun was left in his stuffy black space listening to silence. It could be a trap, Jun thought. They could be waiting, swords raised, smirks on their ugly faces, ready to slice him apart when he emerged. So he waited, waited a little more—then, to his surprise, he fell asleep.

He awoke to the gray light of dawn and a voice calling his name from outside the crawl space. "Jun, where are you, my prince?"

It did not sound like one of the marauders. He thought the voice sounded familiar, one of the servants, perhaps. And his muscles were cramped from the night on the dusty stone floor and his bladder was full. Cautiously, he slid the rice-straw basket from the mouth of the crawl space and peered out. He saw a very old man, fat in the belly but of dwarfish proportions, wrapped in a raggedy gray sarong, leaning on a thick wooden staff and smiling amiably down at him.

As he crawled stiffly out of his hole and stood, the little old man said, "Are you hurt, my prince? Have you suffered a wound?"

Jun shook his head. He was fairly sure that this was the ancient who had served him his wine the evening before. "You are . . . you are . . ." he said, once again struck by the absurdity of the fact that he did not know the fellow's name.

"I am Semar, my prince," said the old man, beaming. "I have had the great honor of serving your family for many years now."

"Of course you are Semar, of course. Forgive me, Semar, my wits are disordered."

Jun scrubbed his dust-covered face and looked about him for the first time. He was appalled by what he saw. Ruin on all sides. The pavilions had mostly been burned to their bases—all except the Pavilion of War. But that was sagging at one side where a pillar had been tumbled into rubble. Mounds of gray ash with a few upright, blackened stumps poking through marked the groves of palm trees. The surfaces of the square pools were covered in a thick lather of ash and grime. There were bodies everywhere, lying singly and in little heaps. Hundreds of dead. Jun looked over to where his father had been killed and saw the form of the man he had loved most lying on the stone beside the Moon Pool covered in gray snow.

"What happened?" he asked the old man. And realized the stupidity of his question.

"They came from the sea—these pirate scum—and they came in numbers. Two hundred fighting men, maybe more, in a single ship. They killed and burned everything. And took the Kris of Wukarta Khodam with them. It seems that is what they came for."

"Is everybody dead?" Jun whispered.

"There's you and there's me—and I suspect some of the sea villagers may have survived," said Semar cheerfully.

Jun looked over at the huge double doors that made up the gateway of the Watergarden. They had been ripped off their iron hinges and partially burned. Through them Jun saw that the devastation was equally bad beyond the walls and as far as he could see. His stomach rumbled, incongruously, telling him that it was time for breakfast.

"What do we do now?" he said, looking down at the smiling old servant.

"What would you do, my prince, if you could do anything in the world?"

Jun looked about him; he looked at his father's body, the other piled corpses, the mounds of ash, the shattered buildings—and for the first time anger glowed in his bowels.

"I would punish those who did this," he said. He felt the rage grow, warming his whole body. "I would punish those who slew my father and take back the Khodam."

"And how would you do this?"

"I would take men, armed men, trained warriors, and go after these pirates—"

Jun stopped. His shoulders dropped. There were no armed men left. War-Master Hardan was dead and the tiny royal guard had been annihilated before his eyes.

"Your cousin has soldiers in the city of Sukatan; as you know, he rules much of eastern Yawa and has grown rich on the fruits of the Konda Pali mine there. He may help you, if you ask him," Semar said. Then the old man said something quietly, so quietly that Jun felt he was speaking inside his head. "You cannot stay here, my prince. Not now. We must go after them. There's nothing here for you now."

The fishing boat was narrow and uncomfortable. Not much more than a long tube with a thin wooden outrider on each side and a single grubby triangular canvas sail stretched between the mast and the boom. Its owner, a scrawny slip of a girl named Ketut, was only just past puberty but already she had grown into one of the most unpleasant people that Jun had ever had the misfortune to encounter. She was a tangle-haired, flat-chested thing, with skin burned dark brown by the sun, and blazing black eyes and a quick, harsh tongue that she wielded with no thought given to courtesy, decency or Jun's exalted rank.

A mile out to sea and Jun was seriously thinking about slipping over the side and trying to swim back to the shore.

"Get your head down, richboy, we're going about," shouted Ketut, and Jun immediately did as he was ordered. He had learned the hard way that when she put the tiller over and the boat suddenly changed direction, the heavy wooden boom would come swinging across onto the other side of the boat and was likely to crack his skull if he didn't hurriedly duck. He had little idea why she kept changing the boat's direction of travel like this, only that it had something to do with the wind. And they had traveled in a series of zigzags to get out beyond the reef before settling on a course northwest, with the jungly coast of Taman on their left-hand side and in the far distance on the right, no more than a dark shadow, the neighboring Island of Molok. That island had also once been ruled by a prince of the Wukarta, but he had been a cruel man and arrogant, and more than ten years ago the peasants had risen up in anger and briskly put him and his entire family to death. A Taman princeling would find scant help there today.

Jun looked left over the whitecapped waves at his homeland. It was beautiful, the jungle green and glossy, the sand here a pristine white, the sea that lapped it a brilliant aquamarine. He wondered if he'd ever see his beloved island again.

He still wasn't quite sure how he had been persuaded by Semar to come on this mad voyage. It had made sense at the time, for sure. He had been angry at the death of his father and the destruction of his home but he had agreed to everything that Semar had suggested—the hiring of the boat to take them to Sukatan, the packing of a few possessions, the gathering of food and drink—with a meekness that now seemed almost dreamlike.

The old man's singsong voice had been soothing and oddly compelling, too. He had even abandoned his father's corpse and the cleanup of the Watergarden to the few servants and villagers who had escaped the massacre. Semar had assured him that his father would be cremated with all the proper rituals and that all that could be, would be salvaged from the wreckage of the Watergarden, when news reached Basar, the administrative capital in the south of Taman, and the courtiers of the Son of Heaven came north to gather up his bones.

He recalled making some kind of wild, impassioned speech to the survivors in the ruins of the Watergarden: something about avenging his father and returning with the Khodam, but grief and shock seemed to have clouded his mind and he could not remember the exact words he had said.

Jun knew that he was not a man of iron will but his own docility and obedience to Semar's gentle stream of suggestions surprised him. If they were to catch up with the sea raiders, if they wished to regain the Khodam, they must leave today, Semar had said—otherwise the pirates would disappear into the vastness of the Laut Besar never to be seen again. To Sukatan, then, to his cousin the Raja. There to raise fighting men and confront these sea scum. To punish them, and bring home the Khodam in triumph. It would make a story worthy of a hero: and Jun would be that hero. That thought lifted his gloom a little. They would make songs and stories about him. No one would mention that he had hidden in a dusty mousehole when enemies attacked his home. They would call him Arjun Pahlawan, Jun the Hero. But could this old servant be trusted to keep his mouth shut about the truth?

The servant himself was now sitting at the pointy front end, the prow he had heard Ketut call it, and gripping his long wooden staff between his knees as the sea wind whipped his unbound gray hair around his face. He seemed to be in a state of extreme joy, as if he were embarking on a carefree jaunt, rather than fleeing—for that is what they were doing, Jun realized with a jolt—fleeing a catastrophe.

"You look very pleased with yourself," Jun said sourly. His head was aching, the effects of the terrible night before and the brazen sun, a golden hammer that mercilessly beat down upon his head in the open boat.

Semar beamed at him. "I love the sea," he said. "It has no past, no future. It just is. It is wet and wide and it is bearing us that way"—he pointed ahead with his staff—"and there is nothing that we can do but submit, and allow ourselves to be carried along by its vastness to whatever we shall find at journey's end."

"Nothing you can do? I don't think so, old man," said Ketut from the tiller. "There are lines, hooks and bait in the locker by your feet—you and the rich boy can start by catching us some supper."

"My name is Prince Arjun Wukarta—my father was the Son of Heaven." Jun felt his cheeks grow red. "That is my kingdom," he said, throwing out an arm to indicate the green mass of Taman. "You will address me in the future as 'Prince'—or if you prefer, 'my lord.' You will not call me 'rich boy' again."

"Do you know who I am?" Ketut spat back at him. "Do you know *what* I am?"

Jun did not deign to reply.

"I am the fourth daughter of a whore. My older siblings all died before they were fully grown, mostly from diseases brought on by years of hunger. I have no idea who my father was—but I was told he was an idle rich fellow just like you, who used my mother for his pleasure then paid her off when the relationship became inconvenient. I . . . am . . . Dewa!"

Jun gave a sharp intake of breath. He had never been so close to a Dewa before. Never spoken to one. These people were the lowest form of mankind, the slaughter men, the tanners, the whores, the buriers of the dead, the cleaners of latrines. The Dewa were said to be the descendants of the Ebu people, the short, dark-skinned, curly-haired tribes that had occupied all the islands of the Laut Besar before the coming of the Harvester folk, Jun's own people, more than two thousand years ago. The skin on his arms and back began to crawl, as if Ketut's invisible contamination had already begun to affect him.

"This is my kingdom." Ketut gave the side of the boat a resounding slap. "You are in it. And in my kingdom I will call you whatever I like—richboy."

"There's a storm coming," said Semar. "A huge one. Praise the Gods, I think the winter rains have finally arrived."

They ran for the shore. A wall of purplish-gray cloud rushed toward them, barrelling in from the east, seeming to chase them. The waves became huge, towering blocks of water, which came in rank after rank, lifted the fragile boat and hurled it over the line of the reef with a man's height to spare. It was calmer inside the line, but not much. The waves chopped and twisted the craft, throwing Jun to the deck, Semar laughing maniacally and clinging to a mast rope with both hands as they were swept along at a fine, hectic speed.

The sea finally thrust them up onto the beach, a forbidding strand of black, volcanic sand, the dark land suddenly crunching below the keel. Jun, dazed by the swiftness of the transformation from placid, blue-water sailing, stepped shakily out of the boat and stood, hands by his sides as Semar and Ketut began to haul the vessel up the beach. That was when the rains hit: with a gigantic crackle of thunder and a sheet of white lightning, the big, heavy drops began to hammer down as if a dozen waterfalls had opened above their heads.

"Don't just stand there like a dumb ox, richboy, lend us a hand!"

Jun found himself gripping the curve of the outrigger and heaving, straining with the weight of the boat, forcing it up the steep, black-sand ridge and feeling his soft palms smear against the hard wood. The rain slashed down, drenching them all, making it all but impossible to see—but between them they got the craft up and under the palm trees, the prow lashed to the nearest trunk. Jun sat down under the half shelter of the tree. He found himself staring at the huge painted eye of the fishing boat, concentric circles of bright red and black, beside the long snout, which was painted with huge, curled teeth and what appeared to be shooting jets of flame.

Ketut was dragging out strips of tarred canvas from one of the lockers; she passed one to Jun, who seized it and cowered under its meager protection at the base of a coconut tree as the wind screamed, the rains pounded the canvas and the fronds of the tree lashed the sodden air around his head. Water seemed to fill the air—it was even difficult to breathe, each gasp having to be sipped through the fingers of a hand covering the mouth. *This is it,* Jun thought. *I'm going to drown on land. Some hero.*

The storm, for all its savagery, lasted no more than an hour. And, as if it had never happened, the rain clouds vanished from overhead, the wind dropped and the sun shone placidly once more. Jun looked up at the clear blue sky. It was late afternoon. A beautiful day. He stood up, shaking off the tarred-canvas strip, and looking around.

Ketut was already bailing out the boat with an old coconut shell, her torso bent over the side, rhythmically tossing showers of gray bilge out behind her.

But Semar was nowhere to be seen.

CHAPTER 6

⸻⸻⸻◦❈◦⸻⸻⸻

The same storm exhilarated Farhan. Five hundred leagues to the northwest of Taman, and an hour or two later, he stood at the prow of the *Mongoose* wearing nothing but a sarong and let the warm rain lash his back and wash the filth of the city from his body. The *Mongoose* was one day out from Singarasam, standing west for Istana Kush, with the Lion Standard of the Lord of the Islands limp but visible through the murk of flying water at the masthead.

Farhan felt a spasm of contentedness ripple through his body: he had Ongkara's letter of marque safely in the drawer of his desk in his cabin; in a morning of very hard labor, he had overseen the dumping of the tangled mountain of old iron that had been rusting in the hold; he had a well-trained crew of Buginese sailormen about him who had willingly helped with the iron-dump and who were now efficiently shepherding the ship through this delightful tempest; and most of joyous all, he had, for the moment, escaped the clutches of his creditors—most notably that monster Xi Gung—and he was free and clear on the high seas and ready to undertake another daring mission for his Amrit Shakti masters. If he succeeded, all would be well now and forever: there would be money, a great deal of money, more than enough to pay his debts, easily enough to retire on, too. He was tired of this rackety life: the danger, the deceit, the endless running from one thing or another. He might buy himself a governorship of one of the prettier obat islands in the Laut Besar, which would mean a generous income for life from his cut of the trade . . .

There had been a sticky hour on the evening before the *Mongoose* had set sail from Singarasam Harbor, when he had been obliged to hide in one of the special compartments in the side of the hold while Captain Lodi denied all knowledge of him to a gang of Xi Gung's thugs, who thumped around the ship muttering threats. But that unpleasantness had soon passed: the off-duty Buginese sailors had congregated at the hatchways, more than a score of them, ostentatiously sharpening their long, steel parangs, as they idled, watching the Xi bullyboys with eyes of jet. There was no love lost between Han and Buginese—they'd been enemies for centuries, ever since the Han had first built their vast obat plantations on the Island of Sumbu, and had co-opted local Buginese farmers into their brutal labor battalions. The Buginese called them Squinters for the narrow shape of their eyes. The Han looked on the Buginese as little better than talking monkeys.

In hindsight, Farhan was rather surprised that there had been no bloodshed. But Captain Lodi knew his crew of old and clearly had them tightly leashed. And after a fruitless hour of stomping about and banging on bulkheads, the disappointed Xi thugs took their leave and Lodi had ordered the crew to weigh anchor and set a course toward the west.

In a dozen hours or so they would dock at Istana Kush, the Gates of Stone, a mighty Federation fortress that guarded the narrow Straits to the north of Sumbu and controlled all shipping that came into the Laut Besar from that direction. At Istana Kush, by night, and as discreetly as possible to avoid Ongkara's spies, they would embark a company of Dokra mercenaries—tough fighting men from one of the poorer, upland parts of the Federation who were permanently stationed there. Once the Dokra company was safely on board, it was away south and the long haul across the Laut Besar to the huge Island of Yawa.

Farhan had no fears of meeting any of the Lord of the Islands'
ships on the journey: no one but the King of Singarasam himself
knew that he was supposed to be heading east to Ziran Atar—he
had sworn the greedy old pirate to secrecy—and the flag fluttering above his head would ensure that any of Ongkara's ships gave
him a respectful greeting. He had secret letters and signs, too, that
would ensure he was unmolested by any Federation shipping,
and why not? He was working for their benefit, even if they did
not know it. And the Han? Well, he could fight—or run from—
any ship of the Celestial Republic that showed interest in him,
except perhaps the new light cruisers that he'd heard the Republic
was building. Besides, the Han these days had almost entirely
given up the practice of piracy among the islands. If they met Han
vessels, they would most likely be ignored. The Celestial Republic
guarded its gum, obat and timber colonies with its own troops—
usually stiffened with Manchu guardsmen or elite Legionnaires—
and its transports, which took the goods north to the homeland,
were slow and ponderous and the *Mongoose* could easily run rings
around them.

The storm passed into the west and sunshine began to dry the
water-glistening deck. Farhan remained half-naked at the prow,
reveling in the heat on his skin. He glanced down at his belly,
which bulged softly over the top of his wet sarong. *Getting fat,* he
thought, *getting old.* He wondered what *she* would say if she saw
his naked body now. Would she be disgusted? He thought not: she
was not interested in boys—she had told him that—she wanted a
man. A man of intelligence, wit and wealth. When he was installed as governor of that pretty little obat island, perhaps he
would summon her and they would live there together, and be
happy. For her, he would exercise more, drink less, give up his
gambling.

"Had an enjoyable bath?" The captain's voice jolted Farhan out
of his delightful reverie. "Because if you are done with your ablu-

tions, our esteemed guest says that she would like to speak to us both in the cabin immediately. We can eat while we talk."

The "guest." Yes. That had all the makings of a rather large squall on the horizon. But Farhan was confident that he could weather it.

The captain kept a good table. He usually fed half a dozen or so of his senior Buginese crew at a time, seated at the end of the board and encouraging them all to eat, drink and make merry. But on this occasion it was only Farhan and Lodi and the captain's guest who gathered under the swaying fan at one end of the long table.

The guest was a huge woman of indeterminate age in a shiny cerise sari, appallingly tight over her arms, belly and thighs, topped with a wide golden scarf. She had a fat pearl mounted on a golden stud in her wide, fleshy nose and a huge blood-red bindi between her heavy, black eyebrows.

"I shall be traveling with you," she had announced, as she waddled onto the deck of the *Mongoose*, a few minutes after the Xi bullyboys had left, accompanied by a tiny teak-colored maidservant who struggled under the weight of an enormous black-leather trunk and two smaller woven bamboo bags.

"Call me Mamaji, everyone does," this vision in pink and gold had announced.

When Captain Lodi had begun to protest, she had seized his left ear between two powerful fingers and whispered into it, and he had collapsed like a pricked bladder and ushered her and her maid aboard, settling them and their luggage in the master cabin, and having the crew shift his gear into the lieutenant's cubbyhole next door.

Farhan had watched her arrival and swift mastery of Lodi with amusement. A relative of some sort, he assumed, a bossy aunt, perhaps, who needed a free passage to the Federation base at Istana Kush. Well, it would not impede their mission. They had to stop there anyway to collect the Dokra troops. It might even be rather fun to see the priggish Captain Lodi being bullied by this formidable Mamaji person. He occasionally got too big for his boots around Farhan, scolding his old friend for his pastimes, questioning his good judgment—the merchant wondered if he might make an ally out of this amusing fat lady.

It was very hot inside the cabin, despite the cleansing rains. Mamaji sat beaming at Lodi and Farhan—she had appropriated the seat at the end of the table, traditionally the captain's place, and Farhan smiled inside at Lodi's loss of authority. The three of them said nothing, while grinning Buginese servants in crisp white jackets brought in a succession of platters of cold food and a pair of dewy bottles, along with plates, cups, knives and so forth, and then left them alone.

"Lord Madani," said Mamaji, turning her huge head and twinkling at Farhan from beady black eyes. "I fear you must think I have been ignoring you since I came on board. No offense was intended, I assure you. I hope you can forgive me."

Captain Lodi moodily picked up a hard-boiled egg, tapped it a few times on the tabletop and began to peel it.

"Not at all. And please, Mamaji—call me Farhan. The title is only a courtesy used in these waters for the head of a trading house; it's really only for impressing the natives," he said. And seizing a large plate, he continued, "Do have one of these pickled sea cucumbers—they are quite delicious, delicate in flavor but very rewarding to the connoisseur."

"I think perhaps we should talk before we eat—if you don't mind, Farhan dear," said Mamaji. "And if *you* don't mind, either, Cyrus," she said, looking at his egg. "You can stuff yourself as much as you like in a few short moments. I won't be long."

Lodi, looking hunted, put down the half-peeled egg and folded his hands in his lap.

"I don't know if Cyrus has told you yet, dear," said Mamaji, smiling coquettishly at Farhan, "but I come here at the express orders of General Vakul himself."

Farhan felt the floor of his stomach dissolve.

"The General has personally instructed me to join your mission—but purely in an advisory capacity. I see by the look on your face, dear, that Cyrus did *not* tell you."

Farhan blinked once or twice but could find nothing to say. General Vakul was the legendary head of the Amrit Shakti. His ultimate chief in the huge intelligence and security organization. Neither Farhan nor Lodi had ever met the General. Very few people had. And neither was his image ever allowed to be seen, by strict order of the High Council. In the dark corridors of the Taj Palace, the sprawling home of the secret organization in Dhilika, his name was spoken only in terrified whispers. Some weaker souls said he did not truly exist, or that he was a ghost or a demon. But everyone knew someone who knew someone who had crossed his path. And there were a hundred stories about him, most of which chilled the listener to the bone. Some Shakti officers claimed that he would sometimes personally attend the interrogation of the most dangerous enemies of the state in the dank cells below the Taj, his face hidden by a black silk hood, and later he would return to his personal quarters with both arms bloody to the elbow. Whether these stories were true or not, no one could say. But no one denied his power. Some said he even dared spy on the Federation's High Council itself, and was not above permanently removing an errant Council member who did not accord with his views. People who opposed General Vakul, or who spoke against him, or even obstructed his policies, swiftly disappeared—and those who asked too many questions about these sudden disappearances also soon vanished forever.

That was who this fat, seemingly jolly matron in the garish too-tight sari represented. That was why she sat at the end of the table in the captain's place.

Farhan swallowed. "An advisory capacity, you say, madam?"

"Call me Mamaji, dear," she said, leering at him, "but yes—I am here to offer advice, which I hope you will accept. I'm here to help. And to sing your praises in the Taj Palace when the mission has been accomplished. As it surely will be. I'm sure none of us wants to disappoint the General. But this is still your mission, Farhan—I couldn't bear to think that I was treading on anyone's toes. The glory will be all yours, dear."

Farhan understood. She was in charge. Her advice had better be heeded—her advice was in effect a command from General Vakul himself. But if the mission was a failure, it would be his head on the block, not hers—and he would find himself chained in the black cells below the Taj awaiting the attentions of the interrogators. He doubted he would merit a personal visit from the silk-hooded General, though.

"Well, as long as we all understand each other," said Mamaji, smiling happily at the two men. "Before we eat, I do have a tiny piece of advice for you—but please do tell me what you honestly think. I propose that we should blood these Dokra troops as soon as possible. We pick them up from Istana Kush tomorrow, yes? We are paying them a lot of the Federation's gold, after all. Let us give them a chance to show us what they can do. Put them through their paces. I know it would greatly reassure the General. He does worry so. What do you think, Farhan dear? Does that sound as if it might be a sensible idea?"

◆ ◆ ◆

Six days later the *Mongoose* nosed around a headland at the
northern end of a wide bay near the southern tip of the Island
of Sumbu. She came in under a single fan-shaped sail, wafted
around the rocky point by a hatful of wind, barely enough to
spread the Lion Standard of Singarasam, which alternately fluttered and flopped from the top of the mainmast.

Her unexpected arrival into Kulu Bay that morning caused a
sensation. On the quay, Farhan could see Han soldiers in their
blue padded-cotton tunics and nodding blue helmet plumes running here and there; he could faintly hear the sound of whistles
blowing. Above the quay, on the walls of the town, pikemen and
archers were gathering in their formations, their officers pushing
men into place and shouting—silently at this distance. Above the
walls, the town climbed up the slopes of a small hill culminating
in a brick-built citadel at the summit. The blue-and-green flag of
the Celestial Republic flew high above this citadel, alongside two
black-and-white vertical banners of the Manchu guards. That
didn't mean much, Farhan thought. The Manchu were inordi-
nately fond of banners. Two banners probably meant no more
than a score of guardsmen. And coupled with a few hundred common Han foot soldiers in the town below, it was not such a formidable enemy as might be assumed. These were not Legionnaires,
after all. The elite, indeed almost-legendary, assault troops of the
Republic would never be left to molder away in a backwater like
this.

The town of Kulu, for all its walls and banners, was not much
more than a fortified trading post. For a generation it had served
as a way station for Han ships traveling up the Sumbu coast to
Singarasam before heading farther north through the Straits of
Kalima to the Celestial Republic. It was a place of dwindling for-
tunes, because the Han merchants' new heavy transports had no
need of a stopping place this close to Yawa. These leviathans could

hold enough stores and water in their vast holds to make the voyage directly across the Laut Besar, south to north, from Sukatan to Banjarput, rather than hopping along the coast like most shipping, and their great size meant they were immune to all but the severest storms.

It might have been an unimportant, provincial outpost—and Farhan had chosen it as a target for precisely this reason—but the merchant was still impressed at the speed at which they reacted to the sight of an alien, heavily armed war vessel cruising into their bay.

There were no other ships of a comparable size with the *Mongoose* in the harbor of Kulu—but then Farhan knew that already. His spy boat had made a thorough reconnaissance on the moonless night before. But a pair of swift schooners were hastily manned with troops, unmoored and darted out from the quay to challenge the far bigger *Mongoose*.

He nodded to Captain Lodi, who issued a string of brisk orders to the waiting Buginese, and six portholes on the landward side of the *Mongoose* popped open and the thick round muzzles of brass cannon appeared, wheeled out by the sweating crews beneath Farhan's feet. It was a declaration of war. In response, on the walls of the town, a signal rocket was fired high up into the air, one of those multicolored Han devices that exploded in blue and green and red showers in the sky above their heads. The combination of colors giving the rocket message its meaning.

There is no turning back now, thought Farhan. *The alarm has been raised.* All along the Sumbu coast Han fortresses would be registering the signal rocket and passing it on. In a matter of hours, more powerful Han outposts to the north, and away south on the long Island of Yawa, would be sending men to investigate. Soldiers from the gum and obat factories inland would be ordered to march on Kulu in strength. Battleships of the Celestial Republic would be sliding down the slips and splashing into harbors hundreds of leagues away.

The nearest schooner was no more than a few score paces away now, and Farhan could see that it was packed with men in blue tunics, the thick fabric reinforced at chest and shoulder with small, square, iron plates, and armed with swords and that curious Han weapon called a Kwan Tao, which was like a short, fat scimitar on the end of a long pole. Fifty or sixty men aboard the lead schooner, and heading straight for the *Mongoose*.

"Destroy the shipping first, Captain, I would suggest," said Farhan.

"You do not tell me how to fight my ship, Madani," said Lodi from his shoulder. "That great grinning sow might have the authority to order me about like a cabin boy—but you do not. Let us be abundantly clear about that."

But, despite his words, Captain Lodi gave a shouted command and there was a storm-like noise of bare feet stamping and running on the deck beneath them. And a few moments later, the foremost cannon roared, followed by the second in line an instant later.

The schooner disappeared in a burst of gray smoke and was replaced by a patch of sea littered with smashed timbers and the sodden blue bodies of men. A few had miraculously survived and were trying to swim in their heavy, waterlogged tunics, the weight of their armor dragging them down. Few of them would make it to the shore, Farhan knew. The ones heading for the second schooner would not fare much better.

A second pair of cannon fired from beneath his feet, and he felt the double pulse through his boot soles. The more distant schooner was hit by one ball that plowed through the packed ranks of Han soldiery on the deck, carving a bloody channel. The second ball missed by a pace and skipped across the blue waves to the boat's right.

It was enough, though. The surviving schooner captain put the tiller about and wind spilled from the sail. As the smaller boat was beginning to turn, the final pair of cannon on the *Mongoose*'s starboard side fired and the schooner was turned to matchwood in the blink of an eye. In less than a score of heartbeats, Farhan had seen two ships utterly destroyed and more than a hundred men killed. He felt sick. It was not the first death he had seen but he'd always been better at the dry discipline of planning an attack than witnessing its execution.

The *Mongoose* had reached the far side of the bay by now and at Captain Lodi's command the ship smoothly went about and began to cross the bay again, a little closer in to the harbor on the opposite tack. Farhan heard the crack of a cannon from the walls of the town and a dozen yards in front of the prow a waterspout kicked up. He glanced behind him at the bow, where Mamaji was sitting in a vast wicker chair beside the Buginese wheelman, her maid holding a black silk parasol above her head to keep off the blazing sun. Neither woman looked at all perturbed at being in the midst of a sea battle; the maid had a face like carved stone— her habitual expression—and Mamaji wore her perpetual smile and was slurping something alarmingly yellowish from a crystal beaker held in one plump hand.

Another cannon fired from the town, just as Lodi gave the order for an adjustment to their course to bring them closer in to the harbor. The ball screamed through the air an arm's length from Farhan's head, severing a single backstay, a thin rope that helped to keep the mast in position, but otherwise passing over the deck without touching a thing.

"About now would be a good time to begin the bombardment, wouldn't you say, Captain?" Farhan realized he was nervous. He talked when he was nervous. He was terrified, in truth. That enemy cannonball had passed so close to him that he had felt its wind on his cheek. One pace to the right and it would have taken his head clean off.

"You keep your damned mouth shut, Madani. Last warning," growled the captain. He was staring ferociously at the town through a battered brass telescope. But he snapped the instrument shut and gave an order to the Buginese lieutenant beside him.

As Farhan looked on, the portside cannon began to fire, one after the other in a rippling broadside that sent the shot screaming across the bay to smash into the brick walls of the town, which was now not much more than two hundred paces away.

The damage done was far greater than Farhan had been expecting. Cannon were not his area of expertise—sometimes he wondered what exactly his area of expertise was, but he knew that it was not cannon. The balls must have been of a particular kind, fitted with an extra destructive element inside the solid iron casing, because, once the missiles had smashed through the brick wall that surrounded the town, they exploded and showered the interior of the fortification with hundreds of shards of white-hot metal.

The effects of the bombardment were horrific. Through the gaps blown in the walls, Farhan could see the blood-saturated detritus of battle, severed limbs, headless torsos, crushed and shredded men, scattered weapons. A few survivors tottered about, dazed and deafened, their smoke-blackened blue tunics contrasting with the gore-splashed town walls.

The *Mongoose* reached the northern side of the harbor and came about, turning smoothly on its own wake to begin the southward pass. The starboard-side guns began to fire. More slowly now, carefully aimed, perhaps one gun every dozen heartbeats. When all had fired along the line, the foremost gun, now reloaded, fired again and so on down the starboard side. The town walls, already holed in several places, all but collapsed under this steady, relentless bombardment.

One cannon fired from the citadel at the highest part of the town: it flew long and wide, soaring over the top of the mast, splashing into the sea a good fifty yards behind the ship. The outer walls might have been reduced to rubble but the upper town was still defiant. The blue-and-green standard of the Celestial Kingdom still flew from the citadel, and the handful of Manchu up there were still working their guns.

Captain Lodi, perhaps regretting his earlier harshness to his friend, put a hand on Farhan's shoulder. "Look up there," he said, pointing beyond the bow of the ship to the headland at the northern end of the bay. "The Dokra have kept exactly to their schedule."

Farhan could see men wearing scarlet jackets, white sashes across their chests and huge scarlet turbans, dozens, scores of men, with long muskets in their hands, sabers at their waists, scrambling over the skyline of the headland and spilling down across the shoulder of land toward the ruined, smoking walls of the town in a red flood.

The blooding of the Dokra had begun.

CHAPTER 7

C aptain Musa Yoritomo sat cross-legged in the center of a pure white square of rice-matting in the courtyard outside the bridal suite in the Palace of Ashjavat. He was dressed in a long white silk robe and nothing else. He had carefully washed every inch of his body before the ceremony, had shaved all the hairs from his face, arms, legs and torso and had trimmed and oiled his long black mane before tying it neatly behind his head with a white ribbon. On the mat in front of him lay the naked blade of a short, slightly curved dagger, called a tanto, about a foot long with a ridged ebony handle. It was his personal, secondary weapon; the weapon of last resort in a battle if his katana were to break or be lost. He had spent nearly an hour before dawn cleaning the handle with sweet oil and sharpening the blade. It was keener than his razor now.

He had said good bye to his men—clasping hands with all eleven of them. And now they stood in a loose circle around the square rice mat, each man immaculate and slightly inhuman in his black-lacquered armor, face mask and wide-brimmed helmet. Each man had a hand gripped on his katana, ready, at the nod from Yoritomo, to draw, slice and make a clean end of this business. But Yoritomo's pride would not let him give that order. It was his death, and he would administer it himself without faltering, without a cry of pain; as his father had, and his father's father before that, all down the long line of the Yoritomo clan.

Yoritomo closed his eyes, his cupped hands resting placidly in

his lap. His eternal spirit, he reflected, had no more need to reside
in this frail body. In a little while he would set it free to join the
nebulous mass of his ancestors' spirits—the Seirei—the collection
of souls which made up the immortal god Yori, after whom his
clan was named. He had begun his journey on Earth as just one
tiny part of that eternal whole, made flesh as a mewling baby,
and growing in power and skill as the years were piled upon his
shoulders. He knew that his mother would weep when she heard
the news of his death, and his wife, too. But he also knew they
would be proud of the manner of his passing. And his son Ari
would surely be proud, too. Now it was time to release the burden of this life and be reunited with his kin.

He dwelled for a few moments on the shame that he had been
accused of, the "disgrace" that had led him to this place of death
in this far southern land. And flicked that thought away: there was
no shame—he had warded the Lady Katerina as well as on any
other night, standing alert and ready outside her door all through
the dark hours. She had claimed that an intruder had broken into
her apartments and slain her new husband in his bed. But this was
not true. None had passed him. None had entered the room. Yet
he had accepted her sentence of death for his "failure" to protect
her without a word.

It was clear, at least to Yoritomo, if not to any of the Southron
fools of this garish city, that the Lady had killed the man herself—
why, he had no idea. It was not his place to make conjectures. She
had killed him and she wished to pretend that she had not. And so
he was to die, not for neglecting his duty, but merely to bolster her
pretense that an assassin had entered her chamber. He would not
protest. He welcomed the order. Even if the reasons were obscure
to him, he was dying for his lord—what greater honor could a
Niho knight wish for? When she had ordered him to make an end
of himself, he had merely bowed his head and made his prepara-
tions.

Yoritomo opened his eyes. He looked about the courtyard. A few of the Ashjavat nobles had taken up places around the walls of the yard, some whispering to their neighbors behind their hands, marveling at the sight of a Niho warrior preparing to destroy himself. He did not despise them. They were not his equals to be judged by his code: they were weak, ill-disciplined sheep, barely human. He was glad that the Lady would rule them when he was gone: they needed a firm and ruthless shepherd.

And there she was: Katerina herself. She had paid him the compliment of dressing entirely in white, the color of death, to show that she appreciated his final sacrifice. That was courteous of her: as befitted the daughter of an Emperor. He caught her eye, and she nodded slightly to him, and gave him the ghost of a smile. Yoritomo understood her perfectly. It was time.

He lifted his chin and spoke: "I, Musa, captain and knight, headman of Clan Yoritomo, shall this day make my death in the presence of my lord, Princess Katerina Kasimirovitch Astrokova, and my comrades of the Niho Brotherhood. I wish to atone for all my errors and wash my spirit clean with the blood of my sacrifice. I thank the Lady for permitting me to serve her these many years, and for granting me this release from the burden of life. I commend my eldest son Ari as the finest of my children to her service. May he prove himself worthy to take up the duties and responsibilities that I gladly lay down this day."

"I shall gladly receive him into my service," said Katerina. "I shall welcome him, secure in the knowledge that he will discharge his duties as faithfully as his father before him, or any member of the Yoritomo, which has served me and my family so loyally down the centuries."

"I go now to my ancestors. I go to join the Seirei," said Yoritomo. He picked up the tanto from the white mat in front of him with his right hand.

"I release you from my service," the Lady replied.

Yoritomo could feel the warmth of the feeble winter sun on his shoulders, like the gaze of a loving mother. He could smell frying garlic coming from the kitchens—and it seemed beautiful to him. The murmuring of the crowd of Ashjavat nobles sounded like the gentle singing of running water over the stony bed of a brook.

Life is sweet, he thought.

He put the blade to his right thigh, resting it on the white skin just below his genitals. With one smooth movement he sliced deeply through the skin and muscle, chopping through the big pulsing artery and lifting the knife clear. The blood, thick and purple, welled from the cut. Yoritomo felt nothing but a slight burn from the blade. He put the point of his dagger into the crook of his left elbow, punched it in and sliced down along the line of his forearm, dragging the razor steel through veins, tendons, ligaments until it reached the base of his thumb. His mind felt clear. The pain no more than a background hum, a minor distraction. *One more cut,* he told himself. *One more and I am done with this Earth.*

He lifted the tanto to his neck. Put the point behind his ear, allowing the cold, blood-smeared blade to dig into his flesh under his chin, and with one sharp, twisting, downward tug, he severed the fat artery that fed the brain, bringing the dagger around in a half circle that almost entirely cut through his windpipe.

A gust of warm lung air blew purple bubbles through his opened throat. His head slumped, chin resting on his chest. His head was spinning now; the darkness encroaching. Through dimming eyes he looked down at his body; the white silk robe was drenched. He looked at the white mat and saw the purplish tide oozing outwards from his crossed legs.

It was done. It was done well. He was free.

◆ ◆ ◆

Katerina watched Yoritomo slump as the spirit left her soldier's body. She walked forward, parting the craning nobles and the gathered Niho guards. She stopped by the body, still as a stone but sheeted in dark blood. She bowed once, bending from the waist until her head was lower than her hips. Then she straightened up and knelt at the very edge of the sodden white rice-straw mat. She dipped one finger in the purplish mess and put it to her lips. It tasted as salty as the sea but also with a tart, vinegary edge. So the tales were true, she thought.

She stood and looked at the Niho guards gathered around her, grim as death in their black face masks, right hands still clutched around their katana hilts.

"You," she said, pointing at the nearest man. "Murakami, isn't it? You are captain now. And your first task is to take the body of your comrade for burning. See that he is given all the rites and honors that are his due."

"He already has earned honor enough for a dozen lifetimes, Lady," said the knight, his voice muffled either by deep emotion or by the black-lacquered mask.

"Yes, well, take him away. Do whatever you think is right. And I want you to double the guard around my person from this moment on. There are turbulent times ahead of us."

"As you command, Lady," Murakami said, and bowed.

That evening, the throne room of the Palace of Ashjavat was as bright as day. A thousand candles had been lit and the golden fittings on the furniture and walls reflected the light in dazzling splinters. Katerina had changed into a peacock silk gown of iridescent blues and greens and her maid, Sara, had made her pale hair into an elaborate tower of plaits, held in place with jeweled pins. She sat in the Chair of State, a carved black oak monstrosity with a towering back and square, muscular arms in the

shape of lions' paws, which was designed for a big-framed Southron warrior to sit in, not a delicate sixteen-year-old Khevan girl.
She looked tiny, fragile even, in its huge embrace. On either side
of the chair, still as statues, stood her two bodyguards Murakami
and Tesso, the new captain's deputy. Around the throne room, the
nine other Niho knights had taken up positions against the walls.

Katerina looked out over the crowd of Ashjavat nobles and
merchants, more than a hundred men and women. Anyone who
was anyone in the city had been summoned and was now packed
into the throne room that evening. Katerina had no intention of
doing this performance more than once. They had been served
wine and sweetmeats by the palace servants, and treated with
courtesy, but none had been told why they had been summoned,
although most could guess.

Katerina recognized a few of the faces from the wedding feast
and she had probably been introduced to some of the greater men
in the throng but she made no signs of recognition; she just sat,
blank-faced and as still as the Niho knights on either side, while
this aristocratic rabble filled the room and stared inquiringly up
at her as she sat on the dais at the far end of the hall. They seemed
reluctant to come close to her, and only the pressure of new arrivals from the big double doors at the far end of the room forced the
crowd toward the throne.

They fear me, thought Katerina. *Good.*

A gong sounded and over the heads of the crowd, Katerina saw
that the doors were being pushed shut by a pair of burly slaves.
Through the closing doors she caught a glimpse of a smirking
Captain Artur of the Palace Guard. She hoped he was not going
to be a problem. The man had taken the news of Khazeki's death
without the slightest sign of distress and had readily agreed to
have the five gates of the city of Ashjavat locked and manned by
his men until further notice. But there was something altogether
too familiar in his tone, and he had made a great play of seizing

her hand and kissing it before he had rushed away to do her bidding. No matter. She would deal with him later. She rose to her feet from the oversized chair and took a step toward the crowd. She held a parchment scroll tightly in her left hand.

"People of Ashjavat," she said quietly. All murmuring stopped and every ear in the room strained to hear her. "Your prince, my noble husband, is dead. Alas! He was slain by cowardly assassins who came into our chamber and stole his life while I lay sleeping beside him. We do not yet know the identity of these assassins, nor do we know the identity of all the conspirators who planned this foul act. But we will not rest until we have exposed them. My prince's spies and your very own heroes of the Palace Guard are working night and day to uncover the truth."

She lifted the scroll and wagged it at the crowd. "It pains me to tell you all that we already have evidence that suggests that some of the conspirators who arranged this black deed are in this very room, at this very moment, wearing the masks of friendship and loyalty to Ashjavat. They are among you, even as I speak. At your very elbows. But, this I swear to you, they will be rooted out. All of them. And when they are discovered there will be no mercy for them. Death is coming for them all."

Katerina paused and was gratified to see several members of her audience eyeing their neighbors with a newfound suspicion.

"We talked, my prince and I, in the sweet but too-short time we had together, about his plans for Ashjavat and the direction that he wished to take this land. And I hereby pledge to you that I mean to follow his plans for this great nation and, as the new ruler of Ashjavat, to carry through his wise designs with all my strength . . ."

"Hold on just one damn moment!" A short, dark, moon-faced man, clearly a high noble by his gorgeous velvet robe, was pushing through the crowd. He reached the front rank and a small space opened up around him, his neighbors edging away until he

found himself alone. "By the ancient laws and customs of Ashjavat, the ruler, the High Prince of Ashjavat, is chosen by the Gathering of Peers. His widow does not automatically have the right
to rule in her dead husband's name . . ."

"Identify yourself, if you please."

"I am Andrei, Count of Tashkhan. I am—I mean I was—first
cousin to your husband Prince Khazeki. And I have as much right
to the throne of Ashjavat as you."

Katerina unrolled the scroll a handsbreadth and peered at its
totally blank interior. She raised her eyes to the dark-haired nobleman.

"You are Andrei of Tashkhan?"

"I am," said the man proudly, throwing back his shoulders.

"Seize him," she said quietly. And an instant later the man was
immobilized in the iron grip of a pair of Niho guards. "Take him
to the interrogation chamber."

As the man was dragged away, protesting, Katerina looked
over the murmuring crowd and raised the scroll once more. "His
name, along with many others, is on the list of possible suspects.
But do not fear, my people, his guilt or innocence will be determined before too long. My loyal inquisitors will see that the truth
comes out."

Katerina saw that a small commotion was occurring in the
center of the crowd. It looked very much as if a man with the sloping eyes of a Han and a white streak in the center of his shining
black hair was trying to physically subdue a small, elderly Han
woman in a tight-fitting white silk gown. He had his hands on her
shoulders, and he was speaking urgently, desperately into her
face. He lost his battle and the woman squirmed out of his grip
and pushed her way to the front of the crowd.

"Murderer!" she cried. "Coldhearted killer of my son! May you
burn in all the Seven Hells for eternity for what you have done."

Captain Murakami had already taken a step toward the woman. His blade was half-unsheathed.

"No," said Katerina quietly. "Let her speak. Mother Kwan Li, what are you trying to say? You cannot truly think I would do something so wicked to the man I loved."

"You killed him. You married him, bedded him and then killed him in his sleep." The Han woman was weeping unashamedly now, fat, oily tears carving tracks through the caked makeup on her shriveled cheeks. The young man with the white streak in his hair was standing slightly behind her, his arms by his sides. His face a picture of tragedy.

"Highness," he said, "forgive her, I beg you. She is deranged by grief. She does not know what she says. She has lost her son—and her mind with it."

"Take her away, let her rest. She will see things in a new light soon enough." Katerina beckoned to a pair of burly slaves standing by the closed door of the chamber. "Take the lady to her quarters. See she has everything that she requires."

"Deranged, am I? I will show you deranged . . ." The elderly woman reached up into her piled black hair, extracted a gleaming foot-long steel pin and rushed at Katerina.

This time the princess did not stop Murakami. She took a pace backward and the Niho knight smoothly stepped in front of his mistress, his katana bared. As the bereaved Kwan Li rushed forward, the daggerlike hairpin lifted, Murakami took a half pace forward, lunged and simply impaled the elderly woman on the end of his blade. The bloody tip burst out of the back of her white silk robe for all in the audience hall to see. The long, sharp hairpin clattered on the dais. Then Murakami withdrew the steel and, with one swipe, hacked off the old woman's head and set it rolling across the floor.

The room was stunned into silence. The Ashjavat nobility had not ridden to war in two generations; only a handful of the men in the room had ever seen blood spilled in anger.

Katerina stepped forward again. "This has been most unfortunate. We are all suffering grief at the loss of our beloved Prince Khazeki. So unless anyone else has anything they wish to say, I think we should draw this doleful audience to a close."

She scanned the crowd for a moment. "Does anyone have anything to say?"

She tapped the scroll against her left leg. A small movement but enough to draw every eye in the room; enough to make her point.

She sat back down on the massive wooden throne and watched as the aristocracy of Ashjavat shuffled out of the audience chamber, some looking back at her fearfully. Three slaves were dealing with the blood and meat and mess before the dais that had once been her mother-in-law. She felt light, free. It was accomplished. Her course was now set.

She turned her head to the faceless, gleaming, lacquered bulk of Murakami standing beside her, his right hand on his sheathed katana.

"I think that went rather well, all things considered," she said.

CHAPTER 8

———— ✄ ————

Extract from *Ethnographic Travels* by
Professor Tolmund K. Parehki of the University of Dhilika

The ancient Wukarta dynasty of Yawa has many myths and legends that are still recalled in the public shadow-puppet perfor-
mances and told in the markets by professional storytellers to this
day. Perhaps the most famous concerns the family's acquisition of
the Kris of Wukarta Khodam.

One day many centuries ago, a young prince named Arjun was
watching the heavens from his palace in the hills of central Yawa
and he saw a star fall to Earth. The prince was a bold fellow and
bored with his soft life so he gathered his bow and quiver and jour-
neyed far to the west to the place where the star had landed near the
roots of the Black Mountain. When he came there he found that a
crater had been gouged into the vegetation, the plants blackened
and dying all around the rim, and in the center was a vast shell the
shape and color of a mussel, smoking hot and cracked to reveal its
pink interior. As he drew near, Arjun saw, in the glowing heart, a
beautiful maiden lying asleep on a mound of silken pillows. Her
naked body was the color of silver, her hair like a sheet of red flame
spread out upon the pillows. Arjun saw her and knew love for the very
first time. He knelt beside her and kissed her. She opened her eyes,
and seeing his strength and beauty, she loved him in return. Without words, for the lady could not speak in the tongues of men, she
embraced him. And they made love in the shell's glowing heart.

Inside the mussel shell, time had no dominion. In its shelter the
human frame required no food and no water; and for nine days
Arjun and the star princess lay together in joy. And on the ninth

day, a baby was born to them, a beautiful boy with hair the color of flame.

Arjun named the boy Karta, which means "gift from the heavens" in the old Yawa language, and he would have been content to stay with the child and his star princess forever. But it was not to be. The arrival of the shell had roused Grandfather Pande from his Black Mountain lair above the valley. The blacksmith set down his hammer, banked his forge, and gathering his many sons, he came down and approached the shell in stealth. While Arjun and his star princess made love, the Pande watched from the darkness outside, and he desired her. Yet the great Pande had no regard for the love of a woman; he made his own children in his forge, from fat and blood and bone. He desired the star princess for the matter she embodied. He desired her flesh to make a magical sword. The first kris.

On the tenth night, Grandfather Pande and all his sons rushed into the shell. They beat Arjun with iron clubs, breaking his bones. Then, believing him to be dead, they cast his body out into the jungle to be carrion for the Ghost Tigers. But when the Pande's sons struck the star princess with their clubs, they found their blows left no mark. The iron weapons rang like bells against her silver skin. So, instead, they seized her and bound her with silk ropes and, singing their triumph, they carried her up the Black Mountain.

Yet Arjun did not die. He lay for a day and a night in the forest. The Ghost Tigers came and taking pity on him, they licked the blood from him with their rough tongues, and with the power of their saliva they healed his broken bones. Their leader, Raal, brought him fresh meat to eat and watched over him while he healed. And Arjun came back into his strength.

On the twelfth day Arjun came out of the jungle, whole and hale, and he went back to the mussel shell to find the baby crying for his parents. He picked up his son, Karta, and gave him to the

Ghost Tiger mothers, setting him to suckle at their teats. Then he collected up his bow and quiver and full of rage he climbed the Black Mountain in search of his love.

Arjun crept to the entrance of the Pande's fortress and, shooting from the darkness, he slew many of the blacksmith's sons. And when the rest had fled in terror, Arjun entered his enemy's lair, the lust of vengeance upon him. He found the Pande alone in the heart of the mountain, standing before his roaring forge with a beautiful kris in his hands. Its blade was the color of the star princess's skin; the wood of the handle was the color of her eyes.

"I forged her," the Pande said. "I threw her living into the flames. I took her flesh, blood and bone and made it steel and wood—and the world shall never know a blade like this again. It is filled with her soul, her Khodam, filled with the essence of the stars, and no Earth-made material can stand against it. Look!" The Pande took a bar of iron and threw it spinning high into the air. Before it landed, he sliced once with the kris and cut through the falling metal as if it were no more than a cobweb, the two pieces clanging to the forge floor.

Arjun's eyes were filled with tears. He nocked an arrow but so blinded was he by his grief that the shaft missed his mark and sank deep into the Pande's thigh. The blacksmith screamed, dropped the sword and, spouting blood, he hobbled away, fleeing into the warren of his mountain realm. Arjun picked up the kris, he kissed the handle, his tears falling on the silver blade. And as his finger touched the keen edge, a drop of red blood bloomed and the metal began to glow with a fiery hue, the color of the star princess's flaming hair.

In that manner, the Kris of Wukarta Khodam came into the possession of the Wukarta. Arjun took the baby home, riding on the back of a Ghost Tiger, and in time his son grew and had children of his own, and his children called themselves Wukarta, the people of Karta.

They decided to make camp there that night, although there was still a good hour left of daylight. Semar had not been too difficult to find. Jun had taken a dozen steps into the jungle and called his name twice and the little man had appeared, grinning, from behind a large rock. Jun had been alarmed to find his servant gone and had asked him with more than a touch of hauteur where he had been hiding.

"It's not a good idea, my prince, to shelter under a coconut tree in a rainstorm—or at any other time for that matter," said Semar.

"Why not?" asked Jun. "It seemed as good a place as any other."

Semar bent down and picked up a yellow coconut pod from the leaf litter of the forest floor. It was twice the size of the little man's head. He tossed it at Jun, who caught it easily.

"When the wind blows, it shakes the trees and they drop their fruit," the old man said. "They also drop their fruit when the wind doesn't blow."

Jun held the coconut in his hands. He could hear the water sloshing around inside. He imagined the heavy nut falling on his body from the top of the tree as he sheltered against the trunk—and shuddered.

"Why did you not warn me?" Jun asked the old man. But his imperious tone had disappeared. Semar took him by the hand and led him back to the beach, where Ketut had already got a fire going. Semar indicated that Jun should sit and the old man took the coconut from him, went to the boat and after fishing around in its depths for a moment emerged with a parang, a long, broad, steel knife used for cutting back jungle greenery. As Jun sat and watched, Semar, with a few deft strokes of the blade, hacked the top from the coconut and passed the decapitated fruit to Jun, who drank deeply of the sweet juice. Semar sat down beside him.

"I must tell you, my prince, that I have certain skills that perhaps you did not know I possessed. It is one of the few benefits of a long life that one accretes wisdom. You pile it up over the years. I can trim up a coconut neatly, as you see."

He gestured to Jun and the prince found himself handing the heavy fruit to the old man who took a long drink. Jun could never have imagined himself sharing a drinking vessel, even one as crude as this, with a servant at the Watergarden. But much had changed—and although it felt rather strange, it did not feel entirely wrong to him.

"There are certain other things that I can do as well." Semar passed the coconut back to Jun. "I can make a tasty stew from dried fish. I can sew up a tear on a jacket so you would never know the damage had been done. And I can read destiny on people's faces."

Jun was aware that Ketut had joined them beside the fire. She stood looking down at the two men, her hands on her hips.

"Did you say destiny?" Jun asked, slightly confused.

"I can look into people's faces and see their future," Semar said. Jun frowned at him.

"I am rarely wrong," said Semar. By some trick, some combination of bright sun coming off the sea and the shadows thrown by the trees, his eyes now seemed to be entirely black, the white swallowed up by the iris and pupil.

"You saw my destiny?" Jun said. "You know what will happen to me in the future?"

"Not all of it," said Semar. "But I saw enough of it to know that you would not be killed by a coconut falling on your head."

"What did you see?"

"I saw you sitting on the Obat Bale. I saw you sitting in splendor on the throne of the King of Singarasam."

Jun did not know what to say. He hid his face in the coconut. He drank and passed it to Ketut. The silence stretched out and became unbearable.

"So I am to be the Lord of the Islands one day?"

"So it would seem," said the old man.

"Well, if I am to be the ruler of the whole Laut Besar, you had both better start treating me with a good deal more respect," said Jun. He meant it as a joke. But it came out merely as childish petulance. Neither Semar nor Ketut said anything at all.

Jun said, "I suppose that explains why you didn't tell *me* to move in the storm. You knew a coconut wouldn't fall on me. But why did you move?"

"I can see your future," said Semar. "I cannot see mine. For all I know it may be filled with falling coconuts."

And, mercifully, they all laughed.

Semar proved his second boast that night: he made a quick and easy stew out of dried fish and spices from their provisions, translucent coconut flesh and wild green papaya that he tracked down and plucked from the jungle. It was extremely good, Jun admitted to himself, but as he had not eaten since a rushed bowl of rice at breakfast before they had set sail he was ravenously hungry, and that perhaps made all the difference.

As the sun began to sink, the three of them sat drowsily by the fire, which Semar had fed with green leaves and grasses so that curtains of smoke wafted to and fro in the light sea breeze and kept the mosquitoes at bay. After the delicious fish stew, Ketut had made tea in an old battered iron pot and they passed it around and sipped the fragrant liquid as they lay watching the shadows lengthen and the sky turn from orange to pink to milky gray.

"Can you truly see the future in a face?" Ketut said. "It is not trickery or a joke or some such piece of nonsense to amuse children?"

"Would I admit it if it were a trick?" Semar said.

Ketut smiled, a quick twisting of one side of her mouth. It made her look much older and more cynical, Jun thought.

"Do me then," she said. "Prove yourself. Tell me what you can see in my face."

"Come and sit before me," said the old man. And when Ketut was settled cross-legged in front of Semar, the old servant stared into her face, and lightly traced her brow with one gnarled finger. Jun, watching from the other side of the fire, noticed that his tiny servant's eyes appeared to have turned entirely black again, but with the drifting smoke and dying light it was difficult to be sure.

"I see love. I see a great passion in your future," Semar said.

Ketut sprang to her feet as if she had been insulted. The transformation in her was extraordinary: she seemed instantly filled with a boiling rage.

"Don't! Don't you do that," she snarled. "Don't do that to me!"

"I only tell what I see."

"Love is for credulous fools. Love leads women to their own destruction. Love is slow poison for the soul."

Semar shrugged. He loosened the sarong around his waist and pulled it up to his shoulders. He lay down beside the fire and settled himself, covered from neck to knee by the sarong, his staff by his side, his head pillowed on a bundle of his spare clothes.

Ketut was pacing up and down on the other side of the fire.

"I think you are a fraud, old man," she said. "I think you tell people what you think they want to hear. I say you are a liar."

Semar said nothing. Jun could see that his eyes were closed.

"And you, richboy—" Ketut was pointing an accusatory finger at Jun. "You useless puppy, you will never sit on the Obat Bale of Singarasam. Much as you might wish to."

Jun was about to protest that he had no such ambitions but by the time he opened his mouth, Ketut was gone, striding away from the fire into the dark jungle.

"Let her go, my prince," said Semar, without raising his head or even opening his eyes. "She won't desert us. She'll be back before the morning."

"Did you read that in her face, too?" Jun's tone was contemptuous.

Semar opened one dark eye. "No, not in her face. In that." He jerked his chin over at the long, low form of the boat drawn up on the sand. "She won't abandon her only means of livelihood just because I blew on her feathers a little."

Semar began to snore shortly after that. Ketut did not return. And Jun, although as tired as he had ever been, did not feel disposed to sleep. He resented being called a "useless puppy" but he knew that looking out through Ketut's eyes he must seem fit for very little. There was not much call for poetry on a fishing boat, and the fact that he could recount all the names of his ancestors back a hundred generations now seemed a less-than-astounding feat. He got up and went over to the boat and, fumbling slightly in the dark, he found the recurved bow that he had hurriedly packed before they set sail. The bow was already damp and he dug in his pack for a tub of wax and a clean cloth and took them all over to the fire, where he sat down and began to wipe the horn-and-bamboo bow free of salt and sand.

He dumped a little more wood from the pile onto the fire, so the flames flickered higher and he had light to work by. It was full dark by now and moths and bats flitted through the trees behind him. He wondered, as he worked on the bow, rubbing wax into all the grooves and corners, what Ketut was doing out there in the black jungle. Probably crying, he thought. Probably blubbering up snot and slime like the dirty Dewa that she was. And all because an old man had told her that someday some dolt would take a shine to her.

But then who was he to sneer at her for weeping? He recalled his own night of shame. He thought about his father, drowning in a sea of flies, his nose and mouth filling until tightly packed with their crawling bodies; he thought about the flames of the burning pavilions, the hacked bodies of the dead servants; he thought about the gray-cloaked demon with his dark face and high cheekbones, that slash for a mouth and the hooded eyes

Jun found he was staring into the flames; the blaze danced and flickered before his eyes, the color of the fire seeming to turn a greenish tinge, and slowly an image of the dark man appeared in its heart. The demon seemed to be looking directly at Jun. He saw that the demon's eyes were in fact gray, the iris veined and cracked with black lines. It was some trick, Jun thought, some horrible deception of his senses. He closed his eyes, opened them again. The cruel face still stared out at him from the heart of the green fire. Without his headdress, Jun saw that his head was covered with a cap of tiny black curls of hair.

"Who are you?" the demon said. His voice was cold and sharp as a blade of flint.

Jun was too surprised to speak. All over his body the fine hairs stood up.

The demon smiled. "I know you now. You are the son, the milksop heir to the Wukarta, who stood and looked on terrified and helpless as your ancient sire fought me."

Jun straightened his shoulders. "I am Prince Arjun Wukarta and I will make you pay for my father's death, demon. I will follow you to the ends of the world . . ."

"You are—what?—you are pursuing me? For vengeance?"

The demon began to laugh, and the horrible sound made Jun want to run away, far, far away into the jungle. He felt hot and cold at the same time. He felt his bladder loosening.

"You are chasing after me. Of course you are. You seek revenge and the return of the Khodam. So where are you, my young vengeance-seeker? Still on Taman, I'd guess . . ."

The green fire was suddenly extinguished. The demon disappeared. Snuffed out like a candle. And there was Semar, standing over him with an uptipped bucket of seawater. The bizarre contact with the demon and the sudden loss of light made Jun dizzy. He sensed rather than saw Semar squat next to him in the new, chillier darkness, and felt the old man's gentling hand on his shoulder.

"It might be better, my prince," Semar said soothingly, "if, on this arduous journey of ours, you did not proudly announce your name and titles to any passing fellow who might ask. Plain Jun will suffice if you want to introduce yourself."

"He was there, in the fire. He was speaking to me as if he were actually here."

"It was but a specter, a projection of himself across the night."

"Who is he? How . . . How did he do that?"

"His name is Mangku. But do not say it aloud, nor too often. Particularly when you look into the heart of a fire. Some people say that fire is the original magic, that all fires everywhere are part of one eternal magical fire. So if you look into a fire and think of him, and he's staring into his own blaze and searching with his mind, then connections can be made. Mangku has learned to do this. But it's no more than a conjurer's trick, really."

"He is a demon." Jun's words were half question, half statement.

"He's no demon, merely an old man, but he *is* a sorcerer," Semar said. "Nevertheless, we shall best him, my prince. He believes himself more powerful than he truly is."

"He knows where we are; he knows we are pursuing him."

"I am afraid he does—now. But do not let him trouble you. He is too far away to hurt us. Sleep now, my prince, and do not think of him. I will watch the darkness for a while."

Jun wrapped a sleeping sarong around his shoulders and lay down on the cold sand. It was surprisingly hard and he wriggled and squirmed for a while until his body had made a natural hollow. *How does one* not *think of someone? It is impossible. By deliberately not thinking of them you are, in fact, thinking of them.* And how did Semar know so much about this sorcerer, anyway? He clearly knew him well. But how? *Stop,* he told himself, *stop this line of thought right now and go to sleep.*

He remembered an old trick that his mother had taught him long ago when he was just a boy. In his head, he pictured the Watergarden as perfect as it had been all his life—except for that last horrible night. He saw a blood-red dragonfly bright as a jewel and watched it hover and glide through his mind, alighting on a waving stem here, a twig there, dipping through shafts of sunlight. It swooped down close to the water, skimming the green surface and landed gently on the lip of a lily pad.

And Jun fell asleep.

CHAPTER 9

———————◦❀◦———————

The Dokra poured down the shoulder of the northern headland and formed up to the right of the fortified town and fifty paces from its battered and gaping walls. The company of ninety men formed two lines, fixed their spike bayonets, raised their muskets and waited for the order from their captain, a tiny figure distinguished by a black cross belt rather than a white one over his scarlet tunic, and two golden epaulets. The company's discipline was magnificent. As Farhan watched, at least three of the men standing stock-still in the two lines were shot down by Manchu sharpshooters on the walls of Kulu. As the men fell, they were dragged to the rear by the underofficers (white cross belt, single gold epaulet) and the line closed up again. Quite what the captain was waiting for, Farhan could not imagine— unless perhaps he wanted to show that his men could die without a word of complaint.

Standing on the deck of the *Mongoose*, Farhan found he was holding his breath. He glanced over at Mamaji, who was watching with interest through a small telescope from the rail a dozen yards away, with her petite maid standing beside her and shading her from the hot sun with a black parasol. It was midmorning and hot as a meat-griddle on the deck.

A cannonball from the town, the first for some time now, screamed in and smashed into the bow of the ship, bursting through the rail and bouncing once on the deck to sail over the other side and splash into the water. A blizzard of splinters from the shattered rail showered the deck, one the size and shape of a javelin sticking out almost vertically from where it had stuck, deep in the polished teak beside the tiller. Neither Mamaji nor her maid flinched when the ball had struck and they barely moved now, the maid idly brushing some flakes of wood from her silk-clad chest. Mamaji merely shifted the focus of her telescope to the upper citadel where the black Manchu banners flapped lazily in the slight breeze.

Finally, the Dokra captain gave the order to fire. A line of gray smoke plumes spewed from the musket mouths of the first line. And the scarlet-clad men immediately knelt and began to reload their weapons. At a cry from the captain, the men in the second line began to march forward, passing through the rank of kneeling men and advancing about ten paces. They straightened their line—one man had been shot out of it—and fired a volley into the gap in the town walls that was only forty paces distant and now lined with blue-clad Han soldiers. The massed volley, forty-odd men firing at such close range, smashed into the blue crowd of Han like an enormous invisible fist, punching a hole through their ranks as bloodied men fell left and right. The second line of scarlet men dropped to their knees and began to reload.

The first line of Dokra, already reloaded, stood and advanced through the ranks of their comrades until they were only thirty yards from the gap in the wall. They fired, sweeping almost all the remaining defenders away, and dropped to reload. The second rank of men behind them now charged through their ranks, screaming their outlandish war cries, plunging through the shattered rubble of brick and masonry and disappearing into the town. The first rank were soon up and ready and, at a word from their captain, they followed their brethren and were swallowed by the smoke.

Captain Lodi shouted a command and there were twin splashes only a heartbeat apart as the two attack launches were dropped from their cradles into the turquoise sea. A swarm of Buginese sailors flowed over the sides of the *Mongoose* and swiftly filled the two boats, the little nut-brown men dressed only in brief sarongs, armed with keen-edged parangs and double-shotted pistols and grinning madly to show teeth stained blood-red from their habit of chewing betel nut before battle.

Farhan knew he must go with them but he felt his dread like a physical weight around his shoulders. Death was all around that sparkling morning. He was surprised, though, to see Mamaji's massive form in the act of climbing over the rail. She was much more nimble than he had ever imagined. Her massive haunches wobbled at the top of the rail, the shiny, bright green fabric of to-day's sari stretched tautly over her vast behind, then she disappeared below. He ran to the rail, looked over and saw that the dark maid was already ensconced in the prow of the attack launch and holding a vast black bag and the Buginese were shoving each other aside to make a space on the benches to accommodate Mamaji's bulk. As Farhan began to clamber over, the long cutlass at his waist tangling awkwardly between his legs and the struts that supported the rail, he heard Mamaji calling up to him, "Do hurry, Farhan dear; or we'll miss all the fun!"

When Farhan, red-faced with exertion and embarrassment—by the Gods he was unfit—was finally settled in the boat, and the oarsmen were pulling for the shore, and the salt breeze was cooling his cheeks, he finally felt the yoke of dread begin to lift and a spark of excitement ignite in his hollow belly. Mamaji was as jolly and carefree as a young girl on her first holiday; she beamed at Farhan and patted his thigh with one meaty hand. It was impossible to believe that anything bad could happen to him while he was in her company. He looked over at the other launch, a stone's throw to their left and twenty paces ahead of them, with Captain Lodi standing with one bent knee on the prow, his face eager, a drawn cutlass in his right hand, a pistol stuffed in his belt.

They were going into battle. It was a beautiful day. And all would be well.

The town smelled of fresh blood and powder smoke. But it seemed that all resistance had been extinguished by the Dokra attack. They passed a herd of Han prisoners, squatting dejectedly in a town square, watched over by two grinning, turban-wearing men, the points of their bayonets still red and glistening. Farhan walked beside Mamaji up the steep and winding stone-flagged street toward the citadel, her maid straying a little ahead, with the black parasol, now neatly rolled, gripped in her small hands diagonally across her chest as if it were a loaded musket at port.

Farhan had drawn the cutlass and held its shining length out in front of him. But he felt ridiculous in the absence of any living enemies to slay. There were plenty of dead bodies in blue-cotton jackets, and the frequency and size of the mounds of corpses increased the higher they climbed. Shots could be heard from time to time from the citadel above them. And occasionally a hideous scream. Through an alleyway to his right, on a small patch of beaten earth hemmed in by tall, whitewashed houses, Farhan saw a gang of half a dozen Buginese sailors crouched over a writhing bloodied figure that was wailing and thrashing under their grip. He thought it was a Han girl—he had caught just a glimpse of black pigtails and a pretty face—and for a moment he considered intervening. He glanced at Mamaji; she did not seem to have noticed. But she gripped his arm and said, "No time to dillydally, Farhan dear, we need to get up to the citadel as quick as we can. Somebody will think to fire the town and we need to discourage that until we have the papers, don't we?"

A Han trooper came charging around the corner holding a Kwan Tao, a curved blade mounted on a pole, the standard weapon for the line infantry of the Celestial Republic. Half the man's face was covered in blood and, under his plumed steel cap, his one visible eye stared crazily at them. Farhan froze with shock, the cutlass forgotten in his hand. The man shouted something in the Han language and raised the Kwan Tao to strike at Mamaji. Farhan recovered himself and poked at the warrior with his blade. It was a halfhearted effort but just enough to be effective. The Han changed his stroke and the Kwan Tao swept down and parried the cutlass, the blades clanging together, the sword leaping from Farhan's fist to clatter away on the stone street. He was now defenseless. But the maid Lila was not. She darted in low, hooked the parasol's curved handle around the Han soldier's left ankle and tugged. The man tumbled to the ground, his weapon now bouncing away on the stones. The maid reversed her grip on the parasol and stabbed the prone man in his good eye, the long sharp point on the end of the sunshade smashing through the eye socket and piercing his brain. Farhan scrambled over to collect his cutlass, gathered it up and turned to see that Mamaji was now holding a huge double-barrelled pistol almost as long as Farhan's arm and pointing it, steady as a stone, at the dead man at her feet.

For five whole heartbeats nobody said or did anything. Then: "Well, that was rather exhilarating!" said Mamaji, smiling at Farhan and pushing the enormous pistol back into the capacious bag that she carried over her arm. "I must thank you both for protecting me so gallantly from that rascal. Farhan dear, you were magnificent, a lion! And Lila, you did jolly well, too, to pull him down like that."

Mamaji beamed and Farhan, although he was no novice at applying a thick buttery coat of praise, could not but feel himself warmed by her words, no matter how undeserving.

"Come along now, dears, not too much farther to go," said Mamaji. "We don't want to be too late. Come along!"

The Manchu had made a determined last stand in the courtyard of the citadel. But Captain Lodi had gathered his Buginese and a large number of the Dokra troopers and they had stormed through the gates in the face of the Manchus' deadly fire and swiftly overwhelmed them. As was their custom, not one Manchu, even those badly wounded, had surrendered. Their eighteen bodies now lay in a bloody heap in the middle of the courtyard.

Cyrus Lodi had taken a pistol ball to the shoulder, a messy, bloody furrow in the top of the meat, but not serious, and the sea captain was cheerful when Farhan, Mamaji and Lila found him. He was sitting on a barrel by the main gate and sipping on a large mug of marak for the pain, having his shoulder roughly sewn up by Lieutenant Muda, one of the Buginese crew, a tubby ruffian who was the captain's second-in-command.

"Our boys did well, I'd say, very well," Lodi called out, as Farhan approached. "Showed those precious Dokra fellows that they're not the only ones who can fight!"

"It's a marvelous victory," said Farhan. "You should be proud of yourself."

"Good of you to say so, Farhan. Very handsome of you. Though, of course, it's not really much of a victory. We had them beaten the moment we came into the bay."

"I am very impressed, Captain dear," said Mamaji. "All that I have been told about the fighting qualities of the Dokra has been shown to be true. Your crewmen were superb, too. I am quite satisfied with the action and I'm sure that General Vakul will be very pleased."

Farhan could have sworn that his wounded friend actually blushed.

At that moment, the Dokra captain came up to the small group. He was a little whippet of a man with a gigantic black mustache. His golden epaulets gleamed in the sunlight. He saluted Cyrus Lodi, and said: "Orders, sir?"

"Ah, Captain Ravi, I must compliment you on the conduct of

your men. A magnificent performance. I trust that the casualties
have not been too heavy?"

"Thank you, sir. Not too bad. Seven dead, twelve wounded. It
could have been worse. And we showed these Squinters a thing or
two about how real soldiers conduct themselves."

"Well, you did magnificently. Now, I am afraid that alarm
rockets have been seen farther up the coast so we must embark
with some speed before the full wrath of the forces of the Celestial
Republic falls on our heads. We must sail before the half hour . . ."

"We will not sail for at least two hours," Mamaji interrupted
Lodi. The little Dokra captain gawped at her in astonishment.

"Farhan and I need at least two hours to go through their papers and pick out the ones that are of particular interest to us."

"But Mamaji—the alarm rockets will bring down . . ."

"Two hours, is that clear? You get the men ready to depart,
get the wounded loaded. Fill the water casks, do whatever you
need to do. Oh, and release the Han prisoners—be sure to tell
them they have been released on the orders of the envoy of the
Lord of the Islands. Draw their attention to that Lion flag on the
mainmast. Is that all understood?"

"Yes, Mamaji," said Captain Lodi, unable to meet her eyes.

CHAPTER 10

Extract from *Ethnographic Travels* by
Professor Tolmund K. Parehki of the University of Dhilika

The remote, rain-drenched and mountainous Island of Kyo to the northeast of the Celestial Republic, off the coast of the barren Manchu horselands, is the homeland of the fabled Niho knights. Five hundred years ago the island had been part of the Republic but the men of Niho finally put aside their traditional clan enmities, united and rebelled against their Han overlords, slaughtering the governors, slaying their regiments of Manchu bannermen, even defeating a Celestial Legion in open battle, and declaring themselves free men, henceforth to be ruled by a council of the patriarchs, one from each of the twelve Niho clans.

The Republic did not lightly cede its territory and a brutal war was waged for nearly a hundred years between the Niho knights in their mountain fastnesses and a succession of invading Han and Manchu armies. Gradually, the soft decay caused by the traditional corruption in the Celestial Republic's corridors of power and the difficulty of projecting that power to such a remote and difficult corner of the world had combined to ensure that the Niho were finally left in peace. Starving on rocky, desolate farmlands, untilled for generations, their rigid society forged by hardship and decades of battle, the Niho were forced to hire their men out as mercenaries to any noble houses who could pay their high fees, promising fidelity down the generations in exchange for the honor of service and a generous stream of silver sent back to their impoverished homelands.

Tung An Shan, Envoy of the Celestial Republic to the Principality of Ashjavat, spread his arms wide and meekly allowed the Niho guard to feel his limbs, armpits, groin, waistband and collar for hidden weapons. The knight in the menacing black mask made him take off the soft leather boots he wore and thrust a hand inside each; finally, he ruffled through his neatly cut, white-streaked hair with hard fingertips, combing right down to his scalp. Tung wondered what this black-armored monster would do if he discovered that the last two cloth-covered buttons on his thigh-length blue silk tunic were in fact made of a solid resinous poison, enough, if dissolved in wine or hot water and merely tasted, to kill twenty men in a few brief, agonizing moments. He imagined he would be immediately put to death. He kept his face carefully immobile as the search continued.

It had been ten days since the Venerable Kwan Li, Prince Khazeki's aged mother, had been killed—was it by this very man?—and the horrible image of her tiny, crumpled, headless body lying before the dais in the throne room of the Palace of Ashjavat was burned into the back of his eyeballs. The Niho were all identically dressed in the lacquered black armor, and with only their dead black eyes showing above their masks, it was almost impossible to tell one from another. But he thought that it probably had not been this one. It did not matter anyway: the brute had merely been obeying the orders of the she-demon he was about to meet, and even if he were to take his revenge on the man responsible, another would spring up to take his place. But there would be a reckoning one day for the death of Venerable Kwan Li, and for her half-witted son, Prince Khazeki, so blatantly murdered in his marriage bed by this newcome ice-bitch from the frozen north.

Tung was ushered into the presence of the ice-bitch, and made his obeisance, kneeling and knocking his forehead three times against the thick-carpeted floor of the chamber. It was sparsely furnished by Ashjavat standards, a single gold candle-stand by the deep purple armchair on which she sat reading a scroll. A pair of paintings of the chase, fur-clad men on horseback armed with spears in the Northron style. A table holding a small, silver-rimmed crystal jug filled with a pale liquid and two tiny cups and a plate of sliced pickled beetroots.

Unexpectedly, Katerina rose from the chair and came over to Tung, extending a white hand to help him up after the obeisance, smiling prettily and thanking him for coming.

"Envoy Tung, what a great pleasure it is to receive you," she said, handing him to a wooden chair beside her purple one. She was wearing a simple, long white dress, a mark of mourning, presumably, but her fair hair and long, pale, slender arms were bared. "You'll take a cup of marak?" she said, gesturing gracefully at the jug on the table. "It is poor, weak stuff, barely fit for pigs, but the best they can manage in these parts."

Tung declined. He sat in the chair and fingered the bottom button on his coat. He wondered if he dared tug it loose and drop it in the crystal jug when she wasn't looking. He decided he did not, at least not yet. He'd see what the bitch wanted first.

"I am most grateful that you have made time to visit me before your departure for the Celestial Republic," Katerina said, pouring herself a tiny brimming cup of the pale liquid and downing it in one practiced movement. She picked a thin slice of pickle from the plate with her long fingers, crunched briefly, then licked them clean.

Tung had been summoned to her by a pair of the Palace Guards while he had been sitting miserably in his quarters drinking tea and contemplating the hiring of a fast coach and six to discreetly take him and his small retinue east. But he had not yet said anything to his servants about his plans. He wondered how she knew he meant to go.

"You will be reporting directly to the Conclave of Venerables on your return, I imagine, to inform them of the unfortunate incident with Venerable Kwan Li."

"I will indeed," said Tung. "Although I do not think 'unfortunate incident' adequately covers what transpired." He spoke the Khevan tongue to her with a slight Ashjavati accent but no trace of his native Han in his intonation. "A more truthful and accurate expression would be 'the cold-blooded murder of the mother of the prince.'"

"You grieve for your mistress, I'm sure," said Katerina placidly. "Do you think that the Conclave will be equally grieved—even angry? And, furthermore, do you think in their collective wisdom there is a chance that in their rage they will be moved to punish poor little Ashjavat? In short, sir, do you think they will consider waging a war against us?"

"I think it almost a certainty," said Tung.

"War is a terrible thing, Envoy Tung. And war with a daughter of the Ice-Bear Throne would be even more appalling. The might of the Khevan Empire pitted against the massed Legions of the Celestial Republic—Ashjavat invaded, perhaps, our lands laid waste, the city burned to the ground, tens of thousands of men dead and maimed, it would be a tragedy of epic proportions, do you not agree? A bloody catastrophe. I would seek to prevent that, if possible. Indeed, I would like *you* to help me prevent that. And I think we might both be able to manage it—if only you could be persuaded to remain with us for a little longer."

"If you think that you can prevent the news of your vile actions reaching the Celestial Republic by imprisoning me here, you are very much mistaken." Tung found the poisoned button had come loose in his hands. He would take it himself if they tried to lay hands on him. He would not allow himself to be imprisoned, beaten, tortured . . .

"Oh, nothing of that kind, Envoy, certainly not for a man of your talents. You and your retinue are free to leave the moment that this interview is concluded. But I merely hope that you will listen with an open mind to what I now have to say. When I have finished, you have my permission to pack your things and go— and the deaths of tens of thousands of men and women, Han and Khevan, will be on your conscience, not on mine."

Tung stared at her. She was little more than a girl and yet she spoke of wholesale slaughter as calmly as if she were speaking of a lost kitten.

"What do you wish to say to me?"

"First, if I may, Envoy, I will discourse a little upon the history of this region. I believe it will shed some light. The Principality of Ashjavat is a recent addition to the Khevan Empire, as you know. It was acquired a hundred and fifty years ago by Vladimir the Great, and the Emperor wanted it, chiefly, because it holds the great warm-water port of Ostraka, a gateway to trade with all the fabled wealth of the Laut Besar. Indeed, this province was once called Ostrakavat, when the southern port was its capital city. The Celestial Republic and the Empire had long skirmished, and even fought two short, bloody wars, over possession of what later became Ashjavat. And I know that the Celestial Republic desires her still—do not attempt to deny it."

Tung said nothing. He knew the history as well as she did.

Katerina said, "So, let us imagine, for the sake of argument, that because of all that unpleasantness with Venerable Kwan Li and her son, war is declared between the Empire and the Republic. The Celestial Legions or possibly the Manchu guard battalions will pour over the border into Ashjavat. The Emperor's Cossack regiments will be mobilized and thousands will come southwards over the Ehrul Mountains to counter the invasion. This principality will be ravaged. Thousands will perish. The war may last a year, or five, it does not matter. The end result will be the same."

Tung stared silently at her but despite himself he slightly raised one eyebrow.

"The Empire is weak," she said. "The Khevan nobles do not make themselves richer and stronger with trade; they guzzle and gorge and fuck their mistresses and abuse their peasants, happily ignorant of the rest of the world. The Celestial Republic is strong. Her Legions are the finest troops in the world. Added to that, the Emperor is dying, as you must know, and the next man who will mount the Ice-Bear Throne is an arrogant idiot who, if he ever thinks beyond his belly, thinks only as far down as his prick. Nevertheless, he will order the Cossacks south to meet the Legions; and they will fight bravely but, because of the incompetence and indifference of the boyars at home in Khev, they will undoubtedly lose the war. The new Emperor will be sorely humiliated but, unless he wishes to risk the whole of his Empire, he will be powerless to do anything but sign a peace treaty with his enemies. Then the victorious Celestial Republic will gladly take possession of Ashjavat, including her all-important warm-water port Ostraka. I foresee no other possible outcome."

Katerina paused and looked Tung squarely in the eye.

Then she said, "I plan to cut out all that pointless bloodshed in the middle of this painful scenario and go straight to the end of the game. I plan to give Ashjavat to the Celestial Republic—just hand her over, cede the whole principality, without a fight, without a drop of Han blood spilled. But, naturally, I want something in return for my gift."

Tung found that his mouth was hanging open. Was she mad? He had just heard the *de facto* ruler of a Khevan principality utter rank treason to the Ice-Bear Throne. If the Emperor were to hear a single word of this, she would be impaled within the week, her royal status notwithstanding. Tung closed his mouth. She wasn't mad. Cold as frost. Ruthless as a viper. But not mad. But could he trust her? Absolutely not.

"Do you find anything false in my reasoning, Envoy? If you do, please do tell me now. Because I want you to stay here, and work closely with me over the next few months. I want you to help me deliver Ashjavat bloodlessly to the Celestial Republic. Am I incorrect in any of my strategic reasoning?"

Tung was silent for a moment. Was this a trap? He could not tell. He was already in her power, anyway, so what did it matter? He told her the truth. "I think your reasoning is correct, Highness. I think that the Khevan Empire would undoubtedly lose a war against the Republic. Ashjavat would surely fall to us."

"So, will you stay?" she said. "You will help me avoid a bloody catastrophe?"

Tung said nothing for several moments. He desperately wanted to go home. He wanted to be away from this foul country, this foul ice-bitch with his mistress's blood fresh on her dainty white hands. But he served the Celestial Republic. His family had always served the Republic. If nothing else, he was a man of duty.

"I . . . I will stay," said Tung.

"Good, well, that is enough for now. You will no doubt have secret messages that you wish to dispatch to the Conclave of Venerables. We shall speak again soon."

Tung got up; the button fell from his lap and rolled on the floor to the feet of Katerina. She picked it up and looked at it briefly. She tossed it to the Envoy.

"Take your button with you, sir," she said. "You should not leave something like that lying around. A child might see it, pick it up and put it in her mouth. Then die horribly."

Tung blushed and shoved the button into his pocket.

"Of choking, I mean," said Katerina with a happy smile. "For how else could a pretty little button kill someone?"

◆   ◆   ◆

K aterina rang the bell when the Envoy had left, and as a servant appeared, she said, "Send the General in to me immediately."

General Jan Artur swaggered into the room a few moments
later. His long, beautiful black mustaches were freshly oiled, and
he was looking tanned, strong and pleased with himself, as well
he might. He was now, thanks to his lady's favor, the commander
in chief of all the armies of Ashjavat. It was a grand title but, in
truth, Artur was master of no more than a few thousand poorly
equipped recruits, who were mostly stationed in the rocky broken
lands on the border with the Celestial Republic engaged in a des-
ultory struggle with the local marak smugglers, and losing badly.

If his ramshackle troops were demoralized, corrupt and lacking in essential food, kit and weapons, General Artur had no
power to do anything about it. All funds were controlled by the
Ashjavat Treasury and he had been told firmly that no more would
be forthcoming for matters of defense in the next year or two.
So he resigned himself to enjoying the perquisites of his new position, and suffocated any qualms he had about the state of his men.
He had retained the position of Captain of the Palace Guard, and
the generous salary that went with it, and he was the recipient of
a regular flow of bribes from Ashjavati courtiers and foreign dig-
nitaries who believed that he had the princess's private ear. So
long as he kept his eyes shut to the dire state of the army, life
would continue to be good.

He bowed low before Katerina and leered at her gallantly. She
merely said, "Strip!" and then began to take off her own tight
white dress.

Half an hour later, when they had finished, she drank off another glass of marak, gave one to the sweating, red-faced Artur,
and reclined still naked in the armchair.

"I want a discreet watch put on Envoy Tung An Shan at all
hours of the day and night—good men, not your usual incompe-

tents. However, his private couriers to the Celestial Republic are not to be molested in the slightest—no demands for bribes or emoluments—and I want a daily list of the people he speaks to in the Palace and the city. Is that clear?"

"As you wish, my love," said Artur. He came over to the chair, grinning and bending down to kiss her. She shoved him away with surprising strength. He staggered back, confused. "My love?" he said. "Have I done something wrong?"

"I am not your *love*, General," she said icily. "You are merely a bull performing his stud duty. From now onward you will address me as Highness at all times. Now, get out."

CHAPTER 11

There were five of them, five white nicks on the horizon. Sails. Farhan was sure of it now. They were not fishing craft, they were too big for that, and the distance between them was equidistant and unchanging. Most likely they were a squadron of battle cruisers from the Celestial fleet. But whether they were following the *Mongoose* was difficult to tell, even from Farhan's seat in the crow's nest near the top of the mainmast. With the sinking sun a handsbreadth above the horizon behind them he had to squint into its reddening glare even to make them out. The *Mongoose* was sailing almost due east, with the wind blowing strongly on its port quarter and the deck canted over at a fine angle. They were making good progress and shouldering their way strongly through the moderate swell.

Farhan cursed Mamaji—but under his breath. Even up here, forty feet from the quarterdeck where she sat placidly under the parasol held by her maid, he dared not abuse her too loudly. She had insisted, after the fort in Kulu was taken, that they examine all the papers in the officers' mess, despite Captain Lodi's increasingly urgent warnings that the signal flares had gone up hours ago and even now the Celestial Republic's armed forces would be descending upon them.

It was not as if they had found anything of particular interest among the letters, journals and written orders of the detachment of Manchu bannermen and the officers of the Han 16th Regiment of the Line. It was mostly routine stuff, bills of sickness in the soldiery, accounts of the stocks of food and drink that the garrison held, a few private missives containing scraps of gossip about missed production targets of the obat factories farther up the coast—certainly nothing worth lingering so long for.

Farhan had leafed through them all, finding nothing of particular interest: his command of Han, written and spoken, like his grasp of the Common Tongue, the lingua franca of the Laut Besar, and half a dozen other major languages, was excellent—which was one of the many reasons he had been recruited by the Amrit Shakti all those years ago. But Mamaji had seized upon great sheaves of paper and had insisted that they be transported to the *Mongoose* where she could pore over them at her leisure. And she had done so, rarely emerging from her—or rather the captain's—cabin, except to call for more food and drink for her and her silent maid, Lila.

The five ships were definitely coming closer, Farhan thought. Their square sails, piled one on top of each other, three to each of the three masts, could now clearly be seen. He wondered if he ought to come down and tell the captain, but Lodi had recently shown a marked prickliness about receiving advice from his old friend when it came to sailing the ship. He had to do it, though, even at the risk of being snapped at.

By the time Farhan had laboriously clambered down the mainmast and reached the quarterdeck, he knew his intelligence was already obsolete, for Captain Lodi and Mamaji were both standing at the taffrail with their telescopes trained on the five ships following them, which were now much closer.

"Celestial light battle cruisers," Lodi said to his fat companion. "Five of the bastards. Each carrying ten guns, and fifty musketeers. And they're faster then us, if well handled." He thought for a moment. "I could fight off one, easily, maybe two at a pinch. Not five."

"Well, dear, you'd better not let them catch us then," said Mamaji, folding up her telescope, returning it to her bag, turning her back and waddling back to her seat.

"Can you lose them in the darkness, Cyrus?" asked Farhan.

"I certainly hope so," said Lodi. And he began bawling a string of orders to his crew, sending the lithe Buginese sailors scrambling up the masts.

The sun was half-sunk into the western ocean and the Celestial cruisers were closer still, easily recognizable as the slim, deadly, fighting ships they were, when Farhan went below. He needed to go through his belongings and decide which of his papers he might need to discard in the event of capture. Spies were routinely tortured and executed by the Republic; ordinary merchants might be merely imprisoned. But he and everyone on this ship had just sacked a Han outpost, and killed scores of men. They could expect no mercy.

When Farhan went back up on deck he saw that the tropical night had fallen with all its usual suddenness. Captain Lodi had not moved from his position on the taffrail, although his telescope was useless in the darkness. The five ships were close now, perhaps half a league away and each one could be made out by a collection of little orange lights. The captain said a quiet word to his lieutenant, Muda, who nodded and went away.

All over the ship the lanterns were snuffed out, the Dokra mercenaries, a dozen of whom had been standing in the waist, goggling at the oncoming vessels and fingering their muskets, were herded down below, and the word was passed from man to man: "Silence, silence on deck, a flogging for any man who makes a noise."

Farhan ignored the command. He said quietly to Lodi, "Do you mean to make a run for the Yawa shore?" He waved a hand vaguely to the south.

"That's what they would expect us to do. Run for the shore in darkness and hide in a little delta or mangrove swamp till they pass us by. I mean to do the opposite. Now if you want to be allowed to remain on deck, I need you to be absolutely quiet."

"Yes, sir," said Farhan, only a little sarcastically. He walked off the quarterdeck, down the little set of steps into the waist, and seated himself cross-legged on a bale of silk, out of the way. He took out a little wooden box from his pocket, pinched off a large nub of obat and tucked it in his mouth between his teeth and the flesh of his cheek. It was a waste of the precious drug, he knew, for its effects would be far milder than smoking it. But lighting a pipe was asking for trouble on the blacked-out deck and he was damned if he would not enjoy the obat's wonderful soothing effect one last time before he was no more.

As he replaced the wooden obat box in the pocket of his heavy woolen coat, his fingers touched the cool metal of his little solid-iron pistol. He had "borrowed" it from the ship's arms chest when the armorer wasn't looking, loaded it with his own powder and shot in his cabin, and he was ready, if they were boarded by the Celestials and looked to be captured, to put the gun to his own head and pull the trigger.

He had seen the victims of torture who had been released from the dark cells below the Taj Palace—those bloody, limping, forever-ruined wretches who had been found, after all that pain and blood, to be innocent. The guilty, of course, were never seen alive again. No, thought Farhan, stroking the chilly metal in his pocket, he would not be taken alive.

For perhaps half an hour, nothing happened. The *Mongoose*, now in total darkness and further cloaked with an unnatural hush, save for the creak of taut ropes and wooden masts and the wash of the sea along her flank, proceeded on her course unchanged. By leaning out into the freshening breeze off the port side, and looking back, Farhan could make out two clusters of orange lights, the two northernmost cruisers. Then he heard Lodi whisper an order and there was the slap of bare feet on wood as a score of sailors rushed to their stations, some nimbly climbing the rigging. The tiller was put hard over and the *Mongoose* began her smooth turn, to port, toward the northeast, as close to the wind as she would swim. As the ship turned through forty-five degrees, heading out into the vast emptiness of the Laut Besar, there was hardly a noise but the light clatter of the booms against the mast and the whisper of orders, and Farhan watched the lights of the cruisers with his breath held down tight in his lungs, to see if they'd make the same turn.

A minute passed, and another, and now Farhan could see all five of his pursuers. Their course was unchanged, blithely continuing eastwards. He let out his breath with a whoosh. He could feel the obat working in his bloodstream and a thrill of euphoria glowing behind his eyes. Half an hour passed, and now Farhan could see the very faintest glimmer of lights appearing across the narrow waist of the ship. The enemy was due south of them, still apparently unaware that the *Mongoose* had slipped away northwards. Then, as the distance between them grew greater still, their lights winked out, one by one, swallowed by the black ocean.

An hour later, and Captain Lodi gave the order to go about, and with the same disciplined near silence the *Mongoose* came into the wind, and swung round farther and the ropes were sheeted home for her new course, south by west, heading back toward the Yawa shore with the enemy cruisers now quite invisible somewhere to the east, far ahead of them. Farhan felt the urge to cheer—but he knew it was merely the obat rushing in his veins. Instead, he got up off the silk bale and stumbling slightly on numb legs, he made his way down into his dark and stuffy cabin, lay down fully clothed on the narrow bunk and allowed the blissful drug to claim him.

He awoke with blinding sunlight streaming through the porthole and the cheerful chatter of the Buginese on the deck above him. He had been dreaming about *her* again and his member was hard as iron. His head, on the other hand, felt as if it was stuffed with wool; his senses were dull, and a heavy, aching pulse beat in his temple. He knew it would wear off in a few hours. He stripped, splashed his face, body and softening prick with seawater, before dressing and coming up on deck.

The scene that greeted him was one of placid domesticity: about thirty of the Dokra mercenaries were lounging around the deck half-naked, scarlet turbans discarded, their long hair piled up on their heads, chatting to each other. Other members of the company were busy with vast tubs of seawater washing their comrades' linens, and those items already washed were hanging from lines strung fore and aft, fluttering in the breeze like little white flags. The Buginese were hanging from the ratlines, running up and down the ropes like children at play, calling out to each other with happiness at their escape from the cruisers. Others were sitting in little groups on the deck, mingling with the Dokra, laughing and playing at dice. On the quarterdeck, Mamaji sat in her customary place in the center, shaded by her ever-watchful servant, Lila. Captain Lodi, beaming, was standing legs apart, riding the gentle swell with ease. The sun shone brightly from an almost-cloudless sky and Farhan noted that the wind had changed direction and was blowing from the north, directly astern, and wafting the *Mongoose* toward the low, green, jungly shore several miles ahead, toward the Island of Yawa.

"Good morning, Farhan," called the captain. "I trust you slept well."

The tubby merchant, in his post-obat funk, did not deign to reply but came slowly up the little set of steps to the quarterdeck and stood beside his friend.

"We lost them, I see," he said, scanning the empty horizon, east and west.

"Yes, with any luck, they will be halfway to Sukatan by now. Or scouring the ocean to the north looking in vain for a sniff of us in all those thousands of sea miles."

"So what is the plan?" Farhan asked.

"The plan remains unchanged, dear," said Mamaji, turning in

her seat and bestowing Farhan with a loving look. Lila scowled at him. "We will proceed along the coast to the Celestial Republic's factory at Tekal and let the Dokra loose to have their fun. Then on to Sukatan to lie in wait for the Republic's gold transport. Nothing has changed, dear. We are just a day behind schedule; that's all. But you've all done very well. And you particularly should be jolly proud of yourself, Captain."

Cyrus Lodi grimaced at her tone, but said nothing.

Farhan was staring off the port bow. He rubbed his eyes. Looked again. The white speck was still there. "Cyrus, what do you think . . ."

Farhan never completed his sentence. A sharp cry of "Sail-oh, Captain!" came down from the crow's nest. Lodi did not hesitate even for an instant. He leaped at the nearest ratline and swung his bulk into the rope ladder and started climbing, as nimbly as any of his far lighter crew, and despite the affliction of his forty-odd years.

A tense quarter of an hour later, and the captain was back on the quarterdeck, puffing slightly. "Hard aport," he said to the helmsman. "Set course east-northeast." Then he yelled, "Muda! Set the wings and flying jib. And be quick about it, man!"

"Captain, what on earth is happening?" said Mamaji, rising ponderously from her wicker chair. "I demand that you tell me this instant."

Lodi looked at her. "There are two—only two—Celestial cruisers five miles to the east." He gestured with his hand off the port bow. "We are going to fight them, cripple them or sink them, before the others in the squadron can come up."

As the ship came around onto its new heading, accompanied by the whistles and shouts of the petty officers and slapping stamp of bare Buginese feet, Mamaji said crossly, "But you assured me, dear, that you had lost them in the night."

Through clenched teeth, Lodi said, "It would appear that I

have not, madam. But the squadron has separated in the search for us, and that gives us a fighting chance."

"I am not sure that I think that is wise. Would it not be better to head in toward the land—perhaps we could hide from them . . ."

"No, madam, it would not be better. If I can see them, they can see us. We must beat them while we have the chance. *Before they are joined by their consorts.*"

"I don't think General Vakul would approve of this reckless . . ."

"I don't give a soggy fart what Vakul thinks. He is not captain of this ship; neither are you. I'm in command. And I will thank you to go below and allow me to do my duty."

Farhan had never seen Mamaji checked in this way before. A mixture of contrasting emotions was briefly visible on her fat face, and then she said, "Very well, Captain. But on your own head be it! Be assured I shall report your insolence to the General."

"Go below, madam, now!" said Lodi. But Mamaji was already stumping away.

With the new sails set and sheeted home, the *Mongoose* seemed to lurch forward like a racehorse straining at the bit. The two cruisers, one half a mile behind the other and slightly to the south, were now clearly visible from the quarterdeck, and coming closer at a terrifying rate as the three vessels converged on each other at their combined speeds.

"What can I do to help?" said Farhan.

"I don't know. What *can* you do to help?" said Lodi. He was clearly very angry.

Farhan frowned at his friend, and Lodi had the grace to look a little shamefaced.

"There is nothing for you to do, my friend. Just keep out of the way of the fighting men, and try not to get hurt," he said. "This is going to be bloody."

CHAPTER 12

⸺ ❦ ⸺

Minister Tung An Shan walked the full length of the throne room, stopping just before the dais and the tiny figure in silver silk on the huge, lion-pawed, oak chair.

"Highness, there is a Niho man to see you, a knight, he claims, who says he has traveled many long, hard leagues to serve you."

Katerina inclined her head fractionally, and Tung clapped his hands. The slaves swung open the double doors and a tall, broad-shouldered figure in a loose and rather dusty white-linen jacket and trousers, and with a long, curved sword thrust through his belt, strode into the room. He marched up to the dais and made a crisp bow, bending low.

"Thank you, Minister, that will be all for now," said Katerina.

As Tung retreated to the wall of the chamber, dismissed, and took his place next to Captain Murakami, still as a black statue in his lacquered armor, he reflected that he had enjoyed far more respect as an Envoy of the Celestial Republic than he did as Minister to Her Highness the Princess of Ashjavat. But he had had no choice about accepting his new role. The Conclave of Venerables had insisted emphatically that he remain in Ashjavat and serve the princess in whatever capacity she might require, until the secret negotiations about the future of the Khevan principality were concluded. He longed to go home to his little rice farm and his wife in the village just outside Nankung and the eleven-month-old son he had never yet laid eyes on. *Not long now,* he told himself. *Not long.* The negotiations were nearly done—made all the swifter because the Conclave had agreed immediately to almost all her demands with scarcely a quibble.

"Ari Yoritomo, knight first grade, at your service, Lady," said the tall young man, smiling easily up at the throne. Katerina was a little taken aback. She had never seen a Niho knight smile before. True, they almost always wore their black-lacquer masks on duty, but even when she was younger and she had taken her guards with her to the swimming hole on long, hot, dusty summer days, she did not ever remember, not even once, one of the naked muscular men swimming powerfully beside her showing any kind of emotion at all. She had been naked, too, in the first budding of womanhood but, even so, none of the knights had ever shown the slightest interest, either by glance or expression, in her smooth white body. Other men had, and for the first time she had become aware of her power over them. For the first time she had begun to collect them, to bind them to her and hold them, as she thought of it, in her pocket. She looked down at this smiling, handsome knight, and realized that she had not, until this moment, thought of the Niho as fully human. But this bold new fellow was grinning at her as if they were old friends. She was not sure she liked it. However, he was a well-made creature, she conceded, a hank of thick black hair falling forward over a wide, strong face, well tanned by travel. She noticed, too, that he did not have the usual ink-black eyes of the rest of them. His eyes were a dark blue color.

"You are of the House of Yoritomo? Eldest son of Musa, my former captain?" said Katerina. She immediately realized that it was a stupid question. Of course he was. He had just said as much. She was thrown by his smile. The younger Yoritomo merely bowed again.

"Can any of you vouch for him?" she said, looking at the row of knights by the wall.

Captain Murakami stepped forward and bowed. "I vouch for the Yoritomo knight first grade, Lady. He was fostered into my House and I personally oversaw his training in swordsmanship, archery, horsemanship, unarmed combat, pole-arm combat, stealth maneuvers, poison resistance, as well as the flower ceremony, the seven tea rituals . . ."

"Yes, yes, all right," said Katerina.

"He is a knight first grade, Lady, the very best of his class and generation." There was unmistakable pride in the older man's words.

"I'm sure he's a paragon." She turned to Ari. "You're ready to take the oath of service to me?"

"Quite ready, Lady," said the young man, again accompanying his words with a boyish smile. He dropped on one knee and began to say the words Katerina had heard so many times before, sonorous phrases about lifelong duty, loyalty to lordship and courage in the face of death. Katerina barely listened to them; she watched his face and the way his mouth moved as he spoke. He was rather beautiful, she realized. He had a grace and quiet strength that made General Artur look like a posturing ape.

Finally the young man pulled his short knife, his tanto, from the back of his belt. He held out his left palm toward her. Katerina sat up in her oversized chair. This had never been part of the traditional ceremony. This was new.

Ari looked directly at her, and said, "I spill my blood today, willingly, as a symbol that I shall never shrink hereafter from spilling mine or that of any man or woman or child who seeks to harm you. Let this blood bear witness to the sacred oath that I make this day and be the ink that writes the contract of life and death between us."

Katerina was aware of a low, rumbling sound, almost a growl, that came from the ranks of the Niho. She realized that the other guards did not like Ari's departure from the ancient formula. She glanced at them and there was silence once more. Ari took the tanto and sliced once hard across his left palm, the thick blood oozing from the cut as slow as honey.

"From this day forward, and forever, I am your man," said Ari, squeezing a fat droplet from his closed left fist, which splashed to the floor.

"I accept your blood offering, Ari Yoritomo, knight first grade," said Katerina. "May you never know dishonor in my service."

"It is perfectly simple, Minister, I must have the timber, suitable wood, cut into the correctly sized planks. How else am I to make my ships? Ashjavat is near treeless!"

"I will ask them, Your Highness," said Tung, "But I believe the Conclave is quite adamant on this point."

He did not believe anything of the kind. The Conclave of Venerables had given in without a murmur to the rest of her demands: the gangs of skilled carpenters and shipbuilders, the miles of rope and acres of canvas for the sails, all the cannon, powder and shot, trained Han gunners to teach Ashjavati men how to use them, the stores of dried goods, trade goods, the huge water barrels. They had provided her with detailed intelligence on the Indujah Federation fortresses in the region, and the dispositions of the powerful pirate fleet of Ongkara, Lord of the Islands . . . They had even promised her, gift of all gifts, a whole Celestial Legion for her to command—an unprecedented move. A thousand highly trained, well-armed elite fighting men handed over to this pip-squeak of a girl for her to play with as if they were no more than a thousand blue-uniformed dolls.

He had delivered her demands and an outline of her plans—an armed trading expedition comprising three ships to the Laut Besar—and her solemn promise not to molest any of the Celestial Republic's factories or plantations nor to trouble its merchant shipping and, within a week or two, which was for all practical purposes instantaneously, the Conclave had given its approval.

"Might we discuss the handover of the Principality now, Highness?" said Tung.

There was the crack of a whip and a terrible scream rang out across the main courtyard of the palace. Tung flinched in his seat under the awning, and kept his eyes firmly fixed on the princess's face. The sun was particularly warm that day, yet it was not the only cause of the greasy drops of sweat that began to slide down his cheeks. He did not care to watch the execution of the prisoner. He decided that he would not look at him at all. He would rather have conducted this stage of the negotiation in the privacy of the princess's chambers, or in the throne room, or *anywhere* but here. And at any time but during this appalling display of Khevan barbarity.

"It should be straightforward," said Katerina. She watched as on the far side of the courtyard the Master of the Lash, a hairy, big-bellied Ashjavati, who apparently preferred to work naked above the waist, drew back his arm for the second blow on his victim: Andrei, Count of Tashkhan, self-confessed traitor and accomplice of assassins.

The nobleman hung bloody and limp by the ropes that tied his wrists to the crossbar. Katerina feared that it would take no more than three dozen blows of the long, heavy, horsehide whip to finish him. The count was a weak man—he had shown that under torture, meekly confessing to everything that his inquisitors suggested he was guilty of when he was only lightly tickled with the hot irons and crushed for a few days under the weights.

Katerina hoped that the Master of the Lash knew his work: this foolish count must suffer a terrible death, long and slow, and very public, to discourage any others who might contest her right to the throne. She hoped the Master would not kill him too soon, feeble as he was. Her Cossacks at home would make a better, longer and more painful job of it. *Home.* She would not see it for many years—perhaps never again. In this endless heat, she longed for the crisp cold, for the clean snows of the Khevan winter.

The whip cracked and the victim gave a gurgling shriek that rounded the courtyard.

"Highness?" said Minister Tung. "The handover?"

"This is for your ears only, Minister, and the Conclave's, of course, that is if you value your life," said Katerina. She nodded toward the bloody wretch swinging by his arms from the cross-bar. "Flapping lips must be sealed with whips, as my old governess used to say."

Tung shivered at this threat but nodded his agreement to keep silent on the matter except to his masters. The lash smacked again. Andrei howled like a demon.

Katerina continued blithely, "When the ships are built at Os-traka and the Celestial Legion has arrived there and been inspected by me, I will order the whole Ashjavati army north to the Ehrul Mountains, stripping all the men from the garrisons on the border with the Celestial Republic. Your armies may then cross into Ashjavat at your leisure. In the high caves, the age-old strongholds in the Ehrul, the Ashjavati forces will dig in and await the Khevan response to the annexation. The new Emperor cannot allow this first test of his new rule to go unchallenged. He might have publicly converted to the Martyrite religion but the fool will still have to fight—did you hear that? He openly became a convert to the Burned God! The imbecile has decreed his regnal name will be Vladimir the Pure? What pompous nonsense!"

The whip struck again. Tung tried to block his ears to the sounds.

Katerina scratched her nose, and said, "Anyway, the Emperor has to fight us if he wants to retain the Ice-Bear Throne. Has to. And the Ashjavati army will face him there in the high mountains and die heroically in the snows of the Ehrul in a futile attempt to hold back the Cossacks. I estimate that they will last a week, two at most if they are extremely determined. While they are holding on so bravely, dying tragically for their homeland, your Celestial forces will occupy the rest of Ashjavat, streaming in through the unguarded border; and if they are wise, they will attack the Cossacks immediately when they come down into the plains. But I will leave all that manly war strategy stuff to the Conclave's generals. So, there it is. The handover will be complete. Is there anything else?"

Minister Tung felt slightly sick. It was not the unguarded glimpse he had just caught from the far side of the courtyard of the naked dangling body, the back and buttocks so deeply lacerated that white bone could be glimpsed through the blood. It was the notion of this pretty young girl—no, this terrible icy woman— casually slaughtering her own troops merely to advance her ambitions. The Celestial Republic had its own share of wickedness, no doubt, many bad, powerful men and women, but he could not think of anyone who could match Katerina.

"No, Highness," he said. "I have no more questions today. Perhaps I might be permitted to withdraw from your presence. I have . . ."

The Master of the Lash swung again and this time the sound of the heavy leather striking flesh was a deeper, louder crack. Andrei made no sound at all. He was limp.

"By all the Gods, I do believe that clumsy fool has broken the count's spine," said Katerina, rising from her chair to get a better look. "Eleven blows, that's all—eleven! Not even a round dozen. The incompetent cretin. I've half a mind to string the Master of the Lash up there beside poor old Andrei and show him myself how it really should be done."

CHAPTER 13

——— ❧ ———

Extract from *Ethnographic Travels* by
Professor Tolmund K. Parehki of the University of Dhilika

Two thousand years ago, there was a vast influx of peoples into the
Laut Besar from the Indujah Peninsula. These sea-migrants were
rice farmers, who kept pigs and buffalo. They craved land and
were bold enough to risk a long and perilous ocean journey to find
it. For there was land to spare in the Laut Besar and those who ar-
rived safely said prayers to their God. For as well as their agricul-
ture, they brought the religion of Vharkash the Harvester, then
unknown here.

The sea-migrants displaced the native people, now called the
Ebu; they cleared the ancient forests and built villages and pens
for their beasts. The Ebu, who lived in small bands and made their
livelihood through hunting game and gathering nuts and berries,
were awed by the New People, as they called the incomers. The
childlike Ebu did not know iron, they venerated their ancestors and
practiced a simple form of blood magic. The Harvester worship-
pers, in contrast, lived in villages of many hundreds of folk; they
generated a surplus in food, and were able to support high-status
members of society who were specialists: priests and soldiers. The
warriors banded together with others from different villages and
regions and made armies, and they were soon able to push the Ebu
into the remotest corners of the Laut Besar, to slaughter them if they
resisted, or enslave them and set them to work in the fields.

In Yawa, once the Ebu were subdued, the incomers' thoughts
turned to their principal God, Vharkash, who had given them this
paradise. To honor Him, and the other deities of their Pantheon,

*they created a vast temple complex in the jungly heart of the island,
with great wooden bells to ring the hours, many altars and a huge
statue of Vharkash in the main enclosure, the Harvester God ever
poised with his scythe to slay unbelievers.*

*Men and women from all over the Laut Besar came there
to serve the deity, to train as priests under the High Priest and
his seven deputies. Some of these were even descendants of Ebu
who, after hundreds of years, had been absorbed into the Yawa
population. In those days, the Harvester religion was far more
bloodthirsty—they regularly sacrificed living folk to Vharkash. Yet
the Temple grew in wealth and power as the centuries passed.
At the height of its glory, a thousand years ago, towns and cities
from the whole of Yawa gave up annually one-seventh of their crops
to the Mother Temple, and each year fourteen virgin boys and girls
were given up to the priests, too, either as blood offerings or to become novices. Sometimes both.*

A s their boat rounded the rocky lighthouse point and
came into the harbor of Sukatan, Jun was suddenly made
aware of just how insignificant a personage he was. The
city, the greatest urban conglomeration on Yawa, when seen from
the water, appeared to be absolutely enormous—a sprawling collection of houses and godowns, temples, palaces, shops and taverns that filled both arms of the bay and rose up the slope behind
it to the magnificent sun-reflecting golden roof of the Raja's Palace. It must have ten thousand inhabitants, thought Jun, almost as
many as in the whole of Taman and all crammed together into
one port and town. Gold and slaves had made this place—and
made it beautiful.

He had been here once before as a child to visit his cousin the
Raja—the present Raja of Sukutan's father—but they had come by

the overland route, across the narrow straits between Taman and Yawa and through the long, twisting, mud roads through the jungle to enter the city from the south, but all Jun could remember of the journey was the boredom, sitting in the palanquin borne by six muscular Dewa porters and playing endless games of chess with his tutor or with War-Master Hardan as the stuffy wooden box jolted along. He remembered the palace itself, a vast, airy space, filled with a permanent hush and the sweet smell of incense, and sitting on a pile of cushions, sipping delicious sherbet, while the Raja, a kindly old man, had asked him endless questions about the health of his family. Questions he did not know how to answer. He remembered being punished, too, beaten painfully on the rear with a rattan cane for shooting his toy bow and arrow down a long, empty corridor and smashing a priceless blue Han vase on a plinth that had been his unthinking target.

"Look," said Semar, standing in the prow, as Ketut guided the vessel toward a large stone pier, one of many that jutted out from the land into the harbor. "They are here, too!"

The old man was pointing to a large ship, square-bowed, but curving up sharply at the prow in the Han style into a carved wooden serpent's head painted gold. A black flag with a broad green stripe through the middle hung limply from the central mast, a sudden gust of wind revealing the emblem of a golden snake coiled in the center. From Semar's excited words, Jun realized that this was the vessel of his enemy—the sorcerer Mangku. He wondered if the Khodam was, even now, hidden somewhere below its crowded deck.

Two of the three masts of the ship, the ones at prow and stern, were entirely bare of spars, sails and rigging, presumably undergoing some sort of refit. About forty ill-looking men, many with shaven heads and scalp locks, others with dark woolly polls and great matted beards, were leaning over the side, spitting blood-red betel and chatting to each other or calling out to the dragonfly-craft, manned by women in round, pyramid-shaped sun hats, and nimbly maneuvered by one long oar at the stern, which whizzed between the shipping offering varieties of fruit, fresh fish or small, leaf-wrapped blocks of obat for sale.

Jun stepped shakily onto the unyielding stone of the pier as Ketut tied up the boat. Semar followed him up and a Yawanese man in a small, tight, orange-brown turban with a leather satchel over his shoulder came hurrying along the jetty.

"Five kupang per day," said the man with no more welcome than a brief bob of his head in greeting. "Harbormaster's fees."

"Two," said Semar. "It should be no more than two."

"Five," said the man, "or be off with you. There's plenty more who would like a nice berth at the Yellow Pier."

"Four, but only if you'll direct us to a clean, reasonably priced tavern," said Semar.

Jun burrowed into his pack and produced a handful of copper coins from his purse. He had a store of money, salvaged from the Watergarden, but it was a paltry sum and he was relying on his cousin to furnish him with a good deal more.

"Why are we staying at a tavern?" asked Jun, as the three of them walked down the pier, following the directions that the Yawanese in the orange turban had given them. "Surely we should go straight to the palace and present ourselves to the Raja. He will give us free lodgings there, not to mention a hot bath, decent food and clean clothes."

"The sorcerer is here," said Semar tersely. "It would be wiser— don't you think, my prince?—to make some reconnaissance, to get an idea of the way of things, before we go barging into the Raja's affairs. By the look of that ship, it will not be leaving for days."

"If we are staying, I want to go to the Temple of Vharkash tonight," said Ketut.

"Why?" said Jun. Ketut looked sullen, said nothing and would not meet his eye.

The tavern, in a dim side street off the main harbor road that ran all along the waterfront, was neither clean nor reasonably priced. It was named The Drunken Sow, and a square wooden sign hanging at head height outside the low building showed a picture of an enormous white pig, rolling on her back, twin rows of nipples exposed with her eyes blissfully closed. It might have been used to depict the tavern keeper: a grossly fat Han, with a single black tooth in her slack, blubbery mouth.

Jun reluctantly parted with fifteen kupang and they were shown into a tiny room with three straw pallets on the floor. After a cursory wash in the slime-walled bathhouse and a hasty meal of rice and gristly fried pork with stringy, bitter, green vegetables, Semar announced his intention to begin his reconnaissance.

"You two stay here, take a little walk along the waterfront, look at the ships, if you must, but try not to get into any trouble. Stay away from the drinking dens, the brothels and the obat houses. I'll be back—but probably not before dawn."

When Semar left in the late afternoon, dressed in his oldest, grayest sarong and a gray baggy shirt, and carrying only his staff for protection, Jun and Ketut looked at each other. They had never felt easy in each other's company, even after five days together in an open boat, and five nights of camping on the shore.

"We could play chess, if you like," said Jun. "I have a fine set in my pack."

Ketut gave him a searing glare of contempt. "I'm going out, richboy," she said.

When the door closed, Jun waited for a count of twenty then set out after her.

◆　◆　◆

Hiero Mangku released a long orange stream of urine into the porcelain bowl on the low stand in the corner of his chamber and gave a vast sigh of relief. His pissing was blissful; the release an almost sexual pleasure. He had long since given up marking the hour and day of his birth, and even, as the generations slipped past, remembering the year of it required an effort of mind. However, due to their extreme age, some of the organs of his emaciated body, including his bladder, occasionally refused to submit to the commands of his will. It had been troubling him all day, and now, as the shadows lengthened, this release was an exquisite pleasure.

As the pungent urine splashed into the bowl, Mangku gazed around his chamber in the Jade Tower of the Palace of Sukatan. It was well furnished, with golden fruit plates, crystal vases and fine Indujah rugs. Gauze curtains covered the wide-open windows, allowing the chamber to benefit from a cooling breeze. It was a mark of respect that he had been given this fine room; it was, he assumed, only a little less opulent than the Raja's own quarters.

Good. They respected him. Or rather they feared him and his ability to bring down the wrath of his master. The performance he had given that morning to the sweaty little Wukarta puppy who now sat on the throne of Sukatan had been a resounding success . . .

Mangku had presented himself, alone, that morning at the doors of the palace and had announced himself to the various guards and servants and insisted that he be shown directly into the Green Withdrawing Room for an unscheduled private audience with Raja Widojo.

The boy—despite the feathery trace of a mustache on his upper lip and his twenty-one years of life, he could not truly be called a man—had been somewhat surprised to see a tall, lean and terrifying priest bursting in on him during his leisure hours. But he had borne it well. The Vizier had announced him as His Holiness

Mangku the Wise and mentioned, only in passing, that his powerful warship, well provided with cannon and filled with a couple of
hundred brutal-looking fighting men, was docked in the harbor.

Widojo had nodded solemnly as if he had been expecting this
wonderful piece of news; he had bid the priest welcome, invited
him to sit and asked exactly how he might possibly aid such a,
um . . . such a well-armed servant of the Gods.

Mangku had taken a high hand from the beginning. "I am the
special envoy and plenipotentiary extraordinaire of Ongkara,
Lord of the Islands, Lion of the Southern Lands, Dragon of the
High Seas, and I am making a tour of all the lands across the Laut
Besar that owe him fealty. I shall remain in Sukatan for only a few
days but I shall require from Your Highness a large quantity of
fresh water and dry food stores for my onward journey."

"You *require* it, do you?" said the Raja, bristling slightly.

"I demand it, Highness," said Mangku, lifting his chin to look
down his broad nose.

The Raja opened his mouth to say something but Mangku interrupted him. "I shall also require—or demand, if you prefer—a
chest of your finest obat and two tuns of marak. And other sundry
ships' items that I will not trouble your ears with. And in payment, I shall be most happy to give you a paper guaranteed by the
Lord of the Islands himself."

The Raja frowned.

"As the special envoy of Ongkara the Fearless, I speak with his
voice," said Mangku.

There was a long, awkward silence in the Green Withdrawing
Room. The Raja looked at his Vizier, a silk-wrapped butterball
with a long, plaited white beard. The Vizier looked back at the
Raja and then merely shrugged helplessly.

"Whatever the Lord of the Islands requires, of course," said
Widojo sulkily. "And, of course, there will be no need for any such
payment. It is an honor merely to be of service."

He knew as well as any man in the room that the paper receipt from Ongkara was worthless. He also knew that refusal to provide the ships' stores for his guest meant inviting immediate brutal retaliation from the most powerful warlord in the whole of the Laut Besar.

"The Raja is most gracious," said Mangku, without a trace of irony. "There is one other thing: I should like, if I may, to view the Eye of the Dragon, perhaps even to be allowed to hold it in my two hands. If Your Highness would consent to that signal honor."

Widojo sat up on his cushions at that point. The Dragon's Eye was an enormous and extremely valuable gemstone the size of a small pig—it took a strong man two hands to cradle its weight. It was the most prized possession of the Rajas of Sukatan, discovered in the Konda Pali mines generations ago when the Gold Masters had burrowed as deep as they dared into the quartz rock below the Gray Mountain, killing a thousand slaves in the process, or so it was said. The Eye of the Dragon had been found, encased in a pure gold nugget, and it had been the centerpiece of the Sukatan royal treasury ever since.

"Ah, I'm not sure that would be . . ." began Widojo. Then he stopped.

Mangku wondered briefly if he would be forced to make a more overt threat to persuade this princeling to agree to his demands, or whether he would be obliged to perform some simple feat of magic to cow him. Perhaps not. He fixed the Raja with his gray, black-veined eyes and saw the boy flinch from his gaze. The boy was clearly a weakling.

"The Lord of the Islands would esteem it a great privilege, if you would consent," he said slowly, twisting his lips into a smile for the first time that morning. "I have been tasked by the Lion of the Southern Lands with assessing all the great treasures of the kingdoms of the Laut Besar—I must report back that they're all secure and being properly cared for."

"Oh, well then . . . I suppose then we might arrange a viewing. Shall we say tomorrow at noon in the Grand Courtyard. If we are getting the Eye out of the vaults, we might as well let the people of Sukatan catch a glimpse of it for once. It is rather spectacular. We can arrange that, Vizier, can't we? Spread the word. Tell the people. In the meantime we must find Your Holiness some suitable lodgings and refreshment."

The Raja clapped his hands.

Outside the slatted windows of Mangku's chamber the dusk was swiftly turning into night. The whine of mosquitoes caught his ear. And the deep booming of the hollow log bells of the Temple of Vharkash. He pushed open the casement and cocked his head, listening. How he remembered that sound! Even now it seemed to call to the marrow in his bones. He had spent twenty years in the Mother Temple, first as a lowly serving boy, then a novice and finally as a priest. All his days and nights had been governed by the sound of those bells.

It was as a serving boy in the Mother Temple that he had first become aware of his inferior blood. He was fifteen, no, still just fourteen when he was first called a Mudskipper by one of the older novices. It had burned his soul then, and even the distant memory of the insult made him flinch now, so many, many years later.

"Hey, you, Mudskipper, get your dirty Dewa finger out of my soup," a senior novice called Lallat had shouted at him as he was serving out the bowls for their dinner at the long communal table in the Hall of Eating.

Lallat was the second son of the hereditary steward of the rulers of the Island of Molok. A snobbish oaf. But his skin was light, his nose beautifully thin and his hair long and auburn, with flecks of red in the sunlight. He was a novice and captain of the dormitory in which Mangku slept, and he never allowed an opportunity for mockery of the new boy's evident racial inferiority to pass him by. Lallat's family were New People, way back for twenty generations, they even boasted a little Wukarta blood—and the novice captain never tired of mentioning it. On the other hand, Mangku—well, he told the other boys and girls at the Temple that his folk were rice farmers from Western Yawa, humble people but honorable. And he lied: his father was a Dewa gravedigger and his mother an obat-addicted occasional buffalo herder who could find no better-blooded husband to share her dilapidated, filthy two-room hovel on the very outskirts of their village.

His Dewa father had never been an issue before now. His part of Western Yawa was very sparsely populated and a worker was valued as a worker—all hands were needed to bring in the rice crop safely—and this had been the case for generations, so the distinctions between the races were blurred and vague. But Mangku's black hair was tightly curled, his nose was flat and broad, and his skin was dark—his looks proclaimed unmistakably his Ebu heritage. And somehow that seemed to matter to people a great deal more in his new home.

He had left his village and traveled all the way to the Mother Temple because he wanted to escape the poverty and tedium of a life in a dusty, forgotten corner of the world. He had heard that the Mother Temple accepted boys and girls from all over the Laut Besar and that if they worked hard, were obedient and devout, they might one day be made priests. That had been his dream—to gain himself a position of respect and spiritual authority in the community. But his first years at the Temple had been closer to a nightmare.

Led by Lallat, the boys and girls had mocked him pitilessly: calling him Mudskipper, Dung Blood and Jungle Boy. But that was not the worst of it. He could have borne a little name-calling, if that was all it was. But they made him do all the menial tasks:

the jobs that the Dewa servants attached to the Temple would ordinarily have done. He slaughtered buffalo and stripped off their skins to make leather in the urine pits—he would never forget the smell of those rancid, eye-watering pits for as long as he lived—he butchered the meat for the kitchens, he buried the dead—just like his father did back in his home village.

The other boys told him he was polluted, that he was inherently dirty and that the touch of his hands would contaminate them with his filth. In the recreation hour, they made a game of running away screaming from him, holding their noses when he came near, as if his body perpetually smelled foul. Although he scrubbed his dark skin with soap and stiff brushes till it was raw every night. The other novices told him that Vharkash despised him and his kind—and that he could never be a priest. Lallat moved his bed out of the dormitory and into the dank ablutions block attached to the sleeping hall.

He complained once to the deputy in charge of the novices and was threatened with a beating if he made a nuisance of himself. "You are here to work and to learn," the deputy had said. "If you do not like it, go back to whatever dung pile that you crawled out from."

Mangku began to hate.

His hatred grew month by month. It was not just his chief tormentor Lallat that he hated—in fact, he dispatched that boy to the Seven Hells with a large dose of a discreetly administered poison just sixteen months after his arrival. He was allowed to move his bed back into the dormitory when he was finally accepted as a novice, and the name-calling and humiliating games eventually stopped. But their effect was indelible. He feared deep inside himself that he *was* inferior. The hatred took root in his heart like some grotesque and evil fungus, feeding on darkness and decay. And it grew. Every year it grew a little stronger. He hated them all—all the carefree descendants of the New People. He hated them for their privilege and their light skins and small noses, for their air of natural superiority. They were all the enemies of his blood, he told himself.

Then, one day, he met his Master.

He recognized him immediately for what he was. And gradually, over many weeks and months, he opened his heart, and he showed him the hatred inside. In turn, his Master showed him the way.

The hollow log bells of the Sukatan Temple boomed again. It was the Hallowed Day today, Mangku recalled, the sacred time that occurred once a month when the Gods were most attentive to the desires of mortals, most amenable to their prayers. It was the day of power, when men and women possessing even the smallest degree of spiritual ability dared to welcome the divine into themselves and become strengthened and purified. Gods walked the Earth on the Hallowed Day and sometimes took on human form.

But Hiero Mangku had finished with the Gods a long time ago. The Gods were not a reliable source of power—sometimes they listened to the pleas of men, sometimes they were deaf. It depended on their childish whims. They could not be commanded, merely cajoled or pleaded with. You approached them on your knees like a beggar whining for alms. That was not Mangku's way. He relied on something far stronger, a secret knowledge, the ancient forbidden practices that his Master had introduced to him early on in his time at the Temple: blood magic. The sorcery of his Ebu forefathers. The wild power that the original inhabitants of the Laut Besar had wielded.

Mangku settled himself on the floor in the center of the Jade Tower chamber. He had already drawn the seven-pointed star in red chalk on the wooden floor. He gripped his left hand over the blade at the top of his staff—grimacing with the pain of the new wound opened in his much-scarred palm, then making a fist, he squeezed a gout of blood onto each of the star's points.

He rubbed the bloody left hand against his right and said the ancient words of power, pronouncing them clearly but quietly without a single mistake. He reached up to his uncovered head and plucked a single, black, curling hair from his scalp, then cradled it in the gore of his cupped hands. He said the words again, and breathed gently onto the twist of hair. As he watched, the strand shriveled, curled in tighter on itself, forming a bloody ball that coalesced, coagulated and slowly changed from dark red to an iridescent green. He opened his hands completely and a tiny black-and-green beetle rattled its shiny wing cases, unfurled the wings inside and humming contentedly flew up from his palms, hovered at the top of the room and then out of the open window into the warm Sukatan night.

Mangku got up stiffly and washed his bloodstained hands. He recalled then the day they had expelled him from the Mother Temple, when his hands had been slick with the blood of another. The diminutive High Priest standing there looking solemn and sad, a knot of young burly lesser priests and novices with their arms folded across their chests, trying to look intimidating. Necromancer, they had called him. Foul traitor to the Holy God.

He was a fully fledged priest by then, and had given twenty years of loyal service to the Temple. It had been a long time since people had called him names.

For twenty years, he had hidden his hatred of them—as his Master had instructed him to do—he had studied hard, absorbed the lessons the priests taught with ease and made his own secret investigations, too, often late at night in the Great Library, reading scrolls written by people who had been dead for centuries. He studied the old magic, strictly forbidden by the High Priest, hiding the cuts to his own body whence he had drawn the necessary fluids. He had sacrificed animals for practice, mice and rats he caught, then newborn lambs and once a fully grown cow, although the power to be drawn from them was so much weaker.

He read about his own folk, too, the histories of his race—about the many Ebu rebellions, brief bloody affairs that always ended with a brutal crushing of the natives' hopes and dreams. He came across a manifesto—a call to arms from one long-dead Ebu general called Ksajak, who said that there could be no peace until all the New People—every one of them—were expelled from the Laut Besar. His enemies, the very same New People, burned Ksajak alive. But the general's manifesto changed his life. A dream was born, a sacred mission—the total cleansing of the Laut Besar of all these arrogant incomers, every one. It was an impossible task. The dream of a long-dead madman. To rid the Laut Besar of hundreds of thousands of inhabitants? It was absurd. Or was it?

On that last night, though, it was he who was got rid of, Mangku remembered wryly. They had all burst in while he was in the middle of the summoning ritual. His first attempt to harness the lifeblood of another human to unleash pure magical power. The victim was a dim-witted serving girl, a Dewa nobody attached to the Temple kitchens, someone who would scarcely be missed. He had drugged the girl senseless, and strapped her facedown to a table in an abandoned rice barn a few miles outside the Temple complex. He had hesitated over using a Dewa; she was of his blood, she was his kin, in a way. But she was of no importance to the Temple hierarchy, and her disappearance would not cause an uproar. And it was fitting, in a way, that her sacrifice should allow him to gain precious knowledge that would eventually help all her people, his people, everywhere. Her little death would not be in vain.

He had anointed the four corners of the barn with the girl's fresh blood, drawn the four complicated sigils on the walls and chanted the required words perfectly. Then, with the air already humming with magical power, he peeled open the girl's back and tore both her kidneys from her body and, gripping the slippery organs, he had summoned Klotha, the bat demon, from the deepest of the Seven Hells. It had worked. He had triumphed. And he would have bound that great flapping, leathery thing to his will, had he not been interrupted.

The New People had come barging in, beating gongs, torches ablaze, shouting Murder! Sacrilege! Priests and novices, people he had known all his life. The little High Priest to the fore—stern as stone. Klotha had flapped away shrieking into the darkness, never to be seen again. And he had been seized and bound and lectured by the High Priest for hours, told in no uncertain terms the evil of his ways. But they were not permitted to shed his blood. Instead, they made him dig the grave of the novice he had sacrificed—dig it like a Dewa—and forced him to stand penitent at the graveside, silently hating all of them, and himself, too, while they prayed earnestly for the dead girl's soul and for the God Vharkash to forgive his so-called sins. And then, when it was over, they dismissed him. Told him to go. Exiled him from the Mother Temple that had been his home for so long.

Mangku finished cleaning his hands, salved the fresh cut on his left hand and bandaged it tightly with a clean white cloth. He felt drained, as usual, empty and weak—the normal effect of performing any feat of blood magic. But he would eat heartily and sleep in a while and all would be well. The beetle was dispatched, and the Dragon's Eye would be brought out tomorrow for him to view. Everything was unfolding just as he had planned it.

♦ ♦ ♦

Jun followed Ketut along the waterfront, staying a good thirty paces behind her and ducking behind the thick wooden poles of the tall lamps that lighted the street whenever she half turned to get her bearings. Dusk had lowered its gray veil over Sukatan and the lamplighters were out, dozens of pairs of men and boys, who refilled then ignited the bowls of oil at the top of the posts against the coming darkness, the man issuing unnecessary instructions to the boy who climbed the wooden pole as nimbly as a squirrel before drawing up the lit bamboo torch on a cord and setting off the oil blaze.

Ketut stopped to ask one of these pairs something and at that moment the wooden tubular bells of the Temple of Vharkash began to toll; a series of dull, almost moaning booms that echoed across the still water of the harbor. Ketut and the elder lamplighter chatted for a few moments and then shared a laugh about something, the little boy joining in from a dozen feet above their heads, but Jun could not make out what they had been joking about, and when he passed he gave the man a ferocious scowl that would have meant, "No dillydallying, on with your work, little man," had he been at home in Taman. Here it meant nothing. He was met by a blank stare.

He followed Ketut into a darkened side road, heading uphill from the harbor front, and it soon became clear where Ketut was going. The tolling of the bells became louder and a stream of people joined him, thickening to a crowd, all seemingly going the same way. The alley opened into a courtyard and Jun looked up at the wide sweeping tiled roof of the Temple of Vharkash. It was full dark now and the courtyard was lit by four burning lamps on poles, one in each corner. The doors of the Temple had been flung open and Jun caught a glimpse of Ketut heading inside.

He stopped at the doors and a young shaven-headed priest in black robes made the holy sign of the scythe with the crooked index finger of his right hand touched to the center of his forehead. The ground at Jun's feet was littered with offerings in tiny woven grass baskets: a few flower petals, a pinch of salt or rice, sometimes a little wooden or paper figurine and a smoldering incense stick. Many of the offerings had been trampled by the hurrying feet of the worshippers. The smell of the incense caught in his nostrils and he sneezed, but suddenly he felt comforted, safe and oddly at home. This was familiar territory for Jun, not so very different from the temples on Taman where he and his father had worshipped on Hallowed Days. What was different here was the crush of the crowd. In Taman, Jun would have been seated on cushioned rattan chairs in the royal enclosure. Here Jun was swept inside by the press of humanity and, tall as he was, he had to crane his neck over the heads of the hundreds of people in front to see anything at all.

There was no sign of Ketut. But no matter; after a little while, the air of familiar expectation in this holy place began to soothe him and he forgot all about her. At the back of the Temple was a stone table and above it an ornately carved plinth with a stone box, open at the front and empty, but draped with bright cloths and streamers of red and green, the entrance covered in curtains of strung flowers. Two huge glowing incense burners stood at either side of the altar, tended by novices in black robes; they fed the coals and wafted the thick gray smoke they produced toward the congregation. Jun took a deep breath, held it in for a count of ten and felt the familiar joyous tingle of obat smoke reaching down deep into his lungs.

A gaggle of old men filed in from the side of the Temple, into a roped-off area on the left, and took their places, cross-legged in front of their instruments: a set of wooden and bamboo drums and several round bronze gongs of varying shapes and sizes. After a long while, after the musicians had chatted with each other, and greeted several members of the congregation, they got up and changed places with each other, passed each other cushions, sipped

small earthenware cups of black tea and smoked long obat pipes—
then, finally, they began to play. And with the first lambent notes,
Jun felt a shiver run down his spine. This was the music of the
Gods—in particular the music of this God: Vharkash—the greatest of them all. A gentle but thrilling booming of the big bass gong
was like the beating of a giant metal heart; then, a light rhythm
tapped out with padded mallets on the bamboo drums over the
top, and the simple sad melody taken up by the smaller gongs, and
repeated, and embroidered upon by others. Each note sounded to
Jun like a splash of sound, as if the music were water dripping
from a gutter into a beautiful sunlit pond. He stopped feeling the
heat and sweat and push of his fellows, all packed around him,
the elbow in the ribs, the trodden-on toe; he felt himself transported back to the Watergarden, to the delights of his home, to
the liquid music of the summer palace of his ancestors.

The hours lost their meaning in the Temple that night. This
was the time and place of Vharkash the Sower, Vharkash the
Reaper and Vharkash the Harvester. Vharkash who brought the
crops forth from the soil. Vharkash who fed the whole world.
This was the time and place of mighty, all-knowing Vharkash and
his beautiful but deadly consort Dargan—who was, in fact, no
more than the female side of divine Vharkash himself.

A short, fat, elderly male priest wearing a red-and-black mask
and accompanied by two unmasked women acolytes shuffled out
from behind a curtain and into the space before the altar, their
arms filled with offerings: a haunch of pig, a pair of golden roasted
chickens, a bowl of saffron rice, fruits of all kinds from prickly
green durian to brown snake-skinned nut-apples, garlands of red
and blue flowers, jugs of rice wine. They made the crooked-finger
sign of the God to their forehead and mumbled inaudible prayers,
then anointed their heads with dabs of saffron and rice. The two
old women were twins, Jun noted, with a delicious little shiver of
awe—identical to each other in dress, manner and feature, and

therefore so beloved of the God that he created two people from a single soul.

The orchestra's tempo increased. Jun felt the obat singing in his veins. The crowd swayed back and forward in time to the beat. Some were shouting out Vharkash's name now. Jun had the curious sensation that he was underwater, everything being muted and fluid but perfectly clear. Then the first dancer emerged from the packed crowd, almost vomited out into the small space before the altar and the three priests. It was a man of middle years, naked apart from a blue-and-white-checkered sarong and lean and brown from labor in the sun, the muscles of his chest and arms corded and powerful. His eyes were closed but his body jerked and twitched in time to the music. He hunched his back and brought his hands up to his temples, index fingers pointed like a pair of horns. The crowd gave a murmur as they recognized Bantung, the great bull buffalo that was Vharkash's legendary mount. As he danced, Jun felt he could see the shadow of the buffalo as an aura around the man's true body; now he could see only a huge, dark, snorting bovine, now a man cleverly imitating an animal. He knew the obat was at work in him, and the power of the music and the holiness of the Temple itself were making magic in his mind, yet when he relaxed and allowed himself to see the divine beast that possessed the dancing man's soul, he felt a sense of exhilaration, a pure and soaring joy: the great God was truly among them.

The two old women, the sacred twins, were the next to be taken by the spirit of Vharkash; they joined the dancing buffalo-man on the floor, strutting and posing like young warriors eager to make a name for themselves. The transformation was extraordinary: gone were the thin backs bowed with age and infirmity, gone the withered, sticklike limbs, gone the doddering grandmotherly shuffle. The two women strode boldly to the front, heads high, arms cocked on their hips, their movements exactly synchronized with the other, one body an exact copy of the other: and Jun truly saw a pair of young men, warriors in the prime of life, the embodiment of divine Vharkash the Harvester himself.

Then Ketut leaped out onto the floor.

The tiny black-and-green beetle flew high above the rooftops of the Palace of Sukatan and perched on a golden spire. Mangku looked out through the insect's myriad, fractured eyes and saw the lights of the lamps on the waterfront and the glowing windows from the obat dens and taverns that lined the road. The rest of the city was darker, but here and there were pinpoints of light, candle-glow leaking from the doors of the dwellings of the richer citizens who had not gone to bed with the sun. Mangku looked down at the courtyard of the Temple of Vharkash, the lit space and the crowds thronging outside, swaying in time to the distant, tinny sounds of the gong orchestra.

Bah, he thought, with the insect's tiny brain, *they think that is magic. A whiff of obat, a swirl of sacred music and the frenzy of a mob eager to be possessed by the Gods—but it's no more than a shadow play compared with the power I will conjure in this world.*

The tiny beetle spread its wings and flapped up into the night. It circled the golden spire once and flew east toward a balcony on the highest floor of the Palace of Sukatan where a gauzy curtain flapped in the breeze. Inside the chamber, on a bed of silken pillows, the Raja lay snoring softly. The beetle alighted on his downy cheek, took a few featherlight steps and crawled inside the royal ear.

Widojo gave a small gasp and half opened his eyes as the beetle entered the deepest part of the auditory canal, gnawed swiftly through a barrier of bone and gristle and burrowed up into his soft brain. Mangku stilled the beetle. It stopped its tunneling and lay quiet for a dozen heartbeats. The Raja of Sukatan turned over, sighed heavily and settled back into his slumbers. Mangku concentrated his power, projecting it across the space between them, and the beetle, snug in the spongy moist tissue, curled in upon itself, shrank and liquefied, the green juices of its body diffusing into the gray matter, flowing into every corner of its folds.

Ketut leaped out onto the floor. And yet it was no longer Ketut. Jun knew that the gigantic figure, twice as tall as a man, with huge bulbous red-and-black-ringed eyes, with curled protruding fangs and claws of an enormous tiger was his Dewa shipmate. She was Ketut. And yet she was not: she was Dargan—the Witch Goddess, one of the avatars of Vharkash's wife. With her toes and fingers turned outwards, she stamped across the floor in front of the altar. The collective indrawn breath of the crowd about Jun was like the hissing of the sea on a shingle beach; the buffalo-dancer took one look at Dargan, straightened up out of his hunched posture, his eyes fluttering, and he collapsed like a dead man—into the arms of two waiting novices, who carried him safely away behind the altar to recuperate, with the old priest in black fussing over him. The twin Vharkash priestesses, both still deeply entranced, bowed courteously to the gigantic figure and retreated to the back of the space, each still shivering and twitching to the beat of the music. Dargan stamped to the center and looked out over the packed ranks of worshippers. Jun felt her terrible eyes alight on him. He felt the atavistic fear sink deep down into him, right down into his toes.

He was aware of a stench, a hideous smell of decaying meat and excrement, and saw that around Dargan's neck was a glistening pink necklace of human entrails, and at her waist a belt of human skulls knotted together with flaps of rotting human skin. The monster beckoned to him with a ripple of her huge, clawed hands—to him alone. And Jun knew that he must obey—even though it meant his death at the hands of the Witch Queen. He began to move forward, pushing through the crowd, which was now swaying and chanting, a few hysterical souls actually scream- ing out Dargan's name in their ecstasy. He had no control over his legs, which propelled him farther forward, always forward, the red gaze of Dargan still holding him tight. But before he could advance to his certain doom, a man jumped out of the crowd, a burly fellow, with round, well-muscled shoulders, naked above his red sarong and with a short, unsheathed kris in his hands.

Jun stopped dead. The man shook the kris menacingly at Dar- gan, and then began making flowing strokes through the air in a figure of eight, traditional patterns that Jun well knew from his lessons with War-Master Hardan. The Witch Queen broke her gaze with Jun and deigned to look down at this leaping fellow who dared to threaten her with a mortal blade. She made one gesture, an open palm punching the air in his direction, and the man fell back a pace. His face was a rictus of pain, eyes wide as saucers, mouth open in silent agony, the cords in his neck taut. He turned the kris in his hands, laying both fists on the wooden hilt and placing the point of the weapon in the center of his naked, sweat-slimed chest, and then he began to push the kris into his own flesh. Dargan raised both hands, claws extended, holding them above her shoulders, commanding the fellow to impale himself, demonstrating her power over him, and the blade slid an inch into his pectoral mass. She opened her mouth and a blast of red flame shot out and singed the man's face but he merely rolled his head to one side and continued to force the blade into his own body.

The little old priest in the red-and-black mask suddenly stepped forward. He snapped his fingers twice and Jun saw the twins pos- sessed by Vharkash shrink back to their crone forms, shaking their heads and looking dazed. The priest made a cutting motion through the air with a flat palm and the orchestra played a few notes more and fell silent. It was over. Two strong novices had appeared by now and were struggling with the singed man with the kris, their hands gripping the blade, preventing it from being forced any farther into his chest. Jun looked at Dargan—and saw Ketut, standing there with her head bowed, sweat running in rivers down her face, arms limp at her sides. The chanting and screaming of the crowd had ceased and been replaced with a dull, awed murmur. One member of the orchestra began picking out a simple soothing tune on his bamboo instrument, almost a lullaby. The kris-man had been safely disarmed and was being led away by the novices to have his cut chest and burns tended. The floor was empty but for the short, masked priest and the ancient twins, the three of them embracing in a cozy family huddle.

Jun looked for Ketut on the performance area—both awed and appalled in equal measure. And saw that she was gone.

CHAPTER 14

———— ⦿ ————

Below in his cabin, Farhan opened the narrow cupboard that held his few clothes and after fumbling for a moment in the back, he brought out a long, slim wooden box. He was stung by Captain Lodi's suggestion that he was not a fighting man. Did he not face the same risks, or even greater ones if they were captured, as any Dokra mercenary or Buginese sailor? He had never actually killed a man—that was true. But he had slain many scores of ducks and geese, and dozens of spotted deer in his youth while holidaying each year in his father's summer hunting lodge high in the cool Caspaan hills. He had even, on one terrifying occasion, dropped a charging boar with a well-aimed shot, when that beast was threatening to disembowel him.

Farhan opened the wooden box and looked down at the elegant lines of the double-barrelled hunting rifle, silver engraved into the metal, the slim cherrywood stock carved with scenes from the chase. It was with this weapon that he had brought down the wild boar, a two-hundred-pound monster with upcurving scimitar-like tusks, which ran fast as a greyhound out of a thicket of bramble and straight at him. Farhan had had no time to think: he had put the loaded rifle to his shoulder and fired and—thank the Gods—he had shot straight, putting a ball through the animal's chest at twenty paces and exploding its heart. The animal had continued to run long after it was dead and had finally collapsed, twitching, drooling and urinating, at his very feet.

Farhan took the rifle from the blue, velvet-lined box. It felt light and balanced in his hands. He cocked both hammers, put the piece to his shoulder and clicked each trigger once. The hammers snapped down and Farhan imagined a huge, battle-mad Manchu bannerman blown off his feet with each dry click.

He looked down at the empty space where the rifle had lain. Something was wrong. There was a compartment below the stock of the rifle, a square of blue-velvet board that lifted with the right pressure in one corner, and he saw that it was slightly ajar, a sliver of the white interior of the cache showing. He was always meticulous about closing it: he hid some of his most treasured objects inside the box. He pushed the levered door of the box and it opened fully. Inside were a few of the early love notes he had received from the Northron girl, a basic Amrit Shakti codebook, a single finger of pure gold—escape money to be used in the last resort—and an envelope of white powder, a deadly poison, which if used in very small quantities could also be a most effective pain-killer. The packet of love notes had been opened. They had been tied up with a scarlet ribbon and someone had undone it, read and no doubt copied the letters, then retied the bow but in a clumsier way.

Am I imagining this? Farhan considered this for a long moment, and concluded that he was not. Someone was spying on him, and it did not take very much of a leap of imagination to work out who it was: Mamaji—or more likely her maid Lila on her mistress's orders. Still, there was nothing in the notes but words of tenderness, nothing he could not explain as sentimentality. Nothing compromising. So, no matter. No damage was done except to his pride. He knew now that Mamaji did not trust him. But he'd nothing to hide from her except the extent of his debts—and there was no mention of that in his letters.

He put the matter from his mind and loaded the rifle: priming both pans with a pinch of black powder, pouring a full measure of powder into each barrel, stuffing leather, wadding-wrapped balls into both barrels and ramming them far down with the long, slim steel rod till they were snug against the powder charge. He took the small silver pistol out of his pocket and shoved it into his boot top—he still had no intention of being taken alive—and filled his coat pockets with a dozen lead balls, a full flask of powder and a handful of little cut squares of leather. For a moment, he considered taking a pinch of obat—it would quell his fears; he knew that. But at the last moment he realized that he needed clarity of thought and settled for taking a leather tea bottle filled with a fine, delicate Han brew. Rifle in hand Farhan left the cabin and made his way to the stairs that led to the deck.

Captain Lodi felt the brisk north wind blowing on his weather-beaten left cheek. He checked the angle of the sails, tugged on a backstay to check the tension of the rigging, nodded with satisfaction.

"Keep her as close to the wind as you dare, Muda," he said to his lieutenant, who with another powerful Buginese sailor had taken the big round, spoked wheel that controlled the rudder. Cyrus Lodi left the quarterdeck and went forward beyond the curve of the fan-shaped mainsail to get an uninterrupted view of the enemy. He passed by the rows of Dokra, splendid in their best scarlet coats, grinning under their turbans at the captain and saluting with their muskets. Their task in the battle would be to add their musket fire to the cannon broadside on the enemy ships as they passed—trying to kill or maim the vital seamen who sailed the ship, rather than the enemy's marine troops. And if they were grappled by the enemy, they were to resist boarders or, indeed, try to board the enemy ship themselves, aiming to secure the enemy quarterdeck and vital steering wheel.

Captain Lodi climbed the foremast as far as the fighting top and pulled out his telescope. Not that it was much needed. The

Mongoose was less than half a league from the nearest Celestial cruiser, and crucially, slightly to the north of the Han ship, or to windward, the two ships converging fast. The second cruiser was closer in to the green Yawa coast four leagues to the captain's right, half a league behind her consort, but she'd packed on all the sail she could to try to close with her companion. Captain Lodi smiled to himself. *This could be done,* he thought. *It could be done.* He needed precise timing, swiftly worked guns and just a pinch of luck, but it could be done. It all depended on the enemy continuing to do what he was doing now—which was always a risky prospect to rely on. But he could do nothing about that and, so far as it could be predicted, the battle was shaping up very nicely.

Captain Lodi was rather surprised to find himself joined in the fighting top by his friend Farhan, who was grasping an improbably long and rather ornate silver double-barrelled hunting rifle in his right hand. In the bucket-shaped structure of the top, it was rather crowded for two big men to stand together, and Lodi courteously stepped outside the wooden rim and perched on a shroud, swaying easily with the roll of the ship. "Well, at least you won't be in the way up here," said Lodi, smiling. "And, who knows, you might even be able to bag a brace of juicy pheasant for our supper."

"Very funny. I thought I might try to take out their captain or some of their senior officers with this thing. I am pretty accurate, you know. Killed a boar once. I understand that their officers can be distinguished by the round glass buttons fixed onto the crown of their hats—red glass for the captain, if I remember correctly, yellow for a lieutenant."

"Yes, that's what they wear. But it's not really very sporting to aim at the officers," said Lodi, frowning. "They will all be on the quarterdeck, standing tall, showing their courage, taking their chances against the cannon and general fire. The Celestials con-

sider it rather barbaric, almost a war crime, in fact, to pick out
officers especially as targets."

"Truly?" said Farhan, quite amazed at this revelation.

"Yes, even in war there are rules of conduct. Anyway, killing
the captain won't do much good as there are a host of lieutenants,
half a dozen at least, all ranked in order and ready to take his
place. The Celestial Republic trains its sea officers thoroughly but
they are all taught the same tactics and responses—individualism
is very much frowned on. If you kill the captain, the first lieutenant will take over and carry on in exactly the same way. It won't
make any difference. But you bang away, if you want to. It can't
do much harm."

Captain Lodi tucked away his telescope and began to climb
nimbly down the rigging. Farhan felt deeply discouraged. In his
mind's eye, he had seen himself dropping an enemy captain with
a single brilliant shot and ending the battle at a stroke, winning
applause, medals, honors. In his fantasy, they might even have
given him the Order of the Elephant, the Federation's highest
award.

The enemy ships were close now, three hundred paces away
and, as Farhan watched, the nearest cruiser ran out a huge cannon
in the bow. A few moments later it spoke. A cloud of gray smoke,
then a bang, and Farhan fancied he could actually see the ball
hurtling through the air toward them. It flew two yards wide of
the foremast and roared past to starboard, cutting through a
dozen backstays but doing little other damage. He had felt the
wind of its passing. That was something that Farhan had not properly considered: that he, here in his seat in the fighting top in the
prow of the ship, might also be a target. It was not a pleasant
thought. The cannon was now being reloaded, the Han sailors
sponging out the hot barrel surrounded by wreaths of steam, and
another pair of men coming forward with a fresh ball, carried on
a wooden hurdle between them. Then, as if a gate were opening

in his mind, Farhan began to move. It might not be gentleman-like—but these people were shooting at him. At him personally, it felt like. He was damned if he would not reply.

Farhan brought the rifle to his shoulder in a smooth, practiced motion. He pulled back the hammer on the right to full cock and aimed at the crew of Han busy reloading the bow cannon, at a man with a yellow glass ball on the crown of his square black hat who was holding a pole with a burning match at its tip and who seemed to be giving orders. He felt the sway of the mast beneath his feet, moving with the roll of the ship. The target was two hundred paces away and closing. He aimed carefully, took a deep breath, released half and held the rest, as his father had taught him many years ago in the cool Caspaan hills.

At a hundred and fifty yards, he pulled the trigger.

The rifle kicked hard into his right shoulder, a gout of smoke shooting out from the barrel and obscuring his view. When it cleared he saw that the man with the yellow button of office was down, his pole with the burning match discarded. Another man was crouched beside him. There was a splash of blood on the deck. The two men with the cannonball on the hurdle looked on in shock. Farhan shouldered his piece again. He cocked the second hammer, aimed briefly, fired and blew the top of the head off the nearest man holding the cannonball hurdle. The man dropped his burden and collapsed twitching. The spilled cannonball rolled across the slanting deck and caught the lower leg of the fellow just coming round with a bucket of water, who fell with a scream and a broken ankle.

I'm doing it, thought Farhan. *I'm really doing it. I am a fighting man. Three men down with only two bullets.* He felt nothing for the men he had killed or wounded—no more than he did for the beasts of the hunt he had claimed in the past. They were not people—sons, fathers, brothers—so much as inhuman puppets. It was only when he began to reload the rifle that he realized that his hands were shaking wildly and his heart was hammering in his chest. He spilled a measure of black powder on the priming pan and it was snatched away immediately by the wind. Perhaps this business wasn't as simple as it seemed. With an effort of will, his whole body now thrumming with a new energy, he managed to get a pinch of powder into both priming pans, and the pans closed tight.

The ships were no more than seventy paces away from each other and it was clear that the *Mongoose* would pass to the north of the first Celestial cruiser. Far below, he heard muted shouting and the ominous rumble of wheels on wood, and the portholes on the starboard side of the *Mongoose* flipped open all at once and the barrels of the six big brass cannon nosed out. Farhan looked forward and saw that the cruiser was doing the same with her four guns on this side: it would be broadside to broadside when they passed each other. The big guns smashing into each other at a range of a short stone's throw.

Farhan caught a flashing vision of hell as he imagined being belowdecks—in either ship—when the cannon roared and the iron balls were blasted into the bowels of the other, smashing through timbers and crushing frail bodies to red pulp. But the *Mongoose* had more guns—fourteen to the cruiser's ten—and consequently threw a greater weight of metal which must surely do more damage at this short range. In a straight-out slogging match, ship to ship, with equal skill on both sides, the *Mongoose* must win the day.

Yet there was the second cruiser to consider. She had come up fast and now lay about five hundred paces behind the first cruiser and a little to the south. It was clear, even to Farhan, who made no claim at all to be a seaman, that she meant to form a two-ship line with her consort and continue the battering of the *Mongoose* after the first cruiser had passed. His ship would be pounded first by one and then by the other enemy vessel—and he wondered whether she could take it. She must certainly be crippled if not sunk by the attentions of two Celestial warships. The cruisers could circle, turning back on themselves, and pass by once more, again in line but heading east this time, easily overhauling the stricken *Mongoose* and smashing balls into her until she was sucked down into the sea.

All this was perfectly clear to Farhan and, at the same time, he knew that he could do precisely nothing about it. Yet in this knowledge of almost-certain death he found a calmness he'd never known before: he would fight his own private battle up here with his rifle, finding targets on the enemy deck and destroying them, if he possibly could. Whatever happened to the ship, he would fight to the last.

Farhan had managed to get the second ball into the rifle's muzzle and was just ramming it home, when he heard the first brass cannon roar beneath him. He looked to his right and saw that the cruiser was beneath the arm that gripped his rifle barrel. It was only a stone's throw away and moving fast. The enemy ship was about two-thirds the size of the *Mongoose* and gave an immediate impression of order and calm. Groups of men in neat blue uniforms stood to attention along the rail. The wood of the deck had been scrubbed to a brilliant white. The brass fittings gleamed like gold. Then everything was blotted out by the roaring of the enemy guns and a vast cloud of gray smoke that billowed up from below.

Farhan felt the strike of the enemy balls hitting the hull of the ship below him. He could see tongues of orange flame ripping through the smoke from time to time, as the *Mongoose*'s guns returned fire, but he could make out little else. Something caught his eye and he looked across at the passing masts of the cruiser. A man was sitting in the fighting top across and a little below from him, a Han in a blue uniform with a square black hat atop of which gleamed a yellow-glass ball. The man smiled shyly at him—

they were no more than thirty paces away from each other—but made no hostile move. Below them the cannon fired again, and the balls smashed into each of their ships. His crow's nest shook and shuddered with the impacts. The noise was hellish. The smoke was dense as a gray blanket six feet below his boots. Yet Farhan could see the passing Han officer in the other top as clearly as if they were in the same room. He felt the weight of the loaded rifle in his arms and knew that he should lift it and fire. But the smiling Han lieutenant raised a hand to his hat and lifted it an inch or two in salute as he glided away—and after that courteous gesture Farhan could no more shoot him than he could shoot his own mother.

The moment passed. The Han lieutenant was drawn away. There seemed to be a break in the firing and the clouds of smoke parted and Farhan looked down and caught a glimpse of the passing stern of the cruiser, the quarterdeck, where a huge man was grappling with the wheel. He looked like a very fierce fellow, bareheaded, with his black hair drawn in a queue at the back, his muscular frame almost bursting out of the blue jacket he wore.

Farhan lifted the rifle, cocked the right-hand hammer, aimed, breathed and fired down at the man. The bullet caught the wheelsman in the center of his broad back, knocking him away from the tiller-wheel and flat on his belly on the deck. The wheel began to spin wildly. Farhan was aware of a bellowing from his own quarterdeck, and the familiar running stamp of bare feet. He felt the *Mongoose* go about, coming round to head south. The sails creaked and shifted and he was aware, disconcertingly, of grinning brown faces all around him, hauling in sheets and hoisting fresh sails.

The green coast of Yawa was now dead ahead and on his right the first cruiser was drifting away, the wheel still unmanned, the craft turning before the wind. The once-pristine deck was now a scraped and bloodied mess, bodies here and there, jumbles of fallen blocks and rigging and—just then—a full broadside roared out from the starboard side of the *Mongoose*, raking the cruiser from stern to bow. Farhan actually saw a pair of balls shoot out from the cloud of smoke and sweep down the length of the deck at chest height, one plowing into a knot of sailors in blue and disintegrating them, the other biting through the mainmast like an ax chopping down a sapling and causing it to topple slowly, sails, sheets, yardarms, all collapsing onto the deck. The stern of the cruiser was smashed wide open by the rest of the broadside and Farhan caught a glimpse of a bloody cave, a hellish space of dismounted guns and tumbled bodies, a thick stream of gore pouring out from the scuppers. The Dokra troops were massed on the starboard rail, pouring volley after volley of musket fire into the carnage of the cruiser's opened end, their balls punching holes in the smoke and whistling into the darkness of the enemy ship.

Farhan had to look away. He turned his head left and saw the second cruiser fast approaching, no more than a hundred paces away now, coming on perpendicular to the *Mongoose*'s path and as yet untouched by her might. The cruiser's bow cannon roared, the ball scorching through the fan-shaped mainsail, leaving a neat round hole. The *Mongoose* replied in kind. The port broadside lashed out: a vast roaring convulsion of gray smoke and stabbing flame. The forepeak completely disappeared. The foremast was torn down by a screaming ball. All along the second cruiser's length were bloodied, blackened men, dangling ropes, broken lengths of timber.

The *Mongoose*'s starboard-side guns had not completed their bloody business either. They were firing individually now, at the will of their crews, balls arcing out and smashing through the hull of the first cruiser, which was now leaning dangerously to port; indeed the port rail was almost underwater. Men were jumping into the sea. Farhan looked right and saw a ball crash into the interior of the hull through a gap under the stern rail and burst out the other side. It was clear the ship was sinking. Most of the stern was now lapped by water.

To his left, the port broadside crashed out once more, the balls smashing through the hull of the second cruiser at the prow and tearing down the length of the ship, causing Gods knew what carnage in the dark belly of the vessel. And now the *Mongoose* was going about again. Farhan could hear Lodi shouting orders from the quarterdeck. The Buginese were once more all around him. Sheets were tightened. More orders shouted. The ship swung around, the north wind now coming onto her beam, her nose pointing east again. As she came around, the second cruiser's bow chaser fired again, missing altogether as the *Mongoose* swung through ninety degrees. The second cruiser was now passing on Farhan's left, almost close enough to touch, or so it seemed. He lifted the rifle, aiming at a man who was directing the fire of a squad of enemy musketeers. The man somehow sensed Farhan in the fighting top and pointed up at him but before the Han musketeers could change their aim, Farhan aimed quickly, fired and blew his right leg clean off above the knee.

The *Mongoose*'s port broadside smashed into the second cruiser at a range of twenty paces, tearing long holes in the side, knocking two of the enemy gunports into one black space. The cruiser returned fire, a faltering volley that nevertheless crashed into the ship at very short range and made her timbers scream. Farhan felt the jolt of it as he tried to reload his long piece, once more spilling precious powder, and the whole ship seemed to lurch downward at an angle. But the second cruiser was mortally wounded, too. The deck was awash with blood and large chunks of the rail and hull were completely missing.

Farhan saw a man with a red-glass button in his hat ordering the green-and-blue Celestial flag to be hauled down. But before the ship could surrender, a massed volley from the forty Dokra lined up on the rail blew him and his fellow officers into a scatter of red chunks. A final port broadside from the *Mongoose* ripped into the second cruiser—it was her death blow, and the whole vessel seemed to shiver under the impact and settle a little lower in the water. She was holed beneath the waterline, that much Farhan understood, maybe in more than one place and the sea was now rushing in through the shattered timbers to fill her holds with salt water and drag her down. But by then the *Mongoose* was past her, sailing free and clear, with nothing ahead of her but wide, blue ocean.

TWO

CHAPTER 15

❋

Extract from *Ethnographic Travels* by
Professor Tolmund K. Parehki of the University of Dhilika

Istana Kush, the greatest fortress of the Laut Besar, is at the entrance of the Sumbu Straits—a corridor of water between the jungle-garbed, mountainous Island of Sumbu, which runs northwest to southeast, and the impenetrable mangrove swamps of Manchatka. For a trading ship, the only way to enter the Laut Besar from the west is through the Straits. Smaller craft may enter through the narrower waterway four hundred miles south between the bottom tip of Sumbu and the Island of Yawa, but there the currents are ferocious, riptides abound and the coastline is rocky. Many a ship, even with an experienced pilot, has had its bottom torn out attempting to make that dangerous passage.

Jinwa the Valiant, the first King of Singarasam, the original Lord of the Islands, realized the strategic importance of the Sumbu Straits and sent his artificers to build a fortress on the north coast of Sumbu. The stronghold, called Istana Kush, was built well with high walls, defensive ditches and many towers and platforms that allowed defenders to shower lethal missiles on any ship venturing through the Straits. For a decade, Jinwa collected tribute from any vessels passing in or out of the Laut Besar and made himself immoderately rich.

However, Jinwa was bloodily toppled from the Obat Bale and his successor had enough trouble in controlling the merchant princes of Singararsam and the plunder-loving sea-peoples of the islands without maintaining an expensive outpost on Sumbu. A generation later, the crumbling fortress at Istana Kush and the lands around had been granted in perpetuity to the Indujah Federation by a venal and, it must be admitted, desperate Lord of the Islands for the staggering price of one million silver ringgu.

Since then, the Federation has expanded the fortifications and made a handsome return on its investment—indeed it took only seven years before it was turning a vast profit. Now it is the Federation that truly controls the Laut Besar. The Lord of the Islands may lounge on the Obat Bale in Singarasam, fifty leagues to the east, but the Federation Governor in Istana Kush controls which ships come in and out of the Laut Besar—from the west—and how much profit they make. Gold and slaves, gum and spices, timber and obat all flow out of the Laut Besar by this route, and silver and guns and goods from the Federation factories flood in. And the man who holds the Gates of Stone oversees them all.

The Royal Watchtower of Ostraka stood on a wide, blunt promontory of land that thrust out like a fist into the vast Indujah Ocean. It was the southernmost point of the whole Khevan Empire, fourteen hundred miles south of the Imperial city of Khev, three hundred down from Ashjavat. The Watchtower lay directly below the curved harbor and a little to the east of the town of Ostraka. Katerina stood on the Watchtower's flat, round roof, crenellated like a castle, and looked out at the vast sea before her. In days gone by, a great beacon had stood here to guide ships into Ostraka harbor; and the rulers of Ashjavat had posted lookouts to warn of the coming of sea raiders from the wilder, northern parts of the Indujah Peninsula. The beacon had not been lit in a generation; and the Indujah Federation, these days, was far more likely to send a trade deputation than a boatful of heavily armed bandits.

Katerina gazed out over the limitless ocean, today a rich greenish blue, with narrow lines of whitecaps rolling endlessly toward the cliffs below her feet. Somewhere across that empty expanse, three thousand miles or more to the southeast, lay the Sumbu Straits, the gateway to the Laut Besar, and the Federation fortresses of Istana Kush.

This was Katerina's target: the Gates of Stone, the key to the Laut Besar and all its wealth. She had begun dreaming about it from the first moment her old governess in Khev had pointed it out to her on the unrolled leather-and-linen maps, and had read her relevant chapters from Golintski's *Ancient Histories,* and later from her own perusal of the works of the renowned Federation traveler Tolmund K. Parehki. She had also read eagerly, late at night by illicit candlelight, about its supposed impregnability from the revered Khevan military textbook *The Craft of Combat.* But it was not impregnable, she had decided, after many hours of intense study. She could take it, she could possess it, of that she was quite certain. With the troops that she had been given by the Republic and with sufficient determination, the Gates of Stone could be hers. And once firmly in her hands . . .

"Highness," said a familiar voice behind her. "Colonel Tsu Wang says that the 42nd is on parade and ready for your inspection."

Katerina turned away from the sea and looked at her Minister, who was standing in the center of the Watchtower's roof, breathing a little heavily after climbing the stairs from the rooms of state below. A few paces behind him stood a black armor-clad figure, hand on his sword. Minister Tung had aged a great deal in the three months since he had entered her service and put on a little weight in the belly. The white streak in Tung's once-raven hair had expanded and spread until only a few black wisps remained above his ears. Tung's face was now deeply lined, and blue bags hung like bruises below his red-rimmed eyes. He looked at least ten years older than his thirty-one years, which was a shame, Katerina thought, for he had been a fine-looking man. Now he looked badly in need of a hot bath, a hard, full-body massage and about a week's sleep. Well, he had worked diligently for her, that could not be denied, and she was grateful. And this constant struggle would soon be over for him—very soon.

"Thank you, Minister Tung," she said, smiling prettily. "That is most gratifying to hear. Let us go down there and inspect them then."

She paused at the head of the steps and looked out west over the harbor of Ostraka: at the pair of stone moles that jutted out like stiff arms and guarded its entrance; at the bays where boats of all sizes were moored, some hauled up on jetties and heeled right over so that the shipwrights could get at and replace the worm-eaten timbers; at the little whore-town of Pirrus on the far side of the water, where the cheapest marak was diluted with turpentine and a man who fell asleep in his cups was unlikely to wake with anything in his pockets—indeed, he should count himself lucky if his throat was uncut. She looked down at the three deep-water bays, cut into the quay beside the road heading north, beside the square wooden blockhouses, where the timber was cut and where the ropery spun its miles of cordage, and smiled to see the three tall ships moored in the slips, newly built, fully rigged and provisioned for a two-month journey. And before that, on the wide, flat parade ground, lined up in ranks and rows like toy soldiers, motionless, their blue jackets and blue-green banners making them a single block of sea-themed color in the center of the ground—there was the army that was hers to command. Her personal army. A thousand well-disciplined, well-armed, fearless Han fighting men. A whole Celestial Legion, no less.

Katerina looked at Tung An Shan. He was a bone-tired man, a frightened man, a man who had performed wonders for her in a very short time: but was he a loyal man?

"We shall walk through the town, Minister. I would like to

stretch my legs before we meet Colonel Wang's magnificent Legionnaires. You hear that, Yoritomo—I'll be walking through the back streets of the town with my loyal chief minister."

The tall figure in the black-lacquered mask standing just behind Tung An Shan made the briefest of nods in acknowledgment.

Minister Tung and Princess Katerina walked side by side with a pair of Niho knights a pace behind her and one knight ranging ahead, looking for potential trouble in the winding thoroughfares of Ostraka town. This small, dingy, fish-stinking port was a far cry from the gilded grandeur of Ashjavat but, in the week since she had moved her court here, Katerina had come to like it. The streets were narrow and cobbled and twisted into unexpected places: closed-off courtyards where chickens pecked at piles of rubbish or into narrow alleys where the upper stories of the houses on either side almost met above the street to create dark, mysterious tunnels. Sometimes the streets headed down to green-slimed wharves and a glimpse of the gray water where a gnarled fisherman might be sitting on a barrel mending his nets.

The inhabitants of this shabby little town seemed to have no idea—and little interest, anyway—in who Katerina was or what she was doing in their midst. She was a great lady who was employing hundreds of local men in the building of three great ships of war—ships the like of which Ostraka had not seen in many years—and the dozens of foreign shipbuilders who bossed the work answered only to her. But, having determined that she was a rich one from the north, who might have a few weeks' work for a sailmaker and his apprentice, or might not, they made no further inquiries and seemed overcome by a strange incuriosity. The men removed their caps and the women curtsied to her as she passed, but they simply did not find her very interesting—and for Katerina, who had always been in the public eye, dressed by servants since she was a child, told always to watch how she moved, how she stood and what she said, trained always to be on display, always to be viewed with a critical eye or an admiring one, it was at first perplexing then deliciously liberating.

Katerina had mentioned this quality of the local people to the Governor of Ostraka at a welcome feast in the Watchtower a week after her arrival.

"It's all the batter they take, Highness," said Governor Hiki, a tiny, balding fellow with moist, pink, mole-like hands, who certainly *did* know who she was and who was perfectly terrified of her. "Comes in on the ships from the south. There's warehouses in Pirrus stacked high with chests o' the stuff. Nothing we do can stop it."

"What is this batter?" she had asked.

He blushed. "You wouldn't know of it, Highness, I'm sure. Some more rightly call it obat."

"Oh, I have indeed heard of it," she said, smiling. "I have heard that it has certain beneficial qualities, calming the mind, cleansing the humors of the blood, and so on."

"Well, these idle buggers—beg your pardon, Highness—these fellows here like to smoke it morning, noon and night. Always a little bit battered is your Ostrakan."

As Katrina and her Minister strolled through the town, she told Tung how pleased and gratified she was with his service over the past few months, saying he'd done wonders in arranging everything with his masters in the Conclave of the Venerables, the swift building of the ships, the collection of the stores, weapons, powder and shot and so on, the smooth delivery of the Legion, and asking him if he had given any thought to a suitable reward.

"A reward?" Tung looked at her quickly out of the corner of his eye. "That will not be necessary, Highness. The only reward I seek is the knowledge that I've served the Celestial Republic and, of course, your Highness to the very best of my meager abilities."

"I don't believe you. And I do not care to be lied to," said Katerina, looking at him coldly. "I would like to reward you with something slightly more tangible than the glow of satisfaction of a difficult task accomplished. So, Minister Tung, why don't you try to be a little more honest and tell me what it is that you truly desire?"

"What do I desire?" said Tung. "I want to go home and see my wife and baby."

"That may not be possible," she said, and she stopped dead in the street. "But I may be able to offer you something much better than that."

A dozen yards away a skeletally thin young man, dressed in nothing but greasy rags, was sitting propped up against the wall of a house, evidently asleep. His head drooped; despite his youth, his hair was almost all gone, revealing a pink scalp beneath the sparse gray-black strands. His long, thin hands were folded in his lap underneath a shapeless green woolen cap into which some kindly soul had tossed a few copper pennies.

Katerina put a hand to her waistband and pulled out a heavy yellow silk purse that chinked as it moved between her slim fingers. She beckoned to one of her Niho knights: "Your tanto," she said, snapping her fingers. "Give me your short blade now."

When she had the Niho dagger in one hand and the purse in the other, she turned to Minister Tung.

"This purse contains a hundred Khevan crowns, or perhaps a little more. A large amount of money anyway. And I happen to know that your ministerial salary from the Conclave of the Venerables is the equivalent of thirty-five crowns a month. So I have here in my hand what for you would represent three months' salary. I will give it to you, if you will take this knife and cut off the little finger of your left hand. Right now. Will you do it?"

Tung backed away from her, and found that his backward progress was stopped by the wall-like body of one of the Niho knights.

"Highness, if I have offended you, I most humbly ask your pardon," Tung said. Sweat was already pouring from him. His silk tunic was suddenly drenched.

"Answer my question: Will you do it? Will you cut off your finger for one hundred crowns?"

"No, lady, I would not willingly do that."

"Very good." Katerina nodded, as if confirming something to herself.

A fat elderly lady was approaching them, leading a donkey by a rope halter.

"Mother," said Katerina. "May I speak with you?"

"Certainly, my lady, how can I help you?" The Ostrakan woman curtsied and looked blearily up at Katerina, smiling happily, a little drool escaping from her slack lips.

"I have a hundred crowns here." Katerina clinked the heavy silk purse up and down in her palm. "And it will be yours if you would cut off one of your fingers, just a little one would do, and sell the separated digit to me right now."

The woman laughed. "You are a queer one, lady; they said you was a strange bird, even for a Northron—but wait till I tell them this! Oh my, how they will howl."

"Will you do it? A hundred crowns for a little finger."

"No, lady, I need all the fingers I's got. But I thank you kindly for the laugh. Oh, they will bray like asses when I tells them this at home . . ."

And she was gone, pulling the donkey along on its bit of frayed rope, chuckling to herself and saying over and over, "For a finger, oh my, for a dab-laddle little-bitty finger—a hundred golden crowns. Oh my!"

Katerina had already forgotten her. She walked forward and stood over the young beggar, shaking his shoulder to rouse him from his stupor. Tung saw the man look up: his face was greasy with sweat, his skin pale as a corpse's; he was trembling. His eyes though were huge, seemingly twice normal size, glossy and black as hatred.

"What? What do you want?" he was saying. "Why did you wake me to . . . this?" He seemed to be weeping, his vast dark eyes brimming with tears, the shudders of his bony body spilling them from his lids and down his thin white cheeks.

"I have money for you, lots of money," said Katerina.

"Gods bless you, lady, bless you," said the young man, shaking even harder in his joy.

"But I want something from you in return," said Katerina. She bounced the clinking yellow purse in her hand. "You may have this—it is a hundred golden crowns—but you must give me something very precious to you."

"Anything, lady," he said. His eyes were fixed on the yellow purse.

"I require your organ. I require your male member. Cut it off with this knife, right now, this moment, and put it into my hand, and I shall give you all this money."

"No, lady, you jest, surely?"

"One hundred crowns—all for you. To spend on whatever you may desire."

"You swear you will give it to me?"

"I swear."

Tung turned his face away as quickly as he could, but he saw the beggar accept the short Niho blade from Katerina, holding it in his right hand and thrusting the questing fingers of his left into his rag of a loincloth.

Tung heard no more than a grunt, and a little sigh, and then the man saying: "Here, lady, take it. Here it is. Now the money. You promised me the money."

Katerina was looking over at Tung when he finally raised his eyes. She was holding the money bag in the air above the sitting man's head. The Niho knight had retrieved his short blade and was cleaning the blood from it with a piece of cloth. The beggar looked between Tung and Katerina, bloodied and now exquisitely fearful.

"If I give him this money," Katerina said, "he will be dead from obat poisoning inside a few days—week at most. I know that for certain. If I give this to him, he is a dead man."

"Lady . . . I swear . . . I won't smoke that much . . ." said the beggar.

"Shh, quiet now, you," said Katerina. "Shall I give the money to him, Tung?"

"No, for pity's sake, Highness, get him to a doctor. A physician, if we can find one, or even a harborside apothecary. We must get him some help."

"He can buy the services of a doctor with that money. If he chooses to."

"Lady, I beg you . . . the money . . ." whined the young man.

Katerina dropped the heavy bag into the man's cupped hands, said, "There!" and turned from him and strode off down the cobbled street, the Niho knights all around her. Tung spared one look at the half-naked man with the gore-drenched loincloth but that wretch too was up and moving fast in the opposite direction, the bulging yellow bag clutched in his bloody fingers. Tung watched him go, a hard, bitter lump forming in his belly—he was watching a doomed young man running eagerly, even joyfully toward his own death—then he hurried after his princess.

Katerina waited for Tung at the end of the street, which opened out into a broad expanse of tamped sand. The princess stood there, waiting for him, staring out at the parade ground and the wall of brightly dressed soldiers, oiled muskets gleaming on their right shoulders, their Han faces impassive, their ranks perfectly aligned, blue-and-green banners fluttering in the sea breeze above a thousand burnished steel helmets.

With Tung at her side, and the three Niho knights behind her, Katerina marched across the ground, the sand crunching under her kidskin slippers, toward a trio of men, all portly and bearing square silk hats with big, colored-glass buttons on the crown.

It was not until they had greeted Colonel Wang and his two majors, and begun the tedious process of walking very slowly up and down the lines of statue-like figures, peering at the men of the 42nd Celestial Legion, that Katerina spoke to Tung again. The Colonel and his two senior officers were a dozen yards ahead, glowering at the men they passed, huffing with displeasure or occasionally giving a nod of compliment, when Katerina said, "You think that I am a cruel woman, Minister. You probably imagine that I am a little mad, or drunk with power. But that is not the case, I assure you. It is true that I am harsh with my enemies and with those who stand in my way. But I do not take any pleasure in inflicting pain on others. I will not shrink from it; but it is not for my gratification. There is always a purpose behind the things that I do; and, however monstrous they might seem to you, my actions are not mindless."

"Highness, I only wish to serve you. I am not in a position to judge . . ."

"Be quiet, Tung. I don't need you to talk. I need you to listen."

Katerina stopped in front of a tall Han musketeer. She slapped him on the chest, a hard flat blow, that raised a puff of blue-dye dust from his tunic. "This is a particularly well-turned-out young fellow," she said loudly. "A fine young soldier. Strong as an elephant. Brave as a tiger. What is your name, Legionnaire?"

"Undercorporal Chin, Highness, at your service."

"Undercorporal Chin, I accept your service with gratitude and humility. I need good men like you. You are a credit to the 42nd Legion, Chin. And a credit to me."

Tung saw the soldier struggling to hide a beaming smile and thought, *She has enslaved him with two dozen words. This man will*

now gladly die for her. What is this strange power she wields over men?
Whatever it is, it is not right and natural.

They walked on a few steps, and Katerina said, "That young fellow back there, the wretched obat-slave—do you know why I made him do what he did? Do you know why I gave him the means to smoke himself into the next life? I do not think that you do."

Tung said nothing.

"There are two reasons for that encounter. Firstly, I made him mutilate himself to show you the unstoppable strength of the craving that excessive obat-taking can provoke. Do not fall prey to that vice. A true obat-slave will do anything—anything at all—for his next pipe. But more than that. Imagine what an army of obat-slaves, or even a nation of obat-slaves would be able to accomplish for the woman who controls the supply of their pleasure."

Tung tried to imagine a slave nation composed entirely of wretched folk like the young man with the bloodied loincloth, but his horrified mind rejected the thought.

"Obat is farmed only on certain islands of the Laut Besar. Only there will the obat trees grow properly. I mean to take those islands. Indeed, I mean to gain control of that whole region. A year from today, and with luck maybe sooner, I shall be the Lord of the Islands. I shall control the obat groves, and the production of all the obat in the whole world. And every obat-slave in the Laut Besar, and elsewhere, will also be my slave."

Tung thought about the scope of her ambition and was not in the slightest part surprised. In fact, the thought of her lording it over a bunch of ruthless pirates and drug-addled natives three thousand miles away made him feel rather better—the key point, he felt, the essence of the thing, was that she'd be three thousand miles away.

Then she ruined everything by saying, "I may be away for

some time but I will surely return. Once I have secured control of the obat production and have the Lordship of the Islands in my hands I will return here, to Ashjavat. And I need to be assured that I will be welcomed when I return. Khev is my home and I shall not abandon it forever. And that is why I need you, Tung An Shan, Minister of the Crown, my loyal and hardworking friend.

"I wish you to become the Prince Regent of Ashjavat. In my absence, you will rule here on behalf of the Celestial Republic—I have already discussed this with the Conclave and all the Venerables are in agreement with me that you are the perfect man for the job. You will occupy the Palace of Ashjavat and rule the province with three full Legions permanently stationed here to support your dignity. Your wife and young son will move to Ashjavat. You may take as your due in taxes, one-tenth of all the trade that flows into Ashjavat through the port here at Ostraka—and that trade will be greatly increased, I believe I can promise you—and you can set about becoming a rich man, a very rich man indeed. With me gone across the seas, with more money than you have ever desired or could ever spend in ten lifetimes, and with your loving family all around you, I think you may have all you need, my dear Minister, to allow yourself to be happy."

Tung was speechless. The whole world seemed to be whirling around his head. He was dimly aware of Katerina slapping the chest of another strapping Legionnaire and saying the easy words that made the soldier swell with pride. He tottered after the small woman as she moved to the next rank of soldiers, watching her look fascinated and nod wisely at some nonsense that Colonel Wang was spouting about the particular quality of this company.

Then she was speaking again in his ear. "And that was the second reason why I had the wretch mutilate himself," she said quietly. "I made a bargain with him. And even though I knew the money would kill him, I wanted *you* to know that I always keep my bargains—always. I made a bargain with my husband the late

Prince Khazeki to be his faithful wife and to submit to his will until the day that he died. And I kept my bargain. And this shall be the bargain between us, if you accept it. Are you listening to me? You become Prince Regent of Ashjavat and rule the principality in my stead, make yourself rich, enjoy your growing family, and when I return—and this part you must swear to keep to yourself—when I return, you hand over the reins of power immediately to me, or to my heirs and successors, and without the slightest quibble or complaint. And on the day I regain the Throne of Ashjavat, you will be free to return to the Celestial Republic with your wealth and your family, to enjoy a well-earned retirement in the land of your birth. Now tell me, my friend, do you accept our bargain?"

CHAPTER 16

It was long past dawn—indeed, it was almost midmorning—when Semar shook Jun's shoulder and roused him from his straw pallet in the tiny, fusty-smelling room on the first floor of The Drunken Sow. Jun sat up and rubbed his eyes. His face felt swollen and his brain soft and cloudy from the obat fumes, but he had slept very well after stumbling home from the Temple alone and falling into his bed. On the far side of the room he saw Ketut rummaging in her pack and pulling out a small gray linen towel and the earthenware pot of soap she used for her ablutions. He stared at her, remembering in full the transformation he had witnessed the night before. But she refused to look directly at him and after a moment or two she slipped out the door.

Semar handed Jun a cup of hot Han tea and he sipped gratefully. The old man seemed to be full of life, gathering up his belongings and shoving them into his pack, rolling up the straw pallets and stacking them in the corner. And even going so far as to seize a threadbare broom from the corner and sweep the dust of the little room from one side to the other. Jun had been moved from his position by Semar and his energetic housework twice, when he said, "You know all about her, don't you? In fact, I'd say, you always knew."

"Knew what, my prince?" said Semar, sweeping industriously.

"You knew she was a Vessel. You knew she was one of those Vharkashta freaks."

"I did know, my prince, you are quite right about that. Well done! I did indeed know that she is one of those rare people who is so blessed that the Gods choose to inhabit them when they come to visit this mortal realm. Yes, I knew. So what? I would think you would welcome the blessings of the Gods on this difficult quest. Moreover, I took pity on her: she's had a hard life, you know. I have decided to help her along her path, teach her a few of the things I've picked up along the way, make her my pupil, for want of a better word. I hope it does not displease you, my prince, that I should seek to help those less fortunate than us?"

"She's dangerous. We have to get rid of her. She might kill us in our beds."

"I don't think that is likely—she can sometimes become caught up in a little religious frenzy. So what? We each worship in our own way, as we see fit. She seems fine today."

"You don't know what happened, Semar. I followed her to the Vharkashta Temple last night and watched as she became possessed by Dargan—Dargan! Queen of the Witches, the embodiment of all that is evil in the female of the race, she was standing right there before me in the Temple. She tried to kill me! And some other poor fellow, she nearly had him impale himself with his own kris. She is extremely dangerous, I tell you."

"Don't tell me you're scared of her, too—a little Dewa fisher girl?" said Semar.

The question flattened Jun. He felt like he'd been gut-punched, all the air driven out of him. For his ear caught on the old man's word "too" and suddenly he was back in the Watergarden that terrible night when he had showed himself a coward and run in terror from the sorcerer Mangku.

He muttered, "Not scared. I'm not frightened of her—as herself. But you weren't there. She was inhabited by the Queen of the Witches. She *became* Dargan."

Semar took pity on him. "I have come across a few Vessels in my time and they are almost all completely harmless—they become possessed in the Vharkashta Temples on Hallowed Day, dance the night away, enjoy a spiritual experience that is denied to most, and then carry on with their lives as if nothing at all has happened. I tell you what, my prince, I shall watch her with particular care and attention. But if she tells us she wants to slip off to a temple from time to time, well, we allow her to, and we stay out of her way when the Goddess is in her. How does that sound?"

Jun made a disgusted noise in his throat. He realized that in this little band of three, despite his rank and lineage, he was the one with the least sway over the others. All that would soon change, or so he hoped, when they went to see his cousin. All would be well then, and Ketut could be dismissed; given a small reward, a little money, for transporting him here and quietly banished from his company, if not from the whole of Sukatan.

"I give you my solemn word that I will do everything in my power to ensure that no unnecessary harm comes to you, my prince," said Semar. "Not from our young friend the Vessel, nor from any other source. Truly, your life is precious to me."

And, surprisingly, Jun did feel a little happier when he heard that.

However, when Ketut returned to the small room, damp and clean, the air between the two young Tamani travelers was still as thick as curd—with neither wishing to look fully at the other. It was as if they had engaged in some disastrous sexual congress the night before and were now trying to pretend it had not happened. Semar broke the tense silence and suggested that they go up to the palace and try to get an audience with the Raja. He also said he had some news to impart.

"The sorcerer Mangku has been to see the Raja already, I am afraid," Semar said. "I had reports of their meeting last night. The evil one has successfully imposed himself on Raja Widojo and persuaded him to refit his ship, replenish her water and stores. And he has demanded a public viewing of the Eye of the Dragon

at noon today in the Grand Courtyard. I think we should join the
throng who will attend and take another discreet look at this fellow. We should be safe as long as we don't draw any undue attention to ourselves."

"What is the Eye of the Dragon?" asked Ketut.

"Why don't you tell her, Jun, while we walk up to the palace,"
said Semar. "I'm sure you know the story as well as I do. And
when he has told you all about it, Ketut, I will tell you both about
the Seven Keys of the Earth, which are also called by some vulgar
historians the Seven Talismans of Power, of which the Dragon's
Eye is almost certainly one—and your ancestral kris, Jun, the
Khodam, is another."

As they walked up the hill toward the palace, the rich boy, in
his precise diction and irritatingly lordly accent, began to
expound on the object that he and Semar called the Eye of the
Dragon. It was, Ketut realized early in his tedious prattle, just a
big rock. That was it. While the three of them trudged onward,
up through the winding streets toward the palace, and the princeling banged on about the Eye, its magical properties and the bizarre legends surrounding it, Ketut was able to focus her mind
elsewhere. The day was irksome. Her skin itched. She felt sickly and
weak, and a little bit ashamed of herself, as she always did after
she had been used as a Vessel by the Goddess. But there was also
that afterglow, the feeling of immense searing power that had
been in her and was now no more than a raw memory.

She remembered vividly the first time it had happened to her,
the first time the Queen had possessed her body. She had found
herself at the little seafront temple in the village outside the
Watergarden in Taman when the Rice Ceremony was taking
place. As a Dewa, she was not encouraged to participate in the
Vharkashta rituals; there was a feeling that her uncleanliness

might pollute the sacred space of the temple. But she was not actually forbidden to enter: the Harvester was the God of all peoples in the Laut Besar, or so the priests claimed, and all might bask in the warmth of his bounty and love. She was hungry, which was not unusual, and was hanging around the temple so that she might have a chance of grabbing a handful of the cooked saffron rice that was offered up to the God on that day.

She crouched just outside the courtyard and looked in through the split gate, watching the people making their obeisances to the altar, the wizened priests conducting the ceremony, the pretty servant-maids bringing forward the big platters of rice in golden pyramids. She caught the burned-lemon scent of the drifting clouds of obat, and heard the small gong orchestra beating out their lambent melodies . . . and she felt it. A spot of intense heat in her lower abdomen, deep in her loins. It was as if a burning coal had sprung to life inside her and soon the heat was spreading to her belly and up into her chest. The gongs were suddenly loud in her ears, louder than thunder. Her limbs felt as if they were filled with a fiery power, seeming longer, stronger. Her whole body seemed to uncurl like a swift-growing fern, her spine straightening, her chin held high. She was on her feet and dancing, her body moving to the slow beat of the gongs. She breathed deeply of the obat fumes and it seemed to her that her exhaled breath was a thicker plume of black smoke. She found herself in the center of the temple, dancing, strutting, twitching in time to the beat. Other dancers all around her—all distinctions of rank dissolved in the frenzy of the God. She heard the voice of Dargan, Queen of the Gods, consort of mighty Vharkash himself, speak inside her head as clear and cold as a mountain stream. "You belong to me now, girl. You are mine from this day forth. You are my Vessel, my Chosen One. All shall fear your righteous wrath. Which is my righteous wrath incarnate."

And then it was gone. And once more she was just a skinny

Dewa fisher girl in a temple courtyard full of her betters, covered
in sweat, feeling dizzy and weak.

Yet the joyful memory of the sheer strength and power of that
brief moment would haunt her for months. The next time it occurred, her soul rushed to embrace the possession. She began to
pray to Dargan, leaving offerings to her at the feet of her statue
inside the temple courtyard, just a few flower petals, a grain or
two of rice, a smoldering stick of incense, if she could afford one.
She attended the temple ceremonies every chance she got, hoping
that the Goddess would favor her again.

And it was there that she had met Semar.

She looked over now to the little old man with the carefree
smile on his wrinkled old face striding beside her listening intently as Jun related one of the more preposterous myths about
the Dragon's Eye. She wondered what her life would have become
if she had not met him. She wondered if she would even be alive.

She was not the only Vessel on Taman. There were scores of
others scattered around the island, men and women of all classes
and occupations, selected by the Gods themselves for this service.
She was not even the only Vessel in the Watergarden village.
There was a boy she knew slightly, a slender and rather girlish
fellow called Madi who was a Vessel for Larung, the Lion God.
When the gongs sounded and the obat smoke rolled across the
temple courtyard, Madi became deeply possessed, and on this occasion the Goddess was absent from her body so she witnessed the
whole event.

The transformation of Madi when the Lion God entered him
was extraordinary. Through her smoke-bleared eyes he became a
man-lion, his hair fluffing out into a tawny mane, his eyes filling
with fire, his limbs becoming lumped with thick muscle, his skin
shimmering like gold, his fingers turning into the cruel claws of
a big cat. He prowled and pounced in the center of the courtyard,
all around admiring him, venerating him as a sacred Vessel of

mighty Larung. Then the mystical splendor of the spectacle turned to nightmare. Larung's movements became wilder, more aggressive. He leaped onto the back of a middle-aged man, one of the priests, and began to savage him, ripping into his flesh with his claws, tearing chunks from his body with his teeth. The music was halted, the crowds cleared and a dozen priests armed with spears and krises rushed forward and hacked the man-lion apart without the slightest hesitation or mercy. It was no sacrilege to attack a Vessel if the lives of the other worshippers were at stake. The Lion God departed; the boy Madi was left dead in several bloody pieces on the temple floor. The priest who had been so brutally savaged by Larung through his Vessel, amazingly, survived as a scarred and crippled thing. His healed wounds were touched by worshippers ever afterward for luck. But it was Madi that she felt sorry for. He died horribly because the God decided to enter him and, for whatever reason, also decided to attack the priest through his Vessel.

Semar had approached her not long after that. He revealed that he was a priest of Vharkash, and that he knew that she was a Vessel of Dargan. He promised that he would teach her—not how to control the Goddess, that would be a gross sacrilege—but how to guide her actions subtly when she took possession so that there could be no danger to any of the other worshippers. And, although this remained unsaid, that there would be no danger to her from the kris- and spear-wielding priests.

She studied hard with Semar, at least an hour every day, learning to feel the mood and tenor of her own soul, even to change it, and now when she went to the ceremonies she almost always felt the Goddess come into her, and that surge of divine power soon became as nourishing and necessary as food and drink. But great power, great strength, is always dangerous to those who wield it, at least that is what Semar preached. And, while the old man could be intensely irritating sometimes and on some small matters distinctly foolish, she knew what he said about power to be true. The night before, in the Temple of Sukatan, she had seen Jun in the crowd and felt an overwhelming desire to command his respect, to punish him for his haughtiness, his insolence toward her. She did not know what she would have done with him if he had obeyed her summons—but she doubted that it would have ended well for the prince of Taman. That endeavor, however, had been interrupted when the man with the kris had challenged her. She had turned the whole strength of her will upon him, dominating his mind, seizing control of his feeble limbs. And had she not been stopped in time she knew that she would have forced him to impale himself on his own kris.

And that would have been the end of him—and most probably of her.

The Grand Courtyard was even more crowded than the Temple of Vharkash had been the night before. This was the largest of several courtyards in the Palace of Sukatan and the one farthest from the royal apartments. It was used for public displays by the Raja and his ministers—dances, festivals, entertainments, banquets and occasionally for the show trials of important miscreants. It was essentially a rectangular arena, with rising ranks of wooden benches on three sides shaded by white-linen awnings, for which members of the public paid a copper kupang to take their seats. Cushions were an extra kupang. There was also a broad, flat standing area between the benches and the low wooden wall, the barrier between the public and the arena, which was designated for the poor of Sukatan and required no payment to enter.

The fourth side of the Grand Courtyard, the one at the south nearest the palace, was the royal enclosure, with a single row of rattan seats, each one piled with cushions and draped with silks.

A table had been set between each chair on which a bowl of fruit and flasks of tea had been laid out. But the royal enclosure was empty so far. The big mat fans that hung above the chairs were still. The Raja, and his guest of honor, had yet to appear.

Jun, whose store of coins was already much depleted, insisted that they go into the free standing area, and the three travelers pushed their way through the crowds and up to the wooden barrier, Semar using his staff to gently maneuver Sukatan folk out of his path, and Ketut and Jun slipping in behind him. However, since the day was hot, Jun did allow himself to be persuaded by Semar into buying three beakers of cool, creamy, mildly alcoholic palm wine from a passing vendor to quench their thirsts.

A troupe of a dozen dwarves, Frankish types from the far side of the world, it would appear, judging by their big noses, fish-belly skins and shocking yellow, light brown and even orange hair, was entertaining the people of Sukatan—tumbling and leaping into the air, juggling with knives and axes, forming human pyramids in the center of the arena.

"It may be some time before the Dragon's Eye is brought out," said Semar. "And if you can tear your attention—Jun, I'm talking to you—off these little buffoons for a moment, it is important for you to know about the Seven Keys."

Jun forced himself to listen to the old man. Ketut, he noticed, was also deigning to give Semar her full focus.

"As I'm sure you know, your people, the Wukarta, once ruled all Yawa and many of the other islands of the Laut Besar, too. They ruled wisely, for the most part, and there was a period of peace and prosperity for hundreds of years."

Out of the corner of his eye, Jun saw one of the tumblers leap high in the air and land, *on his head,* on the head of another of the dwarves. Extraordinary! How had they ever learned to do that? How could you even practice it? He forced himself to concentrate on Semar's words.

"But one terrible year, the idyllic rule of the Wukarta was disrupted by a virulent plague. All the islands of the Laut Besar were afflicted; indeed it was said that the whole world was stricken with this malady. But this disease was unusual in that it seemed to attack the best born, the noblest men and women in the population. Some of the ordinary working folk died, it is true. But the vast majority of the people who suffered were the better classes, the nobles, the warrior castes, the merchants, the priests and of course the Wukarta princes and their families. And suffer they did, most terribly: once gripped, the victims vomited blood and sweated rivers, and black tumors formed in their groins and armpits. By nightfall, screaming, writhing in pain, they all died."

Jun shuddered as he imagined a calamity of this scale. It even made what had happened to the Watergarden and to his father seem a minor disaster. Ketut, he noticed, seemed unmoved by the tale of carnage among the better classes.

Semar blithely continued his tale. "The ruler of Yawa, the Son of Heaven, summoned his ministers and his wise men, his doctors and his sorcerers and asked them what was the cause of this terrifying disease. And not one could answer him truly: some said it was a murrain created by the evil congress of lust between men and monkeys; others said it was a curse from the Gods for the impiety of mankind. But not one of them could offer any cure, nor could they ease the suffering of the afflicted, save by giving them an early, swift and merciful death. The Son of Heaven was in despair—his world was dying, and nothing could be done. Then a lowly priest of Vharkash, a dusty little man, humble but wise, who had traveled far, came to the Palace of Wukarta—he asked respectfully for an audience with the Son of Heaven and, in desperation, was granted it."

"That wasn't you, by any chance, was it?" said Ketut.

"What?" said Semar.

"The dusty little man, humble but wise . . ."

"Ketut, I am indeed both humble and wise, and well stricken with years, too, but this story took place more than a thousand years ago."

"Oh!"

"So did the wise priest have a cure for the plague?" said Jun. "I assume he did or the world would surely have ended."

Semar looked slightly put out to have his story usurped. "He did," he said. "The priest walked into the royal audience room, a plain wooden staff in his hand, a simple sarong around his waist, and he began to speak. 'My brother priests and I of the Mother Temple of Vharkash have been meditating on this foul sickness, and striving to discover its true cause. At last, after forty nights and days of fasting and prayer, the Lord Vharkash himself came to us, mounted on his great buffalo Bantung, brandishing his Scythe of Power and, all praise be to him, the Seed Sower, the Rice Reaper, the Harvester, he himself revealed the cause of this disaster to us in a series of visions.'"

Semar paused for effect. And Jun noticed that the dwarves in the arena had formed a human ladder, six of them standing on each other's shoulders.

"'The origin of the pestilence is an unnatural portal that has been opened by magic which leads from this world into the realm of death,'" said Semar, in the portentous voice of the long-dead Yawa priest. "'The seal of the Earth has been broken. The fabric of the world has been torn asunder. A mighty sorcerer, for it could only be a being of equal power and malignancy, has found a way to open a gate to the Seven Hells and what is spilling out into this good world of men is a host of demons and monsters, a bestiary of blackest evil. And, along with these unnatural, twisted creatures, has come the flood of this invisible sickness, this plague, this very essence of death.'

"The Son of Heaven asked if there were anything that mortal men could do. 'The portal must be shut once more, and locked tight,' the old priest told him. Then he told the Wukarta king how to find the Seven Keys, the Keys of Power, that would seal this unnatural gate forever and protect the world from the seeping corruption of the Seven Hells. 'One Key,' the old priest said, 'you already have in your possession—it is the Khodam, the kris forged from the bone and blood of the star princess. The rest of the Keys you must gather as quickly as you can and, in a ceremony of solemnity and power, they must all be thrust into the Navel of the Earth to close and lock the portal to the Seven Hells once and for all.'

"So the Son of Heaven selected six of his greatest warriors, three strong men and three brave women, and they scoured the Earth for the remaining Keys—and after many adventures, many trials, the talismans were brought home to Yawa, all six of them—each one a strange and wondrous object—and all were transported to the Navel of the Earth and with magic, a mighty spell-making and the help of the ever-living Gods, the barrier between the world of men and the Seven Hells was remade and the Earth was sealed off from the darkness of the other world. The Wukarta were safe once more."

"I do love a happy ending," said Ketut.

Semar ignored her sarcasm. "The plague abated, the demons and monsters were killed by heroes in epic combats or hunted into extinction by men of valor; other fell creatures, those who survived, took refuge in the dark places of the remotest parts of the world, hiding from the eyes of men. There they remain until this day."

Jun nodded approvingly at the ending of the tale. Ketut yawned.

The Frankish dwarves had retired from the arena to warm applause, and they were replaced by a family of Yawa players, dressed in gaudy robes and fantastical masks. As Jun looked on they rolled into the center of the area a little cart that unfolded, sides, back and top to become a madly painted stage and the players leaped up on it and began to tell the story of the discovery of the Eye. It seemed a team of intrepid delvers, all devout Vharkash worshippers, according to this unlikely rehashing of the legend, set out to discover the Key for the glory of the Rajas of Sukatan by exploring deep beneath the Gray Mountain. The Yawanese players made no mention of the sordid search for gold nor of the thousands of wretched slaves who toiled and died there to enrich their masters.

Neither this fanciful story nor the tale of the great plague was unfamiliar to Jun. He was aware of it, in the way that he was aware of dozens of other myths and stories of the Laut Besar that were performed by the shadow-puppeteers or recited by the traveling story-singers at court. He had even been forced to learn by heart some of the epic poems that dealt with this subject matter.

However, now, what he had always believed was mere fable had taken on a whole other dimension, a far more real and frightening aspect. The Khodam, that decrepit, rust-spotted old kris that had always sat at his father's right hand in council was a real object of steel and wood—and real magic: he had seen it glow with power when his father wielded it. It had been stolen from him by someone who was prepared to go to extraordinary lengths to take possession of it, including murdering his father and burning his summer palace to the ground. Myths about the Khodam, bedtime tales for children, had been transmogrified into real life: his life.

And what of the man who had stolen the Khodam and slain the Son of Heaven—and who now, Semar said, wished to view the Eye of the Dragon in his cousin's kingdom: what did he want? It seemed perfectly obvious to Jun, although Semar had not spelled it out. This sorcerer, this Mangku person, clearly wished to collect all or some of the Seven Keys of the Earth for a terrible magical purpose. Jun did not think that the Seven Hells actually existed; they were clearly a metaphor for something or other, a warning to lead a good and moral life. Nor did he truly believe that any so-called dread portal could be opened into another dimension with these Seven Keys. But at least one of the keys, the Khodam, *was* an object of real power, and whatever Mangku wanted these things for it was not for the benefit of mankind. Quite the opposite.

The benefit or otherwise of mankind was, however, not Jun's primary concern. His task was to regain the Khodam for his family and return to Taman in triumph and take up his inheritance. He assumed the Khodam was on that ship in the harbor and well guarded—but how could he retrieve it? First he must defeat, or kill, or somehow neutralize the terrifying Mangku. But how could he go about that? What did he know about the sorcerer?

Very little. He commanded a powerful ship full of hundreds of murderous pirates, none of whom seemed particularly magical. He was able to make raids on peaceful islands such as Taman, murder, rape and pillage, apparently with no fear of reprisal. And then sail calmly into a civilized harbor a few hundred miles away and demand an audience with the local Raja. He had protection— this Mangku—he had a free hand to do whatever he wished in the Laut Besar. And there was only one person who could give a ship full of bloodthirsty pirates that license: the Lord of the Islands, Ongkara, King of Singarasam.

Mangku was clearly in the service of Ongkara. But why would the Lord of the Islands authorize Mangku to attack weak little Taman? For the Khodam? Yes. Certainly. Jun could think of no other reason. But why did Ongkara want to possess the symbol of the Wukarta?

Jun's pondering was interrupted by a blast of trumpets and there, across the arena, was his cousin, with a handful of ministers, courtiers and priests, filing into the seats of the royal enclosure. Cousin Widojo looked different from the last time Jun had seen him: he was a good deal taller and considerably fatter, but there was something else, too. His plump round face with its feathery black mustache looked unwell. There was a greenish tinge to his skin and even from thirty paces away, Jun could see that he was sweaty and uneasy in his self. A touch of swamp fever, he thought, or maybe just a monstrous obat hangover.

The Yawa players were packing up their little cart and with much whooping, waving and bowing they sallied out of the arena. As the crowd yelled, "Widojo! Widojo! Widojo!" the Raja stood, and lifted his pudgy bare arms. The kupang-dispensers, big woven baskets of coins at their waists, began to make their tour of the area, scattering handfuls of money to the cheering crowds like farmers sowing grain in a millet field. Jun was disgusted—it was unutterably vulgar, this Yawa custom. A mere buying of the populace's affection and quite unworthy behavior from a member of the ancient Wukarta clan. He stood dead straight, stone-faced and proud as the kupang-dispenser came past, ignoring the shower of copper coins. Out of the corner of his eye, he saw Ketut, grubbing on the dusty ground like a beggar to gather up the largesse. *Dewa,* he thought. *Breeding will always show in the end.*

Jun looked over at the royal enclosure and saw with a sense of freezing shock that the man seated to the Raja's right, in the position of greatest honor, was none other than his enemy: Mangku. The sorcerer was not looking in his direction but Jun still felt the urge to cringe below the barrier, and only a great effort of will kept him upright. He looked over at Semar but could not catch his eye. The old man had pulled a fold of his ragged gray sarong over his head, as if to ward it from the sun. He looked even more than usually like a vagrant.

The Raja was addressing the crowd now, his voice ringing out over the arena with the help of a brass speaking trumpet. "People of Sukatan, greetings! We gather here today to view the greatest treasure of our fair city, the flower of our community, the talisman that protects mankind from all the evils of this world and the next—the Eye of the Dragon."

The masses cheered their approval. There was another blast of trumpets and a company of Palace Guards marched into the center of the arena in a compact body and then dispersed to the four corners where they stood in groups of twenty men scowling at the crowd. They were big bronzed men, naked from the waist up, clad in flame-red sarongs and bearing steel-tipped spears, each with a ridged iron club tucked in the back of his belt.

More trumpets and a gang of four huge slaves marched in, bearing a large, heavy-looking sandalwood box suspended between two poles. In the center of the open box, nesting on a bed of golden velvet was a large mass of gold-and-greenish stone. The slaves carried the box slowly around the perimeter of the arena and its passage was marked by the sounds of indrawn breath and more than a few cries of joy and wonder. As the box was brought past the travelers, Jun craned his neck for a better look: the treasure did look remarkably like the mythical creature's eye, with a large, round, dark brown pupil in the center of a creamy oval of stone, with green-yellow striations around the edges. The socket that held the Dragon's Eye was a cup of knobbled yellow metal. Jun had only a brief glimpse of the Eye before it was whisked past him by the four big slaves but he felt a warm gust of awe, and a deep and rather unsettling longing to possess it.

The Raja was speaking again, bellowing through the speaking trumpet. "As you all know, my people, the Eye has been in the possession of my family for many hundreds of years." There were more cheers. A cry of "Widojo! Widojo" went up but soon petered out. The Raja boomed, "It is one of the greatest treasures of the Laut Besar. And the Wukarta of Sukatan have been proud to be its custodians. But now, my friends, now the time has come for the Eye to be passed to another, greater power, where it can be used for the betterment of all mankind, for the benefit of the whole world."

The crowd fell almost silent at his words. A ripple of bewildered murmurs spread around the arena. One man was muttering to his neighbor to ascertain what he had just heard. Jun frowned and looked over at his cousin in the royal enclosure. Widojo was sweating even more than previously; he was twitching, making little jerking motions with his arms as if wrestling with some invisible opponent. Beside him Mangku had his head bowed, his eyes closed: he looked as if he were fast asleep.

The Raja wrestled the speaking trumpet to his own lips. "I have been persuaded by my good friend Mangku the Wise, who now sits beside me, that I should render up the Eye to his master and mine: Ongkara, Lord of the Islands. For who is more fitting to possess the Dragon's Eye than the Dragon of the High Seas himself? His beloved envoy Mangku here assures me that the King of Singarasam will use the Eye in a way that will increase the happiness of all the diverse peoples of the Laut Besar, not just a few thousand privileged men and women in Sukatan. It's time to be magnanimous, my friends. It is time to think of all the peoples of Earth and not just ourselves . . ."

Jun was astounded. He could never have imagined anything like this occurring in a thousand years: a Raja giving away his greatest treasure?

He looked over Ketut's head at Semar but the old man was bowed under his sarong. Jun distinctly heard him mutter, "No, the Eye of the Dragon must stay here."

A heartbeat later, out of the now-silent crowd, a man on the far side of the arena shouted those exact words, "No, the Eye of the Dragon must stay here."

There were several more scattered shouts of complaint from the three public sides of the arena but most people were too stunned and confused to react.

Semar said very quietly, "The Eye is ours. The Eye is ours." And a woman with a glittering golden nose ring ten paces to his left leaned over the barrier and shouted the very same words,

"The Eye is ours!" and kept repeating the phrase until it was taken up by all the people around her.

Widojo was still jerking and twitching in the royal enclosure. "Silence!" he shouted through the trumpet. Some of the bellowing of the crowd abated—although not all. "The Eye of the Dragon belongs to the world! It is not ours to keep." Widojo was now waving his hands in the air. Jun saw that the sorcerer had lifted his head. He was looking directly in his direction. Jun lifted a hand to hide his face from the stare.

Semar muttered, "The Eye must stay in Sukatan!" And a man in the middle section of the arena shouted the same words. And suddenly everybody was shouting that, too, thousands of voices, men, women, young, old, all around the arena chanting the words to a regular beat, "The Eye must stay in Sukatan. The Eye must stay in Sukatan. The Eye must stay . . ."

It was as if the whole population of Sukatan had come together in one voice to shout their disapproval of the Raja's actions: the words rolled across the arena like waves, chopped and broken but ever moving across the space. "The Eye"—"Must stay"—"In Su-ka-tan." A hypnotic beat: Ba-bom. Ba-bom. Ba-bom-bom-bom.

In the storm of noise, Widojo was consulting with a splendidly dressed older man with lily-white hair and clad in a military-style blue jacket dripping with gold lace. He was pointing directly at Jun and obviously giving urgent instructions.

Semar tugged on Jun's sleeve, and said, "Time to go!" and the three of them began to push their way through the sea of chanting, angrily gesturing Sukatanese. The crowd was boiling now, almost set for a full-scale riot. "The Eye—Must stay—In Su-ka-tan"—everyone from sedate mothers to snot-nosed children, from slim young men to bowed grandfathers was yelling the same words in the same pounding rhythm. Jun felt the same tinge of mass madness he had felt in the temple the night before. He looked nervously at Ketut, but she was tight-jawed and silent, eyes fixed on Semar's back as she pushed through the throng. The travelers nearly made it to the entrance, so nearly, when Jun felt a hard hand slap onto his shoulder and he was hauled round to face a pair of grim-faced, bare-chested guardsmen. Another seized his arms from behind. Jun saw Ketut struggling with another two huge half-naked men armed with spears. He said, "Unhand me, scum. I am Prince Arjun Wukarta. I am cousin to His Serene Highness Raja Widojo Wukarta, who will doubtless make you pay for your insolence to his beloved kinsman . . ."

Then an iron club sailed out of the blue sky and smashed him into blackness.

CHAPTER 17

———— ✦ ————

Extract from *Ethnographic Travels* by
Professor Tolmund K. Parehki of the University of Dhilika

*The Wukarta Rajas, who were the rising secular power in the east
of Yawa, grew jealous of the vast wealth of the Mother Temple—
and one year boldly refused to give tribute either in goods or in
human lives. And so a great and bloody war began between the
warrior kings, who claimed that the blood of the stars flowed in
their veins, and the priests of Vharkash, who did not fear death
because they knew for certain that if they died in battle, they would
be rewarded with a place at the heavenly court of Vharkash
the Harvester for eternity.*

*The war lasted nearly a hundred years but, in the end, the
massed bowmen of the Wukarta slew the last horde of fanatical
Vharkashta recruits, cutting them down in their thousands and
watering the fields with their blood. And peace came to Yawa. The
Mother Temple was taken under Wukarta control—the blood rites
were banned. Human sacrifice and the practice of magic were made
a crime punishable by a slow, horrible death. The religion of Vharkashta began to change. It evolved into the benign and tolerant faith
we know today, concerned with healing the sick and succoring
the poor, doing good works, bringing the light of Vharkash to the
benighted—although some claim, of course, that many of its atavistic elements remain.*

*The Wukarta Empire waxed full with the downfall of the
Mother Temple and they and the priests eventually became allies in
the ruling of the whole Kingdom of Yawa—and beyond. They created colonies all around the Laut Besar, and gave them princes of*

the blood to rule over them. And wherever the Wukarta went, the
priests of Vharkash went with them. Five hundred years passed.
The Wukarta fell to bickering among themselves—the princes
of the smaller Wukarta kingdoms, Taman, Molok, even the tin-pot
little outposts in the jungles of Kalima and Sumbu, joined forces to
make war against the Kingdom of Yawa. And, as all mighty empires
must do, it fell, tearing itself apart in a civil war that, so the legends
say, lasted a full ten years and stained the whole Laut Besar red
with blood.

The Empire of the Wukarta in Yawa was destroyed. All that
remained were the little kingdoms here and there, where overbred
princes lorded over their docile people, and grew ever more idle and
ignorant of the world with each passing generation.

They manned the pumps all the rest of that day and all
through the long night, too. Even Farhan took his turn
at heaving the iron bar round and round, hour after
hour, in the black depths of the ship, as the water lapped around
his knees and the wheezing pumps surged up and down and
squeezed the bilge up through fat leather pipes to spurt and spew
over the side. At around midnight, it became clear that, after the
frantic efforts of the ship's crew to get a spare sail over the side and
roped into place, less water was coming in through the two
cannon-smashed holes in the hull than was being pumped out.
And in the dawn, with every living man on the edge of exhaustion, a good twenty leagues from where they had left the wreckage of the two Celestial cruisers, the *Mongoose* limped into the
wide mouth of a river.

Using six pairs of very long oars, they maneuvered her slowly,
sluggishly, out of sight from the sea, up a smaller tributary off the
main flow and into the thick Yawa jungle and there they moored

her, lashing her tight between two giant trees, and finally rested their weary bodies.

On more than one occasion during that dark night of fevered labor Farhan had been sure that the *Mongoose* would sink and he had wondered what it would be like to drown. Would he be taken by the sharks before he drowned or after? Another fear had haunted him, too, and that was capture—for the three remaining Celestial cruisers had been spotted in the small hours a league or two away, shooting bright white starburst rockets into the air in an attempt to locate them in the darkness. To have been spotted would have meant certain death or worse. But they had slipped away unseen, thank the Gods. However, it was clear that the Celestial Republic would not forget their bloody actions over the past few days.

At noon, Farhan roused himself and joined Mamaji, Captain Ravi of the Dokras and Captain Lodi in the main cabin for a council of war. Mamaji sat at the head of the table, with Lila in the background wielding a big ceramic teapot and serving each of them with tiny cups of piping hot Han tea flavored with dried jasmine, which in the close jungle heat was surprisingly refreshing.

"You'd better tell us, dear, how bad it is," said Mamaji gravely, looking at Lodi.

Cyrus took a deep breath. "We are holed on both sides," he said. "But by far the worst is the breach on the starboard bow, where it seems two balls struck almost the same spot and staved in a large portion of the hull. We fothered it last night, that is, ma'am, we got an old sail stretched over the gap in the planks, but the *Mongoose* is not fit for a long sea voyage until that is timbered—and the other smaller breach, too—and the best way to do it would be to careen her so that our carpenters can get at the hull. And that means beaching her."

"How long before she would be fit for sea service, Captain?"

"Two weeks, maybe three at most—if we are unmolested and

if I may make use of the Dokra troopers as a workforce." He looked at Captain Ravi, who shrugged, and looked at Mamaji, then said, "I expect I shall need my men to look to the land defenses of the ship."

"You can spare, say, twenty troopers, Captain Ravi dear, can you not?"

Lodi said, "Three weeks, then, it could be done in that time. With luck."

"We are going to need a fortification on land," said Farhan. "And we'll need some of the ship's guns, and gunners to man them. This is lawless country. The city of Sukatan to the east of here is the nearest large settlement where we might find a representative of the Federation. But that's about thirty or forty leagues away. Two or three weeks' hard march, even perhaps longer, as we would have to cut our way there through thick jungle—even if we could actually find our way to Sukatan and not become hopelessly lost. I don't think land travel is a viable option. The forests here are almost virgin and contain many wild animals, not to mention escaped slaves, outlaws, bandits. There are remote tribes hereabouts who've never heard of the Federation, or the Lord of the Islands: some are barely aware of the existence of the Laut Besar."

"So we must remain and repair our ship," said Mamaji. "We will need a week to build a fort of some kind. Captain Ravi dear, that is your department, I believe, and Captain Lodi will provide you with cannon. And then we need another three weeks to careen the ship and mend her timbers. We are here for a month, it seems. How are we off for food and water?"

"Not good," said Lodi. "Most of the rice became waterlogged and is spoiled, and the fresh tack is now all but gone but, on the other hand, we did plan for a long voyage. With half rations, and a little fishing, we should be able to survive for one month—maybe."

"There should be game in the forest," said Farhan. "If I could have a couple of men to carry for me, I might be able to bring in some fresh meat."

"Very good," said Mamaji. "Then let us proceed. Captain Lodi—you will repair the *Mongoose* as best you can, as quickly as you can. We need only to be able to get safely back to Istana Kush in her—the more extensive repairs can be done there."

"We are going home?" said Farhan.

"Yes, due to this unfortunate delay here we will miss the gold shipment leaving from Sukatan by two weeks," said Mamaji, "and the next is not for another three months."

"But the plan was to take the gold shipment—our rewards, our bonus payments are based on us taking the gold shipment from the Han convoy." Farhan knew he was whining. But this was truly appalling news.

"The plan, you will surely recall, dear Farhan," said Mamaji kindly, "was to foment a conflict between the Celestial Republic and the Lord of the Islands. We are *agents provocateurs*, not gold thieves. Surely you recall your orders from the Amrit Shakti. If it has somehow slipped your memory, let me refresh it for you. The plan—the reason why you, dear, so cleverly acquired Ongkara's flag—was to pose as a ship filled with the Lord of the Island's rascally pirates and to create so much outrage in the Conclave of Venerables that it would lead inevitably to war between our two chief rivals in the Laut Besar.

"Whichever side emerges as victor, after the regrettable slaughter when the pirate fleet of Ongkara meets the might of the Celestial Navy in battle, does not matter in the slightest because we—the Federation—will be the stronger either way. We'll be in a position, when the smoke clears, to take the Lordship of the Islands into our own safe hands. *And we have already achieved our primary aim.*"

Mamaji beamed at the table. "We have surely created sufficient outrage among the Venerables by the attack on Kulu—not to mention the sinking of two of their new cruisers—and that was partly, I must now admit, why I encouraged you to do it. There is absolutely no need to attack the Han gold convoy now, dears—our mission is accomplished. All we need to do is bide our time while we mend this vessel then sail home to Istana in triumph. You've all done very well! All of you. General Vakul, I believe, will be extremely pleased."

Farhan felt a void open up beneath his ribs. His debts . . . oh Gods! He was a dead man! Ongkara must know now that he had been tricked into handing over the Lion Standard—and he would make a bad enemy if he survived the coming war—but that was not the worst of it. He'd always known that he would anger the pirate lord. The real problem was his massive, unpayable, ever-growing debt to Xi Gung—which could not now be settled with his portion of gold from the convoy. Unless the Federation was successful in its attempt to seize the Lordship of the Islands, and he managed to persuade the new ruler to banish Xi Gung from Singarasam, unless that could be achieved, Farhan would not dare to show his face there ever again. Owing what he did, if Xi Gung ever laid hands on him, if he was caught . . . it did not bear thinking about. He would not be safe anywhere in the Laut Besar for the rest of his life. Perhaps not even in the Federation. His whole strategy, everything he had privately planned, had been predicated on achieving a degree of protective wealth. He tried once more.

"Surely, we could wait out the three months and attack the next gold convoy. By sea, Sukatan is not so far away, just a few days' sailing. Think how impressed General Vakul would be if we were to present him—and the Amrit Shakti treasury—with a shipload of pure Han bullion! And we would be greatly impoverishing our enemies, too!"

"We are going home, Farhan. Captain Lodi and I agree, and that is the end of it."

As Farhan still looked mutinous, Mamaji said, "If you are concerned about your mission bonus, I believe I can reassure you on
that point. I am authorized to grant a supplementary payment of
one hundred ringgu in silver for your part in this mission, Farhan,
on top of your usual monthly stipend, and the same amount for
each of you, too." Mamaji beamed at Lodi and Ravi. "Each of the
Buginese sailors and each Dokra trooper will receive ten ringgu,
too—all payments to be made immediately after we have safely
dropped anchor inside the harbor at Istana Kush."

Farhan wanted to strangle the fat, grinning bitch: a hundred
ringgu would not pay one-tenth of the debts he owed to Xi Gung,
even before the interest had been calculated. He bit his tongue.
Courage, he told himself. Get a grip: he wasn't in the old monster's clutches yet.

Captain Ravi, although his tiny frame, dashing air and extravagant vanity might suggest otherwise, was a more than
competent fort-builder. He had his men hard at work tracing the
outline of a reasonably capacious square fort in a jungle clearing
a hundred yards from the ship within an hour of the meeting
breaking up. And, by nightfall, eight of the Mongoose's cannon
had been winched out of the hull and set up, one at each corner
of the fort and one in the center of each putative wall. Dokra ax-
men were busy chopping down the bamboo forest on all sides,
clearing fields of fire for the cannon and providing building mate-
rials. Captain Ravi had eighty-three surviving musketeers, and
none of them were idle. By the time supper was served out—a
watery rice soup studded with scraps of iron-hard salt pork—the
shape of the fortress was clear and even a short section of the
south wall, the wall farthest from the river, had been erected.

Captain Ravi's design was simplicity itself: four walls of twelve-
foot-high double-thick bamboo palisade, with a walkway on the

inside that allowed a man to fire a musket over the wall without exposing his own body. There was a single entrance in the northeast corner that was only a little wider than a man is broad. The cannon were to be mounted on specially reinforced bamboo platforms, with the cannonball, canister, wadding and powder stored underneath and the guns served by means of a clever pulley system that raised a square pallet through a small trapdoor.

Inside the fort, tents made from extra sailcloth had been set up—two smaller ones, one for Farhan, Captain Lodi and Captain Ravi, and one for Mamaji and Lila; and two very large ones, one for the Buginese sailormen and another for the off-duty Dokra troopers. Areas had been demarcated for cooking, stores, officers' baggage, washing and two long latrine trenches had been dug against the northern wall. Captain Ravi had even begun digging a deep well in the center of the camp—for, as the energetic little officer said, you could never be too careful, and while they were only to remain in the fort a month, having a good supply of fresh water could sometimes mean the difference between life and death.

The next morning Farhan slept past the rising of the sun and was awoken some hours afterward by the noise of saws and hammers busily at work. He came stumbling out of his tent, yawning and scratching, and found himself to be the only unoccupied man in an ants' nest of activity: the walls of the fort were already half-completed, and looking north to the river, Farhan could see that the *Mongoose* was in the process of being dragged up the muddy bank by gangs of sweat-gleaming Buginese sailors hauling on a complex network of ropes to the shouted commands of Lieutenant Muda.

Farhan was aware of an embarrassing sense of his own uselessness—he had slept in while others toiled. And no one had thought to wake him to ask him to join in their labors. No one considered his efforts to be worth rousing him. With a feeling of humility, he splashed his face with water, drank down a glass of cold tea and wolfed a single sweet rice ball. Then, collecting his double-barrelled rifle, ball and powder, a freshly sharpened parang, his tea flask, and a pair of Dokra troopers, borrowed with Captain Ravi's grudging permission, he set off out into the jungle.

Least he could do was to put some fresh meat in the pot for the workmen.

Farhan's spirits lifted as he stepped away from the bustle and noise, the clanging and the hammering of the clearing and entered the cool, quiet shadows of the jungle. Within a hundred paces he could no longer hear the shouts and cries of his shipmates and the green closed in around him like a vast cloak. The jungle was not especially dense here: the trees were mostly tall, spindly affairs a few paces apart, with thick undergrowth that tangled the feet and, once in a while, a massive trunk with a sprawling ridged base—one of the giants of the jungle, one that had climbed high enough to break through the canopy and reach the life-giving sunlight. There were no tracks, as such, but the feet of animals had created faint pathways through the undergrowth, which Farhan carefully widened with the parang, and every ten paces or so he cut a little notch on the trunk of a tree at waist height, so that he should not have any difficulty retracing his steps at day's end.

The jungle was full of life: the crick and saw of insects, the high-pitched cries of bright-plumed birds hidden in the branches and, from time to time, Farhan heard the sound of stealthy movements of large creatures in the foliage at ground level. Each time he heard something like this he stopped, waved the two following Dokra into stillness and leveled his rifle—but nothing showed itself. Once he glimpsed a burly, red-furred ape, clutching a baby, in the branches above his head but the animal swung away hooting madly with laughter and disappeared into the endless green.

It was suffocatingly hot, and Farhan found himself dripping, itching and craving the cool tea in his bottle. Yet he knew that he had to ration himself: he had been gone no more than an hour and it might take the whole day for him to find and kill something worth eating. They passed orchids of extraordinary variety growing in the crevices of the biggest, grayest trees—from brilliant green to riotous scarlet and yellow, sometimes cascading down out of their niches like party decorations. They stopped and watched spellbound as tiny jewel-like butterflies delicately battled each other in the rare shafts of sunlight, their miniature wings flashing like winking lights. They passed by giant ferns, twice as tall as a man, waving like long, green Manchu banners in the lightest breeze. Something huge growled at them from the undergrowth, a bass rumbling that stood their short hairs to attention and had Farhan hefting his rifle in sweaty hands and scanning the green wall with his heart in his mouth, but then they heard the great beast padding off, the foliage whispering like silk as it moved away. A huge ratlike creature hopped up onto a tree root, stared at him inquisitively for a moment, and then whisked off about its business with a rustle and flash of its long pink tail.

After three hours of fruitless searching, Farhan called a halt and he and the two Dokra sat down gratefully on the tree roots of a mighty banyan tree.

"Might as well wait for the game to come to us," said Farhan jovially, and he stretched out his legs and sipped frugally from his tea flask. The two Dokra nodded and smiled knowingly, leaned their muskets against the tree's massive trunk and reached for their own bottles. In truth, Farhan was already pinched by the dread of failure. He was exhausted and longed to do nothing more than return to the camp by the swiftest route and throw himself on his camp bed—perhaps after taking a cooling dip in the river. Only fear of the scorn of his shipmates kept him in this torrid hell.

A drop of sweat fell from his forehead onto the silver barrels of the rifle across his knees, and he wiped it away angrily with a thumb. He would have to remember to oil the long gun the moment he got back to camp or risk its tarnishing, he thought.

Then he felt a Dokra hand gently touch his elbow and he slowly raised his head to see a fawn standing not ten paces from him nibbling at a shrub. It was a delicate creature with long spindly legs, pinky-brown mottled fur dotted with white, and huge brown eyes framed with impossibly long lashes. It was almost too beautiful to shoot, but Farhan knew his duty and slowly, very slowly he raised his rifle to his shoulder.

Just then its mother stepped out from behind a bush, bigger, more wary, rightfully suspicious of the three men seated on the banyan roots. Farhan eased back the right-hand cock on his rifle, and at the click, so loud in the hot silence, the adult deer leaped forward, putting its body between Farhan and the fawn. He pulled the trigger. There was a snap as the flint hit the steel and a spark lit in the pan. Then nothing. Misfire. The deer and the fawn were gone—and Farhan cursed his luck. The powder in the frizzen pan must have become damp—hardly surprising given the conditions that day.

The two Dokra looked reproachfully at Farhan. He opened his mouth to explain himself and saw that their gaze had shifted to beyond him. Now they were both leaping to their feet. Farhan whirled and saw a man—at least a man-shaped thing—standing not ten paces away beside the trunk of a palm tree.

The body was naked but for a brief belt and loincloth and thickly slathered with white clay, overpainted with broad gray and black stripes. The face was painted black and white to resemble a skull, with a black scythe painted on the forehead between the eyes. The fellow's hair, a matted mass of thick gray ropelike strands, was piled on top of his head, and in his right hand he carried what looked like a long pole painted with gray stripes half as tall again as the man holding it.

One of the Dokras, standing to Farhan's right raised his musket to his shoulder. Farhan half expected the man to dart away like the frightened deer and the fawn—but he did not. He gave a low grunting cry that sounded like an insult or a foul oath to Farhan's half-comprehending ears; his hand flashed to his belt from where he plucked a long, needlelike object with a ball of fluff at one end from a small pouch. All in the space of two heartbeats, he tipped the pole in his hands, shoved the missile into the end, lifted it to his lips, pointed it at the Dokra and blew.

Ffft.

Farhan turned in amazement to see the elder Dokra drop his musket—which went off with a flash and a loud bang—and clutch at his throat, where the needlelike object with its jolly little ball of fluff was protruding from his Adam's apple. Farhan turned back to the painted man and saw that he was in the act of loading another dart into his blowpipe. Farhan lifted the rifle, cocked the left-hand hammer and, as the savage brought the long pipe up to his mouth, he pulled the trigger.

The hammer snapped down, the flint hit the steel, the spark ignited the powder in the pan. The rifle roared and the ball tore across the ten paces between the two men, smashed into the man's chest high on the right and ripped his shoulder and his right arm completely free of his body. The painted man was knocked back against the palm tree, down, looking in awe at the bloody mash where his right arm had been. Then his eyes rolled up into his head and his body sagged.

Farhan looked for the first Dokra who had been struck in the throat—and a dash of cold horror, tempered by the burning mixture of fear and rage, began to moil in his belly. The dart had clearly been poisoned with some powerful swift-acting toxin, for the trooper was already blue-faced and frothing at the mouth, his body convulsing. His comrade tried to help him but the victim was convulsing so hard that his body was bending almost double. He thrashed and spasmed and bent like a fish on land, now wildly arcing his back, now curling his body in a tight ball. Incredibly, his head was now bent all the way back almost to the soles of his boots. The white froth was spattered all about him. The cords in his neck stood out like iron ridges.

There was a loud, rending crack and suddenly the Dokra lay still, his spine snapped by his own dreadful contortions. His mate, eyes wild with grief and fury, got to his feet and walked over to the painted man, standing over his body. He stared at him for a few moments, then stamped once on his bloody chest. The man's eyes opened and, looking up at his tormentor, he gave an awful, blood-rinsed grin, and said something that sounded to Farhan's ears like, "Accept my sacrifice, lord," and then he spat a thick clot of bloody phlegm on the Dokra's white breeches. The trooper went wild: he kicked repeatedly at the man's head, the heavy army boots thumping against his skull and the matted gray ropes of hair. Then, when the body tipped over onto its side, he began to stomp with all his weight on the fellow's face.

Farhan made some inarticulate protests and waved an ineffective hand, but he was as shocked and appalled as the remaining Dokra by the awful chain of events.

Ffft. Ffft. Ffft. Ffft.

Face. Right hand. Right side of the waist. Left thigh. Darts appeared all over the stamping Dokra's body. He stopped kicking and looked down at the thin missiles now protruding from his flesh. He looked mutely over at Farhan—absolute terror in his last conscious gaze. But the merchant was looking beyond him through the trees to the dozen or so looming white-painted shapes, fast approaching, long pipes in hand.

Farhan did the only thing he could: he flung aside his empty rifle and ran.

CHAPTER 18

❦

General Jan Artur had not slept continuously for more than a quarter of an hour in the past five days. And he did not imagine that he would get much in the way of sleep tonight. He came into the warm cave through the heavy leather flap that covered the entrance and handed his snow-covered cloak and fur hat silently to his adjutant, Major Jodul, who hung them on the stand. The candlelight hurt his eyes after so long outside in the darkness. He rubbed his face, feeling the moisture on his bristles. Then Artur walked over to the big wooden desk and the mass of papers piled upon it and rested his knuckles on the hard surface and bowed his head. For a moment he closed his eyes and let his despair have full rein—a feeling of crushing impotence and sorrow, and deep anger, too, at the impossible situation he found himself in. Then he straightened up, opened his eyes, and his right hand groped for the earthenware flask on the desk. He gave it an experimental shake and heard a hollow splashing that told him it was nearly empty. That was the last of the marak. But he would not drink it now, he decided. He would finish the last mouthful when it came to *that* time. The time for him to terminate his command. Not before.

"Any news from the south?" he asked.

"Nothing you want to hear, sir," said his adjutant glumly.

"Damn it, man, we have sent four—no, it must be five couriers demanding, even pleading for reinforcements in the past week, and no reply?"

"We were sent a party of twenty watchmen from the Fire Ministry. Old men mostly, and a few boys. I sent them to what remains of the 5th Ashjavati Guards in Sector 4. Thought they might make stretcher-bearers, although their lieutenant insists they've been trained with pikes and cutlasses and he says they're eager to fight for the Motherland."

"Pikes?" said the General. "Against the Cossacks' howitzers and muskets?"

Major Jodul shrugged. "There is a personal message for you from the Prince Regent, too. This new Han fellow, Tung An Shan. I put it on your desk."

"Doubtless he is urging me to take not a single step backward. To die bravely to the last man and the last bullet for the honor of our glorious homeland, etc, etc."

"Very likely—that's exactly what the last message from *her* said."

General Artur stiffened slightly. He did not allow his subordinates to criticize *her*. Even if she was, by now, several hundred miles off the southern coast of Ashjavat and sailing merrily for tropical parts unknown. She had given him his orders in a personal letter: to hold the line in the Ehrul Mountains and defend the northern border from the Khevan hordes. She had told him she was counting on him. And he had done exactly as she had ordered for the past ten days, with all the skill and strength he could muster. Part of him knew that he was being used, sacrificed. That she had fled to the ocean, leaving him to die. He also knew perfectly well that his sacrifice was in vain. His own scouts had reported that two Celestial Legions had crossed the unguarded eastern border of Ashjavat and were even now flooding into the plains between the mountains and the capital city. The Han battalions were now everywhere. He did not care: he had been given his orders by his commander in chief. Hold the line. Repel the Khevan regiments for as long as you can. She had said nothing

about the Celestial Legions behind him. But he would obey nonetheless.

He sat down heavily in the chair before the big desk. Looked
longingly at the marak flask, and said, "Tell me it, then. Situation
report. How bad is it?"

Major Jodul glanced briefly at the piece of paper in his hand
and began, "On the extreme left Colonel Kippz of the 3rd Foot
reports a near mutiny. His men refused to counterattack the enemy trenches when ordered to do so, claiming that they lacked
sufficient men and ammunition. They have a point. They have suffered nearly fifty percent casualties after an assault against them
by the 13th, 16th and 17th Imperial Regiments yesterday. Powder
and shot is almost exhausted. The men insisted that they must
remain in their own lines and defend them as best they can. The
Colonel considered hanging the ringleaders but reconsidered
when the other officers had a quiet word with him and he allowed
them to remain in their trenches on the defensive. In short, they
still hold the line but are likely to crumble at the next assault."

General Artur nodded.

"The center left is weak, too," Major Jodul continued. "The
Guards regiments have been mauled worse than any other bri-
gade and are still under heavy mortar and howitzer fire from the
enemy. But Colonel Harsi has them dug in deep, and he thinks
they will hold if attacked. The center right is in bad shape, however, and there are still some alarming gaps in the line where our
light companies deserted en masse . . ."

Artur let the words wash over him, his mind refusing to listen
to their meaning. His head was filled with the pictures of suffering he had seen in the past hour or two when he had visited the
makeshift hospital just behind the lines on the southern slopes of
the Ehrul. Hundreds upon hundreds of bloodied young men lying
on the cold hard earth in the hospital tent, the temperature little
higher than the frozen air outside. Scarcely any medicine, ban-

dages or food, and men who were missing limbs or eyes, with their flesh lacerated and bones crushed, being comforted with hot tea and little else. There had been a pile of amputated limbs outside the surgery tent as high as his waist. And the bloody-aproned surgeons were too busy or too angry to speak to him. The sounds of pain had been inescapable: a low weird moaning coming from many throats, punctuated by the occasional wild, drawn-out hellish scream, quickly stifled lest it demoralize the others.

Artur was aware that the Major had stopped speaking.

"Is there any good news?" he asked, hating himself for this show of weakness.

"A fresh consignment of boots arrived this morning, which should make some of the shoeless recruits extremely happy."

"Boots? Good, very good. And when do we expect the next Khevan attack?"

"Anytime, sir. The scouts suggest that assaults so far have merely been probing attacks to test our strength. There are indications that they are massing their full strength in the center right, readying for a decisive push through the Alaaric Pass: Jaeger regiments in the van, then the Imperial Foot Guards, and finally the mounted Cossacks. It will probably come just before dawn—that is their preferred time."

Artur had a dirty, much-creased map open in front of him on the desk.

"We can't hold them there. They'll punch straight through. And then there is nothing—nothing to stop them riding on down to Ashjavat City."

"We could withdraw, sir. A tactical retreat. We pull back all our men and make a line on the Dniepali River. With the marshes on our left, we could hold them for . . ."

"For how long? An extra day? No, Major, I appreciate your concern for the men but we stay here. How certain are you that the push will come through the Alaaric?"

"Fairly sure, sir. In addition to the scout's reports, the 1st Guards captured an Imperial trooper in that area and he said they had all been told to prepare for a full frontal assault."

"Can I speak to him?"

"No, sir. He was—um—shot while trying to escape, sir. The Guards were very upset over the mutilation of their wounded in no-man's-land by the Cossacks."

"Very well. This is what we shall do. I want the rest of the line abandoned—tonight, soon as we can—and every able-bodied man we have concentrated in the Alaaric Pass. A narrow defense but in depth. Get them dug in deep in the Pass and on the slopes on either side. If we can stop them here, if we can blunt their full assault, there is a chance that they will think again about invading Ashjavat. Tell the men that if we can stop them at the Alaaric, we may just save the Motherland."

The General knew that he was speaking utter nonsense. If the attack was halted in the Pass, and that was an enormous "if," the enemy would merely curl around the now-undefended flanks. The Major's raised eyebrows showed that he knew it, too. But what else could Artur do? He had his orders. *She* had commanded him to hold.

General Artur's eye fell on a package on the desk. It was addressed to him, his name spelled out in a virulent green ink. He picked it up and slit the package open with a long, wicked-looking Ashjavati fighting knife that he was using as a paperweight.

He read the letter inside. He read it again. And then he began to laugh. A great eruption of mirth; hysterical, mad, unstoppable laughter.

Major Jodul looked up from his desk, where he had been hurriedly scratching out the orders to the sector commanders for the new defensive position.

"What is it, sir?" he said, smiling. It was good to see the boss laughing again. "The usual guff about fighting to the last man?"

Artur still could not speak for laughing. He handed Jodul the letter, and gasped out, "You read it!"

Jodul tilted the letter toward the candle, and read,

My dear General Artur,

I write to assure you that your gallant defense in the Ehrul Mountains in extraordinary conditions and against an almost insurmountable Khevan enemy has not gone unnoticed, and indeed will not go unrewarded. Neither have your pleas for aid fallen on deaf ears in Ashjavat City. I am very pleased to tell you that, now that the various disturbances in our nation have been quelled by our good friends from the Celestial Republic, I am at liberty to dispatch reinforcements to you, and this day I have given orders for four full Legions, a little over four thousand infantry, and three augmented companies of artillery, to come to your position with the greatest dispatch and place themselves under your command. I am also granting you, by virtue of this letter, a battlefield promotion to the rank of Marshal. May I be the first to congratulate you, Marshal Artur. Your courage in the face of adversity and the noble sacrifice of your men for our Motherland has been an example to us all.

> Yours, in deepest admiration,
> Tung An Shan,
> Prince Regent of Ashjavat

"It's dated three days ago, sir," said Jodul, "which means . . ."

"Which means that they could be here anytime now—we should be in touch with their advance units tomorrow!" The new Marshal was grinning like a monkey.

"And the redeployment, sir, to the Alaaric Pass?"

"Yes, yes, as you were, redeploy everything to the Pass. And with all possible speed—but tell the men, pass the word through all ranks, that help is on its way. I can scarcely believe it but, in truth, if we can hold them tomorrow, if we can just hold one more day, then the danger is past."

Some eight hundred miles to the south, Katerina stood in the forecastle of the ship *Yotun* and let the sea breeze blast her unbound blond hair straight out behind her. To the left and the right and a little to the rear, were *Sar* and *Egil*, the *Yotun's* smaller consorts—the newly built ships all named for the legendary sky giants that the Khevan Emperors claimed they were descended from. The feeling of the wind on her face, and the occasional packet of salt water that doused her body and the simple, loose sea-green dress that she wore, and the sense of thrusting motion as the ship surged forward beneath her feet, made her feel thrummingly alive and somehow freer than she had ever been before.

So far, she had achieved all that she had set out to do: she had her ships, she had the Celestial Legion, and by installing Tung An Shan as Prince Regent, she believed she had left herself a way back into Khev for the final act in her grand design.

Only one thing still troubled her, and try as she might she could not dismiss it as an unsubstantiated anxiety, a silly, groundless fear: it had all been just a little too easy. From her repeated study of *The Craft of Combat*, she understood that overconfidence could be as great an error as timidity. So what was she missing? Her dealings with the Conclave of the Venerables had been astoundingly simple and straightforward: she had asked for what she wanted and—apart from a few minor quibbles, mostly thrown up by Tung himself, she suspected, for reasons of face—it had all been granted to her. This group of aged Han men and women, famed for their wisdom, foresight and ruthless cunning, had meekly acceded to a young girl's every whim. Something did not

feel right. What was she not taking into account? Did they mean
her harm? She did not think so. They were allies. Quite apart from
her gift to them of the Principality of Ashjavat, their interests
were aligned: she would shortly be attacking and degrading the
war-making capabilities of their greatest enemy on the Laut Besar, the Indujah Federation. Her expedition would advance their
position in the region. And if they thought her a danger, and
sought to remove her? What advantage would they gain if, say,
they had one of the Legionnaires assassinate her in her bed? No
advantage she could see. And even the best-trained Celestial assassin would have difficulty breaking through her screen of Niho
knights.

She turned to look at the tall, dark form of Ari Yoritomo, standing a pace behind her, his body swaying easily with the motion of
the ship. Unlike his comrades, Ari had forsaken much of his armor
as the heat had increased on their journey south. His face mask
was gone, allowing her to see his easy smile and admire the blue
depths of his eyes, and he wore only a black-lacquered chest-plate,
greaves and kneepads, over a black silk robe. His katana was, of
course, as always in the sash around his waist, and his right hand
on its hilt.

Yoritomo was not the captain of her Niho guards, as his father
had been—that honor remained with Murakami—but it was clear
to all that he was the knight most personally favored by her. Almost always now, he was given the role of her close protection, on
duty a few feet from her all day and much of the night. The other
knights, who ranged about her, investigating possible dangers,
even tasting her food, did not seem to resent Yoritomo's swift rise
in her affections—but then it was difficult to tell what they
thought, with their faces confined behind those menacing black
masks. Perhaps they hated him. Perhaps they hated her. She would
never be able to tell—and such was the faith that she had in their
oaths of lifelong service that it made no difference to her. These

men would serve her, kill for her, die for her, if she ordered them to do so. And whether they liked her or not was immaterial.

But Ari was different—he was as dedicated as the rest of her knights but he had a warmth and even a sly humor that the others lacked. She watched him surreptitiously, looking at the smooth sun-brown muscled forearm that rested easily on his sword handle. She wondered what it would be like to touch his bare skin, to caress it . . .

Katerina cut her thoughts short immediately. He was a hireling, he was a bodyguard, and such self-indulgent fancies were beneath her.

Instead, she gazed out over the vast, empty sea: somewhere out there, a thousand leagues away, five or six weeks of blue-water sailing, was the fabled Laut Besar—the warm ocean, surrounded by landmasses and studded with lush islands. She had dreamed about it since she was a little girl—a paradise of warm seas and white beaches, of amiable natives and easy wealth, such as could hardly be imagined: obat groves that stretched as far as the eye could see, mountains where gold could be levered out of the ground in great solid nuggets, tall forests of valuable timber, strong slaves to be captured in the remote highlands, spice plantations, rice fields, gum factories, rich fisheries . . .

Ever since Katerina had first heard of the Laut Besar she had been determined to see it, and before long she had dreamed of possessing it. All of it. Somewhere out there, beyond the blue horizon lay her destiny. And now, beneath her feet, in the packed decks of sweating Han soldiery, and on either side in the other two warships equally stuffed with elite fighting men, were the means to make all her dreams come true.

CHAPTER 19

———— ❧ ————

Pain. The first sensation Jun felt was a blinding pain in his head. He opened his eyes to utter darkness and wondered if he had gone blind. A few moments later, as his faculties returned to him, he realized that he was in a small space, packed in tight against several other bodies. His hands were bound. Thick, rancid-smelling rope, he discovered as he brought his wrists up to his face. It was hot and the air was foul. Someone was weeping, off to his left, a piteous mewling sound that grated on his nerves. His head was aching furiously, beating massively and agonizingly in time to his pulse, and he felt nauseous. He shifted his position and realized that his shoulders were in contact with, actually jammed up hard against, someone beside him; he also realized quite suddenly that he was almost naked. There was a rough wall behind his back; his spine grated against it. Probably brick. He needed to piss—he needed to piss very badly. His knees were bent up in front of him and he cautiously extended them and met firm, rubbery flesh and heard a growled warning. He pulled his legs back. The smell in his nostrils was worse than a piggery.

"You awake, richboy?" whispered a voice beside him. He had never thought that hearing *her* voice could bring him so much joy. It suddenly anchored him in a space and time. He was alive. This was real.

"Where are we?" he said, his voice rough from lack of use. He realized he was very thirsty.

"Keep it down, will you? We're in a condemned holding cell.

Southern district of Sukatan." And then as an afterthought, Ketut said, "Underground."

"What? Why?" he said, too loudly.

Suddenly the cell was filled with a blinding light. The roof lifted open, a trapdoor, and Jun saw a dark man shape looming above.

"No noise in the cell—unless you want the boiling water again."

Ketut's fingers gripped his upper arm, hard as claws. "Hold your tongue," she breathed in his ear. In the sudden blinding light, Jun saw that there were a dozen men and women, of all shapes and sizes but all filthy, villainous, in rags, crammed into a small space the size of one of his private bathing pools in the Water-garden, and not much deeper. Six paces wide, by four. Seated, a man had only inches to spare before his head touched the low ceiling.

Above Jun's head, the intense whiteness of the sky. A second black figure came to join the first. There was a mumble of words and a laugh and then a trickle of liquid arced out of the glare and began to spatter down over Jun's head and chest. He caught a waft of the familiar smell, and was stricken immobile by his sudden and quite overwhelming disgust. Every other person in the cell, including Ketut beside him, struggled to get out of the way of the stream, some yelping in terror.

"Only piss this time, you filthy animals. Any more noise and I'll bring the kettle."

Jun's mind could not quite grasp that he had just been urinated on. For several long moments, once more plunged into black-ness by the dropping of the trapdoor, he thought he must be in some terrible nightmare from which he would shortly awake. But after a little time the pressure from his own bladder assured him that this was all quite real. He felt the damp, spongy earth beneath his buttocks and the soles of his feet and realized that there was one slender consolation to having just been pissed on: with a long sigh of relief, he released his own bladder and he let the hot stream flow down the inside of his thigh.

Hours passed, and through a crack in the boards of the trapdoor above his head Jun could see that the day was ending. Ketut pressed her lips very close to his left ear and in short sentences, spoken at an almost imperceptible level of whisper, she told him what had befallen the two of them since the exhibiting of the Dragon's Eye in the Sukatan Arena.

The two of them had been seized by the Palace Guards—Jun unconscious after the mace blow to the back of his head. Semar had disappeared, melted into the crowds and, while the guards had spent most of an hour searching for him, he was long gone. They had both been bound and Ketut had been gagged and they had been dragged to a small chamber behind the Arena where the Raja and his honored guest—Mangku—had looked them over. The sorcerer said nothing during the whole interview. He seemed preoccupied, staring into space or down at his interlinked hands and only once looking at Jun and smiling oddly.

Ketut had told the Raja who they were and had insisted that Jun was his cousin, a member of his own family, but the Raja had said that he did not believe them, he had never before set eyes on Jun—who was slumped in an unconscious heap. They were imposters, tricksters out to gull the Raja with their lies. Furthermore, they were troublemakers, rabble-rousers who had tried to start a riot among the people of Sukatan.

The Raja declared that he was minded to be generous. Despite their lies and their foul crimes against himself and his people, he would not condemn them to death, as they richly deserved. Instead, he sentenced them to only five years' servitude in the Konda Pali mines.

Jun flinched at that. He knew what it meant: it was equivalent to a death sentence only longer, slower and more painful. He had heard only a little of the mines, and save that they provided a steady stream of gold fingers for the Rajas of Sukatan, he'd heard nothing good. The slaves who worked underground in the heat and squalor were the most unfortunate wretches in the Laut Besar. Jun recalled a visitor to the Watergarden saying that the life expectancy of a mine slave was just six months.

"It must be a mistake," he whispered in Ketut's ear. "My cousin would not treat me like that."

"No mistake," she hissed back. "He looked right in your stupid face and said he did not know you. Now be quiet or they will scald us with the kettle."

"I will tell them who I am . . ." began Jun.

"Quiet. Just sit still and keep your mouth shut."

In the gray morning, after a long, hellish and, for Jun, sleepless night, the trapdoor was pulled open and first Ketut and then Jun and then all the rest of the prisoners were pulled out of the cell and lined up against a dirty whitewashed wall. They were in a dingy courtyard and watched over by a score of spear-armed Palace Guards. The two slave-masters, both shambling orangutan-like men, astoundingly alike, with straggling reddish beards but no mustaches, long, powerful arms and legs and coiled leather whips over their shoulders, splashed the prisoners with several buckets of dirty water and fed them salty rice porridge and foul black tea from huge, dirt-crusted cauldrons.

As they ate and drank the filthy provender, it became evident that they were now allowed to talk, and Jun was surprised to see Ketut strike up a conversation with a tall, broad-shouldered, well-muscled prisoner with a broad flat nose, dark angry eyes, dark almost-black skin and tightly cropped curly black hair. There were long pink scars that looked like old sword cuts on the prisoner's shoulders. And other fresher cicatrices that looked like bite marks from a large animal. It took Jun a few moments to realize that she was a woman. Her chest was a bulging slab of muscle. Her carriage spear-straight and proud. A female warrior, then, fallen on hard times.

There was no sign of Semar.

Jun wondered how he should broach the subject of his identity to the slave-masters: he did not want to be punished for insolence, but enough was enough. He was a prince of Taman, shortly to be the Son of Heaven. He was blood of the Wukarta. They could not hold him a prisoner here as if he were some lowborn Dewa trull. He had hoped to choose his moment carefully but when the slave-masters began to roughly harness the prisoners together, two by two, he knew he had to speak.

"Excuse me, good sirs," he said. The slave-masters ignored him: they were strapping the prisoners into wooden contraptions made of a stout log with two Y-shaped end pieces. One prisoner's head went into one Y-shape and was secured there with leather straps; another head went into a similar shape on the far side of the log. Thus, two prisoners were yoked together like oxen, with a yard of thick wood separating their two bound heads. Their arms were bound to the yoke pole but their legs were free; even so, they could only move with the cooperation of their yoke mate.

"Excuse me," said Jun again, louder this time. He saw that Ketut had broken off her conversation with the huge, scarred black warrior and was glaring at him. She made the universal sign for silence, a finger held to her lips. He ignored her.

"Good sir, I hope you will forgive me for addressing you," he said as one of the slave-masters shambled by him, "but I believe that a terrible mistake has been made. You could not possibly know, of course, but I am Prince Arjun Wukarta . . ."

The slave-master stopped and turned to look at him. He slid the coiled whip off his shoulder. "What you say, pretty boy?"

"There has been a dreadful mistake, sir, although I am quite sure you are not to blame. But I am of royal blood; indeed I am a cousin of your own Raja Widojo . . ."

The first lash curled around his ribs in an explosion of agony. He screamed and fell to his knees. The whip struck again, slicing into his shoulder. He gave a bubbling gasp of shock.

"What's 'at, pretty boy? I didn't hear you," said the slave-master, drawing back his long, hairy arm once more. But Jun could not speak for the pain. He saw Ketut start to get to her feet, perhaps to come to his aid, but the big black warrior gripped her right shoulder and forced her back down, speaking urgently into her ear.

The whip struck again, splitting Jun's skin, blood flicking across the dingy courtyard with the backstroke. He found himself curled in a tight ball as the whip slashed agonizingly across his back and shoulders, each blow like a line of fresh fire. Mercifully, it did not last long. After a half dozen or so blows the slave-master lost interest and moved on to continue his work. The pain for Jun was overwhelming—a pulsing mass of fire throughout his whole body. But worse yet was the shock. He had never been treated like this before. Never imagined that he could be so abused. Ketut came over to him, with a dish of water and some whispered words—not of comfort but of pure scorn: "Idiot. Imbecile. Why can't you ever just do what you're told?"

A half hour later, Jun was forced to his feet; his head was roughly shoved into the Y-shaped wooden harness and lashed into place. His hands were tied to the bar of wood between him and the prisoner who occupied the other half of his yoke. He was still dizzy from his whipping but he managed to clear his sight long enough to look at his partner—and saw an ugly, grinning yellow face on a bull neck, small dark eyes and a wide slack mouth. The man was roughly the same height as Jun but twenty years older and twice his weight, thick in the chest and shoulder and very heavy in the belly. A line of coarse black hair ran across his shoulders and down the muscled valley of his back.

"Mm-mm-mee," said the man, running a purple tongue lasciviously across his brown fleshy lips, "aren't you the tastiest little morsel. I bet you clean up nice and juicy . . . Mm-mm-mee, yes, so very, very delicious. Oh yes. Mmmmm. I likes you, boy, I does. Kromo likes you very much."

CHAPTER 20

The sound of hard fists hitting bare flesh came so frequently that it sounded like applause. But the crowd of Ostrakan sailors and off-duty Legionnaires that surrounded the rope circle was largely silent. Only the occasional shout of "Come on, Toma!" or "Hit him, Birku!" rose above the meaty impacts as the two nautical pugilists inside the rope, both naked to the waist, pummeled each other without fear or mercy.

Katerina sat on a canvas stool on a little dais by the starboard rail and watched the fighters labor. She felt nothing much for either of the men, except perhaps a vague appreciation of their courage and hardiness coupled with a growing sense of boredom, as each smashed blows as fast as he could into his opponent's bruised body. An occasional fist would strike a face, and the fighter who received it might step back with a grunt of pain, before the mutual, ritual pounding began again.

It was so much cruder than the previous bouts she had seen on this day of games and sport, a mere display of strength and endurance. She had watched with great enjoyment as two of her Niho knights had given a demonstration of their sword-art with bamboo practice katanas—a series of lightning strikes and lunges, almost faster than the eye could see, which were parried and blocked with equal skill until one of the knights had been rapped on the shoulder of his black-lacquered armor, conceded defeat and bowed to his partner before retiring. Even the three wrestling matches between Legionnaires had shown more grace than this brutal bare-knuckle onslaught. But she knew she was obliged to watch attentively and show a feigned pleasure as the Ostrakan sailors and gunners of the three ships' companies battled it out with their fists. She assumed that both pugilists had dulled their senses with obat before the match but it could be merely exhaustion or the pain breaking through the fug of the drug—for the blows were coming more slowly now, both men, blood-streaked, bruised, groggy and weaving a little before delivering the next powerfully swung fist.

She looked at the crowd and saw that whatever she felt about this savage brawl, the throng around the circle of rope was deeply appreciative of the spectacle. Every man was rapt, some clenching their own fists and aping the blows of their champions. They deserved this day of entertainment. After three unbroken weeks of tedious sailing, the three ships forging through the vast empty ocean with only the occasional squall to break the monotony, the men were due some recreation. She made a mental note to double the ration of marak allocated at mess tonight. And they might slaughter some of the pigs that were penned in the hold, too. A little celebration would raise their spirits at this stage in the voyage. After all, they were approximately halfway there; in three more weeks, two if they were lucky with the prevailing winds, they would reach their destination.

Two men in the crowd, however, did not seem to be as engaged as the rest. A huge, redheaded fellow, who looked like he might himself have been a suitable candidate for the ring, kept sliding glances over at her. And his companion, a shorter, fair-haired fellow in a bulky canvas jacket, despite the heat of the day, was also showing an unusual interest.

The two men—their coloring marking them out as possessing an ancestry from far to the north of Ostraka—intrigued her. They clearly wished to communicate with her in some manner and yet perhaps lacked the confidence to approach the dais. That, even more than the light shade of their hair, made them stand out. Katerina had become used to the general indifference of her Ostrakan subjects—indeed she rather enjoyed it. The Niho almost never spoke. And the Legionnaires were far too well disciplined to gawp openly at her. The only conversation she had was with her two maids Sara and Ilana—and their prattle was often irksomely girlish. She liked silence—it allowed her to think. But these two, these two big Northron men clearly had something they wished to say to her. What could it be?

She glanced down at Ari Yoritomo, who was standing to her left at the foot of the dais, clad in a light silk kimono and the bare minimum of armor, his hand as ever on the handle of his katana. Ari was watching the two men, too. He shifted his stance slightly, moving a little closer to her. There were three other Niho standing around the deck watching the fight.

There was a huge roar from the crowd. One of the fighters—a man named Birku, she had been told—had landed a good, solid belt on his opponent's jaw and the other man was down on his knees on the wooden deck, his head lolling between his shoulder blades, a stream of red drool running from his mouth. He had, she knew, a count of twenty heartbeats to climb back onto his feet and put the big toe of his right foot on the chalk line drawn on the deck. Otherwise, he was done and the fight was over.

The crowd shouted words of encouragement or jeers of derision. She could see bright coins changing hands among its members as bets were placed. As the crowd chanted out the numbers of the count, the downed pugilist climbed awkwardly to his feet, swaying, staggering, and tried to come up to the chalk line. Katerina could see that both his eyes were nearly closed by bruising, his face and body red-purple, puffy and blotched. The man had only just managed to come up to the line, placed his bare foot just so, when his opponent smashed another hard right directly into his face. The blow lifted him off his feet and slammed him down onto his back on the wooden deck. This time he did not move.

The cheering of the crowd was deafening and, as one of the gun captains who had been acting as referee raised the victor's hand, Katerina rose herself and began to clap politely. A space was cleared and the triumphant pugilist—almost as battered, bloody and bruised as his still-unconscious opponent—was led forward to the dais to receive a slim purse of golden crowns and a few words of praise from Katerina.

As she made the required noises of approval to the battered, swaying hulk of a man before her dais, complimenting him on his exceptional skill and valor, she saw that the two fair-haired men had drawn closer to the dais. The big redhead was only a pace from Ari, who was now watching the huge pugilist receive his reward with a wary eye.

Then it happened.

The big redhead lunged at Ari, wrapping his long, muscled arms around the Niho's chest, pinning the knight's limbs to his sides. At exactly the same time, the smaller blond man swept open his bulky jacket to reveal several rows of small gray plump canvas bags strapped around his middle like a girdle and a pair of what looked like pistols attached one on each side. In a horrible instant of clarity, Katerina saw that they were not full pistols, just the handles, cocks and firing locks of two cut-down weapons. The barrels were entirely missing; and furthermore the man did not attempt to draw them. Leaving them at his sides, using both thumbs he merely pulled the cocks on the pistol locks back to full, while his fingers slid into the trigger guards.

Katerina was frozen. She knew exactly what this meant—she had read about this tactic in *The Craft of Combat*—the man was planning to blow himself, and her, into a thousand pieces. The ranks of gray bags around his waist were filled with gunpowder and loose musket balls, and the half pistols were the mechanism for firing them.

She knew all this and yet she could not move.

Ari, however, was not so inhibited. His pale forehead flashed forward, cracking into the big red face of the man pinning him, smashing the bridge of his nose and loosening the fellow's grip. Ari then sank a two-knuckle punch into the man's solar plexus, and plunged an open hand, stiff-fingered into his throat, crushing his larynx with a surprisingly loud pop and dropping the huge redhead to the floor.

The blond man was just one pace away from Katerina now. He looked straight into her face, a curiously blank expression in his wide blue eyes, and said, in good Khevan, "Blessed be the Martyr! May we all burn joyously in the name of His everlasting glory."

Then he pulled the triggers of the two half pistols.

Ari's shoulder caught Katerina full in the stomach. The weight of his diving body, launched upward toward her like a human javelin, lifted her up and backward, the two of them sailing, clasped together as tightly as lovers, over the rail and into the empty air just an instant before the explosion caught them.

Louder than a thousand thunderclaps. A torrent of white noise. The air seemed to be filled with flame and screaming metal. She found she was screaming, too. And they were falling, falling and landing with a bone-jolting crash in the ice-cold sea.

Down she went, down and down. The impact had knocked all the breath from her body. She was flailing with arms and legs, hitting something hard but still sinking. She opened her eyes and felt her chest convulse, her body desperate to breathe, and all around her the icy darkness. Her lungs were burning. Her mind was afire, too. And she was sinking deeper, heading down to the seafloor. *I'm dying,* she thought, more with surprise than regret. *I'm dead. This is the end. What a stupid waste.*

Her chest jerked again. She closed her lips tight, gritted her teeth and fought the urge. *Not yet, not quite yet.* She would hold for just a little while longer—and then open her mouth and let the deadly ocean rush in and take her down into the deep.

She felt a hand, hard as a horse's bite, grip her left forearm. She could feel her slow descent halted. She looked up and there was Ari, above her, in a faint swirling cloud of red and beyond him, far above, the light of the ocean surface. He was pulling her upward, his other three limbs stroking madly but still pulling her, drawing her up, inexorably up. Her chest convulsed again and she nearly gave in. *Not yet.* Instead she kicked her own legs and felt her body rise. With Ari pulling and her own limbs thrashing, even though her chest screamed and her eyes grew gray and dim, she rose. Upward, upward. And broke out through the surface into the air and the light.

I t took them an age to turn the *Yotun* into the wind and get a boat launched. But Katerina did not care overmuch. She lay on her back in the water, her head resting on Ari's shoulder, his strong arms clasped around her middle, and let the sun play on the wet skin of her face. She was not fully conscious and yet she realized that Ari was singing very softly to her in his own language as they waited for the boat full of Ostrakan sailors to splash their way to her. It was only as they were hauling her sopping body aboard that she came fully back into the world and saw the triangular fins in the water a hundred paces away. She called out weakly for them to hurry and get Yoritomo's bleeding carcass over the side as soon as possible. His black kimono was ripped in a dozen places and she caught a glimpse of the red wounds where the musket bullets from the assassin's bomb had punctured his white back.

Somebody put her into her bed. And she must have slept for a long while. But when she awoke, by the knowledge she had in her head, she also realized that she had spoken to somebody, perhaps Colonel Wang, or Murakami, captain of her Niho, at length before she passed out. Both of her attackers were dead; she knew that. The blond man ripped apart from his own blast, with only his head, miraculously, remaining intact. The redhead had been struck by a dozen bullets from his comrade's device and killed instantly. Half a dozen sailors had been killed, and more wounded. And two Legionnaires were also dead from the blast. Her maid Sara, who had been standing on the right side of the dais, had been struck in the belly and chest by several musket balls and would not live another day.

As she lay in her bed, she thought about the words the assassin had used before he pulled his triggers. It was plain as day to her who had sent the killers, and who had arranged for them to join her crew. Her cousin—the new Emperor of Khev. Vladimir. Her suspicions were confirmed when a shamefaced Murakami came to her bedside and made his report.

"On what was left of the bodies, Lady, we found tattoos of the Burning Tree of the Martyrites. And their comrades confirmed that they were both men of the north who had come to Ostraka seeking employment as laborers and who had signed up as sailors when your expedition was announced. They kept to themselves, apparently, and were quiet and very religious, abstaining from obat and even marak. They gave their ration away which made the other sailors tolerate them. That is all we have discovered so far."

"I want you to question every Ostrakan sailor and gunner— again, I want to know about any irregularities. Pay particular attention to those who favor the Martyrite religion. Any who come from outside Ashjavat. Ask Colonel Wang to review his muster rolls for the same in the 42nd. This must not happen again."

"It will be done, Lady."

Katerina felt a wave of tiredness threaten to engulf her. She was bruised in several places and her belly was sore where Ari's shoulder had slammed into her.

"Tell me, Captain Murakami, how is Yoritomo? Is he badly wounded?"

"We have removed eight musket balls from his back, Lady, and he is now resting in his quarters. But he is young and strong. He will be ready to serve you very soon."

"Tell him . . . tell him that I said thank you. Will you do that for me?"

"It is not necessary, Lady. He was merely doing his duty. And if he had been faster, he might even have . . ."

"Tell him anyway. You may go now."

Katerina sank back into her cushions. When she looked up again she was surprised to see that Murakami was still standing there.

"Yes?"

"I have failed you, Lady," said the Niho captain mournfully. "Through my negligence and that of my men you were brought into grave danger."

"Yes, well. You could not have known what the assassins meant to do."

"I have failed you, Lady," Murakami said again. "I must humbly crave your permission to expunge that failure. I beg your permission to go onward to join the Seirei."

"Absolutely not. No! I will not have you destroying yourself over this."

"But I cannot live with the shame, Lady."

"You shall live with your shame, Captain. That is the punishment for your negligence. Besides, I need you. I need every one of my knights. You are dismissed."

Katerina awoke from a sweat-soused nightmare in which Vladimir was lolling in the Ice-Bear Throne with his head thrown back, his red mouth open, and his long yellow hair falling down the back of the throne almost to the floor, and he was laughing, laughing . . .

Lying in her bed, still half-asleep, she pondered what this attack truly meant. It seemed to her that with the assassins Vladimir had declared war on her personally. It was vindictive, pointless, petty—just plain murderous. True, she had sold out a seventh part of his Empire to the Celestial Republic from under his nose, but that was politics. It was not a personal attack on Vladimir. If he showed a strong enough character, and if he was sufficiently determined, he could expel the Celestial troops and take back the Province of Ashjavat. As far as *he* knew, she did not pose a threat to him. She was, by all the Gods, sailing away from Ashjavat, heading off to foreign parts unknown, perhaps never to return again. He could not know what she planned to do in the Laut Besar; he could not possibly grasp the scope of her ambition. Yes, she did mean, ultimately, to return to Khev with a powerful army at her back and, yes, when she did, she would unseat Vladimir from the Ice-Bear Throne and most probably have him dispatched. Yes, she was planning to do all that.

But *he* did not know it.

So by sending his fanatical Martyr-worshipping men to blow her into pieces, he had, at least to her mind, crossed a line of conduct that could not be forgiven. He had declared war on her. And if he thought she could not wage war, she was going to prove him wrong.

None of them, not Vladimir, not the drunken boyar ministers nor the Khevan generals, not even her father the Emperor had ever believed that she might be able to win wars, or even command men successfully, or that her ideas on strategy and tactics might have some merit.

She remembered vividly, nearly two years ago, a state visit by the King of Frankland, a huge, red-haired barbarian from the far west, who had come to Khev with a dozen of his thuggish, mail-clad warriors. They had been lavishly welcomed by her father, feasted, and given gallons of strong marak to make them merry. The celebrations had lasted for days, and while Katerina had been

formally presented to King Karol IV in the Audience Room, and
had made her curtsy, and accepted gruff compliments about her
looks and deportment, she had also been invited to attend a semi-
secret meeting with the foreign monarch, the Emperor and some
of his chief ministers and generals at which the war in Frankland
was discussed.

She had not been invited to make a contribution to the delib-
erations between these old allies but only to serve the marak,
black bread and pickles, or golden millet beer to those who preferred that milder drink. It was an honor to be asked to serve
them, the steward of the royal household had told her, but also a
measure of security. There were many foreign spies residing at
the Emperor's court and she was, quite naturally, above suspicion.

Katerina had been girlishly excited. She knew all about the war
in Frankland from reading the official Imperial reports and from
talking to diplomats and travelers who had been in the far west. In
the south of the region, where the Franks had been seeking to expand their kingdom, building new villages and grazing their cattle
on unclaimed grasslands, the settlers were plagued by marauding
bands of savage Kelti. These bow-wielding horse-warriors, who
were native to the great southern plains, swooped down on the
Frankish farmers in their settlements and killed them, raped their
women, kidnapped their children, burned their farms and stole
their goods and livestock. And there was little that the Franks could
do. They traditionally fought on foot, in armored phalanxes, wielding swords, spears and axes, and occasionally crude firearms, and
even more rarely a few cumbersome short-barrelled cannon.

The Kelti were master horsemen, almost spending their entire
lives on their mounts' backs. They had no notion of civilized warfare. They attacked in hordes, shooting their bows, riding rings
around the earthbound Frankish farmers, stealing what they
wished, killing from a distance and then riding away with their
booty into the vastness of the plains.

When the Franks formed their phalanxes, the Kelti rode around them pouring lethal arrows into their ranks. The savages could not be made to stand and fight—it went clear against Kelti war culture—and if they could be induced once to come in front of the cannon's mouth, they never did so twice. The Franks were being massacred, with several hundreds of civilians and warriors dying every year, yet there were always more settlers who were willing to try to feed their herds of sheep and cattle on the lush grass of the southern plains.

The King of the Franks had come to Khev to seek aid from the Emperor in his endless border skirmishes with the pestilential Kelti.

Katerina had listened with great attention to the discussion, while she poured tiny glasses of clear, pungent marak for the half dozen men in the chamber and brought round trays of sliced cucumber and beetroot. Only Vladimir chose to drink millet beer, ordering it loudly from her, and calling her "serving wench," and sniggering so that everyone could hear him.

Katerina brought his beer, then ignored him. There were far more interesting things to engage her. It soon became plain that what Karol wished from the Emperor was Cossacks.

"With just three regiments, I could clear a hundred-mile-wide stretch then build a great fence to keep the Kelti out," said the Frankish king. "And if they attacked us, I would have the means to follow after them into the wilderness and punish them in a suitable manner."

It made perfect sense to Katerina. What the Franks lacked was competent cavalry. And the Cossacks were far more than competent. They were, in fact, the finest light cavalry troops in the world—according to all the textbooks and military manuals that Katerina had read. Although they were armed with lance and saber, rather than bow and arrow, the Cossack regiments were recruited from the great steppe to the south of the city of Khev, a similar terrain to the grasslands to the south of Frankland, and hailed from a similar horse-centered culture. They were not the same people as the Kelti, but their languages were related and there were other striking similarities. To Katerina's mind, it was an elegant answer to the King's problem. The Cossacks would be more than a match for the Kelti and could follow them anywhere at speeds the lumbering infantry phalanxes could never equal.

"Three regiments?" said the Emperor, apparently appalled. "I cannot spare three prime Cossack regiments for you to run around chasing savages. I have the Legions of the Celestial Republic knocking at my door in the east. How would I answer them if they were to invade the Empire? How, eh? Not to mention the marak smugglers in the southeast, and my own malcontents in the provinces. How do I keep them in line without my Cossacks?"

"Absolutely not! Quite out of the question," said General Pasternak, high commander of the Imperial Cossack Division. "We cannot spare the men."

"Two regiments, then," said Karol. "I'll pay you for them in wine—shall we say a thousand tuns of good Rhonos for a year's service? I can even spare you a little gold. A hundred fingers. I do not seek charity, sire. I mean to make a fair exchange with you."

"I will lend you a single squadron of the Fifth Regiment. They are my finest. And I will sell you two hundred horses. You can train up your own cavalry with the Fifth to help you."

The Emperor turned to General Pasternak. "We could spare two hundred horses from the remount pool, could we not?"

"It could take months, years even to train them," said Karol, "and a single squadron of a hundred Cossacks will scarcely make a difference against thousands of hostiles . . ."

"Caltrops," said Katerina, and every man in the room looked at her.

"My dear," said the Emperor kindly, "is there something troubling you?"

"Caltrops," said Katerina again, enunciating the word clearly.

"Small spiked weapons of war that are scattered on the ground and designed to injure horses' hooves with their sharp tines. General Sigurd Aarnold Golintski particularly recommended their use against enemy cavalry."

The assembled men of war in that chamber just stared at Katerina. She could feel her cheeks beginning to flush and for an instant she hated everyone in that room. Including herself. But she would not be silent. She believed that she had something important, perhaps even crucial to say.

"If the Emperor cannot spare a great number of his Imperial Cossacks to aid you against the Kelti, Your Majesty," said Katerina, looking directly at King Karol, "then I suggest that you heed the advice of General Golintski, a noted Khevan strategist, now sadly deceased, who recommends in his book *Struggle and Strategy* that a combatant who does not have sufficient cavalry, but who does possess a number of serviceable cannon, uses caltrops. These metal objects, no bigger than an apple and resembling a metallic twist of thorns, can be cheaply manufactured in large numbers and strewn in the field to deny that ground to horses. By this method, attacking horsemen can be funneled into what Golintski calls 'corridors of attack': and if the cannon are well situated, then these corridors of attack become killing zones, the horse and riders slaughtered quite easily by cannon fire . . ."

Katerina trailed off. The men were all still staring at her without saying a word. They looked at her as if she were a piece of furniture that had just begun a discourse on religion.

"You are the daughter, yes?" said Karol, frowning at her.

"She is my daughter," said the Emperor heavily. "I think that is enough, Katerina. Leave the marak bottle on the side and you may withdraw. Thank you."

Katerina felt utterly humiliated. She was quite prepared to debate her idea. It made sense to her; indeed she thought it a sensible solution, but she could be wrong. But to be dismissed as if she had not spoken at all was unbearable. She stood still, head hanging, face burning now.

"Katerina," said her father, more sternly, "you will leave us now."

As she made her way to the door, she heard Vladimir say to Karol, "Your Majesty, if we cannot provide you with enough Cossack regiments for your satisfaction, we could always perhaps throw in a noted Khevan general to aid you. A female general, that is . . ."

And the entire room erupted in laughter at the comic absurdity of Vladimir's notion.

The shame of that moment two years ago was still fresh in Katerina. And her hatred of Vladimir still as strong, if not stronger now.

She would have her revenge on Vladimir. She would show him that she knew how to make war. She would make him pay. But not just yet. First she must achieve her goals in the Laut Besar. And there was nothing much for her to do until they reached that destination.

Her belly, where Ari had hit her was still paining her. She felt exhausted and sick and called for Sara—and when Ilana poked her head out from behind the curtain, she realized Sara was dead.

"Girl, bring me the obat box and the rack of pipes. They are over in that chest."

As the smoke from the first pipe hit her bloodstream, Katerina felt the weight of her pain and worry and fear lifting from her. She had not partaken for many weeks—and the effect of the abstinence was to make the drug overwhelmingly powerful. The narcotic extended its gentle tendrils throughout her body, soothing her, lulling her senses, rendering the world soft and flat. She had the sensation that she was floating in a bath of warm, fragrant oil, deliciously sensuous but totally safe. And, in a little while, she slept. And slept. And slept.

♦ ♦ ♦

She awoke to find Ari standing at her door. On guard. Still half-under the influence of the drug, she smiled at him, reassured to see him there, protecting her person. Then she realized that he should not be on duty so soon after the assassination attempt. She knew that his body had been pierced many times by the exploding musket balls.

She sat up in bed. "Ari, come here."

The Niho knight walked easily across the chamber. Katerina could see nothing in his walk to indicate that he had been shot—was it eight times?—a day or two before.

"Sit down, Ari," she said, patting the bed beside her.

"Lady, I prefer to stand."

Katerina was about to order him to sit, when she realized that it might be painful or difficult to do so because of his wounds. She looked carefully at him. He was in black kimono and full armor, but without the face mask. He seemed entirely unharmed, but that could not be. Then she saw that at his sleeve was a peep of white bandage, and a dab of red where a wound had leaked, perhaps even while walking across the room to her.

"Are you . . . all right?" she said.

"I am alive—and ready to serve you again," he said.

"Should you not be resting?"

"No, Lady, my place is here by your side."

Katerina thought about how to go about this. There was only one way.

"Ari Yoritomo," she said, "I order you to cease your duties as my guard immediately and for . . . for three days and three nights. You will rest in your quarters during that time, undertaking no activities, and you will find another Niho knight to take your place as my guard."

"Lady, I would prefer to remain . . ."

"This is my direct order to you. I do not trust you to discharge your duties to my satisfaction until you are completely healed."

Katerina watched Ari's face change. She had often thought of the Niho as expressionless, almost inhuman creatures. But that last remark had hit home; she saw Yoritomo wince, look deeply hurt, just for an instant, before his impassive mien returned.

"As you command, Lady," he said.

"I would also like to thank you from the bottom of my heart for saving me from the assassins. You will always have my gratitude."

Ari merely nodded. Katerina wondered if she could have offended him—could one actually offend Niho?

She said, "Ari, when you first came into my service, you made an oath to me. Do you remember it? You said, 'I spill my blood today, willingly, as a symbol that I shall never shrink hereafter from spilling mine or that of any man or woman or child who seeks to harm you.' You remember those words?"

Ari nodded again.

"There is a man who seeks to harm me—we have seen his handiwork; those assassins were his creatures. He is the Emperor of Khev. Do you swear you'll spill his blood for me?"

"I swear it, Lady," said Ari. "Gladly."

"Thank you. We must delay our vengeance until we have reached our destination. But I shall hold you to your word. And, in due course, I shall send you against the Emperor."

Katerina was about to say more when she noticed that the spot of bright red blood on the bandage at his wrist had grown in size. She must let him go and rest.

"Tell me one last thing, Ari," she said. "Your father's blood was a purple color. I saw it clearly, when he went to join the Seirei. Yet I see yours is red as a poppy. Why is that?"

Some of Ari's poppy-red blood suddenly seemed to suffuse his normally impassive face. *Two reactions in a day,* thought Katerina. *This is unprecedented.*

At first she thought that he would not speak, so long was he silent. Then he said, "I will tell you, if you command it, although it is a source of shame for me."

He paused for a moment, gathering his thoughts. Then, "As you may know, the Niho fought many wars with the Celestial Republic to gain their freedom. And these conflicts were long-lasting and cruel. The Han troops, in order to humiliate us, would rape all Niho women who fell into their hands. Some of these women became gravid, and although most destroyed the fruit of these liaisons, either before or after the birth, some mothers did not have the strength to kill their own children—and the infants were allowed to live, and grow tall, and eventually were accepted into the Niho clans."

Ari stopped.

"Go on," said Katerina.

"The taint of their Celestial blood remained, of course, even after several generations. And they were weaker than full-blooded Niho, but they were also different in the way that they thought. More creative in their minds, more freethinking, more emotional. They and their descendants are called Kangiru. Perhaps one in every hundred Niho has Kangiru blood, which is red, like mine, like a common man's, not the true purple of a pureblood Niho."

"And do the rest of the Niho look down on you for this taint of blood?"

"Some do, a very few, but most Niho recognize that a Kangiru must struggle so much harder to achieve the required excellence than a pureblood. And that is respected."

"And you, of course, are a knight first grade, are you not?"

"I am that, Lady," he said, and smiled.

"Well, Ari Yoritomo, knight first grade, you have my respect—and my thanks—but you will take your leave of me now. I intend to rest—and I command that you do the same."

CHAPTER 21

For Jun, the march was a blur of agony and exhaustion. After two savage beatings in close succession, he did not quite know how he managed to carry on. But he walked with the rest of them, mostly impelled onward by virtue of the fact that he was permanently yoked to the creature who called himself Kromo, who kicked him whenever he dropped, then kicked him harder until he rose once more to his feet.

Jun had never been drawn to the idea of making love with a man, although he had been very fond of an unmarried uncle whose companions were always lissome young men, and he knew that a significant proportion of people enjoyed relationships of this nature. His uncle had been one of the most upright, moral men he had ever known, as well as one of the kindest. Jun had never paid very much attention to his uncle's choice of bedfellows. In truth, he had no strong feelings about the subject at all—but he was alarmed, disgusted and frankly bewildered by the things that came out of Kromo's mouth during that long, long march. A constant dribble of his most disgusting thoughts, largely directed at Jun and concerning what he would like to do to different parts of his body. There was a disturbing element of brutality and violence—but also a secondary theme of hunger, food and eating—about the sexual fantasies that spilled endlessly from this fellow's rubbery mouth, and Jun had no idea how to shut him up. On top of that, the man's breath was the worst Jun had ever smelled: a stench like rotting meat combined with fresh human excrement.

Kromo was a good deal more powerful than Jun and he seemed to be more than a little insane. Jun thought about complaining to the jailers about his yoke mate and then hurriedly abandoned the idea. So he and Kromo were anchored together, day and night, for the three days that it took to reach Konda Pali, as the vast mining complex in the Gray Mountain was known, and except when he was asleep, Kromo kept up a constant stream of obscenities in a low, half-intelligible mumble.

There were twelve prisoners in this coffle, all of them yoked in pairs and destined for service in the mines. The six yoke pairs were all roped together at the crossbar, with about two paces of thick cord between each pair, which meant that there was no possibility of a yoking running away, even if they could coordinate their attempt. All twelve prisoners were joined in one shuffling mass, urged onward by the whip of one of the slave-masters. The second master traveled in a donkey cart, which held a water barrel and few meager cooking items, plus the two men's spare clothes and bedding. The slave-masters took it in turns to ride in the cart or to drive the coffle forward. They rarely spoke, either to each other or to their prisoners: in the latter case, a vicious blow from the whip expressed more than words ever could. The two men expressed neither fury nor joy, just the unmistakable air that this was a dull, routine duty that they had undertaken before, more times than they could count.

Directly in front of Jun, Ketut and the big black scarred warrior were yoked together. But Ketut had her head bound in position and could not turn and look at him, although she did exchange a few grunted words now and then with her much taller yoke mate.

They walked all the first morning, with Jun dripping blood with every step, through gleaming paddy fields, the hot sunlight reflecting from the surface of the water like mirrors. Dirt-poor peasant farmers stopped their backbreaking work and straightened to watch the coffle shuffle past on the raised road, staring with fearful but compassionate eyes at the condemned wretches, flinching a little at the crack of the slave-masters' whips. They soon left the vicinity of Sukatan and the fields that served it, and now they were entering a low, dry scrubby land of hard gray rocks and sand, with trees few and far between. They stopped at noon for a short break. The two slave-masters came around with bucket and ladle and the prisoners opened their jaws and tipped their heads back and received a sloppily poured cupful of rice water directly to the mouth.

Once more Jun thought about trying to speak with the slave-masters but his courage failed and, like the rest, he meekly put back his head and gratefully received his mouthful of slimy liquid.

They were fed that night—or, at least, a dozen bowls of dry rice with a few rancid pickled vegetables on top were put out on the ground for them to eat. But their arms remained tied to the yoke poles. Kromo had his face down in the dirt, wolfing down the meal before Jun was really aware of what was going on. His own bowl was out of reach, in the middle between his yoke mate and himself, so he waited patiently, with the good manners his late mother had instilled in him, for Kromo to finish and allow him to reach his own bowl. But when the big man was done, he merely shoved Jun along, using all his weight and the inflexible yoke and began eating from Jun's untouched bowl.

Jun looked sideways at him. There seemed to be no point in protesting. But something hard and ugly began growing in his gut. For the first time in his pampered life, he contemplated violence against another living human being. He imagined punching the big man in the face; how good it would feel to smear his fat lips against his big yellow teeth. But there was nothing he could do now. His hands were tied to the yoke—and anyway, the creature Kromo scared him. What would he do to Jun in retaliation, if he were to hit him? Jun shuddered. *Let it go*, he told himself. *Just let it go. Soon this will be over. They will realize that this is all a terrible mistake and cut me free. I must endure.* Wearied beyond measure, with his neck stiff, his wounds aching but mercifully now dust-clogged and drying, Jun fell asleep on the ground, still yoked and bound.

In the blink of an eye, it was chilly dawn and the slave-masters were cracking their whips and coming round with the bucket of rice water and the ladle, and Jun opened his cracked mouth, tipped back his head and waited like a baby gannet for his liquid breakfast.

After three days and two nights of hardship of a kind that Jun had never experienced before—almost no food, precious little water, traveling over a harsh, gray, desertlike terrain which chewed through his sandal soles and bruised his already blistered feet, most of the time near delirious with pain, exhaustion and loss of blood, sometimes out of his own head in a nightmarish otherworld of demons and monsters where War-Master Hardan scolded him for his lack of sufficient military enthusiasm—the coffle tottered into a green valley, where crops were growing in ordered rows, a brook chuckled between low banks, and low, whitewashed buildings with red-tiled roofs were scattered here and there. Washing fluttered on lines. There were even flowers blooming in the neat gardens beside the cottages.

At first Jun thought he was still in one of his walking delusions. Then he saw that a vast, dun-colored mountain loomed above the pretty green settlement, the rising hillside punctuated with several dozen grim black towers, like vast, dead, limbless trees. There were a dozen long, wide black buildings set into the gray hillside with a massive double door and thousands of small black windows. A track led to each one and behind each a giant windlass stood like a guardian, the wheels slowly turning. The mine heads. The entrances to the underground complex of Konda Pali. The greatest source of gold in the Laut Besar, perhaps even the world.

The coffle was herded into a large open space, a kind of stock

pen covered with a palm-leaf roof and surrounded by a high fence
made of hundreds of very thin wires, the ground stamped flat by
the passage of thousands of feet before theirs. Their hands were
freed and the yokes were cut from their necks, collected and
borne away by the two apelike slave-masters.

Jun had never felt a sense of release as powerful as when
the yoke was taken from his neck, and with it came a new surge
of hope and strength. He had survived the march. He was free of
Kromo at last—that endless, perverted, mumbling monologue was
silenced. He saw that the other members of the coffle were hurrying toward the far side of the compound where there were tables
laden with bowls of fruit and mounded rice. And water butts, and
some people already washing. He joined the movement and soon
caught up with Ketut, who was trotting toward the table beside
the big black striding warrior.

For once, and only briefly, Ketut smiled at him. "I did not think
you would make it here alive, richboy," she said.

She was indeed surprised at his survival. This slim, haughty
princeling, this soft-handed boy who had never done a hard day's
work in his life had endured the beatings, the lack of food, the
three days yoked to that Kromo person, and here he was unbroken,
uncomplaining, walking on his own two feet. This rich boy was
tougher than he looked.

"So, do we eat first—or wash and then eat?" said Jun, gripped
by a sudden insane cheeriness.

"Eat—in the Hole you eat whenever you can," said the big warrior. She was speaking the Common Tongue, but in a light tone
with a strong, guttural accent.

The three of them selected palm-leaf plates and piled them
high with sticky gray boiled rice and a coarse bright yellow bean-
and-vegetable stew, and they carried them away to a patch of
empty ground where they sat cross-legged and began to eat.

"You have been here before, then?" said Jun.

The warrior smiled at him and lifted one huge, muscular arm. Jun saw that along the black ribs was a mass of pink scarring. At first he could make no sense of it and then he realized that the latticework of thick scars spelled out a word: "Runner."

"I was lucky," the warrior said. "Mostly the bear-dogs get you. But I killed one of those monsters with my hands when they trapped me, and the Mbaru never want to lose any more of their beasts than they have to, so they called them off. They beat me for two solid days, four of them taking turns, they branded me a Runner and had a little rape-fun, too, of course. Then they did the worst thing they could do to me. The very worst. They sent me back here to the Hole."

"Mbaru?" said Jun. He did not care for this scarred woman's conversation at all.

"Those mummy-fuckers," said the warrior, and inclined her head toward the wire. "They call themselves hunters, we call them Mbaru. They track down those who try to run."

Jun looked and saw a dozen figures standing on the far side of the wire.

At first sight they did not seem particularly remarkable, a group of medium-sized men—no women—in drab baggy breeches and shirts, tall dusty boots, most of them a little scruffy, if the truth be told, their long hair tied back with strips of cloth. Some wore broad-brimmed leather hats against the sun. Jun noticed that they were all very heavily armed: knives in their belts and tucked into their boot tops, swords, too, around their waists, pistols shoved into sashes, long muskets draped over their shoulders, one man carrying a bow, with a quiver full of arrows at his belt. Another held a pair of slim javelins. At their feet, by the wire, squatted three huge black animals, and Jun had never seen their like before: short snouts in wide, triangular, fur-covered faces, small, round ears, honey-colored eyes, heavily bunched, muscular shoulders. Harnesses made of pale brown leather encompassed their broad chests, and each animal was leashed to one of the hunters. The nearest of the beasts stood and turned to lick itself and Jun saw that the front legs were long, furry and slabbed with flesh like a bull gorilla, although slightly bowed inward; the back legs were much shorter, the paws edged with long black claws. The beast settled down again and yawned, exposing a blood-red mouth and long, curved yellow fangs.

A pair of long, lean-bellied hounds sat on the far side of the group. They were impressive hunting dogs with big, square, shaggy heads and powerful jaws that looked as if they could easily crunch through human bone but, even so, these hounds looked nervously across at the massive bear-dogs from time to time, and kept their long tails tight between their legs.

"Those slave-hounds track you—the dogs on the right. They are twice as quick as any man, and they can smell your thoughts before you think them, or so they say. They catch up with most of the Runners within ten, fifteen miles. Most folk climb trees to escape getting chewed. Then the Mbaru come up with the bear-dogs. Bear-dogs can climb trees."

Jun was aware that one of the massive beasts was staring at him. The bear-dog opened its black nostrils, showing a glimpse of the pink flesh inside, and took in a huge snort of air. It was smelling him. Taking in his scent.

"See those necklaces?" said the warrior. "See the big brown beads around the Mbarus' necks? Those are dried Kepala beans. They wear one bean for each Runner they've brought in—living body or severed head, the only difference is the pay: the Squinters pay them five ringgu for a live one, only one ringgu for a head."

Jun looked at one of the hunters, a lean, hollow-faced Han with a curiously blank expression. His necklace was thick with beans, maybe forty or fifty of them.

"But it is possible to escape, isn't it?" asked Ketut.

"Look around you—outside of this compound what do you see?"

"There are no walls," said Jun.

"Exactly right," the warrior said. "They don't need walls."

"But some people must escape—some must get away."

"Some do—for a while. Then the Mbaru either kill you or bring you back."

Jun stared down at the ground between him and the woman warrior. He felt the hardness in his gut shift a little; it seemed bigger, more solid. The food had made him feel stronger; he could feel the blood running in his veins. He was not born a slave. He was Wukarta—and from time immemorial the Wukarta had been warriors.

"I'm going to escape," he said. "It is not my destiny to be worked to death in some dirty hole in the ground. You girls can come with me. Or not, as you choose."

CHAPTER 22

Farhan looked down at the piled gray ropes of hair on the white-painted savage twenty feet below him and held his breath. He had the parang gripped in one sweaty hand; the other was tight on the branch of the tree that grew out by his waist.

Don't look up, don't look up, don't look up. This silent mantra was circulating inside his head. He could hear his own heart beating, seemingly louder than a Moon Festival drum. He had not recovered his calm since the mad rush through the forest, with the sound of the blowpipes—ffft, ffft, ffft—giving his feet wings. He had run as fast as he ever had in all his thirty-nine years of life, hurtling through the jungle with no thought to where he was going, his only urge to get away from the hideous men who were hooting to each other and crashing through the foliage behind him. The parang, in its leather sheath hanging from his belt, had tangled with his legs. He had cursed it then and for an instant he considered tugging his belt loose and discarding the blade, just as he'd discarded the rifle. But that would have cost time. Now he was glad that he had not. It was the only weapon he had—not that this clumsy length of sharpened steel would be much good against a blowpipe unless he could get in close.

It had been lack of breath that had caused him to be in this situation. He had never taken much interest in exercise, preferring to spend any leisure time he had at the gaming tables, rather than in a gymnasium or at the running tracks. And he was paying for it now. After only three or four hundred paces he had realized that he could not run at that speed for much longer and had begun looking for places of concealment. Glancing behind him and seeing that he was out of sight of his pursuers, he had swung himself up into a tree and climbed as far up as he could.

Now, as he looked down at the savage beneath him, he prayed to the Gods he did not truly believe in for the man to walk on. It was hot. The running and the terror had combined to overheat his body and he was sweating hard as his system tried to cool itself down. His armpits were drenched; he could feel the beads on his brow form, join with others and run down his cheeks. He lifted his knife arm to wipe his face with his sleeve—but it was too late. A large droplet of sweat fell from his forehead and dropped into the leaf litter below. It made a tiny noise, a little "pat," as it landed. But it was enough. The painted man turned his head to the place on the ground where the noise had come from. Then looked up.

Farhan gripped the parang with both hands and dropped out of the tree.

He fell straight down and would probably have broken at least one of his legs had he not timed his parang blow to perfection. The long thick steel blade sliced down into the astonished savage's head, cutting through the greasy ropes of his hair, punching through the skull and brain and on through the jawbone, dividing his poll into two pieces like an apple under a butcher's cleaver.

Farhan crashed down into the leaf litter, his own body tangled with the instantly lifeless corpse, which safely broke his fall. He staggered to his feet, pulled the blood-slick parang from the savage's split head, raised it for a second blow—and realized that it was unnecessary. He stood there panting and staring at the carcass, unsure what to do next. He collected himself swiftly. Looked around him. There was nobody else in sight. And again he took to his heels. Jogging this time through the forest in the direction in which he believed the *Mongoose* camp lay.

Two hours later, and utterly lost, Farhan climbed another tree. The soft dusk was stealing up on the jungle and he knew that in these latitudes he only had a few moments before it was fully dark. He climbed to the very tallest branch of the nearest hardwood tree and, in the last golden yellow light of day, he looked out over the canopy, a thick carpet of green that seemed to stretch out forever in all directions.

West. The sun must be sinking in the west. He was looking the wrong way. He orientated himself and looked north and there, just before the last glimmer sank over the far horizon, he saw to his relief a flash of blue sea at least a dozen miles away. But at least he had his direction. And he had seen nothing of his painted foes.

After a very long and uncomfortable night in a hard fork of the tree, Farhan checked his bearings again and stiffly climbed down. He began to walk, stopping every hour or so to climb up and check his direction—and quite often finding that he had strayed alarmingly from his path—and so it was not until late afternoon that Farhan, hungry, thirsty, dirty and exhausted, his clothes stained green with lichen and ripped in places by thorns, stumbled on jelly legs into the camp clearing.

He immediately drank two full dippers of water from the barrel, poured one over his head, then, dripping and hollow-bellied, he went to seek out Captain Lodi.

The fortress, Farhan noted with satisfaction, was almost complete—and he made a mental bow to Captain Ravi for his efficiency. But it was down by the river that he found his friend Captain Lodi supervising the reconstruction of the hull of the *Mongoose*, which had been dragged from the river and was lying forlornly on its side.

"We need to get everybody inside the fort—right now," he said. And Lodi took one look at him, gaunt, damp, dirty, and asked no questions at all.

In moments, the Buginese sailors, still clutching their precious shipwrights' tools, and the few Dokra guards around were all streaming toward the fort.

Inside the four stout bamboo walls, with the door barred and double sentries posted on the ramparts, Mamaji was woken from her afternoon nap. She was given a brief account of Farhan's adventure. Then Lila was dispatched to prepare a simple meal for Farhan, and the two men and Mamaji sat down at a small, rickety table inside the big officers' tent to confer.

"You might think that I'm being alarmist, Mamaji," said Farhan patiently. "But these tribesmen are extremely dangerous— you didn't see the Dokra who was stuck by the poisoned dart. He died in a handful of moments. Convulsed so badly his spine snapped like a straw. And, remember, we are the interlopers here. This is their homeland and we have come here uninvited and killed two of their friends."

"It is you who has done all our killing so far, dear," said Mamaji, with a hard smile.

Cyrus Lodi grunted. "What else would you expect him to do? Negotiate? Ply his famous charm—in the few instants before he died of whatever foul poison they use?"

"I am happy to take the blame, Mamaji. That's not important. The question is what do we do now?"

Captain Ravi came into the tent, pulled out a chair and sat down next to Mamaji. "The sentries report no sign of activity," he said. "Are we sure this threat is serious?"

"It is deadly serious, Captain," said Farhan. "Two of your men might attest to its seriousness except for the fact that they are both stone dead."

"Yes, that is unfortunately true," said Ravi. He looked at Mamaji. "I would like to request permission to send out a strong patrol to retrieve their bodies."

"Are you mad?" said Farhan. "They are out there, somewhere,

in the trees. Their body paint makes them very difficult to see. If
they are hostile, they could pick off the members of your patrol at
their leisure. You could end up killing all or some of your men and
learning nothing about the enemy. It's far too risky."

"Taking risks, my dear sir, is what we are paid for by the Federation," said Ravi, his back stiffening, one hand going instinctively to curl his mustache.

"I would like to continue with the refit of the ship, if I may,"
said Captain Lodi. "The sooner she is whole again the sooner we
can get back to sea."

"We can do nothing tonight, anyway," said Mamaji. "It might
be best if we all remained in the fort—with a double guard on the
ramparts. And tomorrow we shall see what we shall see. Shall we
adjourn till the morning, gentlemen?"

The night was uneventful and when Farhan went up onto the
bamboo ramparts after a cursory wash and a cup of tea, the
cool but sunny morning seemed to be nothing but benevolent, so
much so that for a moment he wondered whether the events of
two days ago had really happened. He stared out beyond the
clearing, trying to penetrate the green curtain of the forest and
saw . . . nothing. But there could be a thousand painted men
with skull faces and blowpipes out there and Farhan would not
know it.

Captain Ravi was especially bullish at the morning meeting
and, although Farhan put up a token resistance to the idea of the
patrol, he was overruled. They agreed that Captain Ravi would
lead a strong patrol of thirty men—guided by Farhan—to recover
the bodies of the two fallen Dokra and to scout the immediate
vicinity. Meanwhile, Captain Lodi would continue with his repairs of the *Mongoose*. A sharp lookout would be kept on the walls
for any sign of the painted men.

"It may be that they were a band of itinerant hunters, dear," said Mamaji. "In fact, I think it more than likely. And if that is the case, they will be long gone by now."

Farhan disagreed but held his tongue. In the hour before they departed he found himself a large, shallow wickerwork basket, cut off the handle and spent some time sewing two leather straps on the inside to create a primitive shield. He wanted to be able to put something between himself and those lethal darts if they came into contact with their foes. He also strapped the parang in its leather sheath around his waist, and shoved the loaded iron pistol into his waistband.

It was more difficult than Farhan had imagined to find the place where the two Dokra had died. But after several hours of panting through the roasting jungle, taking wrong turns and having to retrace their steps—with Captain Ravi becoming more short-tempered with every pace—Farhan finally recognized the huge banyan tree where they had encountered the painted men. However, there was no sign of the bodies. He was almost sure it was the right place but Ravi seemed to doubt him.

In the end he was forced to reenact his panicked flight from the blowpipe-wielding savages, much to Ravi's amusement, and try to work out where he might have thrown his rifle as he fled. He found it in a thick patch of high grass and with a huge sigh of relief, and not a little flourish of triumph, he showed it to Ravi.

"If you were one of my troopers, I'd have you flogged bloody for losing your weapon," sniffed the Dokra captain. "Perhaps shot for desertion in the face of the enemy."

Farhan took the iron pocket pistol from his waistband; he cocked the hammer, extended his arm, aimed carefully and shot Captain Ravi in the center of his small, mustachioed face, blowing his brains all over the trunk of the palm tree behind him.

But only in his mind. For a moment, Farhan indulged himself in this delightful fantasy, then he said mildly to the captain,

"I think we should head back to the camp. These savages have taken the bodies. Which means they cannot be itinerant hunters. They've taken the bodies somewhere—to a village, to a farmstead. To their home."

He slung the recovered rifle onto his shoulder, picked up his wickerwork shield, turned his back on the mercenary captain and led the way.

For three days, there was no sign of the painted men. Work on the ship continued, the Dokra kept a watch from the ramparts and toiled on strengthening the walls of the fort. Even Farhan began to relax, wondering if the savages had seen, noted and comprehended their overwhelming military strength and decided to leave them in peace.

But, on the afternoon of the fourth day, they came.

Farhan was sitting by the riverbank beside a spread blanket under a wild fig tree and playing dice with two off-duty Dokra troopers and a Buginese sailor. He had just thrown sevens and was crowing excitedly about his luck, when he heard a sharp cry and looked over toward the fort. He saw a Buginese plucking angrily at a dart with a tuft of fluff at the end that was sticking out from the meat of his bare arm. And then he saw them, beyond the dart-stuck man in the trees, ghostly figures slathered in white clay, overpainted with black and gray stripes. He saw the long blowpipes and heard the eerie "ffft, ffft, ffft" as they put the long tubes to their lips and blew. Three men now were staggering about the clearing, shouting in pain and shock. A Dokra put his musket to his shoulder and fired, a crack and a spurt of flame, and one of the figures in the tree line dropped.

"Back to the fort, get inside, now," Farhan was shouting as he scooped up his rifle in one hand and urged his dicing partners up off the blanket with the other.

Lieutenant Muda was blowing short sharp blasts on a small brass whistle, and Captain Lodi was bellowing at his men to get inside the fort or die.

There was a stream of men now running for the stockade's narrow door, and a thick scrum there, as too many tried to enter the narrow portal at the same time. There were a dozen men in the clearing who had been struck by the darts, Dokra mostly and a few of the Buginese sailors. Some were running toward the fort, not knowing that they were already dead. Others stood and tried to level their muskets at the white figures in the trees. Far-han wasted no time at all and shoved his way through the crush and inside the entrance, running for the stairway that led up to the bamboo walkway behind the bamboo rampart. He looked out over the clearing and saw that the men who had been struck by the darts were now either convulsing manically in that impossible manner or already dead and quite still. And the painted men were coming out of the trees, cautiously, timidly even, making little scuttling runs toward the fort, stopping to put their pipes to their lips, shooting their darts, then running forward a little more.

Captain Ravi had gathered a score of Dokra in the space before the fort and had ordered them in two perfect lines. Magnificent in their scarlet coats, white cross belts and glorious turbans, they were marching from the north, by the river, toward the tree line and advancing on that handful of attacking enemy tribesmen who were out of cover. Ravi halted his men thirty paces from the en-emy and ordered them to shoulder their muskets.

Two of the white savages aimed their pipes at the immaculate line of Dokra and blew. Ffft, ffft. Two Dokra in the front rank were struck.

"Aim," roared Captain Ravi.

Ffft, ffft, ffft. Three darts came spitting out of the tree line to the Dokra's left. One of the troopers began to twitch and froth at the mouth.

"Run," shouted Farhan from the ramparts. "Run back to the fort, you fools."

"Give fire," shouted Ravi. And a ragged volley lashed out from the line of red-coated men. Three of the white-painted men were blown off their feet. Muskets were crackling from the ramparts by now. Farhan lifted his own rifle onto the firing platform and sighted down the barrel.

"Second rank three paces forward," shouted Ravi. And half a dozen men stepped bravely forward and made a new line three paces in front of their comrades. "First rank reload. Second rank make ready!" Ravi was bawling now, but the darts were steadily coming in—ffft, ffft, ffft, ffft—and his men were dropping. Some now curling, writhing, twisting and screaming on the ground.

"Run, you fools. You mad, brave blockheads, run!" Farhan could not help himself. He was shouting at the top of his voice, rifle unfired, forgotten in his hands.

A dart whizzed across the space from the tree line and plunged into Ravi's right eye. The little man clapped a hand to his wound, and shouted, "Second rank, aim."

Farhan was dimly aware that Captain Lodi was off to his left, issuing brisk orders around one of the ship's cannon that had been mounted on a platform there.

"Second rank, give fire!"

Only three men answered his call. Their muskets spat once before the men succumbed. The painted men were coming out of the trees in huge numbers now, scores, hundreds of them even. They were converging on the fort. Farhan saw that all the Dokra in Captain Ravi's force were down now, although some were still moving. Their leader had sunk to his knees and was still clasping the dart in his eye. He was twitching, shaking, the spittle white below his fine black mustache. The savages were advancing, coming across the clearing in a mass. They were murmuring something, a two-syllable word, chanting it over and over, and it took

Farhan a few bewildered moments to recognize what they were saying. It was, "Vharkash! Vharkash! Vharkash!"

Every white-painted man, he now saw, had a black scythe painted on his forehead between the eyes. They were coming on at a rush, trampling the dead and dying men on the clearing floor, rushing at the flimsy walls of the bamboo fort, pipes in hand but some also carrying bamboo spears and crude, wavy-bladed iron swords.

"Fire," said Captain Lodi, his single word seeming to cut through the hubbub.

There was a fizz and a booming crash as the cannon spoke. In a vast belch of flame, two hundred lead balls were blasted at the advancing savages in a wide spray.

Canister, thought Farhan, with one part of his mind. Like a gigantic shotgun, the iron tin filled with lead balls belched out and shredded the oncoming warriors, blowing a score of them into the next life and wounding a similar number, ripping off arms and legs, shattering bone, flensing the living flesh from their clay-caked bodies.

That one cannon discharge stopped the advance in its tracks. The savages stood there in the clearing, utterly dazed, those un-hurt looking down at their own gray- and black-striped bodies, which were now spattered with their comrades' blood.

The second cannon blast, coming from Farhan's right, from a gun captained by Lieutenant Muda, smashed into the stunned survivors, wiping them across the clearing, hundreds of heavy lead balls smashing into faces painted like skulls, dismembering painted bodies, ripping open naked flesh, soaking the earth of the clearing in a rich dark gore.

Farhan lifted his rifle once more. Men were on both sides of him at the parapet now, firing their muskets. But the painted savages were beaten. Those that still lived, and who could still move, were running, hobbling or crawling back toward the tree line.

A ragged cheering broke out on the firing platform as it became clear that the painted men were in full retreat. One of the Buginese began to sing a victory song, a wild ululating sound that made the short hairs on Farhan's neck stand up.

"Silence on deck," shouted Captain Lodi, forgetting for a moment where he was. "Reload your weapons. We haven't seen the last of these devils yet. Reload and make ready, I say."

Farhan looked down at the rifle in his shaking hands and realized that, in all the carnage about him, he had not fired it once.

———⊰⊱———

CHAPTER 23

It was all very well to boast to his friends that he planned to escape, but Jun had no idea how to go about it. For a start, they were moved out of the wire-fenced compound the next morning after a comparatively luxurious night in which they had enough to eat for the first time in days and were able to wash, tend their wounds and sleep unyoked.

During the night, two more coffles came into the compound, were cut free from their yokes, fed, washed and curled up gratefully to sleep in the dust. But while Jun was dimly aware of the new arrivals, he did not let it disturb his slumber. In the morning, a middle-aged Han gentlemen in a fine blue silk robe and a square hat with a golden-glass button on the top came into the compound, accompanied by a dozen giant soldiers—they were a full head taller than Jun—in long green coats and baggy black trousers, one of whom was carrying a long black vertical banner. Manchus, Jun guessed. Bannermen. War-Master Hardan, he recalled, had been particularly impressed with them. These soldiers were armed with muskets, and at the top of each musket, fixed on a ring around the muzzle was a vicious, foot-long, iron spike. At their belts hung the fat brown coils of buffalo-hide whips.

The slaves were all lined up in the compound, shoved into their positions by the Manchu guards, who yelled at them, spittle freely flying, in their own ugly and incomprehensible language mixed with a few simple words of the Common Tongue. For those who did not immediately understand, whips cracked and the slaves cried out. The line was swiftly formed. Pain is a universal language. Jun noted with relief that the Mbaru hunters and their monstrous beasts, who had watched them silently through the wire the evening before, were now gone. But then the tall, scarred warrior—her name was Tenga, Jun discovered—whispered that their absence meant they were on the trail of a Runner, and Jun's sense of relief turned sour in his belly.

The Han gentleman with the golden-glass-button hat was a senior engineer, Tenga whispered, one of the Gold Masters. He walked down the line of slaves, stopping occasionally and squeezing a limb, or peering at a whip laceration or a rash. About halfway down the line of forty or so men and women standing mostly naked in the cool of the dawn, the engineer stopped in front of an elderly woman, who was four along from where Jun was standing between Tenga and Ketut. The crone was a skeletal creature, with a badly bowed back, spindly limbs and swollen joints at the knees and elbows. Her wild gray hair spilled down over her flaccid breasts. The Han barked a single word and pointed a finger at the woman, and the Manchu who was accompanying him stepped forward and without the slightest hesitation punched the bayonet-spike on the end of his musket into her belly. The woman collapsed around the blade, letting out a sighing grunt, and fell to the ground. The Han gave another order, flicking his finger at the bleeding wretch, and the Manchu stepped in and crushed her skull with one blow of his musket butt.

Jun was not sure if he was more shocked by the sudden cold-blooded murder of a frail human being or by the reaction from the rest of the slaves and the Manchu guards. There was no reaction; nobody moved from the line, nobody protested. And neither did Jun. It was perfectly clear the value that these terrifying people placed on human life. The Han engineer barely gave the old woman another glance but moved on down the line. For a heart-stopping moment, the gold-buttoned murderer stopped in front of

Ketut. Jun saw him assessing her skinny limbs and small stature—
there had never been very much of her, Jun thought, but the hard-
ships of the past few days had stripped whatever spare flesh she had
from her lean body. But Ketut glared directly into the face of the
Han engineer, seemingly daring him to kill her, and after a few
long moments he merely smiled coldly and moved along the line.

After the inspection, the slaves were marched off to their labors.
They came out of the holding compound in single file, following
the Han engineer and with the Manchu guards, muskets at the
ready, keeping a watchful eye on them at all times. They were led
up the slope to the nearest mine head set into the hillside and, as Jun
filed in with the others through the double doors of the square black
building, he had a strange fancy that he was, in fact, entering a secret earthly portal into one of the foulest of the Seven Hells.

He was not far wrong.

They walked through wide steel corridors, past several open
doors leading to cavernous rooms—some with obvious functions
such as the dining hall, where they glimpsed dozens of long tables
and rows of benches where a handful of exhausted-looking
wretches were determinedly, almost manically eating from small
wooden bowls, or the dormitories, where men and women from
the night shift could be seen curled up and sleeping like the dead
on wooden two-foot wide shelves stacked up the walls of wide,
dingy rooms. One room was a morgue and crematorium, and Jun
saw a dozen dirty linen sacks clearly containing bodies piled on
top of each other beside a wall. Some of the sacks were only half-
closed and slack, emaciated limbs poked out. A small, white-
coated man in a doctor's mask was standing beside a gurney
looking at the mouth of a roaring furnace.

Some rooms were empty or had the doors shut. Two Manchu
sentries were posted beside every open door—whether the room
was empty or not. And at one point they passed a Manchu squad
of twenty bannermen marching out toward the exit, and were

forced to give way and hug the walls to allow the soldiers to move past without breaking their step. The air in the mine building smelled of cold steel, machine oil and stale sweat, with an under-note of urine. To Jun's mind it smelled of fear and self-pity, sorrow and an indifference to suffering. It smelled of death.

Another hundred paces, after which Jun realized that he must now be underground, inside the Gray Mountain. He was aware of a noise, a deep metallic clanking sound that came up through the soles of his feet. The farther they penetrated into the mine, the louder the noise grew, and Jun was conscious that the temperature had noticeably increased, too. Now, as they were herded onward, they all gleamed with sweat—even the icy Han engineer was seen to mop his face with a black silk kerchief. They were ushered down a series of steep iron stairs, farther and farther down until they came out into a large gallery with a high ceiling. They were ordered to sit by a warm steel wall and wait, with the Manchus looming over them.

Squatting there, Jun got his first proper sight of the heavy machinery of the mine. At first it was too noisy and confusing to make any sense of it: belts on great wheels flapped and clanked; giant metal hoppers ground gears and squealed; great wooden wagons the size of a modest house in Taman were wheeled past, piled impossibly high with chunks of black stone, some showing tiny visible flecks of light. These wagons were pushed along by gangs of sweating, emaciated men and women, twenty folk to each wagon, the raw whip marks on their bare backs making their servile status clear. Eventually Jun began to make sense of it. The ore wagons were wheeled into position by the slaves. The wagons were then seized by gigantic metal claws, lifted and their contents poured into the vast hoppers. These hoppers gave off a hideous grinding noise, audible even over the roar as the black rock was emptied into them, and clouds of fine gray dust billowed out of the tops as the ore was ground into smaller chunks. A trickle of broken rock came from the bottom of the hoppers and onto a long moving belt-track driven by rollers. The broken-down ore traveled away along the belt-track to the far side of the gallery and out of sight.

To Jun's left there was a bank of four vast elevators, giant cages made of thick, greasy, steel bars and big enough to hold one of the ore wagons and the exhausted people who pushed them. When the wagons were emptied, the slaves dragged the vehicles back over to the elevators, loaded them inside and with a slamming of the steel grills and a sucking, groaning, whooshing sound, the full cage disappeared down into the hot earth below.

A long, piercing whistle split the air and made Jun flinch. Tenga leaned toward him, and whispered, "Shift change. Now we go below. Into the Hole."

The elevators clanged, fell and rose and a great wave of humanity—several hundred men and women in varying stages of malnutrition—surged out of the squat steel cages and swarmed up the stairs to the upper floors. They seemed to be racing each other to get to the top, some shoving others out of the way, some even being trampled.

"Rice time," said Tenga. "They feed us after the shift so they don't waste food on the day's crop of dead. There's never enough rice for all and latecomers go hungry. After the shift, don't stay here in the machine level, go straight upstairs to the dining hall. Run, if you can. Don't wait for anything. Not me. Not Tut. Go straight up there."

When the rushing tide of slaves had passed, Jun saw that the Manchu were pushing a smaller wagon out of the steel doors, which had come up with a separate elevator. The big, green-coated men pushed the wagon across Jun's line of sight toward a smaller elevator on the far side of the hall. As it passed, he saw that the wagon was piled with fresh corpses, half a dozen limp bodies wrapped in big, dirty white sacks. The little masked man in the white coat whom Jun had seen in the crematorium waited by the smaller elevator, leaning against the steel bars of the cage casually, ready to escort the piled bodies to their destination in his fiery lair on the floor above.

There was something familiar about the shape of his head, and the way he held his short, fat body, even in the voluminous white gown. Then he pushed off the steel bars and said something to the Manchu guard, who laughed. The little man ignored the wagon full of bodies by the open doors of the elevator and came sauntering over to the newcomer slaves, sitting by the steel wall. He strolled along the front of the seated prisoners, looking them up and down, as if he were inspecting livestock at market and, as he passed Jun for a brief second their gazes met. And Jun found himself looking into the wise, jet-black eyes of his old servant Semar. He opened his mouth, about to exclaim his surprise and joy—and stopped. Semar's soft, familiar voice was speaking—but speaking inside his head. It was answering questions that he had barely formed, let alone spoken aloud.

"Yes, my prince, it is truly me. And no, I cannot explain things just now. But I am here to help you. Have courage. I will see you again soon. In the meantime, do not tell Ketut. Do not tell anyone who I am. Trust me. Have courage, stay strong. In the end, all will be well."

Jun noticed that the old man was already a dozen paces away, heading back toward his wagonload of corpses even as the echoes of his voice died in his head.

They were ordered to stand up, march to the elevators, and were bundled into the giant cages—all forty of the newcomers and their guards squashing roughly inside. With the groaning and whooshing came a curious hollow feeling in his stomach. Jun felt the elevator drop. Down, down, down it went. The steel wheels screeching as they ran on ungreased rails. Down into the black entrails of the Konda Pali mine.

Jun felt a strange insistent pressure on his rear from the man behind him and by turning his head he saw that he was squeezed up against Kromo, the half-mad fellow he had been yoked to during the march. He had forgotten neither the man nor his disgusting ways but there had been so many new experiences that he had pushed the creature from his mind.

"Good morning, pretty one," whispered Kromo. And Jun caught a blast of his rotting-meat breath. Worse, he could still feel something hard rubbing against his buttocks. He hoped with all his heart that it was just the brute's groping right hand.

Crushed in together in the elevator, Jun could not move away, nor could he move his arms. He looked at the nearest of the two Manchu guards accompanying them down into the Hole but there did not seem to be much point in protesting, and he was not sure how he would communicate his distress to the guard anyway. He looked across at Tenga and briefly caught her hard black eyes but by then they were at the bottom of the fall and the steel-bar gates were clanging open and the pressure was relaxed as they streamed out into a surprisingly large area, as wide as the Watergarden, with a low, rock ceiling and the whole place lit with a sallow glow.

As he came out of the cage, Jun reached behind and felt the material of his raggedy sarong at the back and his hand came away wet and sticky. He felt sick and shaky but he knew he must put his disgust and—yes—increasing anger from his mind: *Semar is here.* That is what he must focus on. They would find a way to escape. He wished he could tell Ketut. But Semar had been clear. Tell no one. All would be well. *Semar is here.* He repeated that luminous fact to himself. Jun hoped it would give him the courage to face whatever horror came next.

He looked around the wide cavern he found himself in. A dozen empty wooden wagons of varying sizes were lined up against the far wall. It was very hot and dim—the only light was a few flickering oil lamps set in sconces hollowed out of the rock walls. By their yellow light, Jun could make out four or five tunnels, twice the height of a man and wider than one of the big wagons, leading off into the blackness.

Jun moved as far away from Kromo as he could, but stayed close to Ketut and the warrior woman. Tenga told them both in a low whisper that this was the assembly area, and that if they ever got lost or separated from the rest of the workers, they were required to come back here and wait for their guards. If they did not, they would be treated as Runners. Jun thought of the Mbaru, and the bear-dogs, and felt his ball sack contract. *Semar is here,* he told himself again. The two Manchu guards, with gestures and grunted commands, separated the forty-strong group of newcomers into two gangs of twenty. The first was herded off to the far side of the cavern where they congregated around an empty ore wagon.

Jun's group of twenty, too, was shown the ore wagon they were to use. His work gang contained Tenga and Ketut, but his heart sank when he saw that Kromo was also a part of it. The big man was ten feet away and whispering to another slave, a darkskinned dwarfish fellow, very strong-looking with a large, misshapen head. He had the flattened nose and tightly curled black hair that marked him as one in whom the blood of the Ebu people, the original inhabitants of the Laut Besar, still ran strong. Both men were shooting glances at Jun, then the dwarf gave a horribly dirty snigger.

"You like that one?" Tenga said to him, nodding over at Kromo who was now leering openly at him from the far side of the wagon. "You like to fuck with him tonight? Or suck him? Yes? Maybe, if you suck him good, he'll give you some of his rice and beans?"

"No! By all the Gods, no. I'd rather starve. How can you ask that?"

"This is the Hole," said Tenga with a shrug. "People do what they have to."

Jun thought, *I am Wukarta. I will never be made into that creature's whore. Whatever it takes, whatever is necessary, I will do it.*

"What are we waiting here for?" he asked, mainly to change the subject.

"They've got to blow their drill-holes," said Tenga. For an instant, Jun thought she was naming some disgusting sex act that took place in this dark and humid hell.

He opened his mouth to say something rude but the Manchu guard shouted out a single word, and Tenga said urgently, "Quick, cover your ears and open your mouth."

"What?" said Jun.

"Do it now, both of you," said Tenga, "or you'll lose your hearing."

Both Ketut and Jun covered their ears just in time. A vast explosion pummeled the air, vibrating the rock under their feet. A huge cloud of dust bloomed out of the tunnel directly ahead of them. All the newcomers were stunned by the force of the blast, rocking on their feet. The dwarfish fellow, Kromo's friend, was knocked off balance, tumbled to the rocky floor, but he bobbed up a moment later grinning, jabbering something funny to Kromo.

When the dust had nearly cleared, the group was herded round the ore wagon, and induced to put their shoulders to the huge vehicle and push it into the tunnel. It was a brute to get moving. The wagon was heavy, even unladen, and the thick wooden wheels were uneven and clumsy. The twenty slaves struggled to keep it trundling along at any speed. To pause, however, even for a moment, was to invite the lash, as one poor wretch soon discovered. A short, fattish woman with her hair tied into two braids stopped pushing for a moment to stretch her back and the nearest Manchu immediately began cutting at her with short hard blows of his whip. The guard only relented when the poor creature, now dizzy with pain and one of her braids dripping with blood, resumed her position at the side of the wagon and once again began straining to heave it forward. Jun wondered what it would be like to push when it was filled with the heavy black chunks of gold ore.

As they advanced deeper into the tunnel, the air became thicker and hotter. The two Manchu guards lighted the oil lamps in the sconces along the way as they passed them, but despite their flickering light, and the chain of diminishing yellow glow-spots leading back all the way to the elevators, Jun could not shake the horrible feeling that he was crawling along inside the intestines of a huge subterranean beast. A notion encouraged by the heat, the dimness and the smell of decay, the stink of animal carcasses left too long in a warm room, which grew stronger as they heaved the wagon forward, slowly, into the darkness.

"What is that smell?" Ketut whispered.

Tenga told her. "Slaves run off down the side tunnels, trying to escape, trying to find a way out. They get lost in the dark and die of hunger or thirst or are mashed into jelly by the shock waves when they blow the drill-holes. Nobody bothers to collect the bodies."

After half an hour of struggle, they had reached the ore-face. The wheels of the wagon were snagged now by loose rocks blown free by the explosion and one of the Manchu eventually called a halt. Jun peered forward but could see little more than a vast heap of smashed rock, rising up into the blackness in an uneven slope, with a few wisps of smoke still rising from the jagged surface.

The black dwarf leaped up and into the interior of the wagon, and reaching down he began to hand out long-handled picks and hammers: a hammer for Kromo, and a pair of picks for a man and a woman, both taller and stronger than average. The dwarf took a hammer himself and vaulted nimbly out of the wagon onto the ground.

For just a moment, Jun stood and watched as Tenga and Ketut bent to pick up large pieces of broken rock, heft them onto their shoulders, walk to the wagon and hurl them inside. There was a loud crack and a painful blow smacked across both his shoulders. A Manchu shouted something, drew back his arm again for another stinging lash, and Jun quickly bent to his task, seizing a chunk of ore the size of a man's head and hoisting it up.

Hour followed hour of brutal work. Bending, lifting, heaving the ore into the wagon. His soft hands were bashed and bruised by their constant blundering contact with the rough stone in the yellowish half darkness. His head still ached from the mace blow four days before, his neck was still badly chafed from the yoke, and untreated whip wounds burned all over his back and shoulders. The heat was like a physical thing: a smothering beast that hung from Jun's body, that coated every inch of his skin in a foul slime of sweat and dust. After only a short while, an hour or two perhaps, his back muscles ached like they were on fire, as did his thighs, biceps, forearms—even his fingers. But no pause was allowed and any slowing in the labor was punished with the whip.

Kromo and his dwarf friend attacked the larger pieces of rock, some the size of buffalo or even bigger, slamming their hammers in a steady rhythm into the dark mass until it cracked and splintered into pieces that could be gathered up by the others. The tall man and woman attempted a similar task with the two picks until one of the Manchu became dissatisfied with the woman's work, knocked her down with one smashing blow to the side of her head from the heavy butt end of his musket, and took the pick from her unresisting hands and gave it to a nearby slave, a tall man. Then he lashed the woman till she rose, swaying, and began shakily to collect the ore with her hands.

After what seemed like several days, one of the Manchu blew a whistle, and all the slaves dropped to the ground immediately. Skins full of blood-warm water were passed from hand to hand among the group and their contents gulped eagerly. Jun was almost delirious from tiredness but he found himself sitting on the ground next to a slim girl with a pert nose and pretty eyes. She reminded Jun a little of one of the jolly fisher girls he had chased so happily in Taman, though this one had a coarser, rounder, sweetly dimpled face, a more classically Yawanese-peasant look.

He smiled at her but she ignored him and stared stolidly at the ground between her legs. He touched her arm, smiled again and offered her the waterskin. She snatched the leather sack from his hand but refused to meet his eye.

Jun shrugged and looked at the vast pile of ore that had tumbled down from the face after the explosion. It did not seem to have diminished at all despite their efforts. When the whistle blew again, the pretty Yawanese-peasant girl leaped to her feet long before Jun could haul himself to his and was immediately heaving the slabs of ore as if born to the task. Her example spurred Jun: he was determined that he would not succumb to his own exhaustion.

Jun noticed that Ketut and Tenga worked together as a team: Ketut picking up the rocks and passing them to Tenga, who would toss them into the wagon with one swing of her long, muscular arms. The Manchu did not molest them at all as it was clear that they were moving more than their share of ore in this sensible way. After a while they would switch places, Tenga doing the bending and picking up, Ketut throwing the rocks into the carrier. Jun felt a shaft of envy that the two young women had forged such an efficient team without including or even consulting him.

When the wagon was full, an event marked by much shouting from the Manchu and even more cracking of whips, they put their shoulders to its sides and infinitely slowly and painfully trundled it back along the tunnel. Once at the assembly area, they tugged and shoved it into the elevator and, when the barred doors had clanged shut, they felt a glorious, almost-refreshing, cooling of the air as they rose up from the depths to the machine level.

It was a very short-lived pleasure. Moments later, or so it seemed to Jun, after they had watched the ore wagon seized by the giant metallic claws and its contents poured deafeningly into the grinding hopper, they were pushing the empty wagon back into the steel cage of the elevator, and dropping down, down again into the heat. An instant later and they were once more back at the ore-face, bending, lifting, hurling the sharp rocks once again into the dark belly of the empty vehicle.

They filled the wagon and took it up to the machine level four times that day, with only one water break of about a quarter of an hour in the morning and one in the afternoon. Finally, after twelve hours of bone-breaking work, when Jun felt that he could quite easily collapse senseless from pain and exhaustion, the whistle blew again—a much longer blast this time—and, although the wooden wagon was less than a quarter full, and the great sloping bank of broken ore as undiminished as ever, the two Manchu herded them all back down the tunnel without the wagon and they knew, with unspeakable relief, that for this day at least their shift was done.

"Tenga says that when we get to the machine level we are to run—run, mind you—up the stairs to the dining room," said Ketut to him quietly as they rode up in the wonderfully cooling air of the elevator. "If we are late, there will be no food *at all* for us today."

Jun, who had made sure that he was on the opposite side of the elevator to Kromo, and who was eyeing the yellow man warily, merely nodded. But when the iron gates opened, he joined the stream of men and women surging up the stairs, along the corridor, past the open and shut doors, and the Manchu sentries, to arrive panting, sweating and feeling that he might vomit at any moment, with Ketut and Tenga not far behind him, near the front of the queue for the food in the dining room.

His effort was rewarded when he reached the counter and he

was given a palm leaf of overcooked gray rice, a scoop of boiled yellow beans and a pot of watery soup with some shreds of un-identifiable meat in it. All this was served by a wizened and furi-ous old woman and two younger matronly types who were plainly family and who chattered violently in the Yawa dialect to each other—but spoke not a word to any of the slaves. Jun ate the lot in about thirty heartbeats and, very nearly full, and feeling the warmth of the food spreading throughout his body, he sat back on one of the benches and watched Ketut and Tenga finish their food in a more dignified manner. Jun saw a handful of late-comers standing in dismay by the counter, which was now being boarded up by the angry old woman. One of the latecomers was the pretty Yawanese girl Jun had sat beside during the first water break. Now that she realized that there was nothing left to eat, her round face streamed with tears.

He looked quickly away from her. For the first time that day he felt almost at ease, although his skinned hands throbbed and his back was a long sheet of pain.

The three of them went together to wash in the communal showers—both men and women washing in the icy water that trickled from bamboo spouts in the ceiling—and Jun was alarmed to see Kromo and his dwarfish little friend openly ogling him as he splashed his body and scrubbed the dust and stink of the mine from his skin. Kromo went so far as to blow him a blubbery kiss, cup his wet genitals in his hands and waggle his penis at him.

Later, sitting on one of the lower sleeping shelves, fed, clean but utterly unstrung by exhaustion, Tenga nodded at Kromo who was lounging on the far side of the room, and said, "If you don't want to suck that ugly fellow's cock, you are gonna have to kill him."

"What?" said Jun. "Kill him?" He thought he had misheard.

"He wants you. He is telling everybody he will have you. If you don't want to do what he wants, you'd better cut his throat in the dark of the night."

"I can't do that!" said Jun. "I couldn't just cold-bloodedly murder a person."

"You never killed a man before?" Tenga looked incredulous. "Tut told me you were some big chief, a king or something. And you never killed a man?"

"We are civilized people where I come from," said Jun.

Just then a scream rang out across the dormitory—suddenly cut off. Jun turned his head and saw that the pretty Yawanese peasant girl had been seized by a group of prisoners. She was quickly hauled over a table, held down by two big men; her raglike breeches were torn off her and she was briskly, brutally entered from behind by another slave. Jun looked around for the guards. There were none. He realized he hadn't seen one since they'd locked the dormitory doors after shower time.

"We should help her," he said, looking at Ketut and Tenga. "We *must* help her."

The first rapist had already satisfied his lust. He pulled out, wiped himself on one of her discarded rags and went around to help the two men holding her down. A second man took his place and began plunging away against her naked rear; a third and forth had formed a queue behind him.

Tenga shook her big head. "Not our problem. Against five or six men? One of us would get hurt, sure. Maybe you. Maybe little Tut. You can't work when you're hurt—and that's when you die in here. You might think you're a civilized man, King Jun, but you're not in civilization now. You're in the Hole. And you better listen to me, your Royal High and Mightiness: you gotta put down that mummy-fucker Kromo pretty quick or it will be you bent over the table being ripped and ruined like the poor little Yawa girl there."

CHAPTER 24

———— ⬥ ————

In the Great Cabin of the *Yotun,* a wide space that extended across the full beam of the ship, and which was brilliantly lit by the sun streaming through the wide, glass stern window, Katerina stared down at the pile of maps and charts on the mahogany table. The topmost map displayed Sumbu, and the Straits between that long island and the mangrove swamps of the Manchatka coast to its north.

"Come in a little closer, gentlemen, if you please," said Katerina, and the three senior officers of the 42nd Legion—Colonel Wang and his subordinates, Majors Lu Sung and Xi Chan—craned over the wide table to look at the map more closely.

It was two weeks since the assassination attempt and the long sea journey was nearing its end. She put a delicate fingertip on the map at the north end of Sumbu Island.

"Here is Istana Kush," she said. "The Gates of Stone. Our goal is to seize it and hold it indefinitely. Istana Kush is to be my base of operations for the foreseeable future."

The Han officers said nothing but Katerina noticed that they exchanged incredulous looks. She looked over by the door and saw that Ari Yoritomo stood there, hand on his sword hilt. He had apparently recovered to full health during the three days she had made him rest and had resumed his place at her side. They had not mentioned the assassination since.

"Here, to the northwest of the city of Istana Kush are the twin fortresses that make up the Gates of Stone: the Red Fort on the

Sumbu coast and the Green Fort over the water on the Manchatka side. As you can see, they are less than eight hundred paces apart and all shipping that comes into the Laut Besar by this route must pass between them, under their guns. The eight cannon in the Red Fort, mounted on wheeled caissons, manned by fifty skilled men of the Honorable Artillery Company are accurate to a range of twelve hundred paces. They are defended by a company of well-trained Dokra musketeers. The six guns in the smaller Green Fort on the Manchatka side have a similar range and are manned by thirty Honorable Artillerymen—but guarded by only a single platoon of Dokra. It is an unpopular posting, the Green Fort, being far from the brothels, obat-dens and taverns of the city and stuck in the middle of a steaming mangrove swamp, and it is often used as a punishment post. No one wants to be sent to the Green Fort. It is, I am told, a place of poor order, slack discipline, occupied by bored, resentful soldiers."

Katerina caught one of the majors raising an eyebrow at his colleague, as if to say, "Why is this slip of a girl telling us all this?"

She said, "The morale of the men in the Green Fort is crucial to my plan. Now, if you please, gentlemen, I would like your full attention."

Katerina put a finger on the western side of Sumbu. "This part of the island is impenetrable swamp. Like Manchatka on the other side of the Strait, it affords no landing places for boats or ships, the waters are infested by large saltwater crocodiles and huge snakes, and men cannot travel over it except with the greatest difficulty and danger. We cannot approach the Gates of Stone from here."

She moved her finger down the western coast of the island. "Twelve miles to the south, however, there is a small cove with a gently shelving bottom and a white-sand beach. Kara Bay, it is called. This is where the *Yotun* will make landfall, and here we will disembark a force comprised of two hundred Legionnaires. This is our launchpad for the capture of Istana Kush. I shall require your best troops, gentlemen, if you please. I want you to handpick them for me. Men used to hardship, who can march for days through difficult terrain, fight and win a battle at the end of it."

She had the officers' full attention now. "I also want at least thirty gunners from the ships—again our best; tough, adaptable men—to accompany the Legionnaires on the march. Every member of my Niho bodyguard will also join the landing party."

Now Katerina traced a line down the center of Sumbu, following a long, thin mountain range: "This is the Barat Cordillera, the spine of the Island of Sumbu. And here, in the center, is Mount Barat, the soaring husk of a former volcano, one of the tallest and most remote mountains in the Laut Besar, where, according to local legend, the Garuda birds make their nests and raise their young on the highest peaks."

"Ha, Garuda birds! These people really are simple savages if they still believe in them," said Major Sung. "What's next? Firebreathing witch monsters? Ghost Tigers?"

"If you are neither going to listen quietly nor to make a useful contribution to this briefing, Major Sung, then please feel free to leave us," said Katerina.

"Keep your mouth shut, Sung, and your ears open," snapped Colonel Wang, and he glowered at his subordinate, who was now flushing with anger.

"So we land our men here, at Kara Bay. The terrain is thick jungle—very thick, so we will travel slowly. We march east making for the Barat Cordillera, which is about five miles away. However, I think we need to account a full day for the landing and to reach the southern slopes of the mountain range, where we will camp for the night.

The three Legion officers said nothing.

"Meanwhile," Katerina continued, "the three ships will make their way north from Kara Bay, following the coast and they will come round the headland and anchor at Loku Beach. This is the Federation holding berth for ships wishing to enter the Laut Besar. They wait here until the negotiations, taxes and tariffs on trade goods, suitable passports and so on, have been agreed upon with the Federation officials at Istana Kush. The beach lies under the guns of the Red Fort. Our three ships will stay there posing as the vessels of merchants from Ostraka hoping to make themselves rich trading in the Laut Besar.

"The ships will wait there for two days, no more—any longer and the Federation officials will become suspicious about their true intentions. Meanwhile, the landing force will march north along the Barat Cordillera in stealth, remaining out of view on the western side of the ridge. We will then come down into the farmlands to the west of Istana Kush, ideally during the night of the second day or very early in the morning of the third, and pass through them as quickly and quietly as two-hundred-and-forty-odd men can, and assault the Red Fort from the landward side, a little before dawn. We aim to surprise the garrison, and capture the fort as quickly as we can."

"I beg your pardon, Highness," said Colonel Wang, "but you keep using the word 'we' to describe this landing party. Can you tell us exactly who 'we' is, if you please. Who, for example, will be in command of this extremely difficult and dangerous mission?"

Katerina looked at Wang. "I am sorry if I have not been clear, Colonel. I shall be in command, of course, and one of your majors—I don't mind which, you can choose the more suitable of the two—shall accompany me as my aide and second-in-command."

"My dear little lady," said Major Sung, "I'm not sure that you understand what this mission will entail. The men will have to hack their way through dense jungle—dealing with the heat, insects, snakes and whatnot—then traverse the side of a bare mountain for a dozen miles, some of it in the darkness. Then cross cultivated lands in secrecy. Then assault a Federation fort, manned with their crack Dokra mercenaries and the best defenses that their deep pockets can supply. It is clearly not a task for a young girl, no matter how game."

Katerina's stare was pure ice. "I understand perfectly what this mission entails, Major Sung. I have planned it in great detail, over several months. However, I do think we have just now resolved one of the minor points. Major Chan will accompany me as my second-in-command in the landing party. You, Major Sung, will remain with the ships."

"You think that is a punishment?" said Sung. "Very well, I accept it, but I must tell you that this is a fool's mission. Likely to be a complete disaster. It would be hard to accomplish even if the force were commanded by a seasoned Legionnaire officer. It cannot be done under the command of a girl with no military experience who wants to play at soldiers."

"You begin to irritate me, Major Sung. And if you do not hold your tongue, I am likely to do something that I may regret later—and that you will regret immediately."

Ari Yoritomo took a step forward, his hand still on his katana.

The eyes of the three Legion officers immediately flicked toward him. Their hands went to their own swords. They all knew the tales of the Niho knights and their ruthlessness.

There was an uncomfortable silence for about five heartbeats. Then Colonel Wang said, "My apologies, Highness, for my colleague's inexcusable rudeness. Would you kindly continue the briefing. I can guarantee there will be no more interruptions."

He shifted his shiny boot and trod down hard on Major Sung's toes.

"Speed is crucial," said Katerina. "We must capture the Red Fort before the Governor of Istana Kush or any of his Federation staff are aware of what is happening. If they were able to reinforce the Red Fort in any strength, then our assault would be little more than suicide. We have too few men for a prolonged fight and no artillery. But with surprise and speed, I believe it may be done. I have no military experience, that is true. But I have studied the textbooks—all of the great military authors. I have read numerous accounts of the terrain. And the Conclave of the Venerables was kind enough to give me their very latest intelligence on the region. It can be done, gentlemen. Have faith in me. But I will require maximum efficiency from the men and full cooperation from all members of my staff."

The three officers looked at her but said nothing.

"The next part of the plan also needs to be done quickly," she continued. "Once we have taken the Red Fort, we must immediately train its guns on the Green Fort on the other side of the Strait. The Green Fort is well within range of the Red Fort's cannon and I believe that we can destroy it or drive off the defenders fairly briskly. We do not wish to allow them to fire upon us, so it is crucial that we dispatch or disperse them as soon as possible. Fortunately, they are not well motivated to die nobly at their posts. Their morale is poor, as I said. I believe that they will abandon their posts and run away into the safety of the jungle when attacked." She looked again at the officers, to see if they grasped her point.

Again she was met with silence.

Katerina was speeding up her speech now; she knew it. Their silent opposition to her plan was causing her temper to fray and she wanted to be rid of these three idiots as soon as possible. The plan was achievable. It could be done; she knew that. But that smug prick Sung's jibe about a mere girl in command of a dangerous mission was burning at her like a live coal in the belly.

"I will fire a red rocket to signal that the Red Fort has been taken. Although the sound of the cannon will no doubt alert you to the fact that the assault has begun. The rocket will be the signal for the ships to weigh anchor at Loku Beach and prepare to sail. A green rocket will signify that the Green Fort has been destroyed. At that moment, and under your orders, Colonel Wang, *Yotun*, *Egil* and *Sar* will proceed through the Gates of Stone, completely unmolested by either fort, and will commence bombardment of the harbor defenses of Istana Kush itself, as well as dealing with any enemy shipping. The cannon of the Red Fort will be re-deployed to assist you. With enfilade fire from the fort, and your own powerful ship-based cannonade, Colonel, I believe we should be able to reduce the harbor defenses quickly and land our assault troops in the small boats with little, and possibly even no resistance."

Katerina paused, took a breath. "The final part of the plan is an assault on the Governor's Palace, the city's last redoubt. I am certain that with the combined firepower of the ships and the re-deployed cannon of the Red Fort, the walls can be swiftly breached. Then the Legion will assault and capture the palace and all Istana Kush will be in our hands.

"There is one final thing, gentlemen. There is a small harbor on the eastern side of Istana which I mean to leave unmolested until the rest of the city is in our hands. That will allow the Governor and his staff, and perhaps some of the Federation troops to flee. We want them to be pushed out, gentlemen. I don't want any death or glory, no heroic last stands. We leave them an exit, and hope with all our hearts that they use it. Likewise any shipping that tries to escape—let it go. So, there it is. This is the plan. This is what we will do. And by the end of the third day after the advance force's landing at Kara Bay, or fourth at the very latest, I expect Istana Kush, gateway to the Laut Besar, to be mine."

Was it her imagination? Katerina thought she could detect a slight smile of admiration on the Colonel's face. Or was he just quietly laughing at her?

"Are there any questions?" she asked.

"I think you have done a superb job in planning this operation,

Highness," said Wang smoothly. "Really very competent. I do not think any *man* in the Legion High Command or on the hallowed benches of the Conclave Hall could have done it better. However, I do have one small question—what happens if the dawn assault on the Red Fort fails?"

"You have put your finger on the crux of it, Colonel. I commend you."

"Thank you, Highness. And what is your answer?"

"If the assault on the Red Fort fails—and I must stress that I do not think this likely—then I will *not* send up a red rocket on the morning of the third day and you, Colonel Wang, and you, Major Sung, will oblige me by immediately taking my three ships home to Ostraka, then marching the Legion back to the Celestial Republic, where you will offer my thanks, along with my eternal regrets, to the Conclave of Venerables."

"What are you saying, Highness?" Colonel Wang's smile had now disappeared.

"I am saying that if I do not manage to surprise and quickly take the Red Fort, then I, my bodyguards and the two hundred Legionnaires with me will undoubtedly be wiped out by the vastly superior force ranged against us. Everything, this whole campaign, hinges on the capture of Red Fort. If we do not take it swiftly, we shall all be dead."

CHAPTER 25

The sorcerer looked down at the Eye of the Dragon as it nestled in a bed of wood shavings in a timber box in the dim hull of the *Sea Serpent*. The ship was three days out from Sukatan, on a northwesterly bearing, heeling over at a slight angle with a stiff easterly breeze across her starboard bow. He could clearly hear the hissing wash of the sea along her wooden flank as she surged through the waves.

Mangku put out his bandaged left hand, slowly, and touched the smooth, cool surface of the huge green-and-white gemstone with his fingertips. It was the first time he had laid his flesh on it—and he felt a small jolt of magical power surge up his arm at the contact.

That was a vast relief. His information about the Keys came mostly from ancient palm-leaf manuscripts that were often incomplete and some of which were so decayed that they were almost crumbled to dust. There was plenty of room for error. Indeed, there was one Key that he had very little information about at all. He had only just begun his preliminary studies into the myth of the Seven Keys when he had been expelled from the Mother Temple. For decades he did not believe they truly existed, or if they did, that they genuinely had the kind of power that the old stories promised. In fact, it had taken him ten years even to come up with a list of six of the Seven that he had enough confidence in to act upon. But there had been no error here. The Eye was, without a doubt, one of the Keys of Power—and it was finally in his possession.

Even with Raja Widojo's mind and body under his control, it had been a difficult and bloody task to extract the huge, gold-encased gemstone from Sukatan. Indeed, it had been much harder than he had expected. The common people had rioted in the arena at Widojo's announcement and the violence and unrest had spread throughout the city like a contagion.

He and the Raja had been forced to take shelter in the palace for the rest of that day, surrounded by hundreds of armed guards, while the citizens of Sukatan had raved and roared outside the walls, and demanded that the Eye remain in their city and the necromancer who had poisoned their Raja's mind be handed over to them for summary justice. The only consolation for a wasted day had been the chance to send the ridiculous Wukarta prince-ling and his girl-servant to the mines. That would teach the arrogant puppy to try to extract vengeance from Hiero Mangku. It had been a pleasure to punish him.

He had spotted the boy across the arena, picked him out from the crowds when he sensed that someone was agitating against him. He was the only one who did not grub about on the ground for the copper coins dispensed by Raja Widojo's servants. It made him stand out like a goat dropping in a rice bowl. Pride. Always the downfall of these Wukarta usurpers. He was too proud to gather up the largesse offered by his richer cousin.

After the guards had seized him, he had considered ordering his immediate execution—through Widojo's mouth, of course—but it had seemed more amusing to condemn the boy to a slow death. His own Ebu people were daily sent to the mines in scores—it was fitting that a prince of the Usurpers, a living symbol of the race that had enslaved his people, should suffer as they did. The boy would be beaten and raped until he was no more than walking meat, then he would be worked like a mule in the darkness until his spirit gave out and his wasted flesh was flung into a pit, or whatever they did with used-up bodies there.

One day, Mangku told himself, when he had assembled all the Keys, when he came into his full power, he would close the Konda Pali mine for good—and liberate all the poor damned Ebu souls imprisoned there. But that would be far too late for the Wukarta whelp.

On the morning of the second day in Sukatan, the riot appeared to have burned itself out. So Mangku had summoned fifty men from the *Sea Serpent* as an escort to take the Dragon's Eye back to the ship. Widojo was spent by then; he had retired to his apartments whimpering about a headache. Mangku knew the Wukarta Raja did not have long in this world. The beetle would spread rot throughout his brain after a day or two, as these magical creations always did. It was no matter. Good riddance to another member of that dynasty.

When he finally took his leave of the palace and began to head down to the harbor, the Dragon's Eye safely boxed in a bed of wood shavings and surrounded by his fifty men, he saw the devastation that the riot had caused in the town: fire-blackened buildings, looted emporiums, men and women still drunk on obat or rice wine wandering about in confused states. But it was not long before he realized he had made a mistake—and a bad one.

The riot was not quite extinguished and some of the Sukatan folk he passed recognized him from his appearance in the arena, sitting next to Raja Widojo.

"That's the fellow Mangku, the one they say poisoned the Raja's mind," one fat little old man shouted as he passed them, his gray sarong pulled over his head against the sun, pointing at the sorcerer in the center of his phalanx of sailors.

"He's the one told Widojo to give away our Eye!" shouted a workingman.

A stone or two had been thrown. Someone standing on a rooftop had dropped a slate into the crowd of *Sea Serpent* men, smashing the eye socket of one of the pirates and dropping him to the ground. And a ragged musket volley from Mangku's sailors in return had killed the slate-dropper, as well as an old woman standing a few paces away, who was merely looking out curiously over the rail at the noisy street entertainment below.

It was a spark. And there was tinder aplenty. It seemed to Mangku that, at the death of that one insignificant crone, the whole city erupted again in an explosion of noise and fury. The light shower of stones thrown by mildly angry Sukatan citizens suddenly became a raging storm. Bricks and boulders lashed down on them from the buildings on either side. The fifty men of the *Sea Serpent* were battered, gashed, some hauled bodily out of their formation and ripped into pieces by many snatching hands in the surrounding crowds.

Someone with a pistol fired into the mass of *Sea Serpent* men. The bullet smashed the skull of a big hatchet-man standing protectively next to Mangku, showering the sorcerer with hot brains and blood . . .

They had only been saved from being quite literally torn apart by a bold sally from the ship once they reached the harbor road. A squad of musket men had leaped from the *Sea Serpent*, formed up, and, with a reckless disregard for their own safety, they had advanced on their surviving comrades, now huddled around their master and his prize, shooting volleys into the crowds and stabbing almost at random with their spike bayonets at any man, woman or child within reach. Mangku had grasped his staff, sliced his poor palm again and used his own blood magic to blast cones of green ichor-fire into the mob, incinerating dozens, and creating a lane down which he and his men could withdraw. The crowds had pulled back at this supernatural onslaught, bloody, singed and still furious—but now wary. At last, Mangku and the box containing the Eye had been taken on board—and they had cut their cables, abandoning their anchors, hauled up a sail and got the *Sea Serpent* under way in short order. It had been close,

Mangku knew, and if things had gone a different way, he and all his crew might be dead.

But they were not dead—and he now had the Eye.

Still, he *had* badly miscalculated. As the *Sea Serpent* drew clear of the harbor and headed out into open water, Mangku had pondered his mistake.

The extreme fury of the people of Sukatan might seem to be a natural response to the loss of an object as magnificent as the Eye, but the sorcerer knew that it was not; it was not a natural response at all. He had detected a presence there in the arena, and afterward in the violent city streets, a disruption in the flow of the world, a sensation similar to a bad smell, but purely of the mind, which indicated the activities of a practitioner of the ancient arts. Someone had stirred up the people to attack him and his crew. It was not another sorcerer, Mangku was certain of that: the motions of another of his own kind would have been a blaring disruption to all his senses, like a psychic firework, an explosion of mental sound and color. And there were few sorcerers left in the world, anyway, and none now in Yawa. Besides, this was much more subtle. Someone was working against him and using one of the old techniques of the Vharkashta priests to sway the temper of the crowd. And Mangku knew then who it must be: it must be Semar.

Was that ridiculous old goat still following him around the world? He had thought himself rid of his pestilential presence after Dhilika the year before.

Mangku had been on the hunt for the Key of Wood, a venerable wooden staff carved from a tree that legend said the God Vharkash himself had sat under and prayed for rain, and which his researches had indicated was to be found in a back room of the Dhilika Museum of Antiquities, probably dusty, cobwebbed and long forgotten. However, his quest for the staff had proved fruitless—he had searched the museum and interrogated the curator and all his people—but the antique wooden staff was not there. Then he had discovered the presence of Semar in the same city, watching him, skulking in dark corners, talking to the very same people he was talking to.

He had informed a contact in the local security service that Semar was a spy for the Lord of the Islands; he had even told this agent where Semar could be found. It should have been enough to have the sanctimonious old worm carried off to the Amrit Shakti cells never to be seen again, but evidently Semar had escaped the cells or evaded the attentions of this usually efficient organization. For here he was again, in Sukatan, sniffing around, interfering in Mangku's business, stirring up the people against him. He would make properly sure of the meddlesome old buffoon next time he encountered him: a good blast of green ichor-fire and he would make no more trouble in this world.

He closed the top of the wooden box, shutting out the Eye of the Dragon from the meager light. He tapped it down tight with a pry bar and moved over to a similar box, farther along, where despite generating a flash of pain from his gashed hand he managed to lever open the lid. Inside, once more cradled in wood shavings, out of its sheath, freshly oiled and glinting dimly, lay the ancestral blade of the Wukarta.

Mangku took a grip of the worn wooden handle and lifted the kris out of its bed. The blade was thin and worn with use and pitted with age now, but the lines were still classically elegant. He passed the blade through a beam of sunlight, slicing it through the air. This was undoubtedly the greatest of all the Keys—and he felt a joy in its possession that outweighed any of his concerns about Semar. The ancient weapon seemed to shimmer with its own potential and Mangku was reminded of the ancient legend that the spirit of a woman who came from beyond the heavens had been trapped inside. Perhaps it was even true. He sliced the blade one-handed through the air, once, twice, then gently, reluctantly placed it back in its nesting of soft shavings, replaced the lid of the box and tapped it shut.

Two Keys he had, two of the Seven that he needed. One Key for each of the seven elements: metal, earth, air, water, fire, wood—and Ji or life force, the most precious element of them all. Ji was the element that animated all living things. Some of the ancients had called it ether; some called it the soul. And Mangku was not entirely sure, if he was honest, what form the Key of Ji would take. His research was still incomplete. But he would discover it in time; of that he was entirely certain. One Key of Power existed for each of the Seven Hells. He possessed the Key of Metal, the Kris of Wukarta Khodam; now, too, he possessed the Key of Earth, the Eye of the Dragon. What had once seemed no more than a grand dream was becoming reality. Five more Keys to find—only five. He could feel the spirits of his Ebu ancestors smiling upon him. The Master, the wise friend who had set him on this path all those years ago, would be proud of him.

"Lord," said a voice behind him, and Mangku whirled, suddenly flooded with a kind of guilt, as if he were a Temple novice again who had been caught in some illicit action.

It was Arif, a cringing little man, ugly as a bag of toads, that Mangku had plucked from the crew to be his servant, to cook his meals, clean his cabin and wash his clothes, although he had nothing in the way of magical skill or ability—he was not even a very good cook. He was, however, as pure-blooded an Ebu as one could find these days.

"It's the men—they want to speak with you," Arif said. He seemed to be even more frightened than usual.

"What? All of them?" Mangku had meant it as a mild jest but humor was not very prominent among his talents.

"Yes, lord," his servant said. "They sent me to summon you."

"Summon me? I am not a person to be summoned. What do they want?"

Arif could not meet his eye. "They are all on deck, lord."

"Well, then, we had better go and see what this nonsense is all about."

In the bright sunlight on the deck of the *Sea Serpent*, more than a hundred of the crew had gathered in a murmuring crowd. Mangku clambered out of the hatchway and made his way up to the quarterdeck so that he could look out over the mass of raggedy men below him. He felt a sense of trepidation, almost of bewilderment and fear, when he looked out at the sea of faces. Although he made very sure that it could not be detected. Demons he could command, servants did his bidding or they were dismissed, but this crew was different. They were used to the freedom of the Brotherhood of the Sea, the pirates' code of equality, in which every man, however stupid or ill informed, had his say and could dispute with the captain. These men knew the power at his disposal, they knew that he could destroy any one of them with a flash of green fire, but still they persisted in their stubborn individualism.

Mangku was by nature a man who operated alone. He had had almost no friends at the Temple, although he had some companions whom he tolerated, and since then he had wandered the Earth either alone or with a single servant. He had never needed to learn the art of leadership. He had no idea how to make men follow him. All he had was the fear he could inspire in them. He leaned on his long staff and tried to lock eyes with some of the men in the front rank, one after the other. But they all shied away from his angry glare.

"I am told that you wished to summon me. Summon *me!*" said Mangku. "Well, I am here. What is it that you require of me?"

Nobody spoke. The murmuring began again. He looked over his men—apart from a few up in the rigging as lookouts, and two men on the tiller, they seemed to be all here. It was a depleted company and one that bore the cruel marks of battle. Bandaged men, bloody faces, some with arms in slings—they looked haggard, too. Deeply tired.

"Well? What do you want?" Mangku left the question hanging in the air. No one answered it. "If you have nothing to say, I will ask you to return to your duties."

Mangku turned his back on the men and began to walk to the taffrail, feigning an interest in the long wake that stretched out behind the bow of the *Sea Serpent*.

"Your Holiness," said a voice, and Mangku turned on his heel. "Ah, someone has found the courage to speak!"

A tall, broad-shouldered ebony-black man had pushed through the ranks of his comrades. His face was scarred with the tribal marks of his Ziran Atari clan. A long, vicious-looking chopper hung from a loop of his leather belt.

"Yes, Kanto—what do you wish to say to me?"

The tall man straightened his shoulders and looked directly at the sorcerer.

"We think, begging your pardon, Your Holiness, that is me and my fellows, we think, ah, that with all possible respect . . ."

"Yes, what is it? What do you think?"

"We think there has been too . . . too much fighting for too little reward." The tall man said this all in a rush, as if he could not wait to get it all out.

There was a mumble of assent from the ranks behind him.

"Is that so? Interesting. How can you say there has been too little reward? We have in the hold beneath our feet two of the greatest treasures in the whole of the Laut Besar, perhaps the whole world. I would say that was a magnificent reward for our efforts so far."

The Atari warrior seemed to take heart that he had not yet been blasted with green fire.

"An old sword and a big colored rock," scoffed the man. "Can't eat them; can't drink them; can't fuck them, begging Your Holiness's pardon. We got no big bags of shiny silver ringgu; no fat fingers of pure gold. No pretty little slave girls to play with . . ."

Mangku sighed. "You have sufficient meat and drink aboard, there is obat, too—and if it's silver you want, I can promise that at this journey's end . . ."

"We've lost fifty good men, Your Holiness." Kanto was fidgeting on his feet, his hands twisting against themselves in front of his belly, but seemed determined to say his piece. "Fifty-two men out of the two hundred and ten we set out with is now dead. Meat and drink is no use to them. Neither is obat. And half of us still alive is cruelly wounded, some so badly they'll likely not live. You promised us plunder when we signed on in Singarasam and apart from that shitty old sword and the Eye of Sukatan, we've seen little enough of that."

Mangku looked at the Ziran Atari warrior, dominating him with his cracked gray eyes. The man broke his gaze and looked down at his feet.

"What we have achieved, through your courageous actions in battle, is so much greater than a few sacks of ringgu, a few chests of gaudy jewels—can you not understand that? We are about to change the world—and it is all for your benefit. Must I explain all this again?"

No one answered the sorcerer. He gave another great sigh.

"If we gather the Seven Keys, we will be more powerful than any force in the Laut Besar. Can you not get that through your thick skulls? With the Seven Keys in our possession our kind will rule the Earth. The Usurpers—the Wukarta, the overseers, the merchants, the slave-masters, all the bosses—will be swept away and the Ebu—our people—will be left as the sole inheritors of all the wealth that they have gathered. For too long your people, our people, have been enslaved, despised, worked like cattle to enrich the New People, the Usurpers. No longer. It will all be ours. All of it. Everything. Gold, jewels, slave girls—anything you desire will be yours. The whole world will be yours for the taking!"

If Mangku had been expecting cheers at his speech, he was to be disappointed.

"That's all well and good, Your Holiness. For the future. But in the meantime, we would like to do a little plundering, a bit of good old-fashioned pirating, get some of that silver in our pockets, get a few of those slave girls in our bunks—right now, sir, on account, if you like, or as an advance of us inheriting the whole world. That's what we was all thinking, sir."

Rage boiled inside Mangku's brain. He was within a hair of pointing his long staff at the big black imbecile, cutting his own flesh and blasting him to bloody shreds. But he managed somehow to control himself. *They are but sheep and I am their shepherd,* he thought. Besides, if he started killing his own crew, his own people, where would it end? And they *were* his own people—each man picked individually because of his Ebu heritage, not a full-blooded descendant of the New People among them. And they *would* be the inheritors of the world, if only he could make them understand their true role.

"Very well, if it is plunder that you seek, I shall indulge you this one time. The next appropriate ship to cross our path shall be your prey. We shall attack it and the spoils will be shared out equally to all. And if we see no ship I shall select a small port or coastal town for your attentions in the next few days or weeks. Will that satisfy you?"

Mangku did not wait for an answer. "Now if there is nothing else, I shall be in my cabin. And I would be obliged if you would all now quietly return to your duties."

CHAPTER 26

———— ❧ ————

Jun thought that he would not sleep. The pitiful whimpering
of the Yawanese girl from the far side of the dormitory dis-
turbed him, filling him at first with a scalding guilt, then a
quite unreasonable anger at her weakness. Also there was the
lurking fear that Kromo would come over to pester him in some
revolting fashion during the dark hours. However, after such a
brutal day of unaccustomed labor, his physical exhaustion proved
to be too great and, although he tried to keep one eye on the other
still forms in the dormitory, the next thing he knew after his head
touched the greasy boards of the bed-shelf was the gray light of
dawn flooding into the dormitory, and he was sitting up stiffly,
every muscle and joint aching, and scrubbing his face with his
torn and blistered hands.

He fervently wished, not for the first time in recent days, that
he was back in the Watergarden and his cheerful servants were
busy preparing a hot soapy bath for him and a hearty breakfast of
fried eggs with pickled vegetables, fried rice, just-caught fish and
a big scalding pot of Han tea.

What he actually received, after the doors of the dormitory
were unlocked and they were allowed to hurry along to the dining room, was a bowl of lukewarm watery rice porridge, several
days old, reheated and burned, and smelling strongly of rotting
fish. He swilled it down anyway: he was learning. In the Hole, you
eat when you can. And quickly.

In the elevator down to the cavern, he saw Kromo leering at

him from the far side of the cage. He stared straight back at him, considering the advice Tenga had given him. There must have been something new, perhaps harder, more dangerous in Jun's eyes, for Kromo suddenly dropped his gaze and looked away.

The two musket-armed Manchu herded them along the dark tunnel to the ore-face, as they had the day before, and set them to their labor with cries of, "Work! You work." As Jun bent and began to pick up the first chunks of ore he felt all his muscles protesting but, as the cuts from yesterday's whips were still fresh he did not dare to pause or reduce his pace. Tenga and Ketut formed their usual partnership and swiftly began lobbing lumps of ore in the wagon with a minimum of effort.

Jun looked covertly at Kromo, who was wielding the hammer again today with his dwarfish friend, and energetically smashing the larger boulders of ore into smaller, more manageable chunks. The yellow man looked big and strong and full of life, the muscles of his shoulders swelling and writhing with each stroke of the heavy hammer. Could he actually kill this fellow? Jun wondered as he worked. Was he capable of the act—not just capable morally, but in terms of physical strength? Could he defeat him? No, was the short answer. While he might have been incessantly nagged by War-Master Hardan to do his exercises, he had never used any of the skills he had learned against a real, live opponent. An opponent who would fight back. A big, ugly, brutal opponent well versed in the violence of the Hole. He couldn't do it. He couldn't kill Kromo. It was just not possible. Or was it? What would Hardan have done in this situation? What would he advise his pupil to do?

He noticed as he bent and heaved up and dumped the ore in the wagon that the pretty Yawanese girl was struggling—her face was white and tear-streaked and her movements had a shaking, random unsteadiness as if she was fevered or on the very edge of collapse. Then, quite suddenly, she stopped work and fell to the floor, curled into a tight little ball and began to sob, her thin frame shuddering with every wet, tortured breath. The Manchu guards were on her like weasels on a shrew, the whips thudding down on her near-naked body but, to Jun's surprise, she refused to get up, lying there and allowing the blows to cut into her flesh again and again. She wanted to die, Jun realized with a leap of intuition, after being defiled by so many men the evening before, and perhaps during the night, too; after being denied food, sleep and human comfort, and with nothing but more degradation staring her in the face, forever, she wanted this existence to be over as quickly as possible.

He slid a glance across at Kromo, who was leaning on his long hammer a few feet away and watching the savage whipping with a sly grin on his ugly yellow face—this was what that muscle-clad brute had in store for him if he did not submit to his kisses, his caresses, his disgusting desires. He would become a piece of meat just like that poor Yawanese girl: broken, bloody, begging for a swift end to it all.

No. No. A thousand times no.

Jun made his decision.

The Manchus stopped beating the girl. Both of them panting, the sweat dripping down their flat, alien faces. One said something to the other, a joke of some sort, in their own language. The other one laughed. The joker blew his whistle indicating that it was water-break time—although the work gang had only been laboring for an hour or so—and the second Manchu slung a trio of leather waterskins toward the slaves, who had all as usual immediately collapsed on the floor. Jun picked up the nearest skin and drank deeply of the warm, musty-tasting water it contained.

The two Manchus, their muskets on their shoulders, picked up the Yawanese girl, each one taking an arm. Jun could see that she was still alive; indeed she struggled feebly when they hauled her to her feet. Then, half dragging her between them, they disappeared off into the darkness heading back toward the elevators. They did not go far. From out of the darkness, Jun heard the girl give a frightened scream, which was followed by a lustful chuckle, and the sound of a slap.

Here was his chance. It was now or never. Jun picked up the skin of water with his left hand. His right hand closed around a piece of ore the size of a mango. Keeping his right hand hidden, no feat in the dim light, he scrambled over toward Kromo, holding out the waterskin and carefully keeping his face blank. Just as the brute reached out his hand to take the water, Jun dropped it and, as Kromo cursed him and bent to pick it up, Jun leaped forward and smashed the rock in his right hand as hard as he could onto the side of his enemy's face. It was a fine blow, well dealt; the piece of ore shattered into fragments in Jun's fingers, and Kromo was knocked down onto his knees. It was a good hard strike, one that would have felled a normal man. If Jun had received it, he'd have been smashed into oblivion. And it clearly hurt Kromo badly—but it did not finish him.

The big man came up from his knees into a fighting crouch, glaring at Jun, a trickle of blood running from his left ear but saying nothing. He leaped forward, quick as a leopard, and swung, his right fist flashing out toward Jun's face with all the power of his muscle-slabbed shoulder behind it.

Without thought, Jun's left arm came up and round in a crisp block, forearm thwacked against forearm, and the massive punch slipped safely past his left ear. Again without any conscious thought, Jun's right fist shot out like a piston, the two knuckles leading, and crunched into Kromo's mouth, mashing his lips against his teeth. Jun hit him again, this time with his left fist, a more considered blow, with full follow-through, that cracked into his cheekbone and knocked his head right back.

Kromo stepped back, his senses blurred, his face bloodied. He was surprised. Shocked, even. He had taken three hard, punishing blows to the head in a few short moments and he felt dizzy and dazed. Jun was, in fact, no less surprised than Kromo by his own actions. He had never thought that all those tedious combat lessons with Hardan would actually bear fruit. But it seemed those thousands of hours of punching, kicking, blocking, learning the routines, grappling with the War-Master and tumbling on the rice-straw mats, all that sweat and pain, all those afternoons of sheer bloody boredom had actually served a purpose. He could almost hear Hardan's clipped voice ordering him briskly to deliver that kick-punch-kick combination that he favored most.

Jun obeyed.

He stepped in, raised his knee, and his right foot shot out and smacked deep into Kromo's belly; as his opponent grunted and came bending forward, gasping for breath, Jun's left fist chopped down into the right side of his jaw, knocking him around. Then Jun spun to his left, whirling all the way around, gaining momentum; his left leg lashed out, the flat of his sole catching Kromo under the jaw and hurling him up and back, right off his feet, to land with a crunch on the pile of ore.

He sensed danger, spun to his right, and saw the dwarf, with his hammer raised, begin to run at him, snarling. But a long black arm swooped out and seized the little man by the shoulder as he passed, hauling him round. In an instant, Tenga had her thick arms wrapped around the dwarf's neck. She gave one brutal twist, there was a horrible snapping sound, and the dwarf, released, tumbled lifeless to the floor.

"Finish him," growled Tenga, jerking her chin at the big shambling creature struggling to rise from the ore pile. "Do it quick, before the bannermen come back."

Jun advanced on Kromo. The big man rose and swung a fist clumsily at the slim youth—who blocked him easily, dipped and sank a punch deep under his ribs. Kromo sat down hard. Jun snap-kicked him full in the face, crushing his nose, knocking him back

onto the ore slope once more. Kromo got up again—*by the Gods,*
thought Jun, *the man is harder than teak*—and made a stumbling
run at Jun, aiming to ram his head into his belly. Jun dodged, and
drove an elbow hard down onto Kromo's spine as he passed. The
big man plowed into the earth. Jun leaped on him, landing with
one knee and his full weight on his midspine, punching all the air
from his lungs. He straddled Kromo's broad back, seized the
man's greasy hair with his left hand, pulled his head back and
punched hard with two knuckles of his right hand at the point
where his skull met his backbone. He felt the crack of spine under
his fist. It was a killing blow, or so the War-Master had assured
him. But Kromo was still groaning. The man seemed indestruc-
tible. He flipped his body over, stood upright and looked down at
his adversary. The mad eyes were rolling in his head. Blood was
running from his crushed nose and slack mouth. Jun felt the red
rage flood through his whole body—all the indignities, all the
pain, the whippings, the forced labor, the foul food and the constant fear of violence and death. All that fury came out in the one
hard stamp that he delivered to Kromo's open neck. His heel
crunched through cartilage, thumped painfully against the bone.
Kromo's eyes rolled in his head; his face grew dark with blood, a
bloody froth seeping from his lips. His body was still but the head
was moving, jerking slightly side to side. Jun picked up a large
piece of ore, twice the size of the one he had first used, and sharply
pointed at the end. He tipped Kromo's head to one side, exposing
the right ear and temple. He raised his arms in the air, the piece
of ore gripped between his palms, like a man holding up a trophy
in a gesture of victory, then he smashed the rock down onto his
enemy's skull with all his strength.

    "Hai! Stop that!" A whip came from the darkness, the lash curl-
ing around Jun's ribs in a jolt of white agony. The two Manchu
were back—there was no sign of the Yawanese girl. One had his

musket off his shoulder; he was pointing it at Jun, the spike bayo-net glinting evilly in the dim light.

"Back, back." The Manchu was prodding the spike toward Jun, who moved cautiously away. The guard knelt beside the body of Kromo.

He said something to his comrade, evidently reporting Kromo's demise. Then he went over to the dwarf at Tenga's feet.

The two Manchu stood together and looked at Jun. Both had their muskets in their hands. Their eyes were black, hard and shiny as obsidian.

"These two dead," said one of them. "You kill. Now you dead."

The Manchu turned and pointed at Tenga, then at Ketut, who was standing beside her, then at Jun again. "You all dead."

CHAPTER 27

---◦◦◦---

Extract from *Ethnographic Travels* by
Professor Tolmund K. Parehki of the University of Dhilika

*Into the vacuum left by the collapse of the Wukarta Empire stepped
the Han merchant-pirates, setting up their fortified base on the un-
inhabited marshy island of Singarasam some three hundred years
ago and slowly spreading their tentacles all across the Laut Besar.
So the Wukarta faded away, and the Lords of the Islands rose in
their place—but the Mother Temple endured the change. It did not
return to its old bloodletting magical ways, nor did it insist on collecting its wealth-creating tithes. It even eschewed trade, relin-
quishing all that to the rapacious Han merchants. Instead, the
High Priest of the Vharkashta embraced the spiritual life and as his
piety grew so did his renown, and with that his spiritual power:
soon he and his successors commanded the obedience of hundreds
of thousands of souls across the seas from the Mother Temple in
Yawa. Daughter temples sprang up like mushrooms in cities across
the Laut Besar.*

*About fifty years ago, however, disaster struck: the Mother
Temple was destroyed by a great fire. No one knows how it happened but the stories go that a great sorcerer in a fit of rage smashed
all the buildings into a thousand pieces and killed or drove off all
the priests and novices. Certainly the Mother Temple is no more:
the jungle has reclaimed it. Alas, such is the transitory glory of the
world, as fleeting and lovely as the life of the Golden Yawa
butterfly. The mighty Wukarta are gone, scattered across the
seas; the Mother Temple is destroyed and with it a thousand years
of learning. But the religion of Vharkash the Harvester is still*

*with us. And there are still devotees in every city across the Laut
Besar.*

*In the deep jungles of Yawa, however, belief in the great Har-
vester God took a different, stranger direction after the destruction
of the Mother Temple. The people who still venerated the God
there—although fewer now in number—became more fanatical
in their beliefs. There are, to this very day, remote tribes such as
the Hantu Harimau people of eastern Yawa who believe, as their
ancestors did, that to die in the service of Vharkash is to gain a
place at His everlasting court in the afterlife. Accordingly, they do
not fear death—but see it as the ultimate sacrifice to their God.
Indeed, death is central to their version of the religion. They kill for
the deity. They hunt down unbelievers to gain merit in the eyes of
Vharkash. And they eat the flesh of their victims, particularly the
heart, which they believe is the seat of the soul. They say they are
doing the will of Vharkash by harvesting the bodies of unbelievers
for the glory of the Great Harvester himself.*

T he most terrible thing about this siege, Farhan decided,
was the disappearance of the bodies. The painted men
came in the night and removed them—their own and
the fallen Dokra—and all their belongings and weapons, and when
Farhan looked out over the top of the bamboo wall the next morning a little after dawn the space between the fort and the wall of
jungle a hundred paces away, which had been filled with a couple
of score of dead and dying bodies at sunset the night before, was
now entirely clear. All that indicated that a battle had been fought
was a patchwork of reddish-brown stains on the dusty ground.
Farhan suspected that he knew why they had taken the bodies—if
these strangely painted savages were who he thought they were—
and suppressed a shudder of fear and revulsion.

The painted men had not gone, though. From time to time, Farhan could glimpse them moving through the trees on the other side of the cleared space. They were too far for an accurate musket shot. Farhan might have tried a potshot with his longer-ranging rifle but it would still have been a very lucky shot that hit a single moving target at that distance and through trees and, besides, Farhan did not have the stomach for killing that morning.

On the other side of the coin, the range of the blowpipes was evidently far shorter even than that of the Dokra muskets. It seemed that the painted men needed to be within about thirty paces to have a chance of hitting their enemies with their lethal darts. Which meant that the situation was one of stalemate. The defenders of the fort could not strike at the painted men without leaving their bamboo walls—which after Captain Ravi's death nobody was eager to do. The painted savages could not attack their foes in the fort without coming in close and risking another mauling from the cannon.

Farhan, upon reflection, could not decide whether Captain Ravi had been unbelievably stupid or quite remarkably heroic. By forming his little suicide squad and marching out to meet the savages in the tree line, he had probably saved the lives of a good many Buginese and Dokra while they were trying to get to safety. His thin double line of red-coated men had stopped the painted men from flooding into the open space and skewering scores of their comrades as they tried desperately to get into the fort and were held up by the crush of people at the narrow door. Captain Ravi had actually held the enemy back in the tree line for many crucial moments by marching his twenty men forward so splendidly, and having them fire off their volleys to such deadly effect—even if it did mean condemning them all to die in such a horrible fashion.

Farhan offered up a mental salute to the dead captain's ghost and wished him well in whatever afterlife he now found himself.

With the Dokra keeping a good watch under the eye of their nervous new commander—a gangling young fellow called Sub-lieutenant Rohit—Farhan attended a council of war with Mamaji and Captain Lodi in the senior officers' tent.

"If General Vakul were here," began Mamaji, "I am sure that he would offer his condolences to all of us for the loss of Captain Ravi. I humbly offer them on his behalf: the noblest sacrifices are made to preserve our fellow men. The gallant captain will long be remembered and honored in the Federation."

"How *very* kind of the General," said Captain Lodi, his voice dripping with sarcasm. "And do you think our great commander might have any platitudes to offer to remedy the fact that we are now marooned in the jungle with two holes in the sides of a beached ship, very little food and a horde of savages armed with poisoned darts all around? I'm sure he would have some marvelously original words of wisdom on our predicament: to fight on and die nobly for the honor of the Federation, perhaps."

"There is no need to be rude about our good General, Cyrus dear," said Mamaji, "He has all our best interests at heart."

"What are we going to do?" said Farhan.

"We will just have to wait them out," said Mamaji. "They cannot attack us without risking very heavy casualties. And I would strongly suggest that we do not attack them, unless they come close to our walls. We sit and wait. Perhaps they will grow bored and leave us in peace. They must have other things to concern themselves with. They can't just sit out there forever. They must run out of food at some point."

"They have plenty of food—now," said Farhan. "Lots of fresh meat, at least."

The other two stared at him, horrified.

"What do you know about these people, Farhan?" said Mamaji. "If you know something relevant to our situation, perhaps you'd be so kind as to share it with us."

So Farhan told them everything he knew about the painted people, everything he had learned in his studies at Dhilika University. He was not trying to show off his erudition, at least not only that; it was important for these two to understand who they were facing, and why these white-painted enemies would not meekly walk away when they tired of the fight.

"You are saying, Farhan, that these people are religious fanatics," said Captain Lodi, "some obscure and forgotten sect of the Vharkashta religion—and that as part of their foul religion they eat their enemies?"

"In a nutshell, yes."

A servant came into the tent with a tray, and began to lay out plates of food. None of them felt like eating. Sublieutenant Rohit chose that moment to report that he had nothing to report. The enemy could still be seen moving about beyond the tree line but they had made no hostile moves. He said he planned to relieve the sentries who had been on duty all morning. None of the three people to whom he made this report had anything to say.

"The point I'd like to emphasize," said Farhan, when the Dokra officer had gone, "is that, from the savages' perspective, we are not so much enemies engaged in a ferocious battle with them as obstinate livestock they have managed to pen in a convenient bamboo corral. They are merely waiting the opportunity to harvest some more fresh meat."

Farhan enjoyed the reaction to his words. It felt extremely gratifying to be able to knock the self-satisfied smirk off Mamaji's plump face.

After a very long pause, she said, "Well, Farhan dear, it sounds as if you are quite the expert on these poor, misguided souls. What do *you* suggest we do?"

"I have absolutely no idea; ideally, we should kill every last one of them. But I don't know how to achieve that without most of us dying horribly as well."

"Could we talk to them, Farhan dear? You are such a clever-boots—would *you* be able to talk to them? Perhaps come to some arrangement?"

Farhan said, "All I know about them comes from reading the old travel diaries of Federation explorers in the library at Dhilika University. And that was twenty years ago when I was a student there. But it does seem that these people speak an archaic form of Yawanese. I have been able to understand some of their utterances."

"There it is," said Mamaji. "That's the answer. You pop out and talk to them, make them understand our position, see if we can't find a way out of this mess."

Farhan's jaw sagged. Was the woman mad?

"Pop out and talk to them?" he said. "With the greatest respect, Mamaji, have you been paying attention at all? These people would slaughter me on sight."

"You could go under a flag of truce."

"A flag of . . ." Farhan stopped. Something emerged from the dusty tangles of his capacious mind. "Actually, there was a symbol that used to be in currency in Yawa. It was back in the old Wukarta days anyway . . . I wonder. A pair of palm leaves, crossed. If they reciprocate the signal, it means the truce will be observed. It'd be an enormous gamble . . ."

"It is an absurd gamble," said Captain Lodi, suddenly very frightened for his old friend. "They'd fill Farhan full of poisoned darts before he had a chance to say a word."

"What would you have us do then, Captain?" said Mamaji. "Wait until our rice runs out? Or until they come at us one dark night and swarm over the walls?"

Captain Lodi said nothing. Farhan was now desperately wishing he had never tried to display his erudition. What had he got himself into?

"I know that General Vakul would be very impressed indeed if you were to undertake this bold mission for our company," said Mamaji. "He is always so grateful to brave men who are willing to put the good of others, indeed of the Federation itself, before their own personal safety. He has been known to be generous to them as well. Very generous. What do you say, Farhan dear? Will you bravely step forward and save us from our predicament?"

There was a long, uncomfortable silence.

"Let's talk about my mission bonus," croaked Farhan. His throat was tinder dry. *Can I do this?* he thought. *Can I actually do this thing? If they accepted the truce . . .*

"Ah yes, your bonus," said Mamaji. "I believe I have already promised you a hundred ringgu. And I will double that amount, if you will undertake to parlay with the savages and find a suitable accommodation that will get us all out of here. Two hundred ringgu."

"Twenty thousand ringgu," said Farhan, his voice now squeaking like a child's.

Mamaji laughed. "I do enjoy a joke, Farhan dear. But you cannot be serious."

"Twenty thousand ringgu or *you* can go out there and try to talk to these white devils."

Mamaji looked at him for a moment. "All right. Ten thousand ringgu, and not a kupang more," she said. "I mean it—not one kupang more."

For a moment Farhan could not believe his ears. Ten thousand ringgu would clear all his debts with Xi Gung and others and give him a healthy sum left over to begin a new life of leisure anywhere in the world. Perhaps that governorship of a pretty, obat-producing island was still within reach. Perhaps he might yet be able to entice *her* to come and share his life in a remote paradise. She must be tired of her existence in the frozen north—and the company of all those dull, drink-sodden, fur-clad barbarians. She'd love being the Governor's lady, in effect, the queen of the whole island; that he knew for sure. She had always said that she wanted to rule.

All he had to do was avoid getting stuck with poison darts, persuade a horde of blood-crazed religious cannibals to let the *Mongoose*'s company go away uneaten, and get back to Istana Kush in one piece to claim his reward. That was all.

Still, he'd always liked a flutter, he told himself mirthlessly, always been a keen gambler. And this would undoubtedly be the greatest gamble he'd ever taken; the greatest stake of all for the greatest prize: his very life, perhaps even his soul, to be wagered against enough money to make his wildest dreams come true.

"All right," he said. "I'll try."

CHAPTER 28

For the twentieth time in the past hour, Katerina slapped her neck hard and then looked at the tiny spatter of blood and mosquito fragments on the palm of her hand. Ahead of her two Legionnaires were slashing rhythmically at the dense jungle with long, steel parangs, cutting a narrow path for the landing force to follow. Ari Yoritomo stood a little behind her, silent and seemingly unmoved by the heat and the insects—although she had seen a tiny bead of perspiration slide down the side of his uncovered face. Behind her, a long tail of nearly two hundred and fifty men, most in identical blue-cotton tunics and heavy packs, carrying long brown muskets and swords buckled to their black-leather belts, struggled and sweated up the incline, their heads bowed under the weight of their equipment. She caught the eye of Major Chan marching alongside his troops, a short, slight, mild-mannered man with large, watery eyes who seemed to be suffering more than the rest of his Legionnaires. However, she noted that he had not complained once about the speed of the march in this foul heat, nor had he tried to take command from her. He would do, she decided.

She looked once again at the brass compass in her hands, checking the bearing, then at what little sky she could see. The fragments of light that she could make out through the leaves above her had changed from the bright white of noon to the yellowing color of late afternoon and still they seemed to be some distance from the dry, bare slopes of the Barat Cordillera, where she planned to camp. This was her first time trekking through jungle—and she very much hoped it would be her last.

The landing at Kara Bay on the western side of the Island of Sumbu had gone well. The Legionnaires selected by Colonel Wang had been disembarked onto the beach by the small boats without too much fuss and, as the three ships filled their sails and headed north out of the bay, they had formed up on the sand in two blocks of a hundred men each. They were not handpicked men, something Katerina had decided to overlook; they were instead the two specialist companies of the Legion: the Scouts, who were light, fast men, all exceptional shots with their longer muskets, who were highly trained in reconnaissance, ambush and mobile-battle tactics. They were an elite company, and Colonel Wang said they were among the best and most intelligent soldiers in the Legion. The second group of men was the Storm Company, all tall, well-built, older men of proven steadiness under fire. These men, known as Stormers, were usually held in reserve but also used to punch through well-defended enemy fortifications when other attacks failed, or provide stubborn rear guards for retreating Legions. They were paid more than the other Legionnaires and a man could not become a Stormer until he had served in a Legion at least seven years. They were, Colonel Wang told her, a proud, extremely tough company and the bravest men of all.

The gunners, by contrast, were an ill-disciplined rabble of seamen, mostly from Ostraka, who slouched along dressed any old how, chatting, bickering or daydreaming and occasionally wandering off the path to look at interesting species of flora and fauna that the column encountered during the march. They came at the tail of the column along with a dozen light baggage carts pulled by Legionnaires designated for punishment. Sometimes, at the breaks for water every two hours, the sailors fetched out clay pipes and small tin boxes and indulged in a little communal obat smoking. Katerina, very close to a murderous fury, had been forced to post most of her Niho knights beside them, with orders to urge them on, make sure that they kept up with the column and that they did not fall into an obat stupor—or disappear off into the jungle chasing pretty butterflies, as three of them already had.

However, the Niho were under strict orders not to use lethal force or, indeed, injure them severely or permanently under any circumstances. She would need all forty of these men, obat-sodden or not, when the Red Fort had been taken. Then—she told herself—then, when the mission had been accomplished, she would happily have them all executed, slowly and painfully, while she sat in a comfortable chair and watched, with a long, cool, marak-heavy drink in her hand, being fanned by a couple of naked muscular slaves and smoking up all their confiscated obat.

Katerina called a halt. She summoned Major Chan up to her side with a crook of her finger, and allowed Yoritomo to pass her the capacious water bottle he carried. Katerina tipped her head back and drank deeply, and immediately she felt the sweat begin to run—gush might be a more accurate word—from all her pores.

"A quarter of an hour's rest, Major Chan: water bottles but no food, and definitely no bloody obat!" she said. And to Yoritomo, "Go on ahead, Ari, if you please, and find Murakami. Bring him back here. I want to know how much farther we have to travel to reach the mountains. If it's more than an hour or two, we will camp here tonight."

Ari saluted crisply and loped off into the jungle, moving swiftly, agilely, through the green fronds in his half armor and disappearing within moments. He had completely recovered from the musket wounds in the flesh of his back and now he had only half a dozen pink dimples on either side of the twin ridges of back muscle. She knew this because she had watched him strip completely naked and dive off the prow of the *Yotun* and swim ashore when he made his lone reconnaissance of the beach at Kara Bay. She had not meant to linger at the rail and watch his lithe form cutting through the water—Gods knew she had enough to do—but for some reason she could not take her eyes off him. Did she want him as her lover? Of course not. It was a ridiculous idea. Quite absurd.

Katerina sat down on a tree root and contemplated her thin bare arms: they were scratched and bruised, and raised in big red lumps where they had been bitten by insects, and smeared with green lichen, sweat and mud. She very much regretted not choosing to wear a linen shirt with long sleeves. But it was hardly worth changing it now: the day was nearly done. She did not want to think what her face looked like—red and swollen like a hideous troll, probably. She wondered what Ari thought of her, looking like this. *Stop it!*

She looked down the hill through the freshly chopped path, through walls of green and over her small command: the Legionnaires were for the most part sitting quietly, sipping from their water bottles, although some were talking in low tones with their friends—some men, she noticed, had placed themselves on sentry duty, standing by thick tree trunks and facing out into the jungle with their muskets readily to hand, scanning for enemies. *Good troops*, she thought. *Very good*. At the far end of the column she saw that a Niho knight had picked up an Ostraka sailor in his two hands. The little gunner's legs were dangling a foot off the ground, and the knight was shaking him violently. She wondered if she ought to go down and see what the problem was, but realized she was too tired to move. They had only been marching through this green world for five hours, but such was the density of the foliage and the uphill nature of the path that they had covered less than three miles as the crow flies and Katerina was ready to curl up in a ball on the path and sleep for a week.

She forced herself to stand up. She'd better go and see what the problem was between the gunner and the Niho knight. Maybe she could spare just one of the gunners and have him bloodily executed on the spot, just to encourage the others. She took two steps down the hill and stopped. Ari was at her shoulder with Murakami, the Niho captain, his lacquered armor gleaming with moisture and smeared with lichen.

"Not far, Lady," said Murakami. "Half a mile—maybe one more hour and we are out of the jungle. I have found us a good site."

"Thank the Gods for that," said Katerina. "Good, Murakami. Good man. Now, let's get them up and moving. I want to feel sun on my face before nightfall."

Katerina stared up at the imposing mountain range. She stood on a small, rocky knoll about fifty paces from the tree line and looked south toward Mount Barat. Behind her the exhausted, sweaty Legionnaires filed out of the jungle and were guided into their designated camping places by Major Chan and his two captains. Murakami had indeed done well; he had discovered a reasonably wide, flat piece of grassy ground for them to bivouac on, and it even had a small stream that ran across it and down into the jungle, heading toward the sea. A stiff breeze came down off the Barat Cordillera, a wonderfully refreshing rush of chilly air after a day in the muggy closeness of the forest.

Katerina looked up at the bare flank of Mount Barat, the jagged top outlined by the blue sky in the last hour of daylight. It looked like the gray serrated blade of some enormous weapon, thrusting up through the green blanket of the jungle on its lower slopes. The sheer sides were striped with thousands of gullies, ravines and crevices, the remains of ancient lava flows, great and small, and the upper reaches were wreathed in banks of mist almost thick enough to call themselves clouds. She turned and looked along the line of the edge of the jungle, which headed north and a little west from where she stood—her plan called for a march along the edge of the green, skirting the heights of the mountain range and remaining on the lower slopes. She had assumed that it would be easier going than hacking through the dense foliage and she had allocated just a day and a night to reach the farmlands before the Red Fort. Her plan depended for its success on timing: on arriving before the dawn of the third day, before her three ships would come into action in the Sumbu Straits.

That calculation had been made only with the aid of a map in the great cabin of the *Yotun*. It was only about ten miles as the crow flies from here to the Red Fort, but now that she could see the terrain, she knew she had miscalculated. They would only know when they got into those deep ravines how tough it was going to be, and how fast they could travel, but she knew she would be asking a huge amount of the men just to get there. And once there, they had to surprise-assault and capture one powerful fortress filled with enemy troops—and subdue another. Then capture a whole city.

Well, she had known it was going to be difficult. The Federation clearly believed an approach from this direction was impossible, which was why this route to the back door of Istana Kush was left unguarded. She'd show them their error. Besides, there was no going back now. What was she to do? Return to Ashjavat with her tail between her legs, admit that she had been defeated by the slopes of a mountain and beg Tung An Shan to give back her throne? That was not going to happen.

Then she saw something, a tiny black line, little bigger than a dot, circling one of the craggy peaks on the shoulder of Barat. At first she thought it was an eagle. But it was far bigger than that.

The creature, spotting the movement of the Legionnaires as they flowed out of the jungle, banked and flew closer to take a look. Entirely unafraid, it approached on red-golden wings a full six paces wide, circled twice a couple of hundred feet above the encampment, watching with interest as the mass of Legionnaires milled about, setting up their tents and clotheslines, building cooking fires, washing themselves in the stream. Katerina was entranced. She turned to Yoritomo, beaming with happiness. "It's a Garuda, it's a real live Garuda bird," she said. "I thought they existed only in the storybooks, in old myths and legends. I didn't think they were actually real!"

Her face darkened. She seized Major Chan by his lapels. "Spread the word, and quickly now, that if any Legionnaire shoots at the Garuda, I will have him beaten to death by his comrades. These birds are not to be harmed, do you understand?"

"Yes, Highness," said the little man, looking even more terrified than usual. "But, with the greatest respect, no Legionnaire would ever fire his weapon unless they were ordered to do so or were under attack. We are not . . ." He struggled for a way to describe soldiers that merited such a deep level of contempt. ". . . Dokra mercenaries."

"Tell them anyway," grated Katerina. "Beaten to death, you hear, and I mean it."

Her sudden fear passed as she looked up again and resumed contemplating the bird with a heart so full of joy, it almost made her weep: her exhaustion was forgotten, her aches soothed. The sight of the creature's lissome form soaring on thermal currents high above her lifted her spirits so far that she felt she could almost take off and join the creature in its effortless, elegant flight.

It was a male of the species; that was an easy guess. From what she had read, the Garuda were all male save for a single Queen who ruled their colonies and produced the eggs from which all the Garuda were hatched. The Queen, she knew, could be distinguished by its much larger size and a spray of golden crest feathers atop its head. This male bird was white on the head, breast and loins and had white-feathered legs, tucked up under his belly in flight, which both ended in cruel-looking six-inch-long blood-red talons. The long, needle-sharp beak was a rich golden color, and the huge wings were golden too, but shading to red toward the edges, so that the long, fingerlike pinions that controlled flight were scarlet. A similarly bold spray of long feathers sprouted from the base of its spine.

The Garuda circled above the camp half a dozen times, occasionally giving a beautiful cry, a sad, high note that fell in both pitch and volume, and then, having satisfied his curiosity, he flapped his vast wings once and soared off back toward the peaks of Mount Barat and was quickly lost from view in the drifting clouds. By the magic of the legendary bird's visit, Katerina's dejected mood was quite transformed. If myths were real in this strange snowless land, then her dreams could certainly come true. She would lead these men over the flank of this mountain, make it to the Red Fort in time and wrest Istana Kush from the Federation—and then the Laut Besar would be hers.

She would not let anything, anything at all, stand in her way.

CHAPTER 29

—————⊰✦⊱—————

With leveled muskets, the Manchu forced Jun, Ketut and Tenga to walk down the tunnel, away from the rest of the other slaves in their work party. They marched on and on through the dim passage, counting the oil lamps that marked every ten paces until they came out into the wider, better-lit assembly area, where they were stopped by the guard beside a smaller, empty wagon.

"Now you dead," said one of the Manchu guards. He was smiling in a strange manner. Jun was watching the musket, which was held in his hands at about hip level. Jun did not know much about firearms—War-Master Hardan had disdained them as unworthy of a gentleman—but he was fairly sure that you needed to fully pull back the little right-angled piece of steel, the cock, it was called, before you could fire the weapon. On this guard's musket, the cock was not pulled back, which meant that he could not fire at him without giving ample warning of his intention. If the Manchu touched the musket's cock, Jun thought, he'd immediately attack and subdue him.

The other hazard was the spike bayonet that protruded a foot from the end of the muzzle, and which made the weapon no better than a very heavy and clumsy spear. Jun knew how to combat spears—that was something Hardan *had* taught him. He would knock the blade aside as the man lunged and get in very close. Or, if the Manchu didn't lunge, Jun could grasp the barrel, pull and step in. He thought an upward strike to the nose with the heel of his palm might be effective, followed by a hard hand-sword to the throat. But he was prepared to be flexible.

To his surprise, Jun realized that he felt no fear. None at all. It was as if the killing of Kromo had unblocked a barrier inside him, opened a gate, releasing in a flood all the skills he had trained in almost all his life. Now, instead of being paralyzed by the thought of his own death, he was thinking how he could best defeat his opponent. The bayonet was a problem of the kind that Hardan had set him on many occasions. One he knew perfectly well how to address. He did not concern himself with the second guard at all. If necessary he would deal with him after the first guard. But he was sure that Tenga, a seasoned warrior, could tackle him on her own once battle was joined; and Ketut was no milksop. She would weigh in effectively, too.

Jun glanced at Tenga, saw that the big woman was tensed and ready. *All right,* he thought, *let's do this. No point waiting.*

A voice spoke in his head. "Don't do it, richboy," it said. "Don't attack them. These two are sent by Semar. Just do what they say. They are Semar's creatures."

Jun had been on the very lip of launching his assault and the words completely unstrung him. For the voice that spoke in his head was not his own; nor was it Semar's. The voice belonged to Ketut. He looked at the small, scrawny Dewa girl to his right in bewilderment. She said out loud, "Just do what they say, Jun. It will be all right." He looked beyond her to Tenga, who was nodding at him, and smiling slyly.

Jun's confusion took the form of a meek silence, all his bellicosity suddenly wiped away. One of the Manchu delved into the empty wagon and drew out three white-linen shroud-sacks, and with gestures, and words in their own harsh language, they persuaded the three slaves to climb into the sacks and lie down in a row on the floor beside the wagon.

"You stay. Don't move. You dead now. No talk," said one of the

Manchu, and then to Jun's astonishment he heard their footsteps walking away back down the shaft to the ore-face. Then there was silence.

"What's going on?" whispered Jun. He could see nothing, for the white linen was covering his face, but he could feel Ketut's shoulder hard beside his. "And how did you learn to talk inside my head like that?"

"Sssh," said Ketut, "we have to play dead until they deliver us to the morgue. Semar will be there. Lie still and keep quiet."

"But how can you talk in my thoughts," Jun insisted.

"Semar has been teaching me. He talks to me inside my head all the time. He wants me to learn from him. Now be quiet, rich-boy. Or this will all be for nothing."

Jun lay there, marveling that his traveling companions had been conducting a secret dialogue of which he had no inkling. He wondered what else he did not know about Ketut—or about Semar . . . He had said he was an old family retainer, who had served his family for many, many years, and yet he was someone whom Jun had no memories of *at all* before that terrible night in the Watergarden. Who was Semar? Where had he come from? Jun had no idea. But he was kindly disposed toward Jun and his family, that was clear. Or was he? Semar had persuaded him to come on this mad quest to find the Khodam. He had allowed Jun to be enslaved, whipped, even pissed on. But now, evidently, he was helping him to escape. At this point, exhausted in spirit, mind and body after the many horrors of the past few days, Jun dozed off.

After an hour or so, the rich boy began to snore. Which was typically selfish of him. Not just a little heavy breathing, but a full-bore snorting, chopped and strangled rattle, almost a roaring noise that could almost have woken a genuinely dead person. Ketut tried the technique that Semar had so painstakingly taught her: bringing her soul's voice-power to the front of her mind, concentrating her thoughts, smoothing her message into a sleek missile and hurling it at the essence of the target. "Awake, fool, and lie quietly!" But, apparently, she was not now able to communicate to an unconscious arrogant brat in this arcane manner. Sleep had closed his mind to her. Jun continued to snore like a drunken rhinoceros.

"Make him stop that noise," said Tenga, a solid, comforting presence, lying in the white shroud beside her. "Make him quiet or we will be discovered."

Ketut elbowed Jun in the ribs. Hard.

"Wake up, richboy, you are making too much noise," she whispered.

Jun grunted, turned on his right side inside his shroud and slept again. At least now he was quiet.

Another hour passed, and Jun held his peace, but for the occasional deep sigh. However, Ketut was growing ever more aware of the left side of her body, which was pressed up hard against Tenga. It was not quite comfortable but she realized that she enjoyed the feeling: the hard rubbery flesh of the warrior squeezed against her arm and leg, the warmth of the big woman, the contours of her thigh muscles, the heavy club-like forearm.

From almost the first moment they had met in the slave yard in Sukatan, Ketut had felt a powerful pull, a drawing of her to the older woman's side. She felt quite safe the first time she sat down beside her, and pleasantly light-headed; she found she could not stop herself from staring into her scarred face. Not that Ketut cared a jot about scars—she could feel Tenga's strength like a campfire blaze. It nourished her, made her feel at home, loved and protected all at the same time. And the feeling had only grown stronger over the next few days. Now, lying on the floor of the assembly area, pretending to be corpses under the big, looming ore wagon, with Tenga's hot, strong flank pressed next to hers, she felt a happy glow inside her, all the way from her loins to her belly and up into the center of her chest.

Ketut thought about all the conversations they had shared—very few, no more than a handful of exchanges, and yet they had seemed to contain all the necessary information for this precious intimacy. Tenga had told her how she had been wounded and captured in a great battle in her homeland of Ziran Atar against the neighboring tribe, and sold as a slave to Han merchants and shipped to the mines, how she had escaped and been recaptured and tortured and brought back to the Hole again. She had told her of her brothers and sisters, at home in Ziran, and how she did not know if they were alive or dead. She had told Ketut about her dream, one day, of becoming a weapon-smith, learning the art, becoming a maker of blades—of working with iron, forging the metal in a sacred fire, bending it to her will . . .

And Ketut had told her a little of her own life in Taman, how she had been chosen by the Goddess Dargan as her Vessel, and before that, of the hunger and the cold lonely nights, and the shame and self-disgust at her own polluted Dewa blood, and of the pretty boy from the sea-village, one of the New People, who she had once thought she truly loved. She remembered her own words to Tenga about the jagged pain of that affair, unusually fluent for her: ". . . he was so handsome, so perfect—looking just a little like our rich boy here—and he told me that he loved me, and would always love me, and I gave myself to him. But once he had enjoyed me, he made a whore of me and shared me with his friends, as if I were no more than a common bowl of fish stew that they could all stick their spoons into . . ."

They did not speak, Tenga and Ketut, all that long day in the shrouds while they waited for the shift to end, but the touch of their flanks, the feeling of their mutual heat, the pulse of life that passed between them like a current, was better than a hundred voices singing together in beautiful harmonies. And so the day passed. From time to time, Ketut heard the creaking of the wheels and the crack of whips as work parties came past with loads of ore. She heard the clanging of the lift doors and the squeal of unoiled steel. She wondered how her own group was faring: with Kromo dead, the dwarf dead, the Yawa girl dead and the three of them here shamming death, it was a much-depleted work gang. She wondered if the Manchu would allow them to half fill the ore wagon, given their lack of numbers. But most of the time, hour after hour, she wallowed in the proximity of her love, and the power that radiated between them.

Then, at last, there was noise, and the presence of people and Ketut felt her feet and shoulders being lifted and her body thrown, suddenly weightless, and her shoulders thumping hard against the wooden floor of the death-wagon. She felt Jun move beside her, then her beloved, heavy but springy with life, tumbling down on top of her. And then to her disgust three other limp bodies were piled on top. Something wet was dripping on her legs.

Then they were in the elevator, the steel groaning, but the air was becoming cooler; they were being pushed somewhere, the wagon wheels juddering and protesting. And, after a length of time, a long, long wait, the bodies were being lifted off her, the weight was gone, and she was sitting up. There was bright light, and a very hot roaring fire somewhere near, and Semar's kindly face, peering down at her, asking her how she did.

The escape from the mine head was almost laughably easy, after all Jun had endured at the ore-face. With the door of the morgue locked by Semar from the inside, he helped Tenga feed the other, real corpses into the furnace and then all three of the living ones and Semar slid down a chute designed to take the used, soiled shroud-sacks. They landed in a softly malodorous pile of linen in a large, empty room. Semar led the way out of a pair of double doors and they were suddenly in the soft and ordered settlement of the Manchu guards and the Han engineers. Jun could smell the scent of roses in bloom. It was full dark now and there was a need for stealth, but after a few tense moments of creeping through the shadows, Jun soon found himself in a well-lit cottage with a red-tiled roof, where there were clean clothes for him to put on and food and tea set out on the kitchen table as if for a party.

"Whose house is this?" asked Ketut. And Semar told her that it belonged to the Han doctor in charge of the morgue, who had been "persuaded" by Semar that his elderly parents in Singarasam were sick and needed him. Semar, claiming to be a fully trained Han doctor, had volunteered to take over his duties in the mine, and his house, too, till he could return. Nobody asked Semar how he had managed this feat. Jun was just grateful to be out of the Hole. When Jun had washed, dressed and eaten a large but hurried meal, Semar handed him his old traveling pack—the big canvas-and-leather satchel that he had last seen in The Drunken Sow boardinghouse in the alley off the harbor in Sukatan. It seemed about ten years since he had seen his chess set, his sleeping sarong, his spare sandals and all his other belongings.

"When I get back to the city, I will demand that my cousin punishes all those responsible for this evil place," said Jun. "I *will* have my revenge. How long do you think it will take, Semar, for us to get back to Sukatan? Two, three days?"

"My prince, we are not going to your cousin's palace. That road back there is the first place they will look when they find that I'm gone without an explanation—and they will soon discover that you have escaped, too. Those two Manchu guards will confess that they helped us—even if they will never be able to explain exactly why."

"How long have we got before they start after us?" said Tenga.

"So you will join us, miss?" said Semar. "Good, we'll need your strength."

Tenga looked taken aback to be called "miss" but merely said, "How long?"

"I imagine they will sound the alarm a little after dawn—we should expect them on our heels anytime after that."

"Then we'd better go now," said Tenga.

"Why are we not going to Sukatan? Where *are* we going?" Jun felt confused.

"We don't have time for too many questions," said Semar. "But it grieves me to tell you, my prince, that Raja Widojo is dead. You are the last of the Wukarta. Your cousin complained that an evil spirit had entered his brain and infected it with some kind of madness and then, just a few hours later, when he could stand it no longer, he blew the back of his own skull off with a pistol."

Jun did not know what to say to that.

"I garnered that knowledge while I was collecting your things from The Sow. I also learned that our enemy has left Sukatan, with the Dragon's Eye in his possession, and his ship is even now sailing for the Pengut Delta, according to gossip in the taverns. Sailors, even pirates, talk freely when they drink and smoke. So we know he's heading for Sumbu and most likely for Mount Barat—and I think we can guess why."

Semar and Ketut shared a significant glance. But Jun had absolutely no idea why the sorcerer should wish to visit this place called Mount Barat.

"So where are *we* going?" he said.

"We're going west. The direction they would least expect us to go," said Tenga.

"Very good, miss," said Semar. "Quite correct. They will expect us to go north to Sukatan. Or, given Jun's background, southeast to get a boat across the strait to his home in Taman. But we'll

confound them by going west and then northwest. We will head
for the coast. There are some fishing villages up there, even a few
small ports where we might catch a ship for Sumbu. With luck we
can be there in less than a week. But no more questions now.
Haste is required, my friends, haste and stealth!"

In truth, there had been little necessity for stealth once they
had left the scatter of mine officials' villas and begun to climb the
slopes of the Gray Mountain, which was just as well, as the path
was steep and rocky and Jun and his three companions constantly
dislodged small pebbles that rattled down the mountainside behind them. But, as far as Jun could tell, no alarm was raised by
their clumsiness. Certainly there was no flaring of lights or shouting in Manchu or sudden trumpets, bells or whistles. And when
they reached the summit and looked back down at the square
bulks of the mine heads, with their little pins of yellow light from
the small square windows, and the high towers with their slowly
rotating wheels, Jun felt a soaring sense of liberation very close to
actual joy. The cold mountain wind exhilarated him—it was the
breath of freedom. They would come after him, sure: those hideous bear-dogs and their blank-faced handlers, the Mbaru. But he
was free now, and he was confident that if they went fast and
far, he would remain so. It was much, much better than sweating
out his life in the Hole, anyway.

This pleasant sensation was entirely dissipated by the time he
had spent an hour in the jungle. The massive heat came on with
the creeping light of dawn and, even though he had slept long in
his shroud the day before, the hard climb over the Gray Mountain
had taken its toll. They took turns leading the way through the
forest with Semar indicating the direction of travel with his long
wooden staff. But they were sparing with the use of the two parangs that Jun and Ketut had found in their packs. On Tenga's
advice they slipped through between the fronds of the plants
whenever they could, or went around thick patches of vegetation,

or better still followed existing game trails. It was exhausting work, even when they were not obliged to cut a way through, and the heat sapped their strength even further. But Tenga urged them onward, haranguing them to hurry, to hurry if they wanted to live!

She knew better than any of them what was behind them.

When they paused midmorning for a drink from their water bottles, with Tenga anxiously watching their backtrail, Semar handed out a few dried leaves, gathered he said from the young obat bush, which he carried in a little leather pouch. He showed them how to make a wad and hold the leaves between their teeth and the flesh of their cheek. Very soon Jun's cheek began to tingle, then grow numb, but he felt a new surge of energy running through his body. It was a little like the usual obat effect but subtly different and oddly, wonderfully refreshing; his head was clear as crystal and he felt strong and clever, even witty. They plunged on into the jungle with renewed vigor.

It was midafternoon before they first heard the baying of the slave-hounds.

The noise was not unlike the howling of a wolf. They stopped, wiping the sweat from their brows and looked at each other. Jun was shocked to see that Tenga was terrified: her big scarred face was an odd gray color, and drawn much more lean over its bones. Her eyes were huge. "The Queen of Fire protect us," she said. "I thought we'd get farther than this. They're only a mile behind us and they have found our scent."

They ran.

They blundered through the trees at full speed with Semar leading, staff in his right hand, his gray sarong hitched up and his skinny white legs flashing underneath. Then came Ketut, then Jun, with Tenga bringing up the rear. Semar seemed to know

where he was going—at least he did not hesitate for a second
when faced with a choice of two game paths, picking one and har-
ing down it as fast as he could go. After a night on the mountain
and most of a day slogging through the thick jungle, Jun knew
that his strength was near its end. But he saw no sign of tiredness
in any of his companions, and he could still hear the wolflike baying of the slave-hounds, more distant now but still quite audible.
He had little choice but to grit his teeth and carry on running.
After three or four miles, Semar abruptly came to a halt. He stood
there, hands on his knees, panting under a vast baobab tree, and
Jun and Ketut collapsed onto the ground, also heaving for breath.
Tenga stood staring at the trail behind her, the long, steel parang
she still held twitching in her massive fist.

When their breathing had returned almost to normal, Semar
said, "I know where we must go." He breathed a little more. "It is
a place I used to know a long, long time ago and we can hide ourselves there or, if need be, defend ourselves more easily. But to get
there we must run all night."

"We have no choice," said Tenga. "We must run. If we stay
here, they'll find us and you will be taken back."

"Won't *you* be taken back, too?" said Jun.

"I will not allow that to happen to me," Tenga said. "Never—so,
I say we run."

"I really don't know if I can . . ." said Jun.

"It's run or die, richboy," said Ketut. "I'm not staying to be
eaten by bear-dogs."

Jun said nothing. In the far, far distance a slave-hound howled.

"Good," said Semar. "Eat and drink all you can; we cannot afford to carry any extra weight." And from his pack, he began to
pass out sweet, glutinous rice cakes, which were studded with
dried fruits. And thin strips of chewy, dried meat.

Jun forced down his rice cake, and swallowed his strips of
beef jerky—although his stomach nearly rebelled—and then he

downed as much of his water as he could and discarded the rest. He went through his pack, throwing everything out that he could bear to part with—including the beautiful chess set—but keeping a spare light sarong. And his recurved bow and full quiver of arrows. He wasn't sure if he was ready to die, like Tenga, before being recaptured. But if they were caught, he meant to take as many Mbaru down with him as possible.

Finally Semar handed out more of the young obat leaves, which they stuffed in their cheeks, and, at a slower pace than before, but still a respectably fast jog, they began to run.

After a mile or two with the light dimming and the dark forest closing in all around him, and with the rhythm of the run pounding in his ears, Jun fell swiftly into a trancelike state. His focus narrowed to Ketut's thin back, which was bobbing steadily in front of his eyes. He listened to the heave of his lungs and the pounding of his feet. And he seemed, on occasion, to be outside his body watching a running youth, the third in a line of four running folk. After about ten miles, and heading due west, as far as Jun could tell, the jungle seemed to become thinner, a good deal thinner, as if sometime in the recent past it had been cultivated land, now reclaimed by the wild.

It had been full dark for some time, and Jun had not heard the slave-hounds now for an hour or more. Gradually, a half-moon rose in the southwest that gave them enough light to see the path, and make looming shadows of the foliage on either side. But Jun did not pay much attention to the moon or the path or the shadows; he merely ran, his whole being focused on putting one tired foot ahead of the other. His breath was a slow, chugging pant, but perhaps it was the dried obat leaves, or perhaps it was the knowledge of what would happen if they stopped, but he found the strength somewhere inside him to carry on.

Mile after mile, hour after hour, they ran. At one point Ketut stumbled and he had to pause and help her to her feet—and he found himself foully cursing her clumsiness, wanting only to carry on with his run unimpeded.

Semar never hesitated in his direction—neither did the old man tire. But Jun had no energy to ponder why this should be so. He ran. He ran with all his heart and lungs and stomach. He ran as if running was living, as if being alive meant only running, and running meant staying alive—which, of course, it did.

He was thirsty, that he knew. His knees were weak and wobbly. His lungs burned as if he were breathing in fire. Yet his torso and limbs were ice-cold. He ran. He began to see visions, monsters and ghosts. War-Master Hardan ran alongside him for a while, criticizing his style. "Keep those arms tucked in, boy," he said. "Longer strides now. Longer, I say."

Jun lengthened his stride, and ran on.

His father stood by the side of the path, and said sadly, "They took the Khodam, Arjun, they took it from me—from us. So sorry, my son, but I could not resist them."

Jun ran on. Now his head was clear of visions. But he could not feel his legs below the knees. The air was subtly changing, the darkness lightening. The jungle was getting even more sparse; now that he could see, there was barely a tree in sight, just scrubby bushes, clumps of thick grasses, some of which had grown to head height.

Jun looked over his shoulder and saw the drawn gray sweating face of Tenga behind him and beyond her, the red rim of the sun coming up on the eastern horizon.

He blundered into Ketut, stopped and saw that Semar was also still, head down, lungs working madly. Then the old man stopped and, still lightly panting, lifted his gray head. Now he was looking about him eagerly. Jun looked, too—he saw huge blocks of shattered masonry strewn about the scrubby landscape; some of it seeming to be marked with black scorches. There were tumbled-down walls, snapped columns and even whole collapsed houses, blackened, broken and with plant life growing through the windows. Here and there was a splintered statue—some of fantastical animals, some of elegant young men and women. And the rubble and destruction seemed to go on as far as the eye could see. Jun realized that he was standing in the ruins of a large town, even a city.

"What is this place?" he asked Semar.

"This place used to be my home. This was once a place of devout worship and earnest study, of goodness and piety. This was once the home of an ordered and holy community of men and women, priests who venerated the great God and worked to spread His message of love to the four corners of the Laut Besar." Semar seemed infinitely sad as he said these words, as if he were speaking the oration at a funeral of a dear friend.

"This was the Mother Temple of Vharkash," said Jun.

"Does your temple have any water?" said Tenga. "Tut needs to drink."

"Yes, and yes," said Semar. "And I know just the place where we can camp."

Jun slept. Curled in a thick bed of dried grasses, in the shade of a high wall made of gray volcanic rocks, he slept like a dead man for most of the day, waking only in the late afternoon, as the sun was yellowing and falling in the west. He sat up and saw that Ketut was still fast asleep, a dozen yards from him, under the largest piece still standing of a smashed stone table. He got up and walked to the rear of the compound, where a spring bubbled out of a rock face at head height and collected in a pool below.

The Temple of Burunya was one of the few that had not been totally destroyed in the cataclysm that had leveled the rest of the Mother Temple complex. Burunya was the Goddess of Water, of oceans, lakes, rivers, waterfalls and springs, like the merry little trickle that fed the pool in her temple. She was a healing deity, nurturing the weak and the sick, and also the mother of Vharkash—his father, of course, being the Sun God Turunya— and like an elderly, much-loved matriarch she was given her own small home inside the compound of her great son's domain.

The temple was a small, square box, twenty paces on each side, open to the sky and walled with gray volcanic stone, with a square offering block in the center, which had once supported a tiny but elaborately carved wooden house for the visiting God, now long gone, and a few tumbled-down wooden buildings around the walls, now overgrown with grass but still providing fuel for those prepared to dig for it. The walls had crumbled slightly but were mostly intact on all four sides. At the entrance, the traditional split-mountain shape on the south side, a pile of thorny brush-wood had been piled up by Tenga—her last act before she, too, succumbed to sleep—to create something of a barrier.

Jun mumbled a half-remembered prayer to Burunya and knelt to drink from her pool, scooping up water again and again with his cupped hand until his stomach was full. Then he briefly washed his hands, face and neck, and went to seek his friends.

He found Semar making tea from his dried obat leaves at a small fire. Jun waved briefly at him but his eyes were drawn to Tenga, who was standing on a huge piece of cracked masonry, the uprooted foundation of a temple building beside the east wall, and looking out at the ruins of the Mother Temple. He scrambled up beside her, and stared out at the field of broken stone and bushes, of reeds, grasses and stunted trees.

"Any sign of them?" he said.

Tenga shook her head. "And I haven't heard anything from those slave-hounds either, which is more important."

"Do you think we lost them?"

"Maybe."

Jun felt the beginnings of a wave of relief wash through his body.

"Or maybe they've just muzzled and leashed those dogs a mile or two back and are creeping up on us silently right now. They're good at that."

Jun's relief was snatched away. He looked out over the terrain. He had done a certain amount of training in clandestine movement with Hardan, the old man getting him to spend all day, his body shape disguised with grasses and twigs, to advance two hundred paces unseen through landscapes not too dissimilar to this one, just so he could get close enough for a killing shot with his bow. He knew it could be done. Were the Mbaru out there? Or was Tenga taking fright at shadows?

"Semar is making obat-leaf tea," he said. "Why don't we join him?"

"You go. I'd rather watch."

"I'll bring you a cup, then," Jun said, and slipped off the foundation stone.

He found Ketut sitting cross-legged opposite from Semar with her eyes closed. A small metal pan of water was simmering merrily on the edge of the fire. The old man, also with his legs folded up in his lap, had his right hand extended, palm flat against her chest. He was saying, "Feel my beat, girl, can you feel it? Picture my gnarled old beating heart in your mind. Watch the blood pulse in and out, in and out."

"I can see it. I can feel it throb. Bom, bom, bom, bom."

"Good. Now bring your heart into sequence with it. Match your pulse to mine."

"Yes," said Ketut. The two of them sat in silence and Jun was uncomfortably aware that they were communicating in a way in which he could never be part.

He coughed loudly, and Semar opened his eyes and looked at

him. The pupils seemed to have expanded so that the black void filled the whole of his eyes.

"Tenga was wondering if there was any tea," he said.

"All right," said Semar. "That is enough for today, Ketut."

Jun drank his tea with the other two and, while it took the edge off his hunger and filled his veins with a cold, thrumming energy, he was aware that his strength was massively depleted. He got up and took a bowl to Tenga, and as he passed it up to the warrior, he wondered if he had ever, ever in his life, served another living person with food or drink. He thought not. He had certainly never served a bowl of tea to a massive, scarred, foreign slave woman on the run from the authorities.

He was about to make some joking remark along these lines, when he heard a sound. It was a howl like a wolf in agony. It was the call of a slave-hound.

CHAPTER 30

Extract from *Ethnographic Travels* by
Professor Tolmund K. Parehki of the University of Dhilika

The Laut Besar is a treasure trove of myths but one of the most fascinating is the legend of the Garuda birds. It is said that the God of the Wind, Shuruda, grew tired of her lonely life whistling around the top of the world and she desired to have a family. So she transformed herself into a gigantic bird, a magnificent creature of red and white and gold, who called herself Garuda and gave birth in time to thirteen eggs, which she nurtured, kept warm and hatched to create twelve sons and one daughter.

Her children grew up to be as magnificent as she, and none was more glorious than her daughter. When her sons came of age they naturally searched for their own mates and finding no creatures that could compare to themselves, they vied for the attentions of Garuda's only female offspring. They brought her gifts of bright flowers and sang songs of love to their sister—and Garuda was jealous. She flew into a rage at her own child, who had deprived her of the love of her sons, and she slew her daughter, rending her with her great talons. And Garuda decreed that her sons should love no other female but her.

The other Gods were angered that Garuda had killed her only daughter, a great sacrilege, and the Lord of Gods, Vharkash, sought to punish her. He made a magic spell that bound her in her birdlike form, so that she would no longer be immortal but age and die in time; furthermore they decreed that her talons would forever be stained red with the blood of her child and they exiled her to the high mountains where men do not go.

*So Garuda grew old, as all mortal creatures must, and yet the
love of her sons never faltered. And one day she built herself a huge
egg made entirely of myrrh and she hid her ancient, failing body
inside the egg and sealed it from the inside. After thirteen days and
nights, while her twelve sons grieved for her, the myrrh egg cracked
open and Garuda emerged, young and fresh again, in her full
strength and beauty, and with a golden spray of crest feathers atop
her head to mark her magical rebirth.*

*From that day onward, the Garuda have only ever had one fe-
male in their colonies and she is their Queen. The males love her
and serve her, and she mates with them and lays eggs to make more
sons; and from time to time whenever she grows old and tired she
renews herself in the magic myrrh egg that keeps her forever young.*

T he icy wind whipped through Mangku's padded-cotton
tunic as though it were made of cobwebs. But the sorcerer did not feel the cold. He was gazing up at a sight
that he believed had been seen by only a handful of men in the
past hundred years. There were two of them, dark red forms
against the white of the clouds over the peak of Mount Barat. His
heart began to beat faster. Garuda! Two living, breathing Garuda
birds.

Mangku turned to his servant, a short, shaven-headed figure
whose normally swarthy skin had taken on a shade of light blue.

"See them, Arif? That's where they nest, up there, beyond the
crest. That is where we will find the Queen." He pointed with his
long staff. "If we hurry, we can make it there by noon and be
down again well before dark."

The servant said nothing. He was too cold to speak. He scrambled on up the steep rocky slope behind his master, silently cursing the loyal impulse that had led him to agree to accompany the

sorcerer on this freezing climb. They had left the path far behind them and now under their hands and feet was nothing more than crumbling volcanic rock that shifted with every step they took. He was hungry, frightened, and when he looked down at the tiny *Sea Serpent* moored in the delta of the River Pengut, he felt dizzy.

His shipmates would be carousing today. They had declined Mangku's invitation—all of them—to join his climb to the famous summit of Mount Barat. Instead, they informed their angry and disappointed captain, they would rather be merrily spending the silver they had taken from the small Han trading vessel they'd attacked five days previously.

It had not been much of a fight. The *Sea Serpent* had pretended that it was mortally wounded, blackening the sides of the ship as if it had suffered a fire, leaving the sails draped over the sides, ropes and sheets hanging loose, artistically placing a few visibly bloodied bodies on the deck . . . The Han vessel had approached cautiously, slowly inching toward the *Sea Serpent*, and when she was a few paces away, grappling hooks had been hurled out and hauled tight, locking the ships together and a yelling horde of Mangku's crewmen had erupted from a hatchway and swarmed over the rail into the other ship. The crew and passengers of the captured ship had all been slaughtered, their bodies tossed into the sea for the sharks. The lone woman on board, the captain's wife perhaps, a pretty young thing, had cut her own throat with a straight razor in the main cabin and bled to death while Mangku's men were trying to break down the big teak door.

However, despite this small disappointment, there had been a decent amount of silver—heavy canvas bags of shiny ringgu in two chests in the ship's hold—as well as a cargo of fine Han silks worth thousands and some expensive gum and spices, too.

How Arif wished he had remained with his shipmates—there were obat dens and whorehouses aplenty in the small Federation outpost on the Pengut Delta. But when the rest of the crew had declined to spend their precious time ashore panting up this mountainside, Arif had felt that his master needed him and his place was at his side. Not that he had received the smallest thanks for his loyalty. The old bastard took his company entirely for granted.

It took another hour to scale the crest, during which they crossed the snow line, and now their boots crunched through the thick white crust, and sank more than a foot deep. Yet once they had reached the top, and stood panting together, breath pluming in the frozen air, Arif was filled with a glorious sense of exhilaration. He felt he was on top of the world. To the north was the pyramid shape of the summit of Mount Barat, bleak and white, with the Barat Cordillera, the spine of the Island of Sumbu, tailing out beyond. To the west, the earth fell away precipitously, a few hundred paces of snow, then black rock, cut with hundreds of deep ravines and gullies, and at the base the deep green of tropical jungle. The sea to the west was a placid royal blue—it was the wide Indujah Ocean, Arif realized with a start, a body of water that he had never set eyes on before despite thirty years of seafaring, a vast expanse of sea that stretched two thousand leagues westwards all the way to the Federation peninsula. He saw something moving below. "Look, lord. People!"

Mangku had his eyes fixed on the snowy crags at the bottom of the final peak, at a collection of sticks, rags, feathers and bones perched on a snowy shelf, black against the blinding white. Then the sorcerer looked to where his servant was pointing and saw three warships in a wide bay, and boats filled with men rowing in toward the beach, and more men gathering in neat formations on the sand, ant-figures at this distance, but clearly soldiers— hundreds of them. Here and there on the beach, toylike flags and banners could be seen, flapping bravely: blue and green, the colors of the Celestial Republic.

"That *is* interesting," said Mangku. "What in all Seven Hells are they doing there?"

Arif had no answer but Mangku did not require one of him. The sorcerer knew after only a few moments' consideration what he was seeing down there. It could only be an assault force. And what were they going to assault? That was obvious. They were going to march a dozen miles north and come up on the Gates of Stone by the back door. *The Celestial Republic is attacking the Indujah Federation at Istana Kush,* Mangku thought. *How does this affect my plans? It is good news, surely.* It meant war between the two greatest forces in the Laut Besar—and war meant chaos, which should make the task of obtaining the rest of the Keys of Power without interference a good deal easier.

"Ha! And they said that route was impassable!" He slapped Arif on the shoulder. "We shall see whether it is! But I salute whoever came up with this audacious plan of attack."

But do I want it to succeed? Mangku thought. *War is good, certainly, but the capture of the Gates of Stone by the Celestial Republic would not make my task easier. No, I do not think I want them to succeed.* "We must make more haste, man!" he said aloud. "This news will earn us much goodwill when we report it in the Federation outpost in the delta tonight. And if there is some small reward for the information—it shall be all yours, Arif!"

"Oh, thank you, master," said Arif. And when Mangku looked away, he rolled his eyes.

They approached the nest cautiously, Arif cradling his loaded, primed and cocked musket in his hands, now clammy despite the cold.

The last part of the climb was almost sheer, and Mangku was forced to abandon his staff and use both hands to scale the last few feet of icy rock, with Arif waiting below, looking up fearfully as his master, long-limbed as a spider, hauled his way up to the shelf. Mangku peered over the lip, nose wrinkling at the ammoniacal reek of ancient feces. He saw it. His mind glowed with joy.

Inside the large nest was an egg. The sorcerer rolled into the nest, came up onto his knees in the soft bed of feathers. He reached out his long arms and picked up the large egg in both hands—it was lighter than he expected, and warm. An egg was good, very good. It meant the Queen could not be far away.

"Master! There's one of them!"

A huge shadow blocked out the sun and Mangku ducked. There was a rush of wind and an outraged maternal cry. The Garuda slashed with its long red talons as it passed, the needle-points catching on the warm sheepskin hat Mangku wore and tearing it free, but doing no more damage.

"It's the Queen. Shoot it, Arif. Kill her now!"

The Queen of the Garuda was circling, red-gold wings spread wide. She was shrieking in fury. She turned and came in for another pass, scarlet talons reaching for Mangku's unprotected head. She slashed at the sorcerer's bowed back as he curled over the egg, ripping through the cotton robe, her cries deafening. A fury of beating wings and wind. And then she was past him, hovering in the air twenty paces away, spitting her hatred. Mangku could clearly make out the spray of golden feathers on her white head.

His prize. The Key of Air.

The musket barked, a spear of red flame, and the ball smashed into the center of the chest of the enormous bird, knocking her back. The Garuda hovered in the air for a moment, long wings still flapping and Mangku could see the punctured flesh and blood oozing on the white breast feathers. The Queen dropped like a bag of sand, giving one last heartrending cry as she plunged and crashed on the rocky slopes below.

"A fine shot, Arif. You took her like a marksman."

The sorcerer tossed the egg aside and stood peering down at the creature, still tumbling slowly down the mountain, rolling over and over, wings flopping loose. It came to rest in a loose bundle of red-gold and white feathers near the tracks in the snow that they had made on their ascent, blood spilling brilliantly red out onto the frozen ground.

Then he began the task of climbing down the sheer face of the rock shelf.

The male Garuda attacked from below. He came up over the crest unseen and, still rising, struck Arif with both talons full in the chest as the man was in the act of reloading his musket. The bird's long claws sank into Arif's chest, punching all the air from his lungs, and with one lazy sweep of its wings the male bore his captive away, Arif's legs kicking uselessly, the musket tumbling into the void, terrified screams bouncing off the mountainside. The bird carried Arif a hundred paces out into the thin air, heading westwards, its talons locked in his rib cage, high over the rocky slope—and then released him. Arif fell for three heartbeats before his body smashed against a spur of stone a thousand feet below.

Mangku wasted no time grieving for his servant. He gathered up his long staff and began to hurry, stumbling a little down the trail of footsteps that he and Arif had left in the snow on their ascent. He had to get to the Queen before anything happened to the corpse.

The male Garuda came at him, swooping from almost directly above, screaming his rage. Mangku lunged up with his staff, the pointed end slamming up into the soft white feathers of the bird's chest, and the creature retreated, flapping away toward the peak, cawing angrily. And suddenly there were more of them, five, six, seven huge, flapping monsters, wheeling overhead and swooping to slice at Mangku with their razor talons.

He ducked, ducked again, tripped and found himself flat on his face in the drift. He rolled as a huge, screaming bird came sweeping in, the long claws scraping the snow like the tines of an enormous rake where he had lain just moments before. He scrambled to his knees, cuddling the staff to his chest. There was a flapping whoosh and a searing pain in his left shoulder as another attacking bird slashed through the padded-cotton tunic and ripped deep into the meat. He was knocked on his face in the snow by the force of the strike, the blood pulsing hot and wet, soaking the cotton material and the pure white bank around him.

Another bird slashed across his vision and he was burrowing down, tunneling into the snowdrift, like a mouse beneath a kestrel. His mind was all red panic; terror filled his soul. This was no way to die—his great task of liberation not even half-completed. Torn apart by flapping monstrosities on a frozen mountainside. He rolled on his back in the snow. His shoulder was screaming in pain. He pressed the metal blade at the top of his staff into the wound, felt it sink into the already deeply lacerated flesh. He sensed the staff almost gulping, sucking at his flesh, drinking down his lifeblood, filling itself with his magical essence.

The green crystal glowed with power. He could feel its dark heat against his chest. He wiped the snow from his face and immediately saw the bird. The Garuda came hurtling in, flat and low this time, talons reaching out again, beak gaping to expose its bright pink maw. Mangku shouted the word of command, and lifted the staff toward the incoming creature, holding it out extended in both hands like a spear.

A bolt of green fire leaped from the iron tip and crashed into the bird's right wing, the feathers immediately bursting into sickly green flames. The bird fell suddenly, right wing now a charred, useless wreck, its body thumping into the snow just yards from Mangku's own body. It tried to rise, floundering with only one good wing, unbalanced, yet hopping on its talons toward the sorcerer, long beak carving furrows in the air. Mangku, still on his back and half-covered with snow, pointed the staff once more, aimed, uttered the word, and a sheet of green ichor engulfed the stricken animal, the red-gold wing feathers popping like fireworks. A blackened shape, strangely humanlike, flopped in the snow, twitched once and was still.

Mangku sat up. He felt sick and weak; his shoulder was sheer agony. But he forced himself to push the blade of his staff back into the mouth of the wound. The green jewel pulsed again. The staff in his hands felt heavy and hot. He slowly levered himself to his feet with it, letting the staff carry his weight. The Garuda were still there—three, no four enormous birds wheeling all around, shrieking like gigantic, furious seagulls.

Now one came swooping down, talons reaching out but Mangku was ready for it. He lifted the staff, holding it like a musket in both hands, said the words, and a bolt of sickly green energy speared out from its tip. The Garuda dipped a wing and slid sideways in the air, and the jet of magic missed it completely.

Mangku swore, aimed the staff again, but another creature was on him now, out of nowhere; its right talon arced out and sliced into his face, cutting a deep gash from the corner of his eye down to his jawline. He fell to his knees and yet another bird passed inches over his head. He forced himself back up onto his feet. A bird was screaming in his face: he swung and smashed at the Garuda with his staff, catching it on the side of its beak with the jewel end. The animal exploded in a ball of green ichor-fire and crashed to the ground a few paces away, sizzling and stinking in the snow.

Enough was enough. He was Mangku the Sorcerer. Master of Demons. He would not be conquered here. Not by a gaggle of oversized geese. He pressed the blade around the jewel at the end of his staff to his bleeding face, widening the cut, and felt the stone swell and grow, pulsing as it fed on his blood, renewing its power once more. He scratched a rough circle around him in the snow with the tip of his weapon. He wiped at the blood now streaming freely down his face, ignoring the pain in his shoulder as he moved his left arm, and scattered a few drops of blood all around him inside the circle from his dripping fingers. He uttered the ancient mantra—his voice growling with a harsh new puissance—and a wall of ichor sprang up all around, a shield of emerald flame. Now protected, he took careful aim with the staff at a passing bird, skimming along the crest of the ridge. He said the words, the staff discharged, the Garuda disintegrated in a cloud of blood, feathers and raw green magic.

He targeted another, blasting it with a jet of green and tumbling it away over the edge of the mountain. He aimed at a third, farther way—and the bolt of green power fell short.

And it was all over. The surviving birds flapped away, cawing their hatred and grief, leaving Mangku in a blackened circle, his face a bloody mask, his left shoulder ripped to the bone, wreathed in a virulent smoke, his staff as hot as a glowing poker in his shaking hands.

He made it down to the corpse of the Queen without being further molested by the Garuda males. He knelt trembling in the snow and used the blade on his staff to hack out the spray of golden feathers from her narrow head; he tucked the gory bundle into the pouch at his waist. Then he began to stumble, with a drunk's lack of limb control, back down the mountain.

After a hundred yards, his vision was blurring, the pain of his shoulder made the whole of his left side a slab of raging fire, and his badly sliced face was swollen twice its size and throbbing like a Temple drum. He was weak from massive loss of blood but also from the expression of so much raw magic. He could not recall when he had last used so much power in so short a space of time. He was desperate for food, for fuel and for sleep, his exhaustion almost complete, his eyes closing as he lurched along, one foot clumping down in front of another, sinking deep into the snowdrifts. If he could just go a little farther, just a few more steps, if only he could make it to . . .

Three hours later, in the golden light of late afternoon, Mangku awoke. He was alive, plainly, and at some point he had crossed the snow line and made it down to the crumbling black rock, where he had collapsed and passed into unconsciousness. The Garuda were nowhere to be seen and he breathed a sigh of relief for he knew that he could summon no more magic—and would not be able to for some days. And he had no other weapon.

Somehow, he got back up to his feet, levering his body up with the staff, and continued the shambling descent. Stumbling, slipping on the friable volcanic path, falling painfully to his skinned knees from time to time. But on he marched, determined, on and on, down and down, sometimes in a sort of weird dreamland with phantom birds screaming in his ears, sometimes in the agony of absolute reality. Down he went, one hesitant, shaking step after another.

A little after nightfall, he found himself staggering along the main street of the Federation border outpost on the north bank of the River Pengut, using his staff as a crutch. There was a huge, dark, vaguely human shape looming in front of him, with two smaller shapes on either side. He lurched closer, very near to the end, and saw with some surprise that it was Kanto, one of his Ziran Atari crew, and two slight Han prostitutes, one on either of his heavy muscular arms.

"Kanto. Happy to see. You. Must . . . must take me to . . . Federation officer, immediately," he said. Then his knees sagged and he slipped out of the world for a time.

Typically, Kanto did not obey him. He came to again in some slut's boudoir, a fragile bamboo hut that smelled of rancid sex and cheap perfume, with a Han girl clumsily sewing up his torn shoulder, and Kanto trying to feed him some chicken broth laced with a good deal of sour marak.

"I must see the Federation official, Kanto," he muttered. "Utmost importance."

He felt himself falling back into the abyss, and forced himself to sit up. He pushed the Han girl away and tried to stand. His legs gave way and he fell back into blackness.

He was not all that much stronger in the morning. But for a silver ringgu, the Han girl allowed him to clean himself up in her washbasin and made him a portion of fried rice with eggs and a bowl of spicy fish soup. Next, he persuaded Kanto to take him to the Federation office. It was not long after sunrise and supporting himself between the huge, black-skinned sailor's arm and his staff, he made his report to the very young captain in charge of this tiny military post, which marked the southern limit of the territory directly controlled by the Federation, a hundred miles as the messenger-pigeon flies southeast of Istana Kush.

The Dokra captain, looking like a child dressed up for a pageant in his scarlet coat with white cross belt and gold epaulets, was incredulous when Mangku told him that he had seen a large number of troops landing on the inhospitable western side of the Barat Cordillera. In fact, he refused to believe a single word that the tall, gaunt, terrifying man, clearly exhausted and badly wounded, had to say. But Mangku was most insistent.

"I climbed Mount Barat yesterday morning and near the summit I looked down on the western side and saw a force of Celestial Legionnaires, perhaps two or three hundred men, disembarking from three ships."

"Is that so?" said the captain.

"It is. I presume they are an assault force and will be heading north," Mangku said.

"Indeed?" said the captain. This was obviously nonsense. No infantry force could march north on the western side of the Cordillera. The terrain was famously impassible.

"I would think the Federation might be interested in this intelligence. Legionnaires heading toward Istana with hostile intent. You might wish to report it to your superiors."

"Well, thank you, Mister, uh, Mangku. I shall pass on your concerns. Is there anything else I can help you with today?"

Mangku looked at him with loathing. If any living creature deserved a blast from his staff, it was this idiotic puppy-in-uniform. But he knew he simply did not have the strength.

"No, nothing. I shall take my leave now. Good day to you.

"Take me back to the ship now, Kanto," said Mangku, when they were outside the Federation office. Once more his body was betraying him; the world was blurring and twisting at the edges. His knee joints felt dangerously liquid, his feet heavy as boulders.

He put a hand on the leather pouch at his waist and took strength from one thought, one wonderful thought, as they staggered out into the blazing sunshine: the Third Key, the Key of Air, was his.

CHAPTER 31

⸏⸙⸏

Farhan felt curiously light as he stepped out of the gate of the bamboo fort and began to walk across the open ground toward the trees. True, he wore nothing but rope sandals, a pair of short, linen breeches and a loose, linen shirt—he had abandoned any thought of trying to armor himself against the poisoned darts—but it was more than that. It was as if all the great burdens of his life—his debts, his deceptions, his secrets, his failures, his appetites, his fears, his painful, unquenchable love for *her*—all the sad and wonderful things that made him the man he was, all of them were gone. Stripped away by this one grand gesture.

I'm going to my death, he thought. *All my life has been leading up to this point. This is the best and the worst thing I have ever done. This is the apex of my existence—or is it? In a moment I shall know whether there is an afterlife and if all the threats and promises of the soul-merchants are true or, as I have always suspected, a pack of self-serving lies.*

They had fired an unloaded cannon to command the attention of the savages, and hung a pair of crossed palm leaves, stripped from the roof of one of the shelters that Captain Ravi had built, over the side of the bamboo walls. After a long pause, more than an hour, a horrible period for Farhan who spent it writing letters in the tent and drinking most of a flask of marak, a white-caked man emerged from the trees, dumped a pair of crossed palm leaves in the dust and stalked back into the jungle.

Farhan remembered just in time to draw a large scythe on his forehead with a piece of charcoal from the kitchen fire pit, and then Captain Lodi was heartily shaking his hand with, astoundingly, the glint of tears in his eyes; Mamaji was enfolding him in a sweaty, motherly hug; Lila was looking solemnly at him—and was that a new respect in her big, dark eyes? The Dokra were saluting him, stamping and presenting arms with a violent precision that would not have disgraced the High Council parade ground in Dhilika, and he was stepping—light as air—across the clearing and heading for the trees and toward his certain doom.

He stopped at the edge of the clearing, his skin itching, at every moment expecting to feel the sting of the darts in his flesh. Then he stooped and picked up the crossed palm leaves. Shaking the dust from them and holding them across his body, like a fan or a shield, he walked slowly into the jungle. Farhan felt several dozen pairs of eyes on him but it took a moment for his own sight to adjust to the gloom. A tall, painted man walked toward him; he reached out and gently took the palm leaves from his hand. The man said, in a language not very far from the ancient Yawanese that Farhan had been forced to study at school, "You are now under the protection of the Great Harvester. You live at the pleasure of his mercy."

Once Farhan's brain had deciphered the meaning of his message, a surge of relief ran through his body from his crown to his toes and, unable to stop his face from beaming—and suppressing an urge to throw his arms around the man and hug him—he said, dredging his memory for the correct form, "All honor and praise to Vharkash. We live in his shadow."

A pack of a dozen of them gathered around Farhan, either to guard him from others or make sure he did not escape, each man carrying a long pipe with a little pouch of darts at his belt and

all slathered in the white clay decorated with gray and black
stripes. Each man, Farhan noticed, had his own distinct pattern
of stripes, with no man's the same as another's. They led him
deeper into the jungle along paths that Farhan could see had been
well trodden by human feet. After about a quarter of an hour—
much farther away from the clearing, the fort and all his friends
than Farhan liked—he found himself being led into a village, a
settlement not very different from a dozen he had seen in Yawa
on previous trips. To be honest, Farhan was astounded. An area
of forest had been cleared; he could see the chopped-off stubs of
bamboo and the stumps of bigger trees, too. Two dozen long and
low mud-walled huts had been thrown up, thatched with broad,
shiny bright green leaves as big as Farhan's shirt, and there were
women and children sitting about—all naked but for brief loin-
cloths but none of them painted with the white clay of the warriors and, indeed, looking like perfectly ordinary Yawanese
peasants. One woman, her heavy breasts swinging with every
stroke of the ax, was chopping firewood by a stone-lined hearth
outside one of the bigger huts. A slender young girl, with exquisite
natural grace, was carrying a large pot of water on her head across
the outskirts of the village. Older children cried out and came
running to the knot of painted men, clamoring for a sight of the
mysterious stranger with the pale skin in the outlandish linen
breeches and shirt. Owlish babies, sucking on sweet roots or just
their own thumbs, stared up at him from the dust. But every one
of them from the smallest baby to the most decrepit graybeard
had a scythe drawn or tattooed in the center of his forehead. And
they all seemed very interested in Farhan, eyeing him curiously
with what seemed to his scrambled, fevered mind very much like
hunger.

    Then he saw it. A gibbet—a simple bamboo pole with two
A-shaped supports keeping it ten feet in the air. And hanging from
it by the heels was a human form, his long black hair hanging

down almost to the ground. Not a gibbet, Farhan thought, a gralloching frame. He had used similar structures for the deer carcasses when out hunting with his father. And like the stags of his
boyhood, the naked body hanging from the frame had been evis-
cerated, the chest and stomach contents removed, and it flapped
open obscenely. Most of the left leg between the knee and hip
had also been taken away and Farhan, swallowing bile, determined not to show his revulsion, could see the thighbone, scraped
almost clean of flesh. Black flies crawled all over the purple surface of the meat.

Then his mouth flooded with scalding vomit as he saw the
upside-down face: it was the Dokra trooper he'd been playing dice
with two days ago on the blanket by the river. Kishan had been
his name. Sergeant Kishan. He swallowed down the acid and
averted his gaze. Where were the rest of the bodies? In this heat,
they would not last long. The answer to his question came in a
drift of gray vapor. As they walked through the center of the village he saw a large building at the edge of the circle with smoke
gently seeping through the shingle-leaves on the roof. A smoke-
house.

His brain still whirling with horror, Farhan was led to the largest hut in the circle of dwellings in the village. A mat of woven
palm leaves had been placed on the ground in front of the opening,
which was covered by a screen of long, dried grass. There was a
tiny stool beside the entrance, square, almost solid and made of
some heavy, dark wood and beautifully carved with water buffalos
and tigers, scythes and phallic shapes. It was indicated to Farhan
that he should sit on the mat, and once he had done so, crossing his
legs and trying to give the impression of perfect ease and confidence, he was given a cup of water to drink. It was surprisingly
cool and sweet-tasting. His mouth was bone dry—fear, he
supposed—and he drank it down in one draft.

One of his honor guard went over to the door of the hut, poked

his head through the grass screen and reported his arrival. The
rest of the painted men either settled down in the dust to wait, or
wandered off. The tall warrior sat down just behind Farhan's back
on the same mat with a proprietorial air, as if to say this is *my*
prisoner. To pass the time—but also to divert himself from his
own terrible thoughts—Farhan tried to work out the strength of
the enemy. By looking at the mud-walled huts and seeing more
than one warrior entering and leaving—recognizable by the different patterns on their white-painted skins—he calculated that
each hut held an extended family group, with fathers, husbands,
brothers and sons taking their role as warriors. The village, he
thought, might contain as many as three hundred people, and that
meant that there were perhaps a hundred of these white-painted
devils. Not as many as they had feared back in the safety of the
fort, which was good news. However, the fact that they had gone
to the trouble of building a village here, so close to the fort, and
that they had brought their own wives and children with them,
meant that they were not planning to leave anytime soon. Farhan's own words about human livestock in a bamboo corral came
back to him. These white-painted folk wanted to be near their
food source. There must be very few people to hunt for food in
the dense jungles of Yawa and the arrival of the *Mongoose* must
seem to them like a great windfall—a wondrous gift from Vharkash, a reward for their devotion. What could he say to them to
make them give up this holy gift from their God?

The food they had already gathered would not last them forever. About twenty Dokra had died and a handful of Buginese.
And three hundred hungry folk could easily eat one or two carcasses a day. Maybe even three. Assuming they did not eat their
own folk—and cannibals, he knew, seldom did—if you took the
worst scenario, this village would run out of food in about eight
or nine days. Maybe a week.

Another way of looking at it was that there were a hundred and sixty walking food carcasses trapped in the fort a mile or so away from here. Why would they ever give that up? Farhan racked his brain: what could he offer these people that would make them forgo two or even perhaps three months' worth of free meat? Nothing he could think of.

Farhan's increasingly insane calculations were stopped by a movement in the grass curtain at the front of the hut. A long, thin, gray hand emerged through the dried fronds, followed by the long, gray emaciated body of an ancient man. Farhan stared at him, agog. He had the usual scythe on his forehead but the whole of the rest of his body was also covered with markings, old tattoos once in black, now faded to a dusty gray: scythes, yes, many, many of them in all different shapes and sizes but also charging buffalo, leaping tigers, sinuous cobras and several images of a muscular and rather beautiful young man with long black hair, sitting with his legs crossed and his eyes lowered. The old man's groin was covered with a tanned leather loincloth, of the same kind that everybody else in the tribe wore, but every inch of his long legs, long arms and shrunken belly and chest was covered in these marvelous designs. Even his face, his eyelids, his earlobes were marked. Though the color had faded with age these tattoos still looked magnificent, and the way the man held his skinny body, proudly, carefully, as if he were an actor on a stage, gave Farhan, despite his disgust with these people and their vile habits, a powerful sense of the majesty of this patriarch. Indeed it almost seemed as if the images of the divine Vharkash printed on his sagging skin had given his person a touch of godliness.

The old man seated himself on the tiny wooden stool, extended his arms and legs to display them, laying his heels a pace apart on the ground and putting his hands on his bony knees. He said in Old Yawanese and in a surprisingly deep voice for someone so seemingly fragile, "I am Patka Du, Father of the Hantu Hari-mau, priest of Vharkash the Harvester—I grant you an audience under the Palms of Peace."

He looked into Farhan's eyes, and said, "Speak, long pig, that I may hear your squealing plea for mercy and consider it with the wisdom of all-mighty Vharkash."

Suddenly, out of nowhere, Farhan felt an insane urge to laugh. The respect, even awe, in which he had held the old man fell away, crumbling to nothing. The old man's conceit, his self-puffery, his ridiculous papery skin, the smeared, fading tattoos, his fragile, ancient body. The parochial absurdity of thinking himself a great lord of men. A power in the world. Farhan felt an urge to reach over, grasp the ancient arm before him and snap the bone like a stick of kindling. And to all the Seven Hells with the con-sequences. Who did this spindly octogenarian think he was? Far-han was a representative of the Indujah Federation, the greatest trading power in the world. A single regiment of Dokra, suitably armored against their darts—or provided with a viable antidote—could wipe out these half-human ghouls in one short campaign. These folk could be expunged from the face of the Earth—they *should* be expunged from it—in a matter of days and weeks. And yet this rheumy-eyed old worm had the temerity to call him a "long pig."

Farhan's courage rose like a pot of water boiling over. They might kill him—so what? He was ready to die. He would not bow down to these ridiculous monsters. His honor, the honor of the House of Madani, the honor of the Federation would not permit it.

Farhan stared haughtily at Patka Du. He did not speak, delib-erately letting the silence stretch out painfully, until at last the old man began fidgeting and broke the silence by saying peevishly to one of the white-painted men sitting at his side, "This fat beast does understand our tongue, does he not? I was told he spoke the correct words of the Palm of Peace to Ngushu earlier."

"I can speak your degraded tongue," said Farhan in Old Yawanese. "I sucked that skill from the souls of the men we slaughtered
in battle. And there were so many of these dead souls to learn
from that I nearly choked on the lesson."

The old man goggled at him. Farhan smiled.

"I am Farhan Madani, Lord of Dhilika and Singarasam, General of the Amrit Shakti, traveler, gambler, man-killer and merchant prince. And I come before you with a dread warning from
President Madani of the High Council of the Indujah Federation,
my esteemed father and the most powerful man in the Laut Besar,
indeed in all the wide world. My father says: 'Do not meddle with
my son or his people or you will be utterly destroyed, flicked from
the world like a troublesome fly. You have seen the power of their
weapons. You will have seen that they are able to wipe out scores
of your warriors in the blink of an eye. Know that you could, all of
you, easily, be put to death, if it pleased my son.' And I tell you
now, we have only stayed our hand because we share your devotion to Vharkash the Harvester. We worship Him, too. All praise
to Him. But know this, also: our patience is not infinite."

Farhan was rather pleased with his nonsensical bombast—the
high hand, that was the only way to deal with these ignorant cannibals. He also knew that his own long-dead father, a moderately
successful provincial merchant, would have enjoyed being post-
humously promoted to President of the Indujah Federation and
the most powerful man in the world.

Patka Du was conferring in a furious whisper with one of the
white-painted warriors. It seemed that they were arguing, although Farhan could not make out what they were saying.

The old man turned back to him. "We prayed to the Harvester
to feed us. We had been hungry for a long, long time. We used all
our magic, all the wisdom we possessed to persuade all-mighty
Vharkash to send us food—and he answered our prayers. I heard
the God myself. He came to me in a dream and he said he would

send us sustenance—but that the gift would come at a price.
When you came, we believed that you were that gift, and the
price was the lives of our warriors, which we gladly sacrificed for
the Harvester. Now, you say we were wrong. That our sacrifices
have been in vain and you offer insults and threats. And you claim
you are not human swine, but also the people of the Lord of All
the Gods."

Patka Du looked at Farhan and something in his rheumy gaze
disconcerted him.

"Some of the warriors here believe that you are truly
Vharkashta—how else could you harness the power of lightning
in your terrible weapons? Your people are warriors, as Vharkash
himself once was, and you fight with great courage. That is what
some of my own warriors say. Those who have faced you in battle.
I am not so certain—pigs in the herd do not willingly bare their
necks to the slaughter man. I believe you might say anything to
preserve your lives, even pretending to have more power than
you truly possess, even claiming the protection of the God to
whom you owe no allegiance, and for whom you have no love.
So . . . we will put it to the test."

Farhan said, "There is a fleet of Federation ships, not ten miles
off the coast of Yawa—thousands of fighting men with guns, cannon. I will not hesitate to call . . ."

"Be silent, long pig. And listen to my judgment. You will
answer one question, and only one. If you are a true child of Vharkash, you will surely know the answer. If you are a liar, Lord
Vharkash will reveal your deceit to me through your own failure
to give the only true answer. Are you ready?"

Farhan's mouth was ashy. He thought briefly of summoning
more of his threats, more imaginary hordes of Federation troops,
but that mental well was now dry. He merely nodded dumbly to
the old man's mild inquiry. What else could he do?

"The Lord Vharkash always rides into battle on a great fierce beast. All who worship the Harvester know this legendary animal and revere it, along with all its lesser brothers and sisters. Tell me, Farhan Madani, you who claim the mantle of Vharkashta, what manner of beast is this?"

Farhan's mind went blank. He had studied the religion of Vharkash at his university in Dhilika—as he had learned about all the ancient religions—but it had all been so very long ago. He looked at the old man's skin, at the aged tattoos on its gray, sagging surface: he saw the image of the handsome young man with the crossed legs and the long hair, Vharkash himself, of course, and the myriad scythes and tigers and cobras and the strange phallic symbols and . . .

He had it. It came flooding back: he knew the beast on which Lord Vharkash always rode to war. Anyone who had even briefly studied the religion did so, too.

"The beast is Bantung, the Great Bull Buffalo," said Farhan triumphantly, looking directly at the image of the same buffalo which was tattooed on the old man's belly.

There was a murmuring from the group of seated white-painted warriors. The old man stared at him for several long moments, and then he said, "Bind him!"

Farhan's mouth dropped open, and suddenly he was at the center of a scrum of white-painted bodies. His arms were seized and lashed to a bamboo pole, and then his wildly kicking legs were quickly subdued and bound there, too. And two big warriors grasped the ends of the pole and hoisted him into the air. Hanging under the pole like a terrified sloth, Farhan tried one more salvo of bluster, "What is the meaning of this! I have answered your question—and correctly. Furthermore, I have been granted audience under the Palms of Peace. I warn you that there will be repercussions if you do not release me immediately! Fire, plague, the slaughter of all your children . . ."

"Stop that pig's squealing," said Patka Du. And a filthy rag was shoved into Farhan's mouth and tied there with another around the back of his head.

The old man came to stand next to him: his eyes were burning with a dark, fiery rage. "You are not true Vharkashta. Our Lord does not ride into war on Bantung the Buffalo—any child knows that. Bantung is his creature, yes, but never his war mount. That is the foul heresy of the Western Lands, as if the Lord would defile himself with a dumb slave of the rice fields. The war beast of Vharkash is the Ghost Tiger Raal—the mighty gray jungle cat after whom we take our name—the Hantu Harimau—and from whom we are descended. If you were a true follower of Vharkash, you would surely know that. But you are not. You are a liar, a deceiver—you and your kind are merely two-legged swine sent to us to be harvested by the Great Harvester himself."

Patka Du stepped in. He put his skinny thumb on the charcoal scythe on Farhan's forehead, and with a hard sweep he wiped the mark away. Then he poked a stiff finger into Farhan's soft middle, the digit sinking into the fat around his waist.

"You'll make fine eating, my lying little pig, in a day or so, when the Hantu Harimau have finished with the other carcasses the God has generously provided."

CHAPTER 32

———— ✿ ————

Jun sprinted for his pack and in moments he had the bow in his hands and the full war quiver of thirty-six arrows strapped to a belt at his waist. He jumped up onto the masonry foundation block beside Tenga, and gazed out over the field of rubble and grass. He could see nothing at all. No sign of the Mbaru, no sign of slave-hounds or bear-dogs. He looked questioningly at Tenga. The big woman's face was bleak.

"Yes, they have found us," she said. "It is only a matter of time, now." She had a stone in her left hand and she spat on the long, steel parang in her right, and began to run the stone, slowly, carefully down the edge.

Jun turned to look for Semar. He saw that he was in earnest conversation with Ketut. She was shaking her head and he was insisting.

Eventually, she agreed, got up and came over to Jun and Tenga. She handed the older woman the parang. "I won't be using this," she said. "But you might find it useful."

"What are you doing, Tut? You know what will happen if they catch you."

"Semar wants me to try . . . something else." Ketut turned away from them and walked over to the offering block in the center of the temple. She settled down on top of it with her legs crossed. She took a deep breath and closed her eyes.

"Is she mad?" said Tenga. "They're out there now. It is no time to take a nap."

"She is trying to summon the personage you would call Queen

of Fire," said Semar, who had come close to them. "You and I know her as Dargan," he said to Jun.

"Can she really do that?" Tenga looked genuinely shocked.

Jun was looking out over the wall—there was still no sign of the Mbaru. "She has done it before," he said, without looking at her. "She is what we call a Vessel. I saw her do it in a temple ceremony in Sukatan. She was inhabited by the Goddess."

Jun turned to look at Semar now. "But can she do it, cold, like this, with no orchestra, no drums, no obat smoke—no *religion*, at all?"

"I have been helping her to open her heart to the Goddess. I think she might be able to achieve it—cold, as you put it. Perhaps. Anyway, it is certainly worth a try with the Mbaru here. What use would one small girl with a parang be against them?"

"Could we run?" asked Jun.

"Can you run anymore?" Semar countered.

Jun thought about it for a second. "So we fight," he said.

"You two will fight," said Semar. "I shall pray."

Jun stared at him, incredulous. Semar caught the look. "I told you that I was once a priest here at the Mother Temple. In fact, I was the High Priest, lord of all the others. I took my vows as a novice no more than two hundred paces from here, over there where the main temple used to be. I made the same vow that every novice has made there for hundreds of years: I swore that I would spill no human blood."

"Yes, I understand," said Jun, "but these people are Mbaru— they are killers, murderers, man-hunters. They would drag us back to that hell under the mountain. Surely you could spill *their* blood—surely you could make an exception. Vharkash would forgive you. I know he would."

"Are they not human? I swore I would not spill their blood. I shall never break my oath. Even if it be the cause of my death— and a thousand other deaths."

"Couldn't you blast them with fireballs, or explode their heads with a wave of your hand, or turn them into frogs or something?"

"No," said Semar, smiling. "I don't do that. I'm not a sorcerer. I'm a priest. I pray."

Jun found he had nothing to say.

Semar said, "That does not mean that *you* cannot spill their blood. You have taken no oath. Spill as much of their blood as you like—splash it all over the temple walls. Shoot them full of holes. Chop them into little pieces. You have my blessing. I shall be just over there praying, humbly asking my God to come to our aid."

The slave-hounds sounded again: they were very close now.

"It's just me and you, King Jun," said Tenga, scraping the blades of the two parangs that she held, one in each hand, together. "One last good fight before the end."

Jun was not listening: he realized that at some level he had long known that Semar was more than a servant. He was a man of power, clearly. The way he persuaded people to do things; the way he could speak inside one's head. He had always thought that when it came to the extreme, Semar would have some magical trick, or at least some clever stratagem to save them. His disappointment was a vast hole in his being.

He watched Semar, frail, ancient, his wispy hair wild about his wrinkled old head, settle himself against a block of gray stone. He put his crossed feet up in his lap and settled himself, eyes closed, staff at his side. He pressed his hands together in the attitude of prayer. And Jun could hear, very faintly, the sound of his humming. And something strange and magical did happen: Semar seemed to merge with the gray stone. His gray sarong, his gray skin and hair were the exact same color as the broken rock at his back. Jun found that if you looked away and looked back, it took a few moments and the certain knowledge that the old man was there, before he could make him out. He was almost invisible. He was like one of those lizards who take on the colors of their backgrounds to hide from enemies.

Was *that* what Semar was doing? Was he planning to hide from the Mbaru in plain sight?

"There they are," said Tenga. They were both crouched behind the wall, only the tops of their heads visible from the outside.

Jun's attention snapped back outside the wall. There was a man in a wide-brimmed, black-leather hat coming across the field of rubble, picking his way carefully, with a long, lean hound with a massive square head straining at the leash in his right hand. The man was about fifty paces away, and he came on cautiously, stopping every few paces to look around him. The hound was eager, pulling the man forward, and sometimes stopping to let out the wolflike howls that had spurred the fugitives on in the jungle. When he was thirty paces away, the man stopped: the hound was pulled back onto its haunches and began to give off a different sound, a series of short, high, chopped barks. Then it stopped. Its blunt nose pointed at the Temple of Burunya.

"They have us now," said Tenga.

Jun shot the man in the stomach. He stood up, nocked, drew and loosed, and the man in the black hat was looking at a shaft of straight bamboo, with a narrow steel tip, that was stuck right through the center of his body. He fell to his knees, the blood blooming on his grubby white shirt; he released the leash and grasped the bamboo shaft with both hands. The hound, suddenly freed, leaped forward, racing toward the temple at a terrifying speed. Jun loosed again, and missed.

The dog was a mere five paces away when Jun's arrow took it in its hindquarters, striking just below its pelvis and knocking the animal over to tumble into the rocks. The animal was howling, screaming, its back legs useless, its front paws pulling it forward toward the stone wall. Jun shot it again, at a sharp downward angle, and the shaft punched through its skull and quieted it forever.

"Good kill, King Jun," said Tenga. "But don't waste arrows on mercy shots."

"Don't call me that," said Jun sharply. "I'm not a king—not yet. If you want to be respectful, my correct title is . . . oh never mind that, just call me Jun, all right?"

Tenga grinned at him, her face resembling a dark skull.

They watched the man with the arrow in his belly bleed to death. He called out piteously to his friends and tried to crawl back to the edge of the field, to the thicker cover, but he only got so far before the loss of blood made him too weak to continue. They saw one or two figures moving about, dodging quickly between thick clumps of head-high grass, well out of range of Jun's bow. But no one came out to help the man in the black hat. His screams dwindled, faded and died.

After an hour, Jun found to his surprise that he was growing bored. He looked at Ketut; she did not seem to have moved from the spot before the big offering stone. It took Jun a few moments to find Semar, but once he had a fix on him Jun saw that the old man did not appear to have changed his position either.

"Maybe they have gone," said Jun to Tenga. "Maybe they've been discouraged and have given up and gone home."

"No. They never give up. They are just waiting for the . . ."

At that moment, three large black objects catapulted out of a clump of trees on the far side of the field and came hurtling toward the temple.

"Bear-dogs!" shouted Tenga, and to Jun's surprise she leaped off the foundation block and went to stand half a dozen paces away before the spilled gate, taking up a wide-legged pose with the two raised parangs in her hands called The Crab that Jun recognized from his own training. Tenga stood still, directly between the split gate and the offering stone where Ketut was oblivious in her trance state.

Jun's attention leaped back to the three bear-dogs, now fifty paces away and closing as fast as charging horses. Jun nocked, drew and loosed. He hit the foremost bear-dog in its meaty shoulder, burying the shaft deep into the muscle. It did not check the animal in the slightest. It came hurtling on forward, the bamboo shaft standing proud from its shaggy black coat, heading straight for the spilled gate. Jun loosed again; the arrow hit the animal's hindquarters, pushing it off its line and making it stumble, but on it came. A third shaft, stuck in its ribs, caused it to howl, but by then it was bounding through the gate, knocking the thorn barricade away as if it were no more than straw.

It leaped directly at Tenga, up, up, its red jaws open, displaying huge yellow teeth—and the big woman moved to one side, neat as a temple dancer, the two parangs describing shining arcs in the air. Slice, slice, and the beast's outstretched right forepaw, then its whole head, leaped from its flying body.

The second bear-dog was already through the gate now. Jun got one slim arrow into its hairy side, sinking the shaft in right to the fletchings. But now it was leaping at Tenga.

And the third bear-dog barrelled through the gate, saw him and angled right, directly at the big block of stone on which he was standing. Jun loosed and shot but the beast must have had bones of iron. The shaft cracked into its broad muscular chest but only sank in a few inches. The beast checked, clawed at its chest, dislodged the shaft. Yet Jun was reaching for another. The huge animal gathered itself, snarled, leaped up on the flat surface of the stone, its claws scrabbling wildly to keep a grip. It found its balance, tensed its massive muscles, opened its huge mouth wide, foam dripping from its curved yellow fangs, and gave a roar that shook the clouds . . .

And Jun put an arrow right into its open red gullet. The animal was bowled over, knocked off the stone, falling hard on its side on the grass floor of the temple. Its back legs were still kicking, long claws scything the air, bamboo protruding from its mouth. And

Jun nocked, drew and punched another shaft through its hairy ribs, then slammed in another one next to that for good measure.

He looked over at Tenga. Her right shoulder was a glistening mass of blood. But the second bear-dog was lying on its back at her feet, its body hacked open in places to reveal the purplish flesh. One of the parang blades, still quivering, was sticking up proudly from the center of its chest.

Tenga was grinning through the pain. "At least we know now what's for dinner," she said.

Jun frowned at her.

"Bear-dogs make good eating, if you're hungry enough," she said, then sat down heavily.

The Mbaru called for a parlay at dusk. A flat-faced, Han-looking fellow with long black hair, black boots but no visible weapons stepped out of the scrub carrying two crossed palm leaves, and even Jun knew that this was the old sign for a truce, and he beckoned him forward. The man stopped ten paces short of the temple gate, at Jun's command, and the prince of Taman stepped out through the gate to meet him.

"So you got the better of those nasty old bear-dogs, eh?" said the Mbaru, craning his neck past Jun to look through the spilled gate where Semar was kindling a fire beside the carcass of one of the animals. Ketut was dressing the bites on Tenga's shoulder. Her attempts to summon Dargan, Queen of the Witches, outside of the frenzy of the Hallowed Day ritual had evidently been a failure. Semar's prayers had been ignored, too, as far as Jun could tell.

"You got all three of them, eh? You have my genuine respect, sir. Real respect. But then that mad black bitch has some experience with these beasts, eh? Killed one once with just her own bare hands. Did she ever tell you that?"

The man had a gentle, folksy, familiar voice, like a beloved uncle.

"What do you want?" said Jun. He still had the bow in his hand but no shaft nocked.

"And they are expensive, you know that, very dear animals, those old bear-dogs. My, are they pricey. You got to buy them from the sea traders, you know? And they come all the way from the black forests of Frankland. Then you gotta train them up, get the smell of slave in their snouts, keep 'em hungry but not too hungry or they just go plain wild. It all takes hard-earned cash money."

"Tell me what you want, sir," said Jun. "Tell me before my patience wears thin."

"All business this evening, son, eh? Good, I do like that. So . . . we hunters are now substantially out of pocket. I just want you to know that. We are down three very expensive bear-dogs, thanks to your courage, your grit and your very fine skills with a bow. We want to recoup our money. So this is what I propose—you know we gets more for a live Runner than just a head, yes?"

Jun nodded. He could hardly believe he was having this conversation.

"Well, me and the boys—we got twenty good men out there, just so you know, and another two hounds—we think you should give yourselves up to us nice and peaceful. We'll treat you right; we'll take you back to the Konda, sure, but we'll treat you real gentle on the way there. The beauty of it all is this: we get to recoup our money, by sending in live bodies, 'stead of just heads, and you—you-all don't get anybody messing with you on the way home—none o' that ugly raping and beating and whipping and stomping and cutting off of delicate parts, know what I mean?"

"I know what you mean," said Jun. "And our answer is no."

"Because we'll get you, you know that. We got twenty men, night's drawing on, and there's a half company of Manchu, fifty musket men, on the trail behind us. We'll get you-all, in time. What you got? One good man—which is you, sir—one crazy black bitch, an' she's wounded, an old man an' a little girl. You like them odds?"

"I'll make sure I pick you out personally and skewer you when you do come," said Jun. "You'll certainly be dead, even if you do get us. How d'you like those odds?"

"Now, friend, no need to be like that. I came here to make an honest proposal, and I've been more than respectful. The deal stands. Come in quiet and we'll treat you real gentle."

"No, thank you," said Jun.

"Come now, sir, I beg you to reconsider. We don't want any unnecessary bloodshed, I'm sure. I recall making a deal with another gang o' hotheaded Runners, why, must ha' been more'n a year ago . . ."

Jun realized something was wrong. The man had had his answer, and it had been given quite clearly, and yet he was still talking. What did he want?

". . . and everybody was satisfied in the end. Why, they finished up their sentence at the Konda Pali and went home to their families in five short years. Five little years . . ."

"Time for you to go now," said Jun. "No more talking."

"I'm going, sir, I'm surely going. I just wanted to say one more—" The man stopped talking abruptly. His face changed shape. His mouth dropped open. In that instant he looked utterly terrified. "What in the name of the Seven Hells is that?" He lifted a trembling finger and pointed over Jun's shoulder at the wall of the temple.

Jun whirled and looked where the man was pointing. He could see nothing but the last rays of the westering sun casting long shadows on the wall. A heavy weight landed on his shoulders. He reacted instinctively, reaching behind himself to shrug off the Mbaru who had seized him from behind. And stopped. He felt the chill of cold steel at his neck, a sharp blade splitting the soft skin below his jaw. And a friendly, folksy voice saying, "Hold very still now, youngster. I'll take back your head, if I must. I'll cut it clean off right now, if you make me do it, but I'd far rather have you walk back there on your own two feet, just for the extra money, ya know?"

Jun had never felt more of a fool. Tenga exploded out of the split gate, the two parangs in her hands, and Ketut right on her heels.

"Keep your distance, blackie. Or your pretty boyfriend loses his head."

Tenga stopped, one of the parangs raised to strike, the other out in front. The Locust pose.

Ketut sank to the ground, closed her eyes and began to chant, a hum too low for Jun to make out. Out of the corner of his eye, he could see a score of men rising right out of the ground, or so it seemed. They were much closer now, no more than fifty paces away, and he knew then that the talkative man had deliberately held his attention so the Mbaru could creep forward unobserved.

Tenga said, "You let him go now, Willuk. Take that big knife from his throat. Let him go and you can fight me. One to one, as if you were a real man. I'll let you keep hold of that ugly blade and, to make it properly fair, I'll rid myself of these slashers." She shook the pair of parangs at him.

The man, Willuk, merely laughed.

Jun's gaze was drawn to Ketut. Her humming chant had got much louder—something was changing; her shape was becoming blurred. Was there something wrong with his eyes? There was a foul smell in the air, shit and fleshly corruption. And Ketut seemed to be growing, expanding . . .

"You put down those grass-choppers, blackie, or you won't live till moonrise."

"Let the boy go, Willuk," Tenga's voice grated.

A single musket shot rang out. Ketut gave a cry. Tenga cursed and swung round to look at Ketut, who was now slumped back against the outer wall of the temple, bleeding, then she swung back to face the oncoming Mbaru slave-hunters. One man at the front of the pack had a long gun to his shoulder, smoke trickling from the muzzle. Tenga gave a wild ululating yell and, ignoring both Jun and Willuk, she charged, running full pelt straight at the oncoming hunters, both parangs lofted.

Then for Jun it all became terribly confused. The Mbaru were hurrying forward; Tenga was madly rushing out to meet them. And suddenly there were huge, low, gray, agile shapes bounding out of the broken stones to his left, coming in from the east. Tigers. Enormous tigers, with white fur striped with black and gray, were charging into the mass of the Mbaru, their hair-raising roars ripping through the twilight. There were at least four of them, Jun saw. The first one leaped, a gray arc in the air, and landed on the nearest Mbaru, knocking him to the ground. The massive striped head went down into the prone man's body; there was a flash of white teeth, a splash of red as the tiger's head ripped back, tearing free a chunk of flesh. The animal swallowed.

Another tiger swiped at a passing Mbaru, its muscular paw and massive claws catching the fellow in the small of his back and sending his rag-doll body spinning away. A third tiger leaped on one of the hunters' backs, knocking him to his knees. Jaws crunched through his skull. Elsewhere the Mbaru were running, steaming across the field of broken stones. A tiger sprang out of a clump of long grass and easily caught one of the runners, knocking him tumbling with a paw-swipe and then leaping forward to bite, its massive teeth sinking into the man's leg as it kicked in the air.

Tenga had abruptly stopped her wild charge and was standing, quite still, staring at the tigers and their terrified, fleeing prey. One of the tigers, perhaps the biggest of them all, his white mask heavily marked with black stripes and splashed with fresh blood, looked up from the remains of the man he had been feeding on, saw Tenga standing there a dozen yards away and, abandoning his half-eaten meal, began to come toward her, creeping low on his haunches in the classic stalking gait of the cat.

Semar came sprinting out of the split gate of the temple, he flashed past Jun and Willuk, ignoring Ketut, who was slumped bloodily by the outside wall, eyes closed, mouth open; he rushed straight into the field of stones, shouting, "Not her, Raal, not her. No! She's one of ours!"

Jun felt the arm around his neck loosen its grip a little, and the blade come slightly away from his skin. He reached back, grasped Willuk's right elbow with his left hand, seized his right shoulder with his right hand, put his right hip out, twisted his back and pulled.

Willuk shot over his shoulder and crashed to the floor, the heavy hunting knife spinning from his grasp. The man sat up groggily, breathless, stunned. Jun bent, scooped up the long blade in a hammer grip and slammed it into the fallen hunter's waist on the left without the slightest hesitation. He punched the sharp steel into the man's belly, right up to the hilt, then standing over the man, he ripped the blade all the way across to Willuk's right hip, eviscerating him in one hard, grunting swipe, and causing the man's glistening, bloody guts to dump out across his own thighs. Willuk screamed, gasped once and screamed again and again.

Jun stood tall over his victim, the bloody knife in his right hand. The last light was fading from the day. The other Mbaru were in full flight. He saw the last disappear into a stand of scrubby trees, swallowed up by the green. The field was littered with the bodies of those who had not run, half a dozen at least. Semar was standing placidly beside an astonished Tenga and the biggest of the great tigers, the little man resting his old hand familiarly on the giant carnivore's soft gray head.

CHAPTER 33

————— ✦ —————

I t was not even noon and Katerina already wanted to call the whole expedition off, to halt and huddle up in a rocky hollow out of the sun and quietly expire.

She had never expected the march to be this hard. The ravines on the western side of Barat Cordillera were brutally steep, almost vertical, the soft volcanic rock carved into deep V-shapes by ancient rivers and streams. In order to advance, the column had to make its way carefully down to the bottom of each gully, each man watching his step on the friable, gray rock that was likely to slip and slide under his boots, and then clamber up the other side, using his hands as often as not, to reach the opposite ridge.

It was like climbing down a long and treacherous ladder and then climbing up another equally unreliable, shifting one. Up and down, up and down, hour after hour. Katerina had never hurt quite so much in her life. All the muscles in her legs, back and behind were screaming after they had traversed only six ravines. In terms of forward direction of travel, she estimated that they were managing to advance less than five hundred paces every hour. At this rate—if they ever actually got there—they would arrive at the Gates of Stone sometime after noon tomorrow. And that would be too late. The three ships were now at anchor in Loku Bay, awaiting her arrival at dawn tomorrow morning and the firing of the colored rockets to indicate that the assault on the Green and Red Forts had been successful. When dawn broke the next day, if there were no signal rockets, Colonel Wang would dutifully weigh anchor and depart, heading back to Ashjavat where he would march the Legion home to the Celestial Republic. Just as she had ordered him to do. By the time she got to the Gates of Stone, tomorrow afternoon, her three ships and the rest of her Legion would be long gone. Perhaps just about visible as flecks of white on the western horizon.

How could she have been so stupid? It was arrogance, sheer arrogance, to think that she knew better than the greatest military minds in the world. The conventional wisdom was that these ravines on the western side of the Barat Cordillera were impassable to an infantry force of any size—it was the reason why the Federation did not bother to guard against an attack from here—and conventional wisdom, as was often the case, turned out to be correct.

After two grueling hours, they stopped to take water. She stood on the ridge they had just climbed and looked back at the way they had come. She could clearly see the camping ground where they had spent the night after the sweat-drenched day in the jungle: it was not even a mile away. She could see a leather bucket abandoned by some careless Ostrakan gunner lying beside the stream where she had washed her face this morning.

For the first time in many weeks Katerina felt like weeping. Was she mad even to attempt this impossible task? Was she merely leading her Legionnaires, her Ostrakans, the Niho knights—and Ari, too—on a long and appallingly punishing road to certain death?

She looked at her favored Niho bodyguard, standing at her elbow and looking backward over the same dispiriting vista of last night's camping ground. He did not look any the worse for wear after half a morning of extreme hard labor. He looked cool and fresh, alert even. The sunlight reflecting off the planes of his tanned face. His blue eyes glowing like jewels. His presence gave her strength, calmed her soul. They were not dead yet. And if they died in this desperate attempt to reach the Gates of Stone, so be it.

"Major Chan," she said, summoning the officer to her side. "We must make more haste. We are falling behind schedule. You will kindly order the men to increase the pace."

Chan stared at her with his moist eyes; his face was flushed pink and slicked with sweat. He seemed taken aback by her words, quite astonished, in fact.

"It shall be done, Highness," was all he said before bustling away to deliver his orders to his own subordinates.

The pace did increase—but so did the level of punishment. With the sun high in the sky, the heat was like a vast weight pressing down on the toiling column. Up and down the ravines they went, Katerina's legs protesting at every agonizing step. She was lucky, she told herself, that she was not burdened by a pack or baggage, just a light Cossack saber and a leather pouch of necessities at her waist and her water bottle. The Legionnaires labored under a full pack and harness, although she could see that many of them had removed their heavy blue coats and bundled them on the top of their knapsacks. Even the Ostrakans had small mountaineering packs strapped between their shoulder blades.

At noon they stopped again, and she had to stop herself from emptying her water bottle in one long draft. She forced herself to take only two swigs. Then chewed down cold rice and dried meat and a final swig of cool water. And then, after fifteen minutes' rest, they were off again, down the next steep ravine and up the other side.

The sweat came off her in rivers; the extreme pain in her legs had by now dulled to a rubbery numbness, and there was always another ravine to scrabble down, and then haul her trembling body up the other side. She had a sense, occasionally, that they were not moving forward at all, just traversing one piece of hellishly steep rocky ground before being returned to the starting point and being forced to traverse it all over again. On and on they toiled. On and on. The dust raised by her boots was fine and

ANGUS MACALLAN

choking, sticking to her sweat-drenched limbs and forming a thick kind of gray paste, almost a dough—when she looked around at her companions she saw an army of ghosts, trudging on all sides of her. Even the shiny, black-lacquered armor of the Niho knights was painted a powdery gray.

She wondered if she had done the right thing. She could have left the attack on the Red Fort to Major Chan, or that woman-hating fool Sung. She could have sailed up to Loku Bay with her three ships to wait there in comfort for news of the success or failure of this mission. She played with that delicious but illicit idea for a while, while her battered feet automatically climbed the shifting rock of the next ravine and stumbled down the following. Waiting in comfort. What would that be like?

No. It was far better this way. She would not put her life, the success of all her plans, in the hands of another. Particularly not Sung. Major Chan had a whiff of weakness about him. And Colonel Wang was far too old. No, it was better this way. She had to do it this way. Her way. She had to make this march, and make it all the way to the end. She would not value the siren song of comfort over the trumpet blare of victory. This was her struggle, here, now. And she *would* triumph.

She stumbled and crashed down painfully to one knee. But she was up again before she knew it, hauled upright by Ari's fist clutching a handful of her shirt.

A vision of Vladimir, Emperor of Khev, popped into her head. He was laughing, just as he had done so many times in her dreams. If she failed now, he would laugh again; if she died miserably here on this inhospitable hillside, he would hear of it, hear of the ridiculous, impossible task she had set herself and laugh some more. A blast of rage lifted her head up. If she survived this march—and she would survive it—she would crush Vladimir and take sweet joy from his utter destruction. And the fresh anger she felt in her belly gave her a little more strength to carry on. Down one more ravine. Up one more, too.

A brutal hour later all that had changed. She felt sick but too weak to vomit. Her head felt as if it had been split by an ax then bound together with a red-hot iron band. She felt she could not take another step forward. What she wanted now, most of all, was for it all to stop. Forget the mission. Cancel all her ambitions. Forget crushing Vladimir. Forswear the Gates of Stone. All she wanted now was to lie down, to just sleep forever. But she could not allow herself that glimpse of failure. Still she marched, on and onward, putting one foot in front of another. And then again, one foot in front of another. She was too tired to think. And thinking was useless now anyway. She needed all her will just to take one more step.

I n the terrible heat of the late afternoon, one Legionnaire died. He just dropped in his tracks and passed away without a word. They left him where he lay, Major Chan closing his staring eyes, and saying a few solemn words in his own language. The Legion officer collected his water bottle and some identification documents from his pockets and the whole column lurched to its feet like a vast dusty blue caterpillar and stumbled onward.

She felt she had been on those murderous rocky slopes all her life—or rather that she had never had any other life than the existence she endured on this torture march. And, as the orange sun began to dip into the waters of the Indujah Ocean on her left, she truly felt that her soul was now sinking down into inevitable death along with that fiery orb. *Come, sweet Death, come,* she thought. *Come now and end this agony called life.*

They struggled on into the twilight, and Katerina, to her astonishment, found a second—or was it a third or even fourth?—wind. They marched on. One more hour, and then another. The cool of night made things marginally better, and as the moon began to rise—a great, full, silver disk that made it nearly as bright as day—she ordered a halt and a two-hour rest. She was too tired to eat and collapsed into a deep sleep, asking Ari to wake her when the time was up. It was not fair, she knew, asking him to remain awake. But she did not care. The sleep, brief as it was, revived her, although her legs were stiff as spears and her tight-laced, booted feet felt as if they had been crushed in a press. Major Chan and his officers, aided by the Niho knights, roused the whole column. She ate a little, sipped frugally from her water bottle, got unsteadily to her feet, and they forged onward.

In the moonlight, the ravines were huge pools of darkness. At one point she slipped on a loose patch of scree, thumping down on her behind and beginning to skid down into the black well of the gully's bottom. An iron hand gripped her shoulder, stopping her descent, and then Ari was there, lifting her up to her feet and asking if she was hurt.

"Would you like me to carry you, Lady?" he whispered, his face just inches from hers. She laughed—she actually laughed out loud—and shook her head. She would go on on her own two feet until she could go on no longer. She had heard no complaints from the Legionnaires, and while the Ostrakans never ceased their low-level grumbling, they had not fallen behind, as she had feared they might. Perhaps it was all the obat they smoked. Perhaps they could not feel the pain. She did not care as long as they remained with the column. As long as they marched. And if these awkward, silly, self-indulgent men from the most remote backwater in the Khevan Empire could continue to march, then so could she.

In the middle reaches of the night, she was dimly aware that the ravines were becoming less precipitous, that the land was flattening out. Here and there were small bushes and stunted trees. An exhausted Legionnaire tripped over a boulder in the darkness and fell, breaking his leg. He screamed with pain, and she heard

Major Chan ordering him roughly to stop his damned noise. They left him there in the lee of a large rock, with a flask of marak, a tin of obat and a loaded pistol, promising to return when they could.

And on they marched.

The moon was long gone but the night was no longer pitch-dark. A grayness was seeping into the air. Dawn was perhaps an hour away. And with what felt very much like the very last drop of her strength, Katerina—with Ari lending a powerful arm—climbed to the top of a stack of flattish rocks, the highest point around. She looked west toward the ink-dark sea and a bank of thick cloud on the far horizon, and then up at the descending peaks of the Barat Cordillera, jagged and black against the faint lightening of the sky in the east.

And then north.

In the distance, she saw a pinprick of light. A hearth fire, per-haps, kindled for a hot breakfast before a long day in the fields. She waited, the minutes passing, her whole body swaying with fa-tigue. There were other lights, red and orange, now appearing, popping up like tiny, static fireflies. She could even make out, right at the very edge of vision beyond the winking lights a thick block of ruler-straight stone stretching across the land. Something definitely man-made. A wall. A fortification

"You know what that is, Ari?" she whispered, suddenly sag-ging against his hard body. The Niho knight said nothing. But she sensed his smile in the gloom.

"That," she said, "is the Red Fort. We have come at last to the Gates of Stone."

THREE

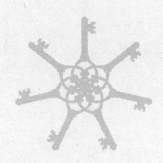

CHAPTER 34

———— ⬦ ————

Extract from *Ethnographic Travels* by
Professor Tolmund K. Parehki of the University of Dhilika

Perhaps the most extraordinary legend of the Laut Besar is that of the Ghost Tigers of the Island of Yawa. These huge creatures, twice the size of a natural tiger, and extremely long-lived, have always been associated with the Wukarta Dynasty, and more recently with the great God Vharkash the Harvester. They were the traditional guardians of the Mother Temple in Yawa, protecting the priests from all manner of harm—although they were also said to eat the flesh of men. Their leader, called Raal, generation after generation, was the greatest of the Ghost Tigers and is descended from the first Raal who succored the first of the Wukarta line back in the time before history began. It was said that the High Priest of Vharkash was trained to speak the language of these great gray-and-black-striped beasts and that he could summon them at will to do his bidding. Of course, the Ghost Tigers are no more than a myth, although their folk memory lives on in the remote tribes of the jungles of Yawa, some of whom venerate them as the battle beast of Vharkash himself and claim a kinship with these animals, even going so far as to partake of the flesh of their enemies . . .

Farhan had not known, honestly and truly, how much he did not want to die until this day. He was slung upside down from a bamboo pole, the blood pooling in his face and neck, the ties on his wrists and ankles cutting in agonizingly.

From the corner of his eye he could see the gently swaying corpse of Sergeant Kishan. Somebody had come to the gralloching frame perhaps an hour past, a smiling, plump-faced matron in a simple hide skirt, and she had cut off the whole of Kishan's left arm and borne it away. Farhan had vomited a sour spray onto the earth beneath his head, the liquid trickling into his nostrils and over his forehead. Horror and disgust. Sheer coldhearted fear, in truth.

He trawled through his misspent life, the adventures, the scrapes, all the fun he had had. The bad times, too. He thought again about the Khevan girl. In his mind she had been elevated into a beacon of shining love, an ideal of pure joy. But he would never see her again, never kiss her cool lips or hold her in his arms and feel her soft skin pressed against his, feel her small heart beating under his hand. They would never share an island paradise and a life together of ease and luxury. Perhaps her Northron blood and fair skin would have reacted badly to the heat of the Laut Besar anyway. She was a child of the snows. Those few weeks with her in the capital of the Empire had been a time of happiness for him and, he believed, for her. But could they ever, truly, have been repeated? Perhaps he'd been deluding himself. Perhaps love was nothing more than a delusion. Did she ever think of him now? Did she even remember their lovemaking?

He thought about all the other joys he would never know again. The nights of marak-fueled laughter. The obat parties. The other women he had enjoyed. The glorious, improbable wins at the tables. The losses, too. That greedy old monster Xi Gung was never going to get his money now, and it served the bastard right. It did not help to think of it: he was going to be dismembered, hacked apart like a feast-day ox and consumed by these appalling white-painted savages, and before that there would be a long red road of agony and waiting.

What had he done to deserve this—had he angered some God? Had he angered Vharkash himself, that the Harvester should allow this cruel indignity to be his fate? He did not believe in the Gods, anyway. He'd always said so. He remembered his grand posturing at the university when he had brilliantly debated the absence of any divine beings outside the human imagination. How he wished he could take that back now.

"Help me now, Lord Vharkash," he mumbled through a raw throat and cracked lips. "Come to my aid and I shall sing your praises forevermore. I will devote my life to good works and spreading your Holy Name across the world. Or, if you wish it, I shall return home to the Federation and never set foot outside my family home and hearth again. Only come to me, Lord, save me, I beseech you with all my heart."

The placid business of the little village went on around him. Children played in the dust with sticks, straws and old bones. Fires were lit and tended. The white-caked, gray-and-black-striped warriors lounged about. He once saw the skinny old devil, Patka Du, walk slowly across the open dusty space between the huts, leaning on a staff, and tried to call out to him, thinking to beg for mercy: but the words stuck in his parched throat.

Patka Du paid him no more attention than Farhan might have paid a ham in the larder. The headman disappeared into a large hut and did not come out. The dusk was beginning to fall, the shadows lengthening. Perhaps Mamaji would order the Dokra to sally out of the bamboo fort and rescue him: they must know that he was in trouble. But he knew deep in his heart they would not come. They would reckon him dead by now. The time of the parlay was long over. And what would be the point? They would be struck down with a hundred lethal darts before they even made it into the village. He was lost. He was a dead man, still breathing. A tethered beast awaiting the knife.

As the day yellowed and the shadows grew, he dreaded the coming of night. His blood-filled head felt that it might burst. His wrists and ankles were on fire. The joints of his shoulders and hips ached with the strain. He did not think he could make it through twelve hours of darkness with only the ghost of Sergeant Kishan for company. But the alternative . . . the alternative was worse. Far worse. He wondered if they would kill him before they began to chop parts off his body or would they try to keep him fresh as long as possible. He wondered if he could will himself to death.

Make an end to it all. Come to me, Lord Vharkash, if only to make my end swift.

He must have passed into something of a stupor because when he next came to it was full dark and the village was lit only by the cooking fires outside each hut and long bamboo torches set around the central space. Something was happening. There were loud cries of fear or joy; he couldn't tell which. People were pouring out of the huts, old men, children, nubile girls, all gathering at the far end of the village. The warriors were in a frenzy, leaping high in the air, shaking their blowpipes. They all seemed to be shouting one word, over and over again: "Raal, Raal, Raaaaaal!"

He craned his neck to see the far side of the open space, where every member of the tribe was now assembled. And saw a huge gray animal shape step carefully into the torchlight. It was an animal, a tiger, but far bigger than any of the creatures he had ever seen before. Its fur was white, with black and gray stripes, and as it padded into the center of the space he saw that it had a rider, a jolly-looking little man, with wild wisps of gray hair floating around his head. And behind the first tiger, three more similar but smaller animals, also bearing humans: a huge, scowling, black-skinned woman, naked but for a white bandage on her shoulder, a girl, also wounded, her chest bound in bloody linen and, last of all, a beautiful young man, slender as a willow but muscled like an athlete.

I am dreaming, thought Farhan. *I have lost my senses at last.* His faculties rebelled and he retreated back into the blackness.

When Farhan awoke next, he was lying in a bed of freshly cut leaves, a blanket covering his naked body. His head was pounding but someone had washed and cleaned his wrists and ankles. He was alone. There was daylight leaking past the edges of the blanket covering the door. He sat up. Beside his bed was a clay jar full of water; he sniffed it and smelled nothing. If it was poisoned, so what? Better dead than hanging by a pole and waiting to be eaten. He took a sip and found he could not stop himself from finishing the whole vessel, down to the last drop.

The blanket covering the door was hurled back and a tall, white-caked warrior came in, crouching under the low lintel. Farhan found himself cowering back on the bed holding up the blanket for protection. The warrior laughed. He said something to Farhan and it took him a few moments to understand the archaic tongue. The man had said, "Come out when you are ready. We have guests—very special guests."

The warrior left and Farhan got very shakily to his feet. He looked about the hut for a weapon but there was nothing but the empty water jar. He left it where it was, wrapped the blanket around his waist like a sarong, and came out into the blinding sunshine.

When his eyes had adjusted to the glare, the first thing he saw was the young man he had seen the night before in his dream. This time he seemed made of flesh and blood and he was standing with a group of white-caked warriors holding one of the long blowpipes in his hand and obviously discussing its merits as a weapon.

At the urging of the white warriors, the young man put the blowpipe to his lips and—ffft—a dart flew across the space to the gralloching frame, where a man-sized log of palm tree was dangling as a target. There was no sign of Sergeant Kishan. The young man had done well; the dart was now sticking out from the center of the log, and the Hantu Harimau were congratulating him loudly, cheering, slapping his back.

On the far side of the open space he saw that the little old man was sitting in front of Patka Du's hut, in the same place where Farhan had been given the test the day before and once again the headman was with him. However, the strange old fellow had been given the carved stool to sit upon and Patka Du now knelt before him on the mat in a position of deep reverence, head lowered. The old man spotted him and gave him a cheery wave, clearly calling him over. Farhan walked across the dusty earth, still almost unable to shake the idea that he might be in a dream, and at the old man's urging he sat down. To Farhan's surprise, the old man addressed him in strongly accented but perfectly serviceable Indujah. And at the sound of his own language, Farhan was almost overwhelmed by the urge to weep.

"It is very important, friend, that you do as I tell you," said the old man. "I use your language so that you may understand but that he may not. Unimaginable horrors await us all if you do not do exactly as I say. Can you understand me?"

Farhan nodded. "Good," said the old man. "First, smile—smile and bow to me as if I was your most revered grandfather. You must treat me with the utmost respect at all times until we are out of this mess. If you disrespect me, or shout out, or complain about how you have been treated—you and all your companions will be lost. We stand on a knife-edge here. Do you understand me?"

"I understand," said Farhan, and he went down into a deep obeisance, knocking his forehead three times on the mat before him. Then he smiled lovingly at the old man. It wasn't hard. This wrinkled little fellow was offering him life for the price of a grin.

"This headman tells me that you have a seagoing ship, and a couple of hundred well-armed companions in a fort not far from here. Is that true?"

"It's true; we have men and a ship but it cannot put to sea. It is beached and has a very large hole in the side. But who are you?"

"Smile, smile all the time. And remember—you are speaking now to a most revered old gentleman. Think of me as someone as near a divine personage as is possible to get in human form—I'm nothing of the kind, of course, just a humble old priest—but can you do that for me?"

Farhan smiled and made another low bow.

"My name is Semar and—well, I'll introduce you to my friends later. For now just tell me two things, and I must ask you to be as honest and accurate as you can: first, how long would it take to make the ship seaworthy, and second, if you were free to do so, would you be willing to take me and my companions with you to Istana Kush, if we were to extricate you from this present situation?"

"That's where we are heading anyway—but I believe we would be most willing to take you almost anywhere you wish if you can get us all out of this hellish place. I think, though, that it will take us at least two weeks to mend the ship."

"Two weeks, well, I suppose it can't be helped. We accept. Thank you, the bargain is struck. Now bow and withdraw to your hut. You will not be molested. Wait there till I call for you. We should have you back with your companions in the fort by nightfall. Oh, one other thing, I would advise you strongly not to accept any food, particularly meat from these people. But I think perhaps that you know that already."

Farhan smiled, a little more grimly this time. But he knocked his head three times on the matting, got up shakily and, refusing to even look at the skinny monster Patka Du, he went back to his hut. But, as he crossed the empty space at the center of the village, in his heart, in his private and most secret heart, he was singing a half-remembered schoolboy paean to the great God Vharkash the Harvester.

CHAPTER 35

———— ✦ ————

J un rubbed the oiled cloth gently over the buffalo-horn-and-bamboo recurved bow that he held in his lap. He had found himself a comfortable niche in the waist of the *Mongoose*, under the port rail and on a mound of old sacking, and over the past few days he had made it his personal territory. The bow had survived the rigors of the escape through the jungle pursued by the Mbaru, and had shot well at the fight at the Temple of Burunya, but now he was worried about the cords. He had only two left and the sea air was bad for them; it made them swell and soften. He worried that they might be saggy and useless if it came to a fight. Not that there was much danger that he would be called on to do battle out here in the empty vastness of the Laut Besar.

Moreover, the ship was clearly a powerful war machine, one that made a joke of a single man with a bow and arrows, and he had been awed and slightly deafened three days ago when the captain had given a demonstration of the fourteen cannon that she carried, firing broadsides and individual shots at a pair of empty pork barrels that had been heaved over the sides and used as targets for the enthusiastic Buginese crew. The cannon were cheerfully and briskly served and even fairly accurate and the pork barrels had been duly blown to matchwood. However, and Jun was by no means an expert, the ship seemed to be moving sluggishly in the water; her hastily patched hull—completed in less than ten days by the sailormen and the Dokra—made her run unevenly in the water. The water flowed more smoothly on the less damaged side, which made her continually veer off her course, and this had to be continually and carefully compensated for by the two tillermen on the big wheel on the quarterdeck. Nevertheless, she swam bravely through the dark blue water and, while the pumps still had to be manned for several hours each day, after an initial period of nervousness, Jun was confident that the *Mongoose* would bear him across the Laut Besar to Istana Kush without sinking.

Jun was not entirely sure what had taken place when they met the Hantu Harimau. But they had been treated like Gods incarnate by these strange, white-caked warriors when they had arrived at their village, borne there on the backs of the four Ghost Tigers. Indeed, that whole episode had a rather foggy, fantasy-like quality.

His shock in discovering that Ghost Tigers really existed had been profound; and that they still guarded the ancient Mother Temple; and that they had responded to the call of Semar, once the High Priest of that sacred place. He was also profoundly grateful that they had saved them from the Mbaru. And when these great beasts, who spoke in grunts and coughs that only Semar could understand, had carried them with swiftness and silence through the jungle for a night and a day to the village—more than twenty leagues, he calculated—he had been both profoundly terrified and exhilarated. And the reception there by the white-painted tribesmen, who seemed to revere Semar as some sort of deity, had been quite marvelous. Jun had not been treated with so much respect since . . . well, not even in his days in the Watergarden. He had reveled in it. A little guiltily, at first, and then with a feeling of homecoming. He was a royal prince once more.

He grasped that Semar had persuaded the Hantu Harimau, who had been at odds with the men of the *Mongoose*, that they must cease hostilities and leave the incomers unmolested while they repaired their ship. He also knew that these people had irregular, even revolting, dietary habits—the eating of human flesh. But he could not truly hate the simple people who had made him feel so welcome, so honored and even perhaps so loved.

They had gathered, the whole chattering, laughing tribe, to see them off when the *Mongoose* was finally launched, bedecking Semar, Jun, Ketut and Tenga with wreaths of flowers, calling out blessings and singing ancient hymns to Vharkash.

As they chanted their farewells, and begged Semar to visit again soon, Jun could not help but notice that Captain Lodi and the whole crew of the *Mongoose* had been in a most unseemly, almost discourteous, hurry to depart.

The plump merchant fellow, Farhan he was called, seemed to have been most affected by his contact with the Hantu Harimau. He was now refusing to eat any kind of meat at all aboard the ship and had visibly lost weight even in the few weeks that Jun had known him. Yet he seemed to be a likable, intelligent man. Well mannered, cultured but a little distant and cool and with an air of deep, indefinable sadness.

This Farhan was now on the quarterdeck talking with the captain of the ship, Cyrus Lodi, and the fat Indujah lady in the garish sari who seemed to be the captain's mother or possibly his aunt. At the other end of the ship, Semar and Ketut were sitting on the prow, facing each other in silent contemplation, the wind blowing the old man's hair out in a fluttering stream behind him. They were speaking to each other silently, Jun realized; part of a long conversation they had been having ever since they had left Taman.

Ketut had now mostly recovered from the musket ball that she had taken at the Temple of Burunya. But it had been a close-run affair: she had barely been conscious for most of the past two and a half weeks and Tenga had attended to her for hours every day, washing her, talking to her, trickling thin soup into her mouth, cleaning up her shameful evacuations.

Semar had removed the musket ball in a short, bloody opera-

tion in the bamboo fort and treated her injury with many poultices and prayers. Now the wound was nearly healed and a raw,
pink, star-shaped scar adorned her skinny chest, above the band
of cloth she wore over her small breasts. Jun had visited her only
once in her sick berth on the ship, finding himself embarrassed by
her weakness and revolted by the all-pervading smell of blood,
shit and pus in the small cabin. He had sat with her for an hour or
two, allowing Tenga to get some much-needed sleep, and Ketut
had surprised him by waking suddenly, seizing his arm, pulling
his face close to her blazing eyes, and saying, "You must swear to
look after Tenga if I die."

Jun had mumbled something about her inevitable recovery, only
a matter of time and rest. But Ketut had gripped him harder, surprisingly painfully, in fact, and extracted his solemn promise.
"When this is all over, she can come and live in Taman with us, if
she chooses to," Jun said. "She would make a good War-Master, I
think."

Ketut had smiled then. "She says you did very well with your
bow, richboy, at the Temple of Burunya. Killed a bear-dog all on
your own."

Jun had preened a little until Ketut added, "I'm glad there is
something you can do well." And she closed her eyes and sank
back into her blankets.

As Jun watched the recovered girl and the old man in the prow
of the ship, Semar lifted his hand and placed his palm over the scar
on Ketut's chest. It was part of the healing process, he assumed.
Neither of them moved or spoke but Jun thought he sensed something invisible passing between them, like a shimmer of heat in
the air above a hot rock.

"Can you spare me some of that sweet oil?" said Tenga.

Jun looked up to see the tall Ziran Atari warrior looming over
him. She held a Buginese long-hafted boarding ax in her big hands,
a vicious-looking weapon with a broad blade on one side of the

shaft and a curved spike on the other. The top of the haft was mounted with a spear-like prong.

"Help yourself," said Jun, nudging the oil pot toward her with a finger. Tenga folded herself on the deck a half pace away from Jun, and reached for the pot. Pulling a rag from her loincloth, the only clothing she wore, she began to clean the weapon.

"Rust," she muttered. "Iron is good, better than good, but rust is an evil red demon."

Jun watched her in silence for a while. She was big, clumsy and ugly, and covered in scars—her bear-dog-savaged shoulder now capped with a thick, dried scab. She was a savage brute, in truth, not the sort of person that he would have even glanced at in Taman, let alone sat down with in this comradely way, but he realized that he liked her. The fight at the temple had forged a bond between them. He respected her courage, envied her ferocity, and was simply awed by her willingness to die for her friend Ketut. Perhaps for him, too. She would make a very good War-Master. And she, it seemed, had not found him wanting in either skill or spine when battle showed its ugly face.

Tenga lifted the ax and examined the play of sunlight on its oiled blade.

"They tell me we will reach this place, the Gates of Stone, tomorrow," she said.

"Yes," said Jun. "We should be docked at the grand harbor of Istana Kush by noon, wind and tide permitting, or so the captain says."

"You been there before?"

"No. But I've heard it's an impressive fortress."

"You think your daddy's old sword is there?"

Jun said nothing for a moment. He knew Tenga had been told of their mission but it still made him feel a little uncomfortable to hear the thousand-year-old Kris of Wukarta Khodam, the sacred blade of his ancestors, described as "daddy's old sword."

"I don't know. But we should be able to get word of Mangku there. Semar said he was heading for the Sumbu coast and in Istana Kush the Indujah Federation spy services pride themselves on knowing about every little thing that moves in their waters."

Tenga grunted something unintelligible.

"What will you do when you get there, Tenga? Take another ship back home to Ziran Atar? Or will you stay with us?"

"I go where Tut goes."

Jun frowned at her. "Why?"

"I belong to her now; she belongs to me."

"Do you"—Jun fumbled with the word, the whole idea—"do you love her?"

Tenga looked directly into his face, her own expressionless. "She is so tiny, so weak. She must have someone to look after her in this world. That someone is me."

Jun found himself embarrassed by this declaration. Yet his own feelings for Ketut had mellowed in recent days and he realized that now he felt a certain warmth for her, too, despite her perpetual disrespect for him and her general spikiness of manner. He realized that he almost never thought of her merely as a Dewa now. She was one, of course, would always be one, and back in Taman, that stain could not easily be ignored. But, if he examined his feelings honestly, he had to admit that he felt a brotherly affection for her.

"If Tut goes with you to find this wizard, I will come, too. I'll help you. Maybe I will cut his head off for you!" Tenga grinned and shook the big, shiny ax under his nose.

When they opened the bay of Istana Kush the next morning, turning past the Grand Mole, which jutted far out into the sea, and gliding into the huge harbor, which was packed with shipping of all kinds, Jun was once again reminded of how small and insignificant his homeland was compared with the might and wealth displayed here. This place was larger, even, than Sukatan, and a good deal better ordered and more martial.

Jun knew vaguely that the Indujah Federation was a powerful western trading nation from a couple of thousand leagues across the ocean—and he had even met some of their merchant princes who had come to Taman to buy carved coral, pearls and polished conch shells, and huge sacks of rice from the jewel-bright paddy fields that covered most of the lowland areas of his island—but the sight of the five massively fortified batteries on the Grand Harbor, each comprised of a pair of long guns all far bigger than Captain Lodi's little sea cannon, impressed him to an extraordinary degree. These people were soldiers as well as traders, that was evident, and even one of those batteries could destroy the *Mongoose* as easily and quickly as the Buginese crew had sunk those bobbing pork barrels.

He looked to his right and saw the fabled Gates of Stone, the twin fortresses with high, forbidding rock walls that guarded the narrow Straits, once again bristling with big guns. The walls of the one on the Istana side were marked with a blotched dark red color, some kind of lichen, Jun assumed, which gave it an evil, blood-drenched look. The distant one on the other side of the Strait was a mossy, moldy green. On the Red Fort, he could see the tiny figures of soldiers on the battlements, Dokra mercenaries he deduced from their scarlet coats and turbans, and the distinctive white cross belts.

The *Mongoose* was intercepted by a small pilot boat long before it came anywhere near the many quays and jetties that extended from the harbor front like the fingers on a hand. A Dokra officer in a scarlet coat and black cross belts inquired who they were in the Indujah language, bellowing through a speaking trumpet and, to Jun's surprise, it was the fat woman—Mamaji, she called herself—who answered rather than the captain. After a short, shouted exchange, it was clear that they were welcome and the pilot boat guided them into a berth in the center of the harbor.

It was obvious, too, that Mamaji was a person of some consequence, for the instant they docked she and her maid, and a mountain of baggage, were borne away in a palanquin carried by six burly slaves, with an honor guard of a dozen Dokra soldiers trotting alongside, while the rest of the ship's company went about the mundane process of mooring the ship securely against the stone quay.

They disembarked soon enough, and made their way up through the crowded streets behind the harbor to the Governor's Palace, with Ketut moving like an old woman and Tenga hovering around her, and scowling, long ax in hand, at anyone foolish enough to dawdle in their path.

The palace was another small fortress, which had been the original bastion in Istana Kush and had stood sentinel over the Sumbu Straits long before the Red and Green Forts had been built. It was fashioned in the shape of the prow of a huge ship, with two curving sides meeting at a point where a battery of ancient brass cannon looked out over the water. A hundred paces behind the two curving sides was a flat wall—as if the stone ship had been cut in half—which was punctured with hundreds of arrow slits. The rear wall loomed over the Small Harbor, a natural cove in the rocky Sumbu shore that had been a famous pirate haven before the coming of the Federation. Now, superseded by the Grand Harbor to the north, which was four times its size, it held only the smaller pleasure boats and fishing craft of the town. Above the battery at the tip of the prow, and set a little farther back, loomed the Round House, a flat, circular, stone structure at the highest point of the fortress with glass windows on all sides that allowed the Governor and his staff a fine view of the whole of Istana Kush, both harbors and the Strait as far as the jungly Manchatka shore. One curving side of the palace, the northern side, abutted directly with the rocky shore of the sea. The other curving up from the south held the main gate—a massive, old-fashioned drawbridge the width of five men and fashioned from teak planks and iron chains. The drawbridge lay over a ditch that was once connected to the sea but which was now dry and filled with years of refuse from the town of Istana, which was spread out along the palace's southern flank.

The town was far larger than the palace and had expanded over the centuries to fill all the space between the two harbors—it was a bustling metropolis of shops, workshops, taverns, market squares, brothels, teahouses and the ordinary dwellings of the denizens of Istana. As the four travelers approached the palace, they saw that the main entrance in the curving south wall was open, the drawbridge down and portcullis lifted, and the way inside was guarded only by two immaculate Dokra. Semar gave their names and they were all immediately admitted, ushered over the creaking wood of the drawbridge by a servant in a long yellow robe who led them into a vast hall beyond the gate and then up several sets of polished-marble stairs, down long, dim corridors, through tiny courtyards open to the sky where fountains tinkled delightfully and finally to their allocated quarters, a set of rooms on the northern side of the palace overlooking the gray, choppy waters of the Sumbu Strait.

Here, quite wonderfully, food and drink had been set out for them: Rhonos wine, flat bread, yogurt, rice, boiled eggs, fried vegetables and a spicy lamb stew.

An hour later, Jun found himself lying in a very hot soapy bath, having his long black hair washed and then his broad shoulders and arm muscles massaged by a rather pretty Indujah servant girl, who appeared not to speak a word of Common Tongue. He found that if he closed his eyes—and he did, wallowing in the voluptuous pleasure of hot water, a full belly and a rare state of cleanliness—he could imagine himself at home once more in the

Watergarden. He considered inviting the girl with signs and smiles to join him in the bath, the tub was big enough for two, then thought better of the idea. He was too tired, anyway.

He slept a little after that in his own private room and when he awoke after nightfall he found that fresh clothes had been laid out for him--loose silk trousers, a long blue-linen shirt and a short red jacket—and after only a few moments luxuriating in the softness of a real, clean-sheeted bed, he rose, dressed and went to find his friends.

Their quarters comprised four sleeping rooms around a small, square central courtyard with a tiny bubbling fountain. When Jun emerged from his chamber he saw Ketut, Semar and Tenga lounging on low couches around a square table where more food, delicate pastries, fresh fruit, cheese and more wine, had once again been set out for them. Jun joined his comrades, collapsing onto his couch and selecting a sugar-dusted pastry that was filled with a sweet, cinnamon-flavored egg custard.

While Jun had been sleeping, the others had been considerably more active, and Ketut and Tenga were exchanging impressions with each other about the wonders of Istana Kush, the crowds of people in their strange dress, the smart Dokra soldiers everywhere, the incredible array of goods and luxuries available in the street markets and big emporiums, the fine stone buildings and the statues—the many, many statues of all the Indujah Gods. They giggled together like children over a skinny madman in rags who was preaching the new faith of the Holy Martyr on a street corner, who harangued passersby about their sins and when they grew angry invited them to burn his body with a pine torch, to give him his own longed-for martyrdom. More prosaically, Semar had been to see the Governor of Istana Kush in another part of the palace, and been welcomed with kindness and named a Friend of the Federation for helping the people of the *Mongoose* to escape from the Hantu Harimau.

"Governor Bandi promises to afford us any help that he can, within reason," said Semar to Jun, looking pleased with himself. "But I did not, of course, reveal the full nature of our quest but only told him that we were seeking a pirate ship that had brutally attacked Taman some weeks ago, and had burned the Water-garden and murdered your royal father."

Jun took another sweet pastry. He had not spent much time recently brooding on his quest to regain the Khodam. And, if he was honest, clean, comfortable and safe for the first time in weeks, he did not much relish an encounter with Mangku. The death of his father was still a dull pain in the back of his mind but, if he had been granted his heart's desire at that moment, it would have been to sail back to Taman in a leisurely fashion, after a week or so re-laxing here in these elegant apartments, to claim his title and resume his life as ruler of his island kingdom. The Khodam was lost—it was a great shame, for sure—but in truth, what difference would one rusty sword, however ancient and magical, make to his future life? He did not, however, feel that he could voice these thoughts aloud to his companions.

Instead, he asked Semar, "And is there any news of . . . the person we seek?"

The old man began peeling himself a mango. "The Governor says that he has had a report yesterday by pigeon from a tiny bor-der outpost a hundred miles to the south that the *Sea Serpent* had arrived at the delta of the River Pengut. As far as we know she is still there. But the local commander said her master informed the customs men that she was bound for Singarasam and would only stay in the delta a day or two to load fresh supplies."

"That makes sense," said Jun. "Only the Lord of the Islands could have sanctioned the attack on Taman. Mangku must have the full backing of Ongkara to do what he did to me with impu-nity. Otherwise the massed fleets of the Dragon of the High Seas would hunt him down and destroy him for his despicable actions."

"I think you overestimate the sea power of Ongkara, my prince—and his genuine interest in punishing wrongdoers. He has other things on his mind—they say war is brewing between Ongkara and the Celestial Republic. But broadly I agree with you. The sorcerer is heading to Singarasam. He has allied himself with the Dragon of the High Seas, for whatever reason. So we must follow him to Singarasam."

Jun felt his heart sink. To guard his thoughts he kept his eyes low and selected another featherlight, custard-filled pastry. They were, in fact, quite delicious.

"There are two other good reasons for us to go there," Semar continued. "The Temple of Vharkash in Singarasam is the finest remaining Vharkashta establishment in the Laut Besar, and for Ketut's continuing education, I think it would be most beneficial for her to pay it a visit and to worship and study there for some weeks or months. There is a huge library of ancient palm-leaf scrolls that she—and I, to be honest—would greatly benefit from consulting. The Patriarch of Singarasam is a very good friend of mine, one of my old Mother Temple deputies, in fact, and I know he will warmly welcome us."

"So we go there," said Tenga flatly.

"What is the second reason?" asked Jun.

"The second reason is even more compelling, I think," said Semar. Then he allowed for a little moment of silence until he was sure that he had their full attention.

"The captain of the border guard received word—from Mangku himself, it would seem—that a force of Celestial Legionnaires had landed on the western side of the Barat Cordillera mountain range; presumably they intend to make a long march and a surprise attack on the Red Fort from the landward side.

"Another pigeon arrived this morning from the delta. War is coming to Istana Kush, my friends. The Governor is even now reinforcing the Red Fort with more Dokra troops. Whether the defense will succeed or fail, I cannot say. But much blood will be spilled in this city very soon and I think it would be prudent for us to absent ourselves."

A little while later, Ketut and Tenga excused themselves and went to bed—into the same bedroom, Jun noticed with a wry smile. He lay back on his couch and sipped his wine. It seemed that there was nothing he could do to avoid going to Singarasam, short of deserting his comrades. But if that was what he had to do, he thought he knew how it might be done, slipping away on his own at midnight, finding a ship that would take him home on the promise of a royal reward . . . He realized that he dreaded another meeting with Mangku. The vision from the fire of his cruel, knowing face, with the gray, black-veined eyes, was still strong in his mind. He thought of the destruction of the Watergarden, of the loss of the Khodam, and of his poor father. What would he find in Taman when he did return home?

His thoughts were interrupted by Semar, who said, "Tell me, Jun, as one who will one day be one. What is a king?"

Jun sat up slowly on his couch. "What?"

"What is it, my prince, that makes one man a king and another a servant?"

Jun thought for a moment. "It is his blood. It is his destiny, as *you* would say."

"Blood, yes. The blood of the star princess that flows in your veins. And, after the sad demise of your cousin the Raja of Suka-tan, you are the last living prince of the Wukarta. By that token, you are very special. Or are you? Surely, now that I come to think of it, there must be other men and women scattered around the Laut Besar who share at least a drop or two of your blood? The Wukarta princes have not always been entirely faithful to their princesses. Your father, for example, in his youth, of course, before he became king, was a famous lover of women. Lots of women. All kinds of women, highborn and low. And I believe you have known a few girls yourself. There must be many by-blows scattered about, bastards as the common people call them, who share a diluted version of your illustrious star-princess heritage in their veins. And they will have had children, too, over the years."

Jun said nothing.

Semar continued, "Take Ketut, for example. What if her nameless father had been a prince of some sort, the callous one who treated her mother so poorly? Then she could have royal blood running in her veins, even though she is a bastard. Could she not be a ruler?"

"A bastard could not be a king."

"Why not?"

Jun found that he could not quite think of an answer. "It would just be wrong."

"In the great war between the Wukarta and the Mother Temple, many centuries ago, the eventual victor was a mighty Wukarta prince named Mansa. History calls him Mansa the Great for he ended the war and united the followers of Vharkash and the proud warriors of the Wukarta. His reign ushered in a thirty-year period of peace over the whole of the Laut Besar. He was beloved by all his people and is remembered as a powerful and wise ruler. And yet his mother was a laundry maid. Oh, on his father's side, he had generations of star-princess blood but his father had no living sons except with a pretty girl who scrubbed out his dirty undergarments. Mansa became a king—and a great one."

"That was all a very long time ago," said Jun sulkily.

"I am not trying to insult your lineage, Jun. I swear not. I am trying to tell you that what makes a king is the love and respect of his people. Family background helps, of course, and there is certainly some ancient magic in the Wukarta seed. But it is the people who make a king, and they must respect him in order to

allow him to rule over them. Think of Taman's neighbor Molok—
they had generations of Wukarta rule on that island, and it was
suddenly wiped out because one royal oaf thought he could do
whatever he liked in his kingdom. The result? Revolution, chaos,
bloodshed. And now they endure a crushing rule by the greediest
and most ruthless of men who have managed to gather the most
power."

"You think Taman will go the way of Molok? Never. The people know that the Son of Heaven has always ruled wisely and well,
generation upon generation."

"They have always worshipped the Wukarta in Taman, sure.
Because they have proved worthy of the people's respect and
love."

"Are you saying that the people of Taman will not respect me?"

"What do you think? The island was attacked and ravaged, the
Son of Heaven was cruelly slain, the sacred Khodam was stolen,
and the young prince set off vowing to regain it and avenge his
revered father. What will they say if he comes home empty-
handed, unrevenged, an abject failure, in fact?"

Jun took a sharp intake of breath. He had the feeling that
Semar had been peering into his head, reading his most private
thoughts. He did not like the sensation.

"So I must go to Singarasam?"

"What do you think?" Semar asked kindly. "I cannot force
you."

"I think you could, actually. Indeed, I think you have just done
that."

"It is for the best, Jun, and I believe you truly know that without my telling you. But imagine this: coming back triumphant,
your father's killer brought to justice, the Khodam recovered. The
young Son of Heaven home at last. Imagine the cheering crowds
of Tamani folk, the flowers strewn in your path; the paeans sung
to your valor; young girls and their mothers all sighing over you;

men praising your name: Arjun Pahlawan! Arjun Pahlawan! Arjun the Hero. Wouldn't that be splendid?"

Jun allowed himself a tiny smile.

"Good, we're agreed then. We'll look for a ship to Singarasam in the morning."

CHAPTER 36

Katerina crouched behind a thick hedge of bamboo and looked through her spyglass at the walls of the Red Fort three hundred paces away. Behind her the two hundred exhausted men of the Storm and Scout Companies of the 42nd Celestial Legion, and a couple of score of Ostraka gunners, were scattered in a loose arc concealed in various barns, sheds and clumps of vegetation. They were in the rich farmlands immediately south of the Red Fort, with the rim of the sun just peeking above the tapering spine of the Barat Cordillera in the east. Between her and the red lichen-stained fort was a wide area of grassy scrubland, a few bushes and trees, but no obstacles save a tethered goat or two munching placidly. Somewhere to the northwest, only a few miles away, her three powerful warships, and eight hundred more Legionnaires, would be waiting in Loku Bay for her signals—a red rocket for the capture of the Red Fort, green for the other. The hard part was done, she told herself. They were here, miraculously on time. Now all she had to do was put her plan into action.

Safely down off the hellish rocky slopes and into the tranquil farmlands, the men were all suffering the effects of the brutal twenty-four-hour march: hollow faces, glassy eyes, trembling limbs surrounded her. And that was just the Legion's officers. Most of the Legionnaires were now so deeply asleep, they might have been corpses. She wondered if, when they were roused from their short slumber, as they must be very soon, they would have the strength and courage for the assault. She wondered if she would. Although the sight of the Red Fort had revived her, as had the triumph of her arrival, she was still as depleted in bone and brain as she had ever been in her life.

Only her twelve Niho knights seemed unaffected by the rigors of the march. Ari, now sitting at her shoulder and watching the Red Fort, seemed a little paler, but his blue eyes were clear. Barring a few deep creases around his mouth, he seemed as alert and ready for action as always. *These Niho are like Gods come to Earth,* she thought. *Are they even human?*

Half an hour ago, once they were in position, she had ordered the men, through Major Chan and his two captains, to eat their fill of the rations they had brought with them, finish them off if they wished. This attack would either end in success, in which case they could make use of the stores in the Red Fort; or in failure, in which case they would be dead. There was no middle ground: death or glory, wasn't that one of the Legionnaires' slogans?

She scanned the south wall of the fort one last time, noting the placement of the two cannon facing them, twenty-five paces apart. She could see a few red-turbaned heads of the sentries pacing on the battlements. But there should be no more than a hundred Dokra awaiting them inside, most of them asleep at this hour, and a few Honorable Artillerymen. Speed was the key. If they could cover the ground before the walls in good time, and have the grapples up briskly, the men could be up and over the walls before the enemy had wiped the sleep grit from their eyes. The Scouts would be the best men for the job, light, fast-moving troops, skilled in stealth. The Stormers would go in behind them, to support them if the attack faltered, and to mop up inside the fort when the first wave had breached the walls. She must try to make sure that the Ostraka gunners were sober, their minds unclouded by obat; once the Red Fort was taken, they needed to be

brisk about wheeling the eight cannon into their new positions
and laying them to attack the Green Fort on the far side of the
Strait. And then re-laying them once more to batter the five
powerful harbor batteries of Istana Kush. She would send Ari to
take charge of the Ostrakans, once the attack began.

Was she forgetting anything? She thought not. The sun was
half a handsbreadth above the mountains. Nearly full daylight.
The sky was beautifully clear. It was time.

The Scout Company went forward, led by their captain. The
men attacked in pairs, moving forward in short little runs,
one man going ahead and stopping, kneeling in cover, alert, musket ready to fire, while his mate hurried forward to join him. A
hundred men went forward like this, in quick, darting runs, every
second man with a knotted rope and grappling iron wrapped
around his waist. Behind the Scouts, the Stormers were forming
up in five platoons of twenty, blocks of grim-faced, big men in
dark blue coats, helmeted in steel. The Scouts' task was to scale
the walls and open the small sally port in the center of the south
wall to allow the Stormers to rush into the fort and subdue the
garrison. And so far, there was no reaction from the stone walls.
The Red Fort was still apparently fast asleep.

Katerina scanned the walls nervously, and now she saw movement. The number of turbaned heads had multiplied and thick-
ened on the battlements. She could hear whistles being blown in
the fort, reedy, faraway sounds, like the voices of children. The
nearest Scouts were still a hundred paces away; some, she saw,
were already pausing to unwrap the coiled ropes from around
their waists.

Not a single shot had yet been fired.

But something was clearly wrong. The intelligence she had
received from the Council of Venerables had stated that there

was never more than a single company of Dokra garrisoned inside the Red Fort, a hundred men, and another fifty members of the Honorable Artillery Company to serve all of its eight guns. She had planned for no more than twenty-five, perhaps thirty musketeers at most opposing them on this unguarded southern side. But she could see many more than that now; scores of little round heads were popping up all along the parapet, more than a hundred men. A hundred and fifty, perhaps. Gods! Even two hundred. Muskets were being lifted, aimed over the stonework. The shrill whistles were still blowing. The little red-turbaned heads now were thick as berries on a bush.

The right-hand cannon spoke. The muzzle belched flame and a small black ball came skipping across the grassy field and struck a running Scout full in the chest, knocking him flat, one detached blue arm spinning away. His mate knelt and fired futilely in return, his musket ball cracking against the red-blotched stonework. The element of surprise was long gone. Both sides could see each other clearly. The Scouts gave a huge cheer and charged, their captain waving them forward with loud, urgent cries and a brandished sword. They came on in a thin wave, a hundred running men, steel helmets winking in the sunshine, now seventy paces from the walls, now fifty. A wave of little blue men running full tilt toward the high red walls.

The massed Dokra on the battlements fired, every second man discharging his musket in a puff of gray, their bullets scything into the attacking Scouts like a lethal, clattering rain, dropping a dozen men. Some Legionnaires fell to their knees, coughing blood, clutching at shattered limbs; others staggered onward or tried to return fire. The second cannon, on the left of the south wall, roared out and two crouching men, one behind the other, were caught by the same ball and ripped into bloody pieces.

A goat, bleating madly, ripped its tether free and ran away to the west.

The Dokra fired another volley, little blooms of smoke appearing all along the wall. A bullet struck the shouting Scout captain full in the face, blowing his head from his neck. A dozen other Scouts were knocked over. The green pasture was now littered with bodies and patches of blood. Met by superior numbers, superior firepower, the attack wavered. A few Scouts had stopped to aim and fire their muskets up at their foes on the walls; some were still unwinding the grappling-iron ropes from around their waists. Others, now right under the battlements, were swinging the grapples up against the stone, aiming to catch at the top and climb. Katerina could see the Dokra above them reloading. Slim rammers going up and plunging down into hot barrels. She could hear the shouts of their officers, too, and the whine of their whistles.

The Dokra loosed another volley, and at that short range even the poorest shot was making a kill. The climbers were swept from the walls, and their dangling ropes dislodged by hands above. More than half the Scouts were down now, broken bodies scattered on the grass, and more falling with every passing moment. It was clear the attack was failing, had failed. The surviving men, no more than half of the company, were kneeling, firing up at the battlements, then reloading furiously, or just cowering under the lash of the Dokra fire. None were moving forward. Few were now even attempting to climb the battlements. Yet one brave soul did rush to the walls, a small, lean, helmetless Scout, and Katerina silently hailed him as a hero and promised him a vast reward. He whirled and swung his grapple up toward the summit of the stone. The hooks caught, the man tested it with his weight, put one boot on the stone wall—and a Dokra, leaning over from the parapet, shot him through the skull.

"Major Chan!" she called. The smoke of the discharged muskets was drifting over the field. Katerina could smell its eggy, sulfurous stench, and clearly hear the horrible screams and moans of the Scout wounded. She was aware that all twelve of her Niho knights were around her, guarding her from a long musket or cannon shot with their black-armored bodies. "Major Chan—send in the Stormers. Immediately! Send them in now!"

The Legionnaire officer saluted smartly. He began to shout orders and the five platoons of Stormers, each a crisp, neat blue block of humanity, began to move forward, a measured tread, each man's pace exact and the same as his neighbor's.

The Scouts were still firing—and dying—at the very foot of the battlements. There were so few of them left unhurt, twoscore perhaps at most, that Katerina was amazed they did not run. But the Dokra, too, were taking casualties now. She saw gaps in the line of turbaned heads—and now another mercenary was blasted back from his position on the battlements by a kneeling sharp-shooter in Celestial blue.

The Stormers were now two hundred paces from the walls. They broke into a jog, still maintaining their perfect alignment. Five blocks of men sweeping toward the enemy walls. The sun-light reflecting on their mirror-bright helmets. *They were magnifi-cent*, Katerina thought. *Truly magnificent men.*

At a hundred and fifty paces, the right-hand cannon roared, canister this time, and the blast, hundreds of lead balls shooting out in a cone like an enormous shotgun, caught the inner edge of the center platoon, wiping away a dozen Stormers with one vast, bloody sweep. A one-armed man staggered onward, his stump showering blood. His other arm still brandishing his musket, shaking it at the enemy. Other men were sitting on the green grass in puddles of red. Katerina was aware that Ari, ever at her shoulder, was counting under his breath: "Sixteen, seventeen, eighteen . . ."

The Stormers were running at full pelt now. Just a hundred paces out from the walls. The left-side cannon spoke now, a huge orange tongue of flame and a roar that shook Katerina to her boots. An entire platoon of Stormers was destroyed in that single

discharge, the men snatched away, hurled bloodily in all directions by the flying balls of the canister, leaving a patch of gore-
smeared grass and a few feebly twitching bodies. She clutched at
the handle of the Cossack saber at her waist. The Dokra were
firing again, disciplined volleys, half the men on the walls firing,
and then reloading while the others aimed and fired. The volleys
shredded the neat formations of the Stormers, plucking men
out of the blocks and hurling them away. Yet still the Stormers
came on.

Ari was still counting: "Twenty-eight, twenty-nine, thirty . . ."

The right-hand cannon fired once more, the canister balls flay-
ing the almost intact right-hand Stormer platoon, leaving no more
than a handful of dazed, bloodied men still standing. All cohesion
in the attack was gone, the Scouts and Stormers, the cream of the
42nd Legion, now no more than a crowd of deafened, bloodied
men milling around at the base of the walls. Some were still firing
at the walls but it was only a matter of time before they were all
picked off from above.

The attack had failed. She had failed. Once again she cursed
her own arrogance in thinking she might do what the cleverest
men said was impossible. Her intelligence had been wrong. Or she
had been betrayed. That was surely it: betrayal. There were more
than five times as many men facing her as she had planned for.
And they had not been at all surprised by her assault. Indeed, she
had the strongest feeling that they had been waiting for her. It
didn't matter now. It was over. Her dream, her grand, wonderful
dream lay in shattered, bloody ruins before the walls of the Red
Fort with the butchered and broken bodies of her courageous
men.

"Lady," said Ari, "with your permission we Niho would like to
try something." Katerina looked at him blankly. "We believe we
can breach the walls," he said. *Why not?* thought Katerina, in despair. *We are all dead now. Better to die in one last attempt than be*

captured and suffer what must inevitably follow. Then, to her surprise, Captain Murakami stepped forward and bowed.

"It has been an honor to serve you, Lady. But now I must beg you once again to release me from the burden of life. I go to join my ancestors, the Seirei."

"I release you from my service and thank you for it," said Katerina.

Ari, Murakami, Tesso and the other knights conferred briefly. And then Murakami bowed to her once more. He unsheathed his long katana and began trotting toward the walls. After he had gone fifty paces or so, the rest of the Niho, all ten of them save Ari, began to move slowly, almost leisurely, after him.

"I will go with them," said Katerina. She drew the Cossack saber from its sheath

"Lady, it is not wise," said Ari, putting a restraining hand on her arm.

"Do not touch me," Katerina snarled. "Obey me, knight. We will go with them."

When Captain Murakami was two hundred paces from the wall, he went from a trot into a full charge. He screamed his own name, and the name of his clan, lifted the katana high in the air and rushed straight toward the right-hand cannon. The sunlight flashed on his black-lacquered armor, and on the curved blade gripped double-handed above his head. It was a ludicrous sight, a lone man with a sword attacking the walls of a mighty fortress. And yet to Katerina's eyes it was heart-wrenching and utterly heroic—even beautiful. Murakami was moving at an incredible rate now, lengthening his stride to come up to his full speed, running like a deer, and now he was only fifty yards from the battlements. He seemed impervious to the musket balls that cracked against his armor. Murakami flew onward. So nearly there, just a few yards to go. And, inevitably, at that moment, the right-hand cannon belched out its full load of flame and death. The two hundred lead balls inside the canister exploded out of its mouth, hissed through the air and ripped Murakami into a thousand bloody shreds, leaving no more than a mist of red where a brave man had been running.

"Now run," shouted Ari in the princess's ear, and with the ten other Niho, they sprinted directly at the right-hand cannon. Katerina could see the men of the Honorable Artillery Company feverishly sponging out the barrel of the long cannon, a hiss of steam as the damp cloth went into the hot metal. She was aware, over the sound of her own panting breath as they flew over the grass, that Ari was counting again: "Thirteen, fourteen, fifteen . . ."

She could see the Dokra on the walls, and the little puffs of smoke as they fired at her and her tiny running band of black-clad knights. No volleys now, just individual aimed shots. The Niho were all around her, protecting her with their armored bodies as they ran. A ball pinged off the lacquered shoulder of the knight beside her and hissed past her face. The surviving Scouts and Stormers were still below the walls, sadly depleted, only a few score men standing. Some were occasionally firing up at the enemy, some gawping at the charging Niho. They were fifty paces away now. The Honorable Artillerymen were slotting in the canvas bag of black powder, followed by the shiny metal of the canister into the huge black muzzle of the cannon, and ramming the charge and load home. The Dokra were now concentrating all their fire on the running band of knights. Musket balls pinging and cracking against the lacquered armor.

"Twenty-three, twenty-four, twenty-five . . ."

They would never make it, Katerina thought. But at least her death would be quick. The Artillerymen would put match to the touchhole, the gun would roar and it would all be over in an instant. She heard the meaty thud of a musket ball strike at close range. A knight to her left gave a high cry and fell away and she caught a glimpse of his bloodied face as she hurtled past him, breath sawing in her throat. The bullets were cracking all around her now. She felt their hot wind. Another knight was hit, directly in front of her. He fell and she hurdled his body and carried on. She looked up, twenty paces away, and she could see the Artilleryman atop the wall, a gingery man in a flat black cap, with the match glowing, a tiny coal at the end of his pole. The others of his crew were tipping the cannon, depressing the muzzle, aiming it directly at her, or so it seemed. It would roar out its fire, anytime now, and she would instantly die.

But the first Niho knight was at the base of the wall. He put his back to it, bent his knees, laced his fingers together into a stirrup. The second knight stepped straight into the cup of his hands, the first knight heaved and the second was catapulted upward, hands reaching for the lip of the wall, and he was over and gone. Another followed him, and another. Katerina rushed forward, stepped into the stirrup. She felt Ari's steadying hands on her buttocks, and then she was flying, up, up, the vista of the interior of the Red Fort opening before her. She landed catlike on the top of the wall. Saw a red-turbaned face with a huge black mustache, the man lunging at her with a bayonet. She slashed with the saber, knocking the musket aside, and chopped down with the backswing, cutting through the side of his turban, splitting his skull.

There were Niho all around, sleek black figures with darting, shining steel. All the Artillerymen were down, one man's ashen face lying next to the still-smoldering match. Ari was beside her now, and the Dokra were massing, a score of them charging along the parapet, snarling, some firing, others charging with bayonet. A lone Niho smashed into them, a solitary black knight charging home, katana whirling: limbs were lopped, bellies opened, the bayonets scraping noisily over his armor leaving deep white scratches in the black lacquer as he killed them all. That single knight went through a platoon of Dokra like a hot poker through a block of butter. There were bodies falling left and right, as his steel katana carved into flesh, blood spraying everywhere, stricken men tumbling off the parapet, screaming, to land with a thump on the earth floor twenty feet below.

Ari was tugging her sleeve. "The sally port, Lady, we must open the port to let the Legionnaires in."

He led her down a set of stone stairs, hacking two Dokra out of his path with an elegant, almost-contemptuous ease. She found herself at the bottom of the steps. A red-jacketed man rushed at her, a sword arcing toward her face, but Ari's blow severed his arm before he could connect. Her knight took on two men, experienced bayonet fighters, jabbing and staying out of range of his long, curved blade. Ari rolled under one lunge, and came up with his katana deep in the man's belly. He was up in an instant and whirling, slicing the second man's head clean from his shoulders in a hot spray of gore. Katerina saw a pale, shouting face in front of her, slashed instinctively with her saber, feeling the crunch of teeth under her blade all the way up her arm. The man fell away. She wrenched the saber free.

"This way, Lady," said Ari. A musket fired close by and she felt the tug of it in the cloth of the loose breeches she wore. She looked down but saw no blood. Ari was pointing at a small brown wooden door set into the wall at its center point. There were still hundreds of Dokra in the fort; they swarmed everywhere, surrounding the individual Niho knights in struggling knots. The air was thick with musket smoke; the smell of blood and ripped entrails strong as cheap perfume in her nostrils. She swiped at a passing Dokra and he ducked away from her blow. Ari flicked out and sank his blade into the waist of an Artilleryman, nearly severing him in half.

They were by the wooden door.

Four Dokra were charging at her, muskets and bayonets, but using all her strength of will, she turned her back on them, and leaving Ari to defend her while she focused on the little door, began to wrestle with the heavy, horizontal wooden bar that locked it. It was stuck. Immovable. She could not lift it from its bracket. She heard the screams from behind, the panting breaths; a spray of hot blood spattered her cheek. She could not lift the bar. She couldn't do it. She would have to have help.

She forced herself to be calm. She looked again and saw that the bar was held in place by a simple locking pin. Someone barged heavily against her back but she ignored it. Ari was there. She pulled the pin from the wood, lifted the bar easily, and was nearly knocked off her feet as the door swept open and a huge Stormer, face a mask of blood under his gleaming helmet, charged through with his long musket in his hands, bayonet fixed. She stepped smartly out of the way as another man came tumbling in, a slender Scout with shining sword in his fist—then the flood of men began.

The remnants of the Scout and Storm Companies of the 42nd Legion had endured all the torments of Seven Hells. Their ranks had been decimated while they stood helplessly outside the walls. They had stood like sheep and been slaughtered from above for longer than anyone had the right to ask of them. They had endured; they had died. But once inside the walls their store of fury had no limits. The sally port that Katerina had opened admitted perhaps no more than eighty men, many of them wounded, some barely even able to walk, but they poured into the fort in a ravening pack, stabbing, slicing, blowing their enemies to eternity in a frenzy of revenge for the mauling they had suffered for so long.

It was their reckless ferocity that won the day.

The Dokra were pushed back, slashed, hacked and torn apart and, as Katerina crouched by the open port, utterly exhausted, the bloody saber cradled in her lap, she saw that the red turbans were slipping over the eastern wall and then, when the main gate was flung wide, they were streaming out of the Red Fort in their scores, heading back down to the city of Istana Kush.

She called out for Ari, and found him right there, of course, standing next to her, still on guard, a bad cut on the visible portion of his handsome face, above the black mask, next to his eye, the armor of his left arm cracked and hanging loose in places, thick red blood seeping through.

"Lady?"

"I want a red rocket launched. Now. And get the Ostraka men and the baggage up to the fort. The north-wall cannon must be brought into action. Do it now."

CHAPTER 37

———— ✤ ————

Mangku knelt before the Obat Bale and made his obeisance to the Lord of the Islands. Then at Ongkara's gracious command he rose to his full height and smiled.

"I have the blade, sire," he said. "I have the Khodam of the Wukarta."

"My felicitations, Hiero! Have much difficulty obtaining it?"

"Nothing to speak of, sire."

"And yet, I expected you back with it more than a week ago. I heard in great detail of the—uh—collection of the Wukarta Kris from the island of Taman and I presumed that your first concern must surely be to bring it to me with the utmost speed."

Mangku was taken aback by Ongkara's words. But, of course, the slippery little frog would have his spies and informants on every one-palm-tree knoll of the Laut Besar.

"I was not aware that there was a strict schedule, sire—or indeed any urgency at all."

"No? No urgency to bring the sacred symbol of the oldest line of rulers in the world to its rightful owner? No urgency to place it in the hands of the Lord of the Islands?"

"I had some trifling personal matters to attend to, sire. Then I returned with all speed."

"So I hear. I gather that you persuaded the late, but not-very-much-lamented Raja Widojo of Sukatan to part with the Dragon's Eye, saying it was to be a fitting gift to me."

Mangku said nothing. His shoulder and face were both paining him, despite having dosed himself with a powerful obat-based medicine on the ship and having slept for nearly two straight days. *Was this preposterous despot going to be difficult? Perhaps it was time to take direct charge of what he comically called his mind.* So far, their relationship had been fruitful: Ongkara had provided him with a ship and allowed him to recruit a crew of his choice and given him a free hand in the Laut Besar in his self-appointed task to gather the Keys of Power—not that Ongkara knew the truth about that! In exchange, Mangku had destroyed several of his potential rivals for the Obat Bale with his own blood magic and some less-taxing old-fashioned poisons. He had allowed Ongkara to remain on the Obat Bale throne for several years now. Perhaps it was time to show him who was truly master.

"No need to look so glum, sorcerer. I was merely jesting with you. You may keep the Dragon's Eye. I have enough baubles. It is a fitting reward for your loyal services. However, I shall trouble you to hand over the Kris of Wukarta Khodam."

"As you command, sire," said Mangku, and he turned and gestured to two of his *Sea Serpent* shipmates, who had been kneeling respectfully ten paces back, their foreheads pressed to the Audience Hall floor, on either side of a large wooden chest.

As the men carried the chest forward, and levered it open, Mangku decided that he would allow this little pirate frog to keep control of his mind for the time being. When he insinuated himself into the brain of one of his victims, the hosts rarely lived very long afterward—as had been the case with Widojo—and Mangku preferred, on balance, to keep Ongkara alive, at least for the moment. Finding a replacement Lord of the Islands who was as pliable and stupid would have involved a great deal of work and the sorcerer had his task to accomplish and little time to waste. Later, when the Keys had all been assembled, and the ancient powers invoked, when the doors to the Seven Hells had been opened, this irritating little buffoon could be swiftly dispatched and a suitable replacement found.

Mangku picked the Kris out of the box and, kneeling before the Dragon of the High Seas once more, he presented the ancient blade, holding it up with both hands. Ongkara growled an angry curse at one of his Jath guards, who had stepped forward to receive it, and hopped off the Obat Bale himself to accept the sword with his own two hands. He drew the pitted blade from its wooden sheath and held it up to the light.

"Doesn't look like much, does it?" he said.

"It is more than a thousand years old, sire. And while it may perhaps show its venerability, it is still the sacred symbol of a royal line. The man who holds the Kris of Wukarta Khodam must be acknowledged as a rightful ruler—whoever he might be."

Ongkara glared at the sorcerer from under his brows, irked by this reference to the flimsiness of his claim to the Lordship of the Islands. He knew he was a usurper—his father had been a drudge in the obat orchards of Piri-Piri, whose son had only escaped the same fate by taking to the sea and a life of murder and pillage—but he didn't care to be reminded of it. One day this tricksy conjurer would go too far and, when his usefulness was at an end . . .

Ongkara opened his left hand and placed the dull blade against the skin of his palm. Then he thought better of it.

"You, big-beard." He beckoned the nearest Jath guard. "Hold out your arm."

The man did as he was commanded, and Ongkara sliced the old blade into the thick meat of his forearm. The steel cut through the wool of the Jath's sleeve with ease and the man jerked in surprise. "Hold still, damn you," said the Lord of the Islands and, as wetness bloomed through the cloth, he wiped the Kris in the gore and held it up to his face, staring at it intently. The blood glistened on the ancient steel.

"I thought a touch of blood was supposed to turn it to magical flame," he said, his disappointment plain.

"That is merely a myth, sire," Mangku said. "The true power of the Khodam lies in its possession. You are its possessor. No man now can doubt your right to rule."

Ongkara summoned the Jath again and wiped the Kris clean on his other arm.

"I have taken the liberty of constructing a stand for the Khodam," said Mangku. "Might I suggest that the blade is displayed, as is traditional, at your right hand in the Audience Hall at all times? The people of Singarasam must see that you possess it."

A few moments later, Ongkara was admiring the Kris as it stood proudly upright in a little wooden contraption of struts and slots to the right of the Obat Bale.

"It does look rather fine, Hiero. You will forgive my earlier churlishness, I trust. And I thank you most warmly for my splendid gift."

"I am honored to have made it to you, sire."

"You are a good man, Hiero, and a loyal friend. I trust I can count on you in the coming days and weeks? I may have need of your invaluable assistance."

"Sire, I am yours to command. But may I ask what is troubling you?"

"There has been some . . . difficulties . . . with the Celestial Republic. As I'm sure you must have heard. The Permanent Envoy of the Council of Venerables has closed his House and departed from Singarasam, along with all his staff. And there are reports that a powerful fleet of Celestial battleships has been launched from Nankung and is heading south through the Kalima Straits. They mean to make war on me."

"May I inquire what has caused this painful rift with our friends in the Republic?"

"I was tricked, Hiero, tricked by a weaselly liar named Farhan Madani, who is no doubt a secret agent of the Indujah Federation. I gave him my flag and a letter of marque and he has been making mischief all over the Laut Besar, attacking the ships and garrisons of the Celestial Republic and pretending to be acting on my orders."

A neat ploy, thought Mangku. *And how stupid of this dolt to have fallen for it. So the Federation schemes to play the Republic off against the Lord of the Islands. Very good. And yet I saw the Republic's Legionnaires moving on the Federation base at Istana Kush not three days ago. Even better.*

War was certainly coming to the Laut Besar, he concluded, massive bloodshed, cities burned, ships destroyed. Very well—but what did that mean for him? Chaos, he had already decided, would make his task easier, if anything. And if Ongkara was to be defeated, killed or exiled? It would be no catastrophe. Inconvenient, yes. But it would not ruin his plans. As long as he could recover the Khodam before Ongkara met his end, what did Mangku care in the years to come who called himself the Lord of the Islands?

"What utterly outrageous behavior, sire. This Farhan Madani sounds like a monster. He must be punished. And how may I serve you in this matter?"

"I have summoned the fleet, all the captains from across the Laut Besar. They are all, to a man, entirely loyal to me, of course, but there may be some of the—uh—more awkward captains who may require—uh—some extra persuasion that my cause is just. I would like you to, shall we say, stiffen the resolve of all the chiefs for this war against the Celestial Republic. Remind them all where their loyalties—and their best interests—lie."

"Your word is my command, sire. It shall be my pleasure to remind the captains who is the true Lord of the Islands." *Assuming,* Mangku thought, *it does not interfere with my own quest. Or take up too much of my time. Too many things to do. Kalima is next—and the Mountain of Fire. The fourth Key of Power is almost certainly to be found there.*

"What would I do without you, my faithful Hiero?" said the Lord of the Islands.

"What would any of us do without you, sire?"

CHAPTER 38

————————⟨※⟩————————

The lodgings of the Patriarch of the Temple of Vharkash in Singarasam were modest in comparison to his elevated status, as befitted a humble servant of the great God. And the Patriarch was no stranger to humility. Many years ago, more than he cared to count, Ratna Setiawan had served as a novice in the Mother Temple on Yawa. He had pounded the dirty robes of the more senior devotees in freezing river water, he had risen in the middle of the night to prepare breakfast for the priests, he had swept the courtyards, an endless, tedious task, and rung the bells for prayer, work and mealtimes. It had been brutally hard work and he had suffered more than his fair share of indignities, but he had survived. Indeed, he had prospered. He had risen through the ranks of the priesthood over the years, gaining authority and responsibilities, and had attained the rank of deputy, one of seven men and women who were only second in authority to the High Priest himself.

That very man—the High Priest, the man who now called himself Semar—sat on the springy bamboo bench before him with three disturbingly odd companions: a huge, scarred savage, a skinny girl with a fresh, star-shaped wound high on her chest, and a languid princeling who appeared to look down his long nose dismissively at everything in sight.

Ratna remembered vividly the last time he had seen the High Priest. His face had been blackened by soot, his robes had been shredded by the vast explosion of green-and-black fire that had utterly destroyed the Mother Temple, and the little High Priest had been possessed by an incandescent rage so great that it seemed to make his whole body vibrate.

He had gathered his three surviving deputies and given them their orders. They were to collect all the priests and the novices who were fit enough to travel and quit what was left of the Mother Temple. He told them where to go, and from whom they might find help when they got there. He told them that the Mother Temple was no more and, indeed, it had been completely torn apart, left with scarcely one stone still standing on another.

The gold-leaf-covered statue of Vharkash, a thousand-year-old marvel twenty feet high and the pride of every soul in the place, had been the epicenter of the blast. It had been vaporized, leaving only a few shreds of blackened wood and twists of tarnished metal. More than a thousand souls—priests, lay-workers, servants, even a few travelers lodging there as guests—had perished in the blast. The High Priest had embraced Ratna, held him tight, and sent him to make his way across the sea to Singarasam, with orders to present himself at the temple there and humbly beg for admittance. The other two deputies, and all the surviving priests, had been similarly dispatched to other refuges right across the Laut Besar.

Ratna had asked two questions before he set off on his long journey. He asked the High Priest what he intended to do now, and why he could not come with them.

He could still remember every word of the soot-blackened, furious man's reply.

"This place was my life. Now it is destroyed. I will spend the rest of my days seeking the one who is responsible. We all know who that is. I will find him and I will punish him, even if it takes a thousand years. Vharkash is my strength and He will not be slighted. The one who did this thing will feel the full wrath of the

Harvester one day. This I swear on my eternal soul. I shall have my vengeance."

They did all know who was responsible. And when Ratna heard the High Priest's words he remembered the shiver of fear that he felt for the one Semar would seek out and punish—the disgraced priest, the outcast holy man, the individual who had dared to dabble in the forbidden arts of blood magic: Hiero Mangku.

"A little more tea, Your Holiness?" said Ratna, holding up the earthenware pot.

"Thank you, yes, but you must not call me that. I am plain old Semar these days."

Ratna nodded, poured, then raised the pot toward his other three guests in a mute question. None of them bothered to reply although the princeling gave him a condescending smile and a curt shake of his head.

What seemed like mild discourtesy to the Patriarch was in fact no more than tiredness in his four guests. They had arrived that afternoon in Singarasam after almost twenty-four hours in a small open boat not much bigger than Ketut's fishing craft.

On the day of their departure the citizens of Istana Kush had been able to hear the cannon of the Red Fort firing quite clearly and the muffled pops of the Dokra muskets. Word that the Gates of Stone were under attack by land had caused something of a mild panic in the city and the harbor had been crowded with civilians and their families seeking a ship to escape. But the four travelers, unaware of the turmoil in the city, had slept deep and long in their comfortable lodgings in the Governor's Palace and by the time they were down on the quays, and pushing through the thronging humanity, they were too late. They were repeatedly told that there were no vessels that could take them to Singarasam.

They had even sought out Captain Lodi and begged him to carry them but he informed them that the *Mongoose* was beached and careened with the damaged hull being properly repaired by the skilled craftsmen in the Small Harbor. It was only, finally, by the good graces of Governor Bandi himself that they had found even the diminutive craft that was eventually to take them onward. It was, in fact, the Governor's own single-sailed pleasure craft, crewed by one gnarled Indujah sailor. After an uncomfortable afternoon and night and part of the next day—the boat was really too small to take five people and their baggage on such a long voyage—they had arrived in Singarasam and made their way straight to the Temple of Vharkash.

"Perhaps you would all like to have some food," said Ratna. "You must be very hungry. We live very simply here, I am afraid, but I think we can manage some boiled rice and vegetables for you, perhaps even a bowl of spiced lentils, as well."

"That would be most kind," said Semar. "And then if we could trouble you for a place to sleep, that would be even kinder."

"Certainly, certainly, the novices will prepare a place for your friends in the dormitory after we have eaten. But you, Your Holi . . . I mean you, Semar, my old friend, must sleep in my bed. I shall be quite comfortable on the bench there. That will give us time to talk, to catch up. It has after all been many, many years since . . ."

Food was brought, and swiftly eaten and, as the light was dying, the Patriarch got up and went over to a three-pronged candlestick standing in the corner. He did not use flint and tinder to light the candles, nor did he have a taper brought from the fires in the kitchens. He merely chewed his lip, mumbled a few words and blew out a fine mist of his own bloody spittle onto the wicks, which burst into flame, bathing the room in a soft yellow light.

Semar frowned at his old friend. "Magic, Ratna? Since when does a devotee of Vharkash make use of the dark powers?"

"Oh, it is not really magic, as such," said the Patriarch, scratching at the white, tightly curled peppercorns of hair on his head. "That would be quite wrong, of course. This is just a little trick—like a conjuring trick—which I find convenient for my needs. Not magic at all—though I expect it would have been rather frowned upon in the old days. But, you know, Vharkashta is changing, my old friend, we are not all as hidebound as we once were in Yawa. Here in Singarasam, I have sanctioned the use of small amounts of spiritual power, in cases of healing the sick and for temple displays at the festivals, a few fireworks and so on. We find it helps in recruiting a steady stream of novices to our ranks and with impressing the jaded members of our congregation. Just a few simple tricks, nothing dangerous."

"As your guest, it is not my place to bring up matters of doctrine, Ratna, but you know as well as I do that the use of any kind of magic was banned centuries ago."

"You are quite right, Semar . . . this is not the time to dispute doctrine. But, as I say, we must move with the times. Vharkashta is not the only faith in Singarasam—you will have heard that the new western religion, that of the Martyr, is gaining converts here. I expect you have come up against it in your travels. A foul creed of self-harm and superstition. We must ensure that we can hold our own against it, and if the price we must pay is a few simple illusions, then I say it is a reasonable one."

Semar said nothing. He sat forward on the bench, leaning on his staff. Tenga gave a tremendous yawn, her huge mouth opening and displaying dazzling white teeth and a blood-red interior. That set Jun and Ketut off. Even Semar had to fight to keep his mouth shut.

"Your friends are tired. Let them be taken off to bed, while you and I shall have another pot of tea and discuss what you have been up to all these many years."

The Patriarch rang a little bell and a baby-faced Han novice in a long black robe appeared and bore Jun, Ketut and Tenga away, leaving the two old men alone.

"So, old friend, what in the name of the great God have you been up to these past fifty years, and what now brings you to Singarasam? Surely, after all this time, you cannot still be following in the tracks of the one who destroyed the Mother Temple?"

"I am. You witnessed the vow I made, Ratna. And it is the pursuit of him—I shall not say his name—that brings me here to Singarasam to enjoy your generous hospitality."

The Patriarch made the holy sign of the scythe with the crooked index finger of his right hand and placed it between his eyebrows.

"May the Harvester preserve us. Hiero Mangku is here in Singarasam?"

"He serves the Lord of the Islands now. And he is here. I can feel his presence." Semar gripped his wooden staff tightly. "For many long years I followed him fruitlessly as he traveled the world. I nearly caught up with him once or twice, but he always proved too elusive. I picked up rumors that he sought yet more power—the Keys of Power, no less—and that he was studying the lost wisdom of the ancients wherever he could find it—in the filthy back alleys of Dhilika, on the high plains of the Celestial Republic, even in the remote mountains of Kyo. I followed him to all these places and each time he slipped away before I could find a way to deal with him. Sometimes I had no wind of him for several years on end. So, in the end, I decided to try to anticipate where he might go next, rather than merely follow hopelessly in his dust. I lay in wait, you might say. And rather successfully, too. I picked up his trail in Taman and followed him across the Laut Besar to your own fine city. He is here now, brother, and I will destroy him yet."

"How exactly do you mean to do that?" asked the priest. "The means by which you plan to destroy him has long puzzled me.

Have you forsaken our vow? We swore—you and I and all our brothers—to spill no human blood. And loathsome as he is: he is human."

"I shall not spill his blood," said Semar. "But I shall work to ensure that others do."

It occurred to Ratna Setiawan that this, too, might consist of a breach of strict Vharkashta doctrine and he considered saying something tart along those lines.

"How can I aid you in this task, brother?" he said instead. "I, too, have not forgotten what he did to us, to our Mother Temple and our faith. I should like to help you strike him down. My resources, all the resources of the temple here, are completely at your disposal."

"He has at least two of the Keys of Power," said Semar, "one of which is the Kris of Wukarta Khodam."

Ratna raised his white eyebrows. "It actually exists? The Khodam is real?"

"Yes, he took it from the south and he will have it here with him. The boy is a prince of Taman, pure Wukarta blood. We must find the Khodam and take it from the sorcerer; I mean to have the Wukarta boy wield it against our foe. He seems weak and foolish but he has some true strength at his core. The girl is strong, too, a Vessel, and of not inconsiderable ability. Between the three of us we shall confront the necromancer and defeat him, my friend, do not doubt it."

"I believe you—and I will aid you as best as I can. But we must proceed carefully. He is a dangerous opponent. I will inquire discreetly about the one we seek and about the Khodam. I have a good many influential friends in this city. We will know in a day or so if what you believe is true. But I see you are quite fatigued, old friend, so for now let us rest, and sleep and wake refreshed and ready for this contest."

Semar smiled at his host and allowed himself a small yawn. "I knew I could rely on you, Ratna. You were always the most loyal of deputies. Thank you."

"Tell me one last thing, Your Holiness. What does our enemy mean to do if he gathers all seven of the Keys of Power?"

"You know what he will do, brother. He will open the gate to all the Seven Hells and unleash the great plague of darkness upon the world once more."

"Why? In the God's name, why? He would destroy mankind."

"Not all of it. Some would be protected from its poison. If you remember the old legends, the aboriginal Ebu people would be quite safe; only the New People would be affected. It is some ingredient, some weakness of their immigrant blood that makes them vulnerable. Those that we now call Dewa would be unscathed. The peoples of Ziran Atar would be also untouched. But all those who do not have enough of the blood of the original folk of the Laut Besar in their veins would die. All Wukarta would certainly be doomed."

Semar yawned again.

"I still do not understand why he would do this," said the Patriarch. "Even if he preserves a miserable few thousand people, why seek to destroy the rest of the world?"

"I don't *understand* it," said Semar. "But I know what he believes he will achieve. He wants to unmake the past two thousand years. He wants to go back to the time before the New People came to the Laut Besar, to the time when the Ebu hunters ruled the empty lands and rivers and roamed the virgin forests. Before the light of Vharkash the Harvester came here. He wants to return the Laut Besar to the time of darkness and blood magic."

CHAPTER 39

⸺◦⊕◦⸺

The large person who called herself Mamaji smiled lovingly at Farhan Madani as he walked into the chamber. She was resplendent in a yellow sari with a design of huge pink flowers that seemed to light up the dim interior of the Round House at the summit of the Governor's Palace in Istana Kush. It was late afternoon and already the shadows were lengthening. Over her shoulder, through the cracked glass of the broad windows, Farhan could see the gray-green waters of the Sumbu Strait and three large warships anchored in the roads about a mile away. There were dozens of smaller craft out there, too. With the arrival of the enemy vessels and the fall of the twin fortresses that guarded the Straits, the panicked citizens of Istana Kush had taken to the water en masse. Most were heading east, seeking to escape the invasion force in the vastness of the Laut Besar, but a few were slipping past the three warships near the northern Manchatka shore and sailing out west into the Indujah Ocean, beginning the long voyage home to the Federation. The three warships of the Celestial Republic, knowing the boats were filled with civilians, women and children, were obeying their own rules of war and chivalrously allowing them to depart, leaving them unmolested as long as they made no hostile moves.

Farhan bowed courteously to acknowledge Mamaji's wide smile of greeting. She seemed to be in an extraordinarily buoyant mood considering the circumstances. The town below the palace was burning in places, where the enemy ships had bombarded it continuously for several hours—houses had been wrecked, shops and taverns torn apart by the barrage; the five harbor batteries had all been displaced, knocked from their fixtures, their Honorable Artillerymen killed or maimed at their posts; and much of the stone quay had been turned to rubble. Even the old-fashioned brass battery at the point of the Governor's Palace, the prow of its ship-like shape, had been targeted by the ships' cannon, although it was at the extreme limit of their range. The stonework of the redoubt had been chipped and shattered but the old brass guns remained intact. And the palace itself still stood, its occupants swelled by hundreds of soldiers, sailors and gunners, city dwellers and foreign merchants, all seeking refuge from the enemy fire. Indeed, the palace had reverted to its ancient role as the keep of Istana Kush, the last bastion. Its gates were firmly shut against the invaders, its long, curving, cannon-pocked walls now manned with every able-bodied man fit enough to carry a musket or wield sword, bow or spear.

The bombardment was over—at least for now. The ships had not come close enough to seriously menace the palace itself but had contented themselves with destroying the harbor defenses and tearing up the town. Now Farhan could see several longboats being slowly lowered from the sides of the warships, filled with men in the blue coats of Celestial Legionnaires. He knew what would happen next. When the fighting men were disembarked, and safely landed in the now-uncontested town, the three enemy warships would move forward a half mile and begin to batter the walls of the palace itself. When a suitable breach was made— and with three powerful battleships pounding the walls, it could not take long—the Legionnaires would be sent in on foot to storm the citadel. The final assault on the last Federation fortress of Istana Kush was about to begin—and for the life of him, Farhan could not see how the palace could resist it. It must fall. With any luck, he would be long gone by then. Once he had the promised bonus money from Mamaji, in cash, preferably, he'd be down in the Small Harbor, where he had a capacious fishing boat and its venal captain awaiting his orders and a promised fat purse, and then it was away south and to safety.

"I have some excellent news for you, dear Farhan," said Mamaji with a smile.

The fat woman had assumed command of this last bastion of Istana Kush, as easily as she had taken command of the *Mongoose*. She had cowed Governor Augustus Bandi with a letter of authority from General Vakul and had even gone so far as to reprimand him sternly for allowing the two forts to be lost while he was in command—despite his having received a timely warning—and for allowing the three warships into the Straits where they could pulverize the city to rubble. There would be consequences, she told him, dire consequences for his incompetence. The poor man, his once-plump face now gray and drawn, stood by the window in his dark green Artilleryman's uniform looking out over the destruction of his former command and chewing on what was left of his fingernails. He knew what the Amrit Shakti meant by "dire consequences." He was surprised that he was not already in chains.

"I have decided, Farhan dear, that you should be given a signal honor," she said.

"How very gratifying, Mamaji. But that is quite unnecessary. All I require is that you make good on your solemn promise to me of the ten thousand ringgu for parlaying with the white-painted savages in Yawa. If you could pay me now, that would be most satisfactory."

"We will come to that, dear. But first it is my great pleasure to tell you that I have decided to promote you to the rank of colonel, with all the pay and privileges that that rank entails. I was granted that authority by General Vakul himself, if I deemed you worthy of it, before we left Dhilika. I have also decided to award you the

Order of the Elephant, First Class, for your courageous actions in Yawa. Congratulations, Colonel Madani."

"Thank you, Mamaji, I'm most grateful . . ."

And it was true. He was. Colonel Madani had a certain ring to it that Farhan rather liked. And the Order of the Elephant was the highest honor the Federation could bestow on those who labored in its service. However, both the new rank and the medal were quite irrelevant because the moment Farhan had the promised cash in his hands, he planned to resign from the Amrit Shakti and retire in comfort somewhere nice and quiet and remote.

". . . but if we could talk now about the money, I would be even more pleased."

"I have not forgotten my promise, Farhan dear. Of course not. But as you can see events are rather overtaking me at the moment." She waved vaguely at the window and the burning town below. "The thing is, dear Farhan, I need you to perform one more service for the Federation. One last mission. We will discuss the money when you return wreathed in glory and I'm sure we will come to a satisfying mutual agreement."

This did not sound good at all.

"What mission?" he said. "What sort of service?"

"Colonel Bandi, if you would be so good as to join us."

The Governor came to her side. Farhan had never seen a man look quite so hangdog.

"Don't know if you are aware, Farhan, but Colonel Bandi used to have a reputation as one of the finest gunners in the Honorable Artillery Regiment, before he was elevated to his position here as Governor. Indeed, he was considered quite a hero, in his day. Weren't you, Augustus? Almost as much of a hero as you, Farhan dear."

Farhan looked at Bandi, who stared back at him glumly.

"I am afraid that now I need my two heroes to save the day once more."

They both looked at Mamaji. Farhan felt a rising sense of panic.

"I'm not sure that I am up to any more heroics, Mamaji. If you could just see your way clear to giving me the money you promised, then I will be on my way."

"Unfortunately, I cannot allow that, at this time. The Federation needs you."

"But Mamaji—"

"Farhan dear, please don't be difficult. I promise that you will have your money and an honorable discharge from the Amrit Shakti, if that's your wish, in due course. But first I must ask you to do this one little thing for me. Now just listen to me, both of you."

Farhan could think of a thousand retorts. But instead he bit his lip and listened.

Mamaji pointed out of the window at the far side of the Sumbu Strait, beyond the three static warships and the mass of smaller shipping busily fleeing the Straits.

"The Green Fort," she said, "has not been occupied by the enemy. Their strategy has, so far, been most ingenious—perhaps even brilliant. They have taken the Red Fort from the landward side, and ejected our garrison; they have bombarded the Green Fort and silenced its guns and, in a short while, I assume they will begin an all-out assault on the palace. But they have failed to occupy the Green Fort in their rear. And I believe their commander, while extremely imaginative and resourceful, is somewhat inexperienced—and he has made a significant error in this matter. Very significant indeed, I would venture to say."

Colonel Bandi had perked up at this information. His head lifted and he craned his short neck to see out of the window. He snapped open a telescope and trained it on the Manchatka shore and the shattered and still-smoking walls of the small fort there.

"No sign of activity," he said. "They haven't placed any men there—or at least none that I can see. No flags or banners either."

"The enemy has made a mistake," said Mamaji, "and we must exploit it."

"The long guns are still there, too. I can see one, no, two dismounted barrels." Bandi was now sounding almost cheerful.

Farhan's heart sank. He had an inkling of what Mamaji's mission would be.

"I am told, Farhan dear, that you have engaged the services of a fishing boat. Even now, Captain Jamus Hawill awaits your orders in the Small Harbor. Is that not right?"

He could only nod, appalled by the accuracy of her intelligence. But he knew, too, that she must have several dozen spies in the city, especially around the Small Harbor.

"I am saddened that you should think of *deserting* us in our hour of need, Farhan. And I'm afraid I really cannot permit you to do that. Not now. Once you have completed your mission, you will have your bonus money and my blessing to go wherever you wish."

She had used the word *deserting*, Farhan noted. A crime always punishable by death in Federation military circles. He was trapped and he knew it. Whatever this ghastly mission was—and he thought he could make a fairly accurate guess—if he did not undertake it, he could be tried and executed for desertion. But if he did what she asked of him, one last time, he would get his money and be allowed to leave. Maybe.

"What do you want me to do?"

"That's the spirit, Colonel Madani! I knew your love of the Federation would compel you to volunteer for the task. Let me tell you the good news: we're under attack, of course, but I believe the palace has sufficient men of grit to hold out against the forces against it for at least two or even three days. We have plenty of stores and water. Our magazines are full of powder and shot. And I have sent fast boats out into the Laut Besar, heading in all directions to seek out Federation forces and order them to converge on

Istana Kush with their utmost speed. I estimate that we should receive help within a week. Maybe sooner."

If we can only hold out for three days, as she just said, and help doesn't come for a week, it will still be too late. It isn't exactly wonderful news, Farhan thought.

"The enemy's main armaments are on their three ships," Mamaji continued blithely. "If they could be silenced—if that danger could be neutralized—I believe we can last out here for a week, two weeks, perhaps a month. By which time every Federation fighting man in the Laut Besar would be here with us. Troops from the Indujah Peninsula might have arrived, too. The enemy, apparently, has only a few hundred assault troops, a single Celestial Legion, I believe. So, if we could somehow sink or burn or even damage those ships . . ."

"You want me to go to the Green Fort, with Bandi here and a few Honorable Artillerymen, re-sight the cannon and sink those three warships, is that it?"

"I knew you'd grasp it quickly, Farhan. It's your keen intellect that I so admire. That's what all of us in the Amrit Shakti—including General Vakul—value so much."

"It's a suicide mission, Mamaji. And you damn well know it. Even if the Green Fort is not garrisoned by the enemy—which it most likely is—even if we can get those guns functioning again—which we most likely can't—even if we can bring them to bear on the warships, the moment we fire a shot every cannon in three powerful ships of war, not to mention the guns of the Red Fort across the Strait, will rain death and hellfire down on us. We will be blown to smithereens in a few instants. As a plan, it is complete madness."

"I'll do it," said Colonel Bandi. "I volunteer to undertake this mission, Mamaji." The former Governor had seen a way to atone for his mistakes. He might die in the attempt, yes, but if he succeeded he could mitigate the punishment he would receive from the Amrit Shakti. Anything, including being blown to smither-eens, was better than being shipped back to Dhilika in chains to meet his fate in the cells below the Taj Palace.

"You see, Farhan dear, our bold Colonel Bandi is not afraid of a little danger. You wouldn't want me to think you had turned coward?"

"Do you really think I care if you call me a coward? What am I, eight years old? Are you going to dare me to do it next? Double-dare me?"

"Very well, Colonel Madani. You leave me no choice," said Mamaji. Her kindly smile had disappeared. Her chubby face looked as if it were carved from gray marble. "I need you to ac-company Colonel Bandi on this mission. I need your brains, to be honest, and your resourcefulness, your cunning and your cow-ard's instinct for self-preservation. We are at war, if you had not noticed it, and you are still, for the time being, a senior officer of the Amrit Shakti. So these are your orders. At dusk this evening, you will embark on Captain Hawill's boat with Colonel Bandi and a well-equipped platoon of Honorable Artillerymen and engi-neers. I have already arranged Jamus Hawill's payment for this mission. You will proceed to the Green Fort. Once there you will reinstate the cannon and engage the enemy warships for as long as you are able, aiming to sink, cripple or injure them in any way you can. Is that clear? I take it that I do not need to tell you what the penalty for disobeying direct orders is in time of war? It is exactly the same as the penalty for desertion."

"O Gods . . ." said Farhan.

"Do I take that to mean that you accept this mission, Colonel Madani?"

"And the money: if I do this, you will pay me the money you owe?"

"The instant you return, Farhan dear," said Mamaji, her smile suddenly returning.

CHAPTER 40

K aterina stood on the parapet of the east wall of the Red Fort and felt the sea breeze caress her bare arms and face, chilling the wet hair that was loosely tied at her neck. She had bathed and changed and eaten a little from the fort's stores—she had even slept for a couple of hours, not nearly long enough, but nonetheless she felt like a new woman. The prospect of victory would do that, she supposed. To her left, across the narrow stretch of water, the Green Fort was a smoldering ruin, her Ostraka gunners, even half-stupefied with obat, had made short work of it—a dozen accurate salvos had smashed the defenses and sent the handful of troops inside fleeing into the safety of the Manchatka jungle. Then the Ostrakans, giggling with childlike delight, had wheeled four of the Red Fort's guns to this eastern wall and opened fire on the five harbor batteries.

The sensation when she saw the *Yotun* sailing proudly in from the west through the Sumbu Straits had been one of the most intense of her entire young life. And her powerful flagship had been shortly followed through the Gates of Stone by *Egil* and *Sar*. All three were in position within a quarter of an hour and adding their considerable weight in screeching red-hot metal to the destruction of the harbor defenses. It had not taken more than an hour to reduce all the five batteries to rubble. Now, as the sun began to sink behind her, the last boatloads of Legionnaires were disembarking on the deserted harbor front.

The populace of Istana Kush had largely gone or were still fleeing, hundreds, even thousands swarming out from their homes and places of work, clogging the roads and market squares, many making for the Small Harbor beyond the Governor's Palace to beg for a place on one of the few remaining ships, but others were simply running south into the farmlands or farther into the foothills of the Barat Cordillera, there to take refuge until the fighting was over. Some were already afloat and small boats packed with people choked the Strait below her. Her three warships, all moored in a line across the Strait, their guns now silent, were ignoring the fleeing civilians, as she had ordered them to do. Let them run. The final assault would go easier if her Legionnaires were not troubled by citizens vainly trying to protect their stores and warehouses. Let them go, let them all go: they would be back in time when the Gates of Stone were wholly hers. Istana Kush was their home: a change of master would not make any difference to their lives. The brothel-keepers and owners of the marak taverns, the bread bakers, rice sellers and vegetable stall holders, the cobblers, cutlers and tailors, even the priests of the many local religions, would not lack paying customers, when the smoke had cleared and bodies had been carted away.

But there was one final act to come: the Governor's Palace on the far side of the city was still held against her and must be taken. Many of the Dokra from the forts and Honorable Artillerymen from the harbor batteries, as well as most of the garrison of Istana Kush itself, had fled into the palace, pulling up the ancient wooden drawbridge and defying her from the high walls. She estimated that at least five hundred fighting men were now inside this last redoubt.

It was a formidable fortress, yes, and strongly manned—but it would surely fall to her big guns and her brave men. Tomorrow, at first light, her three warships would close in and their cannon would open up a brutal barrage on the northern wall, smashing a

large hole, or several large holes in it, through which her eight
fresh Legionary companies—eight hundred elite fighting men—
would then storm. That would be it. Istana Kush would be hers
at last.

In the hours that followed the fall of the Red Fort, Katerina had
sent a message under a flag of truce into the Governor's Palace. It
promised just and merciful treatment for any who would immediately lay down their arms and quit the fortress. If she was forced
to storm the palace, the message said, after the attendant bloodshed and loss of life, there could be no mercy for those inside
when the palace finally fell. Her formal letter had been answered
by a scrawled note that thanked her for her concern and said that,
in fact, the defenders were quite pleased to stay where they were
at present. It had been signed almost indecipherably by someone
whose name appeared to be Mummy.

She watched from the east wall of the Red Fort with the sun
sinking behind her back as the efficient Legionnaires quickly surrounded the palace, digging themselves in among the smoldering
rubble of the city, just out of musket range and bowshot. Colonel
Wang was down there somewhere organizing the dispersal of his
troops. He had strongly advised against a night bombardment and
an attack on the walls in the darkness. Chaotic, he said. Very risky.
Tomorrow, the ships' long guns would be brought into play, the
walls would be swiftly breached, and the bloody business could
begin.

She knew that she could not spend too long on this final assault. Word of the attack on Istana Kush would have echoed
around the Laut Besar and there were powerful ships and soldiers
of the Federation scattered about the seas who would be coming
as fast as they could. She needed time to repair the harbor defenses and garrison and rearm the Red and Green Forts and she
could not do that while her enemies were taking potshots at her

men from the palace walls. But tomorrow the business would be done. Tomorrow it all would be over. And that would give her just enough time to prepare for the Federation's response.

She summoned Ari with a crooked finger. "I will see the prisoner now."

The prisoner, a junior Dokra officer, had been beaten unnecessarily harshly by the Storm Company, his captors, who were still angry at the cruel losses they had endured outside the walls of the Red Fort. Now Sublieutenant Rohit lay quite still in a bloodsodden heap in one of the cells below the north wall of the Red Fort.

Katerina looked down at the body coldly.

She turned to Major Chan, who looked back mournfully at her from his watery eyes, shifting his weight from one foot to the other. His left arm was in a sling and a little spot of blood was even now seeping through the crisp white linen.

"Is he even still alive?" she said.

"He is. You want me to rouse him?" He walked over and kicked the wretch.

"That might not be necessary. Did you get a list from him?"

"Yes, Highness. It's on the table there. He wrote it all down while he still had most of his fingernails. As you requested, it is a list of all the Governor's staff and the senior Federation officers in Istana Kush. We think most of them are inside the palace now, although it will take some time to sort out the identities of all the dead and wounded."

"Do we know who this Mummy person is?" she asked as she scanned the list of names on the blood-splotched paper.

"She is the personal envoy of General Hamil Vakul of the Indujah Federation. A high-ranking member of their spy organization, the Amrit Shakti. She calls herself Mamaji."

"Does she indeed? How charmingly eccentric."

Katerina's eyes were still fixed on the list of names.

"This will do very well, thank you, Chan." Katerina was smiling. She tapped one name with her small white finger. "Yes, this will do very well indeed."

She looked at the Legion officer and inclined her head toward the motionless prisoner. "Tell me, Major—what is that poor fellow's story? Had he been posted here long?"

"He says he arrived back in Istana only yesterday morning, after a voyage down to Yawa. He had some extraordinary tales to tell of fighting off five Celestial cruisers, and of white-painted cannibals and ghostly tigers, mostly nonsense of course. But we kept at him until he told the truth, at least as he sees it. I do not think we were betrayed, Highness. The Governor received word from a traveler in the Pengut Delta, a man who climbed Mount Barat and saw us coming, purely by chance. They knew we were advancing on the Red Fort from the south. This fellow and his Dokra company, along with another, and an extra platoon of the Honorable Artillery Company were posted here, with orders to expect an attack by us."

"Just bad luck, then. Something nobody can plan for. But luck can sometimes flow both ways." She smiled again, looking at the bloodstained list in her hands.

"Yes, Highness. What do you wish me to do with him? I do not think he has any more to tell us."

"Oh, he has told me enough. Thank you, Xi Chan. You've done well. Have him disposed of—quietly. However, from now on, there is to be no more mistreatment of the captured Dokra, do you understand me? No beatings, no interrogations. I want them decently fed and watered, their wounds tended to. I want them treated honorably, with kindness even. Do you understand me?"

"Yes, Highness."

"And I have a commission for you, Major Chan. These prisoners are mercenaries, yes? I want you to ask among the captives if any would be willing to serve me after the fall of Istana Kush—don't threaten them. Offer double pay and a signing bonus of, shall we say, ten ringgu, to any man who accepts—and that goes for any civilians, seamen or travelers in Istana who have military experience. I want you to form an entirely new unit, Major Chan. Let us call it, hmmm, the Istana Volunteers. I want you to form it, train it and ultimately command it in battle. How does that sound, Major? Or should I say Colonel Chan?"

"Highness, I belong to the 42nd. I can't just . . ."

"I will speak to Colonel Wang about seconding you to the Istana Volunteers. I'm sure he will entirely understand. You are relieved of Legion duties from this moment. Your surviving captain can take over, and promote some of the experienced lieutenants and sergeants while you are at it. I know there are many of them who more than deserve it."

Major Chan stared at her. "I beg you to reconsider, Highness. I do not wish to leave the Legion, not ever. My family is rich—they have connections and interests all over the world and I could have had a career as a merchant or banker or shipmaster or anything I chose. I chose the Legions, Highness. Joining the 42nd was the proudest moment of my life."

Katerina looked at the officer. He looked as if she had just ordered him to shoot his own mother in the face. Yet she also knew that he would surely obey her if she forced the issue. She reflected that there was a great deal she still had to learn about soldiers.

"I will make this bargain with you, Xi Chan; and I always keep my bargains. If you will give me one year as Colonel of the Istana Volunteers; if you will recruit them, train them, get them into something resembling the fighting order of a Celestial Legion, then I will allow you to return—if you choose—to the 42nd at the end of the allotted time and I will select another commander for the Volunteers. And I will make sure that Colonel Wang understands and is party to our agreement. Will you do it? Please, for me?"

"As you wish, Highness."

CHAPTER 41

For a day and a night and half another day they kicked their heels in the Patriarch's quarters of the Temple of Vharkash—resting, eating the monks' bland but plentiful food, exercising or just sleeping—while Ratna Setiawan made his inquiries. On the afternoon of the second day, Semar called them all to the Patriarch's chamber where the old man, dressed in shining white robes, which contrasted beautifully with his rich, teak-colored skin, was waiting for them with a beaming smile of triumph.

"I have news for you, my friends," he said, ushering them to the springy bamboo bench. "The Kris of Wukarta Khodam is indeed here in Singarasam. It is in the First House, not five hundred paces from where we are now. The Lord of the Islands has received it as a gift from the sorcerer Mangku and it stands proudly on the right-hand side of the Obat Bale in the Audience Hall on the first floor of the House. The King of Singarasam has been displaying it to all who visit him, and boasting long and loud of its power and lineage and the legitimacy he believes it brings to his rule."

Jun felt a glow in his belly at the thought of the proximity of the Kris of his ancestors. He imagined once more bringing it home to Taman in triumph, the cheering crowds, the songs of praise, the adulation of all the men and women of his homeland. Pretty young girls sobbing with hysterical joy to see him safely home again. It was a delightful thought.

"What is this First House?" he asked.

"It is the residence of the Lord of the Islands, the first proper brick-and-timber dwelling built here in Singarasam, when it was merely a swampy island and nest of local pirates and head-hunters." Ratna seemed immensely proud of the fact. "It was built by the original Han merchants who discovered that obat trees could be farmed in these waters and it has been the locus of power in Singarasam, indeed in the whole Laut Besar, ever since."

"Is it well guarded?" Jun asked.

"It is a house," said Ratna, "but a large one and guarded by sixty scimitar-men of the Jath tribe of Manchatka, who have protected Lords of the Islands since time immemorial."

Jun's heart sank at the thought. He was no coward—he believed he had demonstrated that to his own and everyone else's satisfaction—but neither did he relish taking on threescore scimitar-wielding bodyguards, even if it was to retrieve his sacred family heirloom.

"But let us set that problem aside for the moment," Ratna continued jovially. "Today, as I am sure you know, is the Hallowed Day. All the faithful men and women of Singarasam will be celebrating in the temple here and we would be most proud to welcome you to the ceremony as our honored guests. I understand the little lady might find that congenial?"

He smiled indulgently at Ketut, who stared stonily back at him.

"After the ceremony, I have arranged for us to meet a few prominent members of my flock—a little celebratory gathering—some of these are influential people, with excellent connections throughout the Laut Besar. I'm sure they'll be able to help you in your quest."

Could it really be Hallowed Day so soon? Jun wondered. *Had it really only been one month since he had seen Ketut reveal herself as a Vessel?* So much had happened since then—the Konda Pali mines, the hellish chase through the jungle, the bloody fight at the Temple of Burunya, the Ghost Tigers, the voyage to Istana Kush and onward here to Singarasam. But when he counted the days in his head, he found that it was indeed true.

The Patriarch bustled away to prepare for the ceremony and Jun saw that Semar and Ketut were once again sitting opposite each other on the bamboo bench, Semar with his hand flat on Ketut's chest, both with their eyes closed. They were doing that silent thing that Jun now recognized as a communion of sorts, a lesson in spirituality. He heard Semar say, "Take control, my child; remember, you must loose your power and yet still control it!" and then they reverted into silence. Jun looked over at Tenga by the door—and saw that the warrior was watching the two of them with an odd expression: half spiritual awe, half longing to be a part of whatever intimate experience the pupil and her master were sharing.

Jun found it difficult to concentrate during the ceremony. They were seated on soft cushions in a special roped-off enclosure in the Temple of Vharkash, a far larger space than the one in Sukatan, and as the Patriarch and his assistants made their offerings, and the gongs tinkled and the obat smoke billowed, he felt nothing of a religious nature but a slight softening of reality from breathing in clouds of the drug. He could not stop glancing sideways at Ketut, watching her almost obsessively to see if or when she would transform into the Goddess Dargan. In truth he felt more than a little apprehensive, and for good reason: the last time she had transformed, she had tried to kill him, and had very nearly forced another man to impale himself on his own kris.

He tried to take comfort in the words she had said to him before they filed into the temple and taken their places in the enclosure beside the scared space. "Don't fret so much, richboy, I'm not

going to hurt you tonight. Semar has been teaching me to understand the Goddess more fully and to guide her actions when she
is inside me. Besides, that was then, and then I felt such anger and
rage against you and your kind . . ."

"And now? Now we are battle comrades, the best of friends?"

"Semar has taught me that your kind are my kind."

"What, that we are both Tamani?"

"No . . . yes . . . well, something like that. Anyway, you will be
safe tonight."

"Why?"

"Mainly because now I don't hate you quite so much."

It was not much consolation. And when he saw the obat smoke
and the lilting gong music working on her, and her small, skinny
body beginning to shift and distort, when he saw her growing in
stature, and smelled the meaty odors of entrails and ordure, he
felt his body tense and a sense of almost uncontrollable panic began welling up in his lower belly.

The floor before the altar was filled with the men and women
of Singarasam, devotees of Vharkash, all in trance, dancing for
their God, slinking like Ghost Tigers, or strutting like young
warriors, one man clearly inhabited by the spirit of a python.
The Patriarch, he noticed, did not dance, but stood to the side
of the open space next to Semar, both old men watching the ceremony with benevolent yet wary eyes.

When Ketut, or Dargan as she now was, rose from the cushion
and strode out onto the floor, all the other dancers made way for
her, and Jun felt something very close to terror.

Dargan prowled across the front of the space, her feet stamping, her long-clawed hands moving rhythmically, the merest
whisper of flame on her lips. But she harmed no one. The dancers
revolved around her, worshipping her, their movements in time
with and echoing hers in a wondrous symmetry. Jun tensed for
violence—he aimed to resist her will with all his might; he would

fight her, kill her if necessary with his bare hands—but Dargan
seemed oblivious to his presence. The ceremony continued and
slowly, slowly, Jun began to relax. He breathed deeply of the obat
fumes; he let the music vibrate soothingly in his chest and, before
he knew it, the ceremony was coming to an end. The python-man
collapsed, writhing sinuously on the floor, and was carried away
by two assistants to be revived. The dancers left the floor one
by one and soon there was only Dargan, both arms raised, her
body swaying, her monstrous red-black eyes surveying the ap-
preciatively humming crowd of worshippers. And then she was
shrinking, diminishing, deflating, folding in on herself and a moment later only little Ketut stood there, alone in that sacred space,
running with fresh sweat but quite ordinary once again, a scrawny
Dewa fisher girl, now completely spent.

"May I introduce you to His Excellency Xi Gung, one of
Singarasam's foremost merchants and moneylenders, a
man of great influence across the Laut Besar, and a stalwart of the
temple community here," said the Patriarch. "Without his gener-
osity our little fellowship of faith would be in dire straits, oh yes
indeed. Why, this summer he financed a whole new wing of the
temple's Foundling House . . ."

Jun found himself shaking hands with a very plump little Han
with a wide, beaming, slightly sweaty face dressed in a long sea-
green silk robe, obviously very expensive but which was far too
tight around his ample waist. His long black hair was tied in a
greasy-looking, skinny queue and was draped over his right shoulder and chest. Jun found himself muttering something about being honored to meet him and privately wondering how long this
little party in the gold-bedecked back room behind the temple
space must be endured.

He had already met about twenty "stalwarts of the temple"

and mouthed simple pleasantries and made small talk with all of
them and now he was wondering when the subject of the Khodam and how they were to recover it would be raised. He wanted
to ask the Patriarch but the old man had drifted away and was
talking to the python-fellow, now recovered and his face glowing
with post-trance bliss.

"It is I, indeed, who is more honored by our meeting," said the
funny little fat man who was still pumping his right hand enthu-
siastically. "I gather from our mutual friend Ratna Setiawan that
you are the rightful heir of the Son of Heaven on the Island of
Taman—a Wukarta of pure blood—what a tremendous honor
indeed!"

Jun coolly admitted that he was, and wondered when this
greasy little tradesman was going to let go of his hand.

"Such a beautiful little island," said the man, at last releasing
his grip. Jun had to stifle the urge to wipe his moist palm on the
tail of his long shirt. "I often visited Taman in my youth—for both
business and pleasure. I had the honor of meeting your father,
once, on a rice-buying trip, oh, it must have been all of ten years
ago."

Jun looked at the fellow more closely. He must indeed be a
person of wealth and influence if his father had condescended to
meet him. Hundreds of merchants visited Taman every year and
not one had ever been brought into the presence of the Son of
Heaven to the best of Jun's recollection.

"I was so sorry to hear of his demise," said Xi Gung. "May Lord
Vharkash set a place for him at His right hand at the eternally
renewing banquet in Heaven."

"Thank you," said Jun.

"I understand that you mean to punish his murderers and are
here in Singarasam to recover the ancestral heirloom that was
stolen from him—a sacred kris. Is that correct?"

Jun was quite taken aback by this sudden change from platitudes to matters of the utmost importance, in fact, of the utmost secrecy. He was not sure how to reply—so chose to tell the truth. This funny little man was obviously trusted by the Patriarch.

"Yes, the Khodam—the Kris of Wukarta Khodam, we call it at home. The Lord of the Islands has it on display in the First House, or so I am told."

"Yes, that is very like our own dear Ongkara; he loves to show off his treasures. Even if they are blatantly stolen from their rightful owners."

Jun could think of nothing to say.

"Let me assure you, Prince Arjun, that the resources of my humble House stand behind you. Should you require a loan, perhaps, or any other small service that I might be able to afford you, please rely on me. I am at your service. Ongkara has become far too high-handed of late and it is time that his wings were clipped, in my opinion."

"Thank you, sir. You are most generous. I shall . . . I shall certainly bear your kind offer in mind."

"There is one small thing that I would like to ask you, if I may," said Xi Gung.

"Yes?"

"I am told that you traveled from Yawa to Istana Kush in a ship called the *Mongoose* with a fellow known as Farhan Madani. Is that true?"

"It is. We did."

"And do you by any chance know where Lord Madani might be at this moment. Is he back in Singarasam, perhaps?"

"Erm, I don't think so. We left him in Istana. As far as I know, he is still there."

"And yet my friends tell me that Istana is now under attack by forces of the Celestial Republic." The little man's eyes had hardened. Suddenly to Jun his soft, fleshy body seemed to be made of stone, a granite boulder in a green silk gown.

"I believe it is so. As we left you could hear the guns firing from the Red Fort."

"Yet Lord Madani is not a man made for the battlefield, I think," Xi Gung continued. "I merely wondered whether he traveled here with you."

"No, no, he was still there, as I say, when we left."

"Ah, poor fellow. I do hope no harm comes to him. We are old friends. I would hate for anything to happen to him if Istana Kush were to fall. Perhaps, if you were ever to see him again, here in Singarasam, or . . . well, anywhere, perhaps you would be kind enough to give him my regards and tell him that I have not forgotten our old relationship."

"Certainly, but I doubt I will be seeing him anytime soon."

"Nevertheless. And once again let me say what an honor it is to have met you, Prince Arjun, and please do not hesitate to call on me if I can be of any service to you."

Xi Gung gave him a little bow and then wandered away into the crowd, leaving Jun feeling bewildered by the swift turn in the conversation but also rather pleased by the brief encounter. It was wonderful to be called Prince Arjun again. And a loan might be very useful since he had almost no money and no prospects of getting any till he returned home. The fat little fellow was obviously a person of consequence and considerable wealth who might make a powerful ally in this city of strangers.

Jun went over to a side table and helped himself to a honey cake and a cup of palm wine. As he was eating and drinking, he looked about the throng to locate his friends. On the far side of the room, seated on an ornately carved wooden bench, Ketut was wrapped in an old blanket, looking pale and withdrawn. Tenga sat beside her glowering at anyone who came too close. Yet people were approaching, coming up one by one to stand in front of Ketut, saying a few words and then bowing very low, as if in the presence of high royalty. Some even went so far as to lay little offerings at her feet, a coin or two, a bunch of flowers tied up with a burning incense stick, a bowl of peeled fruit. It looked almost as if they were worshipping her. Sometimes Ketut would say a few words to the person who approached her, but most of the time, she remained silent, huddled in her blanket. Tenga would shoo away any who lingered too long.

Closer to him, Jun could see Semar in deep conversation with the Patriarch and his new friend Xi Gung, who was gesticulating animatedly. They saw him watching them and Semar beckoned and smiled. Xi Gung nodded at him and slipped away.

When Jun approached them, the Patriarch seized his hand. "My boy, I congratulate you, you have made an excellent first impression on Xi Gung—which is good because he would indeed make a powerful friend. Indeed, he has this minute pledged to help us in the task at hand: the recovery of the Khodam from the First House."

Semar was beaming at him, too. "We have other news, too, gathered from several of Ratna's friends. Tomorrow evening the Lord of the Islands will not be present in the First House," Semar said. "Ongkara has convened a gathering in the Harbormaster's House in the eastern side of Singarasam, where he will be addressing the sea captains of his pirate fleet who are now assembled there. Some sort of meeting to rally his troops against the Celestial Republic, I believe. A large squad of his Jath guards will accompany him to the gathering—as will the sorcerer Mangku. This is our chance!"

Jun gulped. "Really?"

"Absolutely, my prince. I have arranged with our new merchant friend Xi Gung that the scimitar-men who remain in the First House be invited to a nearby house of carnal pleasure in their master's absence, where they will be entertained by some of Singarasam's most beautiful and immoral young ladies—this all at our friend Xi Gung's personal expense, Jun. You must remember that. Our Han friend has also arranged for Ongkara's many con-

cubines to be summoned to a boat party on one of his larger pleasure vessels in the afternoon—a short cruise with entertainments,
which will not return till long after dark."

Jun nodded and smiled vaguely. He could think of nothing useful to say.

"So, it seems that the First House will be largely empty after
dusk tomorrow evening," Semar continued blithely. "Everything
has been organized, my prince. To the last detail. Our friend Xi
even has a man in the House, a spy, it seems, a servant of the Lord
of the Islands. This fellow—apparently he owes the House of Xi
a huge sum—can be induced to open a private side door and then
turn a blind eye to our activities once inside."

The Patriarch, who seemed no less excited than Semar, picked
up the thread.

"With the blessing of Vharkash, my son, I believe we can enter the First House, make our way up to the Audience Hall, recover the Kris of Wukarta Khodam and escape without detection.
The Khodam will be yours once more. Tomorrow it will be in
your hands."

Jun felt a shiver of apprehension—or was that excitement?

"Do you think we can really do this?" he asked Semar. "What
if there are some guards left—or other servants discover us who
are not in the pay of this Xi Gung?"

"It is not without risk," the old man said. "But I honestly think
this is our best chance of recovering the Khodam. We can be in
and out inside a quarter of an hour. And, afterward, we will need
to escape from Singarasam swiftly and silently—Ongkara's rage
will shake the Heavens, oh, that would be something to see—but
Xi Gung knows of a reliable captain with a fast ship that can take
us back to Taman the moment we have the Kris in our hands. I
think we can do it, my prince, I really do."

"Why is the merchant doing all this for us?" asked Jun. "It cannot be merely because I was polite to him at a party."

"Oh, if I know old Xi Gung, there will certainly be a price to pay," said the Patriarch. "You may have to give him some rice-trading concessions in Taman once you have regained the throne, or he might ask for a payment of some other kind one day. And, believe me, it would be best then to pay up quickly without a quibble. But I think he is chiefly hoping to humiliate Ongkara— the money he is outlaying on your venture means little to him. But he and Ongkara have been at odds for years over the annual tribute the Lord of the Islands demands from the House of Xi, which I am told is a truly staggering amount. Ongkara has been bleeding him unmercifully for years, charging him a fortune in silver as the price of doing business in Singarasam. But don't concern yourself with that, Prince Arjun. What matters the cost? This is an opportunity to regain the Khodam. Perhaps your only opportunity."

In truth, Jun was not too worried about incurring a debt with this little Han merchant. He would have silver enough to pay whatever the man asked once he was back in Taman. He was more concerned with the robbery itself. Would the First House really be empty? Furthermore, he did not like to think of himself as a sneaking burglar; it seemed low, dirty, unworthy of a prince of Wukarta blood. But, then again, it was not actually theft: he was merely recovering property that was his by right. Semar seemed to think it was a good idea. And most of all he longed to go home. He wanted familiar things, familiar faces around him again. He pictured once more the crowds of Taman folk cheering his triumphant arrival with the Kris of his father. Jun Pahlawan! Jun Pahlawan! Hailing the hero's glorious return.

"Tomorrow evening, then," he said.

CHAPTER 42

———————⟡———————

They had worked all night, in near silence and almost total darkness, fumbling through their labors by the light of dark lanterns, with many a squashed finger and barked shin and one heavily laden Artilleryman, who had twisted his ankle on an unseen pile of rubble in the darkness, hors de combat. Yet Farhan had been deeply impressed with the efficiency of the Honorable Artillerymen and engineers, and even plump Colonel Bandi had been filled with a manic, almost gleeful, zeal.

Captain Hawill's little ship had taken them without incident from the Small Harbor, round the point of land that held the Istana lighthouse and across to the Manchatka shore. The three warships had ignored them, and Hawill had hugged the northern coast, only narrowly avoiding the submerged and razor-sharp rocks that could rip the bottom out of even a shallow-draft ship in a moment. Then, as dusk was falling, they slipped up one of the many narrow river mouths that debouched out of the mangrove swamps, gliding into the gloom beneath huge, twisted trees, swerving around the roots that seemed to rise out of the water like the swollen knuckles of a hand and grip the foul-smelling river with long, slimy fingers.

They had moored the ship a quarter of a mile upstream, leaving Captain Hawill, a flabby, blustering giant of a man, a far-from-home Frank by the looks of his pale hair and skin, and his two crew members behind with strict orders to wait for them. Then they had trekked through the jungle for half an hour to enter the ruins of the Green Fort from the rear.

The heat and stink of the dank wasteland they marched through was appalling—Farhan had been in public latrines in Dhilika that smelled sweeter—and now and then they could hear the gentle gloopy splash of a great beast sliding into the water somewhere off in the darkness: saltwater crocodiles of improbable size, Farhan was told in a whisper, or serpents with bodies as thick as a man's thigh. He tried not to think about either creature.

The Green Fort was completely deserted, of course; its small garrison had departed en masse when the guns of the Red Fort across the Strait were turned on it. The men had fled into the watery forest or along the mangrove shoreline, some of the stronger ones swimming the Strait to Istana, returning to face the ignominy of their failure. Others simply disappeared. The green, mold-slimed walls of the fort were broken in places and cracked, but not completely destroyed; the guns however had all been knocked from their carriages, one shattered into a dozen iron shards, the other five scattered like a giant child's toys when playtime is over. Colonel Bandi and his men had begun work immediately, lighting the dark lanterns and using ropes and pulleys and hastily lashed frames to lift the huge tubes of metal back into their heavy, boxlike, wheeled carriages. Farhan took his own lantern and went to investigate the stores. He found to his relief that the magazine was at least half-stocked with casks of powder, and iron balls were plentiful on the racks, along with wadding, fuses and so on. He immediately set a crew of Artillerymen to work fetching them up to the seawall.

Now, eleven hours later, with milky dawn lightening the sky over the Laut Besar, they had three of the Green Fort's cannon in position against the broken battlements, two guns on serviceable wheeled carriages and the other, by far the largest cannon in the fort, roped and wedged into position in a gap in the stone wall.

That one, a monster that took a ball bigger than a grown man's head, could only be fired once. The thunderous discharge would surely burst it free from the ropes that held it to the battlements. It was a weapon of last resort but it might do great damage—maybe even to the enemy shipping, or so Farhan hoped. He wiped the work-sweat from his forehead, leaving a smear of green lichen against his skin, and peered out beyond the wall into the half-dark waters of the Sumbu Strait.

It was still a suicide mission, he knew. But so far, he believed, they had been undetected in their efforts. There had been no alarms raised or shots fired, and the three warships—one large one, the flagship, in the center and two smaller vessels on either side—rode easily at anchor, with only a few lights shining in the rigging. The three ships were in a row directly between the Green and Red Forts, out of accurate range from the Governor's Palace. But moving them closer to attack the palace would be simplicity itself—there was no enemy ship to oppose them and the palace was armed only with a pair of antique brass guns called the Two Falcons that were easily a hundred years old and had not been fired in living memory.

All was quiet now on the water but the moment he gave the order for their pathetically small, makeshift battery to open fire, the full fury of the enemy warships and the guns of the Red Fort would be turned upon them and they would all be swiftly blasted into the next life. They had about a quarter of an hour, he estimated, once battle commenced, to strike a blow against the enemy before they were all destroyed. It *was* suicide, plain and simple. But it had to be done. There was no other choice.

His mind turned, as it so often did in moments when death seemed inescapable, to the girl he had once loved, the Khevan princess who he had dreamed would one day share a life with him on some remote island in the Laut Besar . . .

It had been she who had made the first advance; he was almost sure of that. And yet the erotic tension between them had been so powerful, so tangible, that it was almost visible in the days leading up to it. She was young, fresh and beautiful to look at—perfect to Farhan's jaded eyes—and yet her soul seemed to him to be as old as the Erhul Mountains, and her mind was as complex and subtle as a seasoned Dhilika politician's. He had been entranced from the first moment he was introduced to her, in the Emperor's presence in the vast audience chamber of the Ice-Bear Throne. He had shaken her hand and felt the chill bare skin against his own and a surge of something shoot up his arm into his chest. He could not take his eyes from her perfect oval face, high cheekbones, and very pale skin, somewhat resembling pictures he had seen of the mischievous water spirits of his own Indujah mythology.

Her eyes were a pale, alien blue, like the sky in high summer, the mane of her silk hair almost as white as the snows of her homeland. And her smile: her teasing, crooked, minx's smile made all his fine hairs stand on end. "I am Katerina Kasimirovitch Astrokova," she said quietly and took his hand in hers. His soul was lost to her from that moment onward.

For three weeks he loved her silently—how could he speak? She was the only daughter of the Emperor and he was just a middling merchant traveling to the frozen north to buy furs and amber for wealthy Dhilika matrons. She was little more than a child, at fifteen years of age, despite the obvious womanliness of her body—although it was also true that his mother had been the same age when she had married his father.

So for three weeks he had said nothing, only played the courteous, avuncular visitor, interested in the local customs, telling amusing tales of his own land, and of the Laut Besar, of warriors and princesses, monsters and demons and the heroes who defeated them, but never touching her, never crossing the line into crudeness, never importunate or, Gods forbid, making her feel uncomfortable. Then he noticed that she was requesting his presence more and more frequently: they had picnics in the snow, just the two of them—and a dozen guards and servants, of course— swathed in furs and served hot spiced wine beside glowing braziers. There were balls, bright, noisy, alcoholic affairs, full of wild music and reckless dancing, when she insisted that he always give her the last dance of the night—and escort her home to her sumptuous living quarters afterward. They visited the Imperial steam rooms together: taking the heat in separate chambers, of course, but she had conversed intimately with him through the hole in the wall that connected the two rooms and he had been afforded tantalizing glimpses of her body through the mist in between bits of salacious gossip about senior figures at court.

He had written up the gossip, and any other snippets of intelligence he could discover, for his masters in the Amrit Shakti, but somehow he had never managed to mention his growing intimacy with Katerina. She was a glaring hole in his reports, dismissed as "Emperor's daughter, 15, pleasure-seeking and frivolous," although he knew that she was so much more than this. And then, to his surprise and joy, she had taken him to her bed, quite suddenly, summoning him to her quarters and making a show of tears, saying that she loved him and that she was distraught that he did not love her in return.

They became lovers then, and for the next four glorious weeks, insatiable for each other, tireless in their passion, their bodies a perfect fit despite their marked differences in age, temperament and culture. And then he had been summoned back to Dhilika by a curt diplomatic note. He was to be sent to the Laut Besar, immediately, by order of General Vakul himself—it had felt like a death sentence. He had wept, and swore he would desert the Shakti and spend the rest of his life here with her in Khev. But no, she told him, he must be strong and do his duty to his country, but she promised that one day, one day they would be together again . . .

"Colonel Madani," said a voice at his elbow. "I believe it is time."

Farhan realized that he had been silently weeping and he looked blurrily at Colonel Augustus Bandi who was standing beside him, ebullient, brisk, glowing with a fine martial excitement. It was full dawn by now, and Farhan could hear tinny bells ringing from the ships in the Strait signaling the beginning of the naval day.

"Yes, certainly, Colonel," said Farhan heavily. "Let us begin."

Katerina stood in her now-accustomed place on the parapet of the east wall of the Red Fort and looked down at the Sumbu Strait and the city of Istana Kush. She was filled with a wonderful calm excitement at the prospect of the day ahead. Before her the golden rim of the sun was just showing above the horizon of the wide Laut Besar and she could already hear the bells of her three warships summoning the sailors to their duty. In a little while, the bombardment of the Governor's Palace would begin. Her flagship, *Yotun,* would move into position off the flank of the citadel and open fire, joined by her other ships, *Egil* and *Sar.*

During the night they had managed to move only two of the cannon from the Red Fort down into the city and set them up opposite the main gate. She had hoped to shift more of them but the Ostraka gunners, after their victory the day before, had indulged themselves in a heroic obat-and-marak session and at least three-quarters of them had rendered themselves insensible, unable to be woken even with the freely applied boots of the Legionnaires. She would certainly hang two or three of the worst offenders, in due course, but she could not bring herself to be unduly harsh to the rest. They had achieved a notable victory against all the odds and some small relaxation of discipline was appropriate. But still it irked her that only two of the cannon had been brought down.

She had discovered another flaw in her plans, too. The main gate, a wood-and-iron contraption with a drawbridge, could not, it seemed, be fired upon by the warships in the Straits. The southern-curving side of the prow-shaped palace, the side that held the main gate, was not visible from the sea—probably deliberately so—and therefore its weakest spot could not be attacked by water-borne guns. The two cannon from the Red Fort, correctly positioned and manned by a handful of the more sober Ostrakan gunners, could peck away at it, certainly, but it was unlikely that it would be speedily destroyed. And speed *was* important. She was certain that Federation reinforcements were already on their way.

It was no matter, she told herself, the cannon on her three ships were easily powerful enough to reduce the northern wall of the palace all by themselves. *Yotun* carried thirty-six guns, and *Egil* and *Sar* twenty-four each, and such a weight of metal should easily be able to tumble the ancient and somewhat crumbling palace wall down around the defenders' ears, in a matter of only three or four hours at most.

Then her Celestial Legionnaires would go in.

They were already in their places around the Governor's Palace, dug in snugly in a crescent that stretched from the Grand Harbor to the Small, their blue-and-green company flags fluttering gaily in the wind off the Straits, with a concentration of several hundred fresh Legionnaires near the northern end of the semicircle. This was where Colonel Wang had his headquarters, from where he would order the assault at the correct time, opposite the stretch of palace wall where the full might of the cannon of her three ships would fall.

She was perfectly confident that the palace, and indeed the whole of Istana Kush, would be hers by nightfall. And she found herself enjoying a sense of luxury—something that she had not experienced for some time—in the knowledge that she need do nothing but observe for the next few hours as her careful plans unfolded. The captains of her three ships had their detailed orders, as did Colonel Wang and his men. All she had to do was watch.

She turned to Ari Yoritomo. "Bring me a chair and some hot tea and something to eat," she said. And the knight nodded and went off to issue the orders to one of the Red Fort's skeleton garrison—mostly wounded Legionnaires from the Scout company.

Now there was movement on *Yotun*. The big ship's sails were dropped, filled by the wind, sheeted tight, and her flagship began a slow turn into the center of the Strait. There was something inexpressibly beautiful about the vessel, its smooth motion through the water, the curve of its many brilliant white sails, the gleam of the brass work in the early-morning sunlight. And the other two ships were moving now, too.

A distant cannon fired, a barking cough that seemed to come from beyond *Sar*, the closest ship to the Manchatka shore. That was not right. They were too far away to begin the bombardment—was it some sort of naval signal? She frowned and reached for the brass telescope that hung from a cord around her neck. She trained the spyglass on the deck of *Sar*, only half-visible behind the big full sails of the *Yotun*.

Something was wrong. She could see that sailors were running about the main deck in panic, part of the rail was missing, and there were bodies, bloody bodies, parts of bodies lying on the clean wooden decking. A cannon fired again and she saw the whole ship shudder under the impact. A hit below the waterline. She saw, too, where the cannon fire was coming from. The Green Fort. Had they not already subdued that fortress? Had they come back? Her world seemed to shift and slip sideways. She could now see the little figures of men at the broken walls and two, no three black gun barrels pointing out over the walls toward the Straits. There were men working the guns, now, wielding long rammers, another man hurrying forward with a ball in his hands.

This was bad. Over to her right, *Egil* had pulled away ahead of *Yotun*. She could hear the distant sound of orders being relayed from one ship to another by a speaking trumpet. *Egil* forged away south still heading for the palace, a clear stretch of gray-green water now between her and the *Yotun*, which Katerina saw was altering the trim of its sails and coming about. A cannon from the Green Fort belched fire and the *Sar* took another shocking blow to the timbers of her side. The enemy battery could hardly miss— the ship was no more than two hundred paces away from their cannon mouths. A few moments later another cannon roared out from the tiny, enemy-held fortress.

Sar finally got off a full broadside: the starboard side erupting in a sheet of flame and wall of smoke. A dozen balls smashed out toward the walls of the Green Fort, some cracking against the mold-stained walls, others screaming over the top to disappear into the mangrove forest behind. And *Yotun* was still turning, turning, returning to savagely punish the tiny Federation battery that dared to attack its sister ship.

"Put that thing down and get those obat-soaked gunners up and to their guns," Katerina growled to a Legionnaire captain who was lumbering forward with a heavy-looking armchair. "I don't care if you have to half murder them but wake them up and get them to their pieces and firing on the Green Fort. Immediately!"

The captain blanched at her fury and scurried away.

"Stupid! Stupid! Stupid!" Katerina cursed herself uselessly, her small hands balled into tight white fists.

Sar was clearly ailing, the deck now canted at a steep angle. Men were throwing themselves from the ship, diving off and splashing into the water. But *Yotun* was coming up fast, and the eighteen powerful guns on her starboard side were being run out in a rattling crash that Katerina could plainly hear even at this distance.

"Now kill them," she whispered. "Kill them all."

F arhan could hardly believe their luck. The first shot had been too high, crashing through the rail of the nearest ship and only killing or maiming two or three men and ripping up a few backstays. But when the second cannon spoke, their aim had been perfectly true, the ball lancing out and crashing into the middle of the side of the small ship, just at the waterline, tearing a hole in the timbers that was visible for a few moments before it filled with black water.

In truth, it was not a difficult target at this short distance, but Farhan was still filled with a special pride at the knowledge of what they had accomplished. The Honorable Artillerymen knew their business, and even sad Colonel Bandi, the sweat of eagerness staining his green uniform, was proving to be an impressive commander. Farhan had given himself the task of organizing the supply of munitions and he and his team of engineers were bringing up round shot and small canvas bags of powder to feed the cannon. They were really doing it—they really were! They were killing a ship.

The first cannon was reloaded now, and at Bandi's command, the burning linstock fuse was brought down to the touchhole and the piece roared once again. Another lethal hit, low in the bow of the vessel. The ship was ailing, sinking, dying.

The Artillerymen went briskly about the business of reloading, sponging the hot barrel, slamming home the powder, ball, and wadding. Wielding the rammers with brutal precision. The command was given to stand clear and the touchhole ignited. A roar like a giant in pain and another ball crashed out and plunged into the broken timbers of the stricken ship.

But the *Sar* was not without teeth, even mortally wounded. The flaps of the twelve portholes on this side creaked open and twelve brass barrels popped out.

"Get down," shouted Farhan. "Everybody down!"

The enemy broadside smashed out in a deafening storm of fire and smoke and screaming metal. Farhan, who was crouched behind a part of the wall that was still intact, felt a cannonball's impact against the moldy stone as a hard punch against his shoulder. Most of the barrage screamed overhead and into the mangroves. But he glimpsed Colonel Bandi, who had not deigned to duck, struck full in the chest by a ball, his uniformed body exploding in red-and-green shards like a ripe watermelon smashed with a hammer. Another ball hit the wooden carriage of the second cannon and the long gun was hurled from its bed, black-iron barrel spinning in the air and crushing an Artilleryman against a pile of broken bricks, nearly severing his body in half.

It was over, almost as soon as they had begun. With only one functioning cannon left, as well as the big monster lashed directly to the wall, they could not hope to do much more.

Farhan peeped over the wall. The brass muzzles of the *Sar*'s cannon had been run in again and he could dimly make out furious shapes inside the portholes, wreathed in smoke, sponging and ramming, even as the ship lurched downward in the water.

Beyond the *Sar,* Farhan could see the big flagship coming up fast toward them, its portholes open, guns run out, like a row of shining brass teeth on some water monster.

A pair of cannon roared from across the Strait, one only moments after the other. The gunners of the Red Fort had come to join the party. The ball smashed through a stretch of wall a dozen paces from Farhan, showering him with sharp rocks and grit. Another ball whistled overhead and splintered the trunk of a venerable palm tree.

He stood up. "One more salvo, boys, just one more," Farhan

said. "We will fire at the big one over there and then we run." He
remembered Mamaji's words clearly: ". . . you will reinstate the
cannon and engage the enemy ships *for as long as you are able,* aiming to sink, cripple or injure them in any way . . ." Well, they had
done that. Now it was time to go.

He walked over to the biggest cannon, the monster on the far
left; his legs suddenly turned to jelly. He looked doubtfully at its
long barrel secured in an ugly, makeshift manner with ropes and
wedges of wood into a V-shaped crack in the wall, its breech end
supported only by a pile of broken stones. It was loaded, he knew,
and he peered along the massive barrel and saw that it was roughly
aligned with the flagship. Gods knew if it would be accurate, tied
up in this unnatural manner. The other smaller cannon—which
had by now been maneuvered around to face the oncoming *Yotun*
by the surviving Artillerymen—fired and a shot lashed out at the
big ship, firing high and passing ten feet above the deck, slicing
through backstays, severing rope ladders and punching a hole
above the boom on the square mainsail but otherwise doing no
visible damage.

"Give me a match," shouted Farhan to a terrified-looking
Artilleryman. He snatched the burning fuse from the man's hand.
"Now, go, run, all of you, before . . ."

He saw a bank of smoke appear silently all along the side of the
Yotun. And then the world exploded in a storm of noise, blood and
hissing metal. He was blinded by flying grit and knocked to his
knees and all around him he could hear a shocked silence, and
then the screams of mutilated men. He lurched to his feet, looked
down at his body, which was filthy but unscathed save for a deep
cut in the back of his left hand, the hand that was still gripping the
burning match. All the Artillerymen were down, their dust-
covered bodies and some parts of bodies, too, lying scattered all
around. A pool of blood was forming in a depression in the ground
behind the mangled mound of two or three men. The second can-

non had been hit directly, its iron barrel shattered into a dozen pieces; most of the rest of the wall was gone, too. But, somehow, the big cannon was still lashed in the same position. Still poking out toward the Strait. He peered down the long barrel again and saw the big sails of the *Yotun,* directly ahead. He leaned back and put the burning match to the touchhole.

The cannon roared, bucked free of its lashings, and jumped backward, missing Farhan with its lethal bulk by a matter of inches. The iron ball smashed into the rear of the *Yotun,* crunching through the taffrail and splintering the tiller, obliterating the two men who were steering the ship there with the giant wheel.

The rudderless *Yotun* swung around, now heading straight for the Manchatka shore, charging forward. There was a lot of confused shouting on the deck. Men in blue running here and there. The ship was coming straight at Farhan, and he knew he had to run away. Somehow he couldn't move. It seemed that the ship was coming after him, targeting him personally, about to leap from the sea like a salmon and crush him with its bulk. He heard a terrible screech of tortured timbers and the huge ship came juddering to a complete stop. All the seamen on deck were thrown off their feet. Farhan could not understand it. The ship was halted. He was saved. A miracle of some kind. Then he knew: the big ship was impaled on some underwater shoal or rock. Grounded. The flagship was dead in the water.

Farhan wasted no more time. He turned his back on the huge, stricken ship and began to run. He stopped after a dozen yards to help a dazed and bloody Artilleryman to his feet, urged another dust-covered man to follow, and the three of them, Farhan and his companion locked together, arm and shoulder, and reeling madly, staggered away into the jungle.

◆ ◆ ◆

I t had taken no more than a quarter of an hour for everything to go from calm competence to utter bloody disaster. Katerina could scarcely believe it. One moment she had three beautiful ships swimming in the Straits in perfect order, the next one ship was half-sunk, its decks awash two hundred yards from the Manchatka shore, and another, her flagship, by all the Gods, was stuck uselessly on a rock and listing badly a bowshot away from its sister vessel.

The *Egil*—thank all the Gods—was undamaged. It was now standing off the entrance to the Grand Harbor and bombarding the palace, as she had been ordered to do, her cannon ringing out regularly and the balls smashing against the ancient stones of the keep.

She turned her telescope on the Green Fort—now even more of a smoking, shattered ruin, with barely one stone standing on another. To her left a cannon fired; the Ostrakan gunners had finally been roused to their duty and they were now thumping shot after shot into the fort across the Strait with great enthusiasm. Not that it was needed now. The men in the Green Fort were either all dead or had sensibly fled once again, and she could see no serviceable cannon among the piles of steaming rubble. There had been no movement there for a while now. No sign of life at all.

She moved her spyglass to the *Yotun,* which was dropping a boat; a well-armed party of sailors was planning to occupy what was left of the Green Fort. If only she had thought of that earlier. A stupid mistake and one that she had paid, indeed would continue to pay for. There were seamen dangling from ropes over the side by the smashed hull where the ship had struck ground but she could tell just by the drunken angle of the deck that it would be no easy task to haul the ship off the rock and get her back into action. It would take time—and time was something she did not have.

"Tell the Ostrakans to cease firing," she called to a Legion officer who was hovering behind her. "Can't they see that *Yotun* is sending in a party of our men?"

She looked again at *Egil,* her last remaining ship, and felt a flicker of hope. Even under the battering from just one warship, the walls of the palace were taking serious punishment. Visible cracks were appearing in the ancient stonework and every ball that struck chipped another big chunk of masonry away. One of the arrow slits, she saw, had been knocked into a hole the size of a marak barrel. Even as she watched, a shot smashed into the top of the wall and punched out a gap the size of a small house.

Maybe it could still be done. Maybe.

She looked over at Ari, who seemed perfectly unperturbed by this disastrous turn of events. "I'm going down into the city to see Colonel Wang," she told him. "Fetch the rest of the Niho. I believe I shall require all my knights with me today."

CHAPTER 43

———— ❀ ————

Guided by Ratna Setiawan, with a long dark cloak over his white robes, Jun, Ketut, Tenga and Semar made their way down a filthy, stinking back street in the heart of Singarasam and stopped at a tall, wide door made of some heavy wood—the tradesman's entrance of the First House. They were well armed: Jun with his bow and a quiver full of arrows; Tenga with her vicious boarding ax; Ketut had a knife at her waist and the two old men each carried their heavy staffs. Jun hoped that they could be in and out without violence. But if he had to fight for the Khodam, he knew he would do whatever was necessary . . .

However, Jun reckoned that it should be a simple and peaceable enough operation. If Xi Gung had played his part as promised, and both Semar and the Patriarch were convinced that he had, the First House should be almost entirely empty at this hour: Ongkara and the sorcerer Mangku, along with a substantial force of Jath guards, should be on the far side of Singarasam rallying the pirate captains to resist the fleet of the Celestial Republic. The rest of the guards and the household ladies were being lavishly entertained elsewhere.

Certainly the First House looked to be entirely deserted. As Ratna knocked softly on the big door with his staff, Jun looked up at the gray walls of the imposing building, with its many balconies and small, square, barred windows, and he could not see a single light showing. The door opened and a figure poked his head out, a small, clearly nervous man, holding a candle that illuminated the extraordinary quantity of gold bullion sewn into his knee-length coat. Ratna spoke a few quiet words to him, passed over a chinking purse and the servant, after a quick glance up and down the street to check they were unobserved, held the door wide to allow them to enter.

As he filed quietly in with the others, Jun thought: *This golden fellow is taking a bigger risk than we are, for it will surely come out that we were freely given admittance, and if Ongkara discovers this fellow's treachery, then* . . . But that was not his concern: the servant had been well paid; he could look to his own affairs.

They were now inside the First House—Jun felt a quickening of his pulse and a heat in his chest. Was this just normal excitement at this stealthy action or was his Wukarta blood responding in some magical way to the presence of the Kris? The golden servant silently led the way with his candle, taking them down long, dark, empty corridors and up a flight of wide, marble stairs. Jun strained his ears but he could hear nothing but his own quiet footsteps and those of his companions. It seemed the First House truly *was* deserted.

They followed the servant down another passageway, across a carpeted hall with chairs set out by the walls for waiting, and stopped in front of a huge set of double doors.

"This is the Audience Hall," whispered the servant. "Tell Xi Gung that I have done my part. Whatever happens next, I consider my debt to him paid in full."

And he threw open the doors, turned his back on the five intruders and walked away into the gloom with his candle.

Jun looked inside and was immediately filled with a deep sense of awe. *This is how a palace should be,* he thought. *This is truly regal.* The room was empty but brilliantly lit and decorated in the most glorious, extravagant Han fashion. As they all walked into the vast space, Jun saw a double line of red pillars, each pillar circled by bearded dragons of gold with purple spine crests and huge green feet, which made a kind of tunnel through the center of the Audience Hall. There were more golden dragons, silver eagles, jade fish and blue-lacquer bulls on the ceiling. The floor was speckled gray marble, highly polished with purple and green lotus-flower mosaics. It was magnificent—Jun's eye leaped from one treasure to the next, stunned by the sheer drama of the decor. It made the palaces of his father seem like drab hovels. Then his eye fell on an object at the far end of the Hall.

It was a shapeless, roundish, white object, as wide as a mattress and three times as high, with a vast gilded throne placed in the sagging middle—it was the Obat Bale. The legendary seat of the Lords of the Islands. But Jun had eyes only for the rickety contraption of sticks and struts set at the right-hand side of the throne, with a thin and very familiar object standing upright inside.

There it was: the Khodam. The Kris of Wukarta Khodam. The blade of his ancestors. The purpose of this long and painful quest. It looked so ordinary, an old sword with a brown wooden handle in a plain wooden sheath, sitting up on the pale bulk of the Obat Bale, dwarfed by the gaudy throne. But he remembered it so well. He remembered his father sitting in state with his gnarled hand resting on the wooden hilt, pronouncing judgment on a matter of Tamani law or granting a boon to a kneeling supplicant. His poor dead father.

He walked toward the Obat Bale, eyes fixed on the Khodam. Finally, finally he would be able to hold it in his own hand, to take it home to Taman in triumph. Arjun Pahlawan!

The sound of a gong beating three times, the booming filling the huge room, jerked him out of his happy daze. He whirled around, his blood suddenly fizzing with shock, and saw that hidden doors in the walls on both sides of the Audience Hall were sliding back. The walls were opening and people were pouring into the

Hall, dark shapes in black turbans with broad, gleaming scimitars. Dozens of men, scores even. All swarming into the huge room.

Jath guards—who somehow were not on the other side of Singarasam. Nor wallowing in pleasure houses surrounded by whores. They were here, now, pouring into the Hall.

Jun had the bow off his shoulder, an arrow nocked on the string in less than a heartbeat, and he was aware of Tenga beside him, moving lithely forward in front of Ketut's little form, and hefting her big, shiny boarding ax.

He did not hesitate—he shot the nearest man, a huge, bearded lout who was coming straight for him with his gleaming scimitar raised. His shaft sank into the fellow's broad chest, the arrow punching in right up to the fletchings. He had another shaft on the string before the man had fallen. He shot a second Jath in the eye, knocking the man back, his scimitar wheeling away and clanging to the marble floor. He was half-aware of Tenga, swinging her bright ax; the meaty thud as it bit into a huge, black-clad stomach.

He shot again, the slender arrow deflected by a swinging blade but sinking through another man's thigh; and loosed again, his hands moving as fast as thought, the hours and hours of practice repaying his efforts once again. He dropped man after man, whirling, selecting targets, his left hand seizing an arrow from the quiver, nocking, drawing back the cord and loosing all in the space of a moment, but there were simply too many of them.

There were Jath behind him now. Boiling into the Audience Hall from hidden doors on both sides. He saw Tenga spear a man through the belly with her ax-head, pull out and chop through another's reaching arm. Hook the curved blade into another man's eye.

Jun turned and shot a man one pace behind him, who was about to strike, hurling him off his feet. He heard someone yell-

ing, "Take them alive! I command you to take them alive." In all
the violent confusion of battle, to Jun, it sounded oddly like
Semar's voice.

He was surrounded by a crush of men in black robes now, angry faces under black turbans, shining steel, grasping hands. His
arms were pinned against his body. One man had a forearm round
his neck, crushing his throat. He saw that Semar had been envel-
oped by two burly Jath, and one fellow had Ketut by the shoulders
and was shaking her whole body; yet the Patriarch was standing
alone, untouched, unmolested, his black cloak swept back to reveal his distinctive shining white robes, a dozen yards away by the
far wall, ignored by the scrum of black-clad soldiery, and holding
one hand in front of his mouth in horror.

Tenga was still fighting, shouting her war cries and carving the
ax through the air in great bloody swings, hacking at black bodies,
laying open flesh, the blood spraying red. There was a circle of
destruction around her. And any man who came within reach
of her ax died screaming. He struggled in the grip of his foes, trying to bite at the arm round his neck. But a blow to the side of his
head, like a bolt of lightning, dropped him to his knees.

As his senses reeled and his vision blurred, he knew one thing
for sure: they had walked into a trap. A trap set by their kindly
host, Ratna Setiawan, Patriarch of Singarasam.

They were cuffed and kicked and beaten with scimitar pom-
mels and the flats of the blades until they were all on their
knees in a line: all four of them. The Patriarch had not moved
from his spot by the wall. He looked exhausted and very sad but
was ignored by the Jath. The four captives' wrists were tied with
rawhide strings behind their backs. One great black-clad oaf,
shaking with rage, snapped Jun's bow in front of his eyes and
cracked each of his few remaining arrows, too, for good measure.

Then he spat into Jun's face and the Wukarta prince felt the slow slide of his hot phlegm on his cheek.

"That will do," said a voice. "Leave them be for now." And Jun watched a short, ugly little man with yellowish, almost light green skin, and long, spindly limbs swagger through the carnage of the Audience Hall—the floor was now thick with bodies, greasy with fresh blood and stinking like an abattoir—and clamber up onto the Obat Bale, where he arranged himself comfortably on the huge, gilded throne and grinned broadly at his four prisoners.

Ongkara placed his right hand on the hilt of the Kris of Wukarta Khodam, and said, "So . . . you actually thought you could creep in here and make off with my new prize from right under my nose, did you? You really thought I would allow that?"

None of the prisoners said a word. From his position on the end, nearest to the Obat Bale, Jun looked down the line of his friends. Tenga, next to him, had a fresh crop of cuts and slashes and a good deal of glistening blood all over her dark body, not all of it hers, he assumed, but her chin was up, her mouth a grim line and her eyes red-veined and burning like live coals. Ketut, next to her friend, was sunk in misery. Her eyes were closed; her bruised head drooped over her skinny chest. She seemed nearly unconscious.

Semar, last in the line, seemed to be paying absolutely no attention at all to the Lord of the Islands. He was staring with mournful eyes at Ratna, who was still by the far wall, his white robes still shining, but now twisting his hands together as if he were washing them.

Semar said quietly, "You show your true colors at last, Ratna Setiawan. That must be a blessed relief to you. But while you may have declared for a side—it is the wrong side."

"What do you know, Semar? You know absolutely nothing of these matters," the Patriarch replied. "You have never understood anything important at all."

"Silence!" roared Ongkara.

Semar ignored the King of Singarasam. "You seek to bring back the old magic, Ratna. I understand that. But you must know it would be cataclysmic. There is a reason blood magic has been forbidden for so long. You do not fully understand what you will bring into the world. The dark plague, when it comes, will extinguish the light of Vharkash. You will be destroyed, along with thousands of others. You follow Mangku in the belief that . . ."

"You think you know what moves me to action, *Your Holiness?*" There was a sneer in Ratna's final two words. "I told you: you understand nothing. I do not *follow* Mangku—I am his Master. I have been so ever since he first came to me all those decades ago at the Mother Temple and begged me to help him learn the ancient blood magic of the world . . ."

"I said, 'Silence!'" Ongkara was sitting up straight in his throne now.

"Oh, Ratna, what have you done? Have you forgotten our most sacred teachings? The use of this ancient sorcery will lead to the unmaking of the world and everyone in it . . ."

"Not everyone—as you admitted yourself. I am Dewa. I . . . am . . . *Ebu!*" Ratna shouted the last word.

Semar just frowned at him.

"My parents were slaves to the Mother Temple—Dewa filth, they called us, doomed to labor forever for our *betters*. My father was but thirty-one years old when he died. And he died an old man—worn-out by labor and cruelty, exhausted by life. But he was proud, so very proud that his little Dewa boy should have been selected for the honor of becoming a novice at the Mother Temple, so proud that his son should be allowed to serve the very religion that had enslaved him and my mother and killed them both so young. I have risen, yes. I am the Patriarch now. I have come into my own. But I am Dewa and I am Ebu. And I always will be, and when we have remade the world, Hiero Mangku and

I, when we have achieved our glorious aim, my kind will live and prosper and rule here when your foul race has been wiped from the face of the Earth."

"Enough! Both of you will be quiet," Ongkara bawled. "Or I will have you all boiled alive. This is my time to speak."

"I am sorry that your parents lived sad lives. But I never once took even the slightest notice of your birth," said Semar, oblivious to the ranting of the Lord of the Islands. "I saw you only as a man. A good and holy man. That is why I made you one of my deputies."

The Patriarch just glared at him

Semar said, "You have made a terrible mistake, Ratna, but it is not too late to change course. You only have two of the seven Keys of Power, the Khodam and the Eye . . ."

"We have three, you fool. We have the Key of Air, too, the golden crest of the Garuda Queen. Soon we shall have them all. Then we shall destroy you and your kind forever."

"Am I going mad? I will not be ignored." Ongkara was fully screaming now.

"Be quiet, you," said Semar, looking hard at the Lord of the Islands for the very first time. Jun saw that the old man's eyes had turned into solid black orbs. "No more noise, now; it is distracting to us. And you will order your Jath to cut our bonds. Do it right now."

Ongkara's mouth flapped silently for a while. Then he meekly gestured to the nearest Jath guard an order to cut the rawhide thongs that secured the four prisoners. Jun could hardly believe his eyes—but then Semar . . . well, he had long been capable of delivering a surprise. It was clear that his strange gift for controlling the minds of men was not limited to stirring up a riot in Sukatan, or persuading a Han doctor to give up his home and position, or getting a pair of Manchus to collude in an escape from the Konda Pali mines. When he exerted himself, even the Lord of the Islands, it seemed, was not immune to Semar's grip.

"That is all I needed to know," said Semar, standing up and stretching his arms and shoulders, rubbing his wrists. He seemed to be bigger, taller even. All traces of the sad, bound captive were completely gone. He was fully in control of the room. "I suspected that you would betray us, old friend. I read that destiny in your face decades ago. But I was not certain until tonight that you had really joined Mangku's murderous cause, and I could not understand *why* you might choose to side with the sorcerer. I suppose I do, now, and I am better equipped to stop this madness. Anyway, we will be leaving shortly, Ratna, with the object we came for, the Key of Power—Jun, you won't forget to collect the Khodam before we go, will you, my prince?—and so I will bid you farewell. I would strongly advise you, old friend, to pack up your belongings and leave Singarasam this very night. And I earnestly hope we do not meet again. If we do, I greatly fear that I may forget my sacred vows and take away your miserable life."

Semar bent down and picked up his staff from the blood-sticky marble of the floor. He looked again at Ratna Setiawan. "You may have set Hiero Mangku on this evil road, old friend, but if you think you are still his Master, you are sorely mistaken."

"Did I hear someone mention my name?" said a new voice, a voice like flint.

And Hiero Mangku stalked into the Audience Hall.

CHAPTER 44

In the late afternoon, Katerina stood by the entrance to the command dugout, with Colonel Wang at her shoulder. On either side of her in a series of zigzags, the trenches of the Legion extended from the Grand Harbor to the Small. Every few paces there were pockets of men, sitting, sleeping, eating the rice and beans that had been provided as rations, looted from the abandoned city around her. She looked up through the shattered ruins of houses and workshops to the scarred gray walls of the Governor's Palace, three hundred paces away.

The ship *Egil* had done sterling work over the course of the day, pounding the walls of the last bastion under Federation control in Istana Kush. The bombardment had been slow, steady, a measured reduction of the fortifications, and now a V-shaped breach ten paces wide at the top yawned in the center of the north wall, slightly to the right and below the Round House. A spill of rubble from the broken battlements tumbled down from the breach toward the city, forming a rough and treacherous stair up to the hole in their defenses. She could see the forms of men and women inside the breach, working furiously wrestling lengths of timber, tables, chairs, even what looked like rolled-up carpets into the gap to make a makeshift barricade. In the deepest recesses of the hole, she thought she could just make out a very fat woman in a bright pink dress waving her arms about, giving orders. Was that this Mamaji person? What kind of woman was she? Formidable, clearly.

As she watched, another cannon shot roared out from the ship
in the Straits, smashing into the side of the breach, knocking free
a patch of wall, turning a heavy wooden table to matchwood and
showering the workers inside with lethal shards. A man in the
scarlet coat and white cross belts of a Dokra staggered into view
and fell out, limp as a rag doll, bouncing down the slope of scree,
his red turban coming loose, trailing after him, the body cart-
wheeling and thumping into the dry ditch at the bottom of the
wall.

Behind her Colonel Wang was having an urgent, almost-
passionate conversation in his own language with one of the
handful of Legionnaire engineers. It seemed clear to her that
the good Colonel was not getting the answer that he required.

Since the shocking disasters of the morning, the news of the
day had steadily improved. She had received a report that the
Yotun had managed to haul itself off the submerged rock on which
it had become impaled—and it seemed that the ship could be
saved. By dint of hard work, martial efficiency and a fair bit of
luck, with a spare sail strapped tight over the massive hole that
had been ripped in her timber bottom, the *Yotun* had managed
to limp across the Sumbu Strait to the north side of the Grand
Harbor and a vacant drydock. Now emptied of men, stores and
guns, *Yotun* was careened on her side and a crew of carpenters
was crawling all over the hull, fitting replacement planks, replac-
ing the futtocks, caulking seams with hot pitch and generally
mending her poor, broken timbers with as much speed as they
could muster. It would take some days before the huge vessel
could swim again, but Katerina's flagship was not lost to her,
and that was a comforting thought. The *Sar* was another matter.
Divers were at work salvaging as much as they could from the
sunken ship. It would never sail again and, for now, all her naval
power resided in little *Egil*.

"What does he say?" asked Katerina. "Does he think the breach is practicable?"

"Alas, no, Highness. Engineer Fung thinks it needs to be a good deal wider, perhaps five paces wider. He also believes that it would be wise to open a second breach farther along the wall, perhaps even a third, so that the defenders must spread their forces. He says that in another day or possibly two days of steady bombardment the Governor's Palace will be as open and inviting as the legs of a . . ." Wang stopped himself. He sometimes forgot that his commander was a highborn lady not a hard-bitten ranker. "I mean to say that in two more days, at this rate, we should be able to storm the palace with relative ease."

"I don't have two more days. Word of our attack must have reached Singarasam by now. I expect the Federation to be on our doorstep at any moment. I must have the palace, today, tonight at the latest. What say you, Colonel? Can your brave Legionnaires force that breach as it is now?"

"Well . . ." Wang was torn between telling the honest truth and giving his commander the answer that he knew she desperately wanted. "It would be extremely bloody. The casualties would be heavy, Highness, very heavy. Even then I'm not sure they could . . ."

"We don't have the luxury of choice, Colonel. You will order the attack. Tell the men that there will be a bonus of a hundred crowns to the first man through the breach. And once inside they may loot the Governor's Palace to their heart's content."

"Highness, I am bound to say that I don't think this is the wisest course."

"Just do it, Colonel. All my life I have been told that the Legions are the finest, bravest troops in the world. Let them prove it. I shall send word to *Egil* to cease bombardment in one hour, and your assault will go in then. Give the orders, now, if you please."

◆ ◆ ◆

The Legionnaires advanced in two columns. Katerina watched from the dugout as two fat snakes of hundreds of blue-coated men emerged from the trenches, one headed for the left side of the breach, the other the right. They moved slowly, keeping formation, muskets strapped across their backs to leave their hands free to climb, wending through the broken houses of the city, parts of each column temporarily lost from sight, only to reemerge as each obstacle was passed.

The guns of the *Egil* had fallen silent a quarter of an hour ago and the sudden quiet after a day of noise was wonderful. She looked up at the cannon-scarred walls again and saw that a rough wooden barricade had been constructed, a ramshackle-looking thing, in the very mouth of the breach. Spear blades, old knives and broken-off swords had been attached to the beams of the barrier, making the hedge of sharp steel known as an Ehrul Horse that her men would have to negotiate, and farther back she saw scores of dark faces under scarlet turbans, and a wink of a bronze cannon in the light of the sinking sun behind her.

It was going to be bloody. There was no getting away from that. But truly these Legionnaires were exceptional men. They *were* the bravest and the best in the world, and what she had said to Colonel Wang had been true: they had no more time to make a bigger breach. If the Federation arrived now, even just one decent-sized warship, Katerina was done for. There were no reinforcements coming for her; she had no spare troops at her beck and call. She had to attempt this. It was do or die. This throw of the dice or damnation.

The two thick blue columns were nearly at the dry ditch before the rubble slope that led up to the breach. Yet there had been no response so far from the palace. The quiet was eerie now, horrible, to be exact. The traditional calm before the storm of battle.

For a moment she allowed herself to wonder if the defenders had decided to quietly slip away—the Small Harbor was still open to them. She had deliberately told her men to allow any who wished to leave to do so unmolested. There were even still a few small ships moored there. But she knew that it was not to be. She would not lie to herself. If this Mamaji was the person she believed she was, she would not run. She had sent men to the Green Fort—a suicide mission if ever there was one—and they had sunk the *Sar*. Mamaji must know that time was on her side. That if she could hold out, salvation was at hand. No, Mamaji would not run. And she would ensure all her fighting men remained with her, too.

The roar from the left-hand column of Legionnaires snapped her out of her thoughts. The men in blue were charging up the rocky slope in front of the breach, yelling their hearts out, scrambling on the shattered rock, using hands and feet to propel themselves forward, upward. Their shiny helmets flashed orange in the dying light. A flood of blue surging up the rocky stair. On the battlements above, on either side of the breach, suddenly there were scores of heads, hundreds of musket men. Now the first ragged volley from the walls, hundreds of tiny puffs of smoke— and her Legionnaires began to die.

The left-hand column was halfway up the slope now, and the right-hand was beginning its own ascent, too. Musket balls from the top of the wall were smashing into them, thumping into blue-clad flesh, tossing bodies backward into the press of men behind. Some of the Legionnaires were stopping to return fire, and here and there on the walls a turbaned head was snatched away. But most of her men were ignoring the fire from above, scuttling up the steep slope in a rushing tide of human flesh, knowing that safety only lay beyond the yawning breach. Katerina could clearly hear the strike of lead bullets on stone, the thump as they punched into human meat and the screams of the men cut down. Arrows and spears, too, were now lancing down on the attackers, skewering men, pinning limbs to the rubble. A shower of rocks, hurled from the battlements, thudded into the Legionnaires' unarmored bodies, clanging off helmets, but still her brave men came on, driving upward, scrambling up toward the breach, now only a few steps away.

Nearly there, nearly there, and once inside their fury would be unconstrained. The leading man was just feet from the opening, within touching distance of the Erhul Horse. He was unshipping his musket from his back, pointing it into the darkness of the breach. The hundred crowns was his if he could live a few moments longer. A single musket barked from inside and the bullet tore away half his face and he fell back. But his comrades were all around him now, surging forward into the gaping maw of the palace, shouting their fear away, twenty men, thirty, with more coming up hard on their heels, some impaling themselves on the sharp points of the Erhul Horse by the press of the men behind them . . .

The cannon bellowed from inside the breach. A spray of canister lashed out from the brass muzzle, hundreds of musket balls spreading out in a cone of destruction, and wiping the leading Legionnaires away in an instant, hurling a dozen shattered bodies back down the slope, and leaving nothing but a mist of blood where they had been and a few scraps of flesh on the dripping steel points of the Ehrul Horse.

But these men were Legionnaires, the best in the world, and a second wave immediately came surging forward into the blood-dripping mouth of the breach, yelling hatred and defiance—and were met by a massed musket volley from a hundred Dokra waiting inside.

The survivors, a few gore-slathered men crazed with pain and rage, came on again, hauling their bodies over the sharp steel barricade heedless of the cuts from the keen-whetted blades. The Dokra were reloading, furiously slamming bullet, powder and wad down the barrel with their long wooden rammers. The entrance to the breach was filled with men in blue, screaming, shooting blindly into the thick smoke inside.

The second brass cannon spoke, the canister ripping the living flesh from the fragile bodies of the Legionnaires, blasting them apart and once more the breach was cleared.

The Dokra rushed forward into the fog, stopping at the Erhul Horse and pouring their fire into the Legionnaires still on the slope. Loading, ramming, firing, killing.

Through the drifting smoke, Katerina could just make out Colonel Wang, at the head of the right-hand column, almost at the top of the blood-soaked rubble stair, the dead men thick about his boots. A few paces from the breach, he half turned and bellowed to the men behind him, urging them onward. A Dokra sergeant shot him straight through the back of his head, dropping his body in a boneless, undignified heap.

The remaining Legionnaires screamed their rage and boiled up the last few yards of the slope, crashing into the Erhul Horse, and were met by the Dokra, men firing into each other at point-blank range, clubbing each other with empty muskets, stabbing with bayonets, hacking with swords, grappling, clawing, swinging bloody fists. Two thick lines of struggling men separated by a barrier of wood and sharp iron. Through the drifting powder smoke, Katerina saw a Legionnaire hauled forward by two Dokra, his body forced onto the blades of the Erhul Horse. A man in blue reared up from the mass and stabbed his bayonet into the armpit of the right-hand Dokra. He, in turn, was promptly pistoled in the face by a Dokra officer, hurled back into the throng of his comrades. Above the scrum of Legionnaires, the defenders on the walls rained down fire and stones, bullets, arrows, spears—all falling like a lethal curtain, punching into bodies, crushing bones, ripping skin, blood spraying about the breach like a dozen untended water hoses.

The Legionnaires recoiled, pushed back from the breach, then they gathered themselves for one last effort, the dead and wounded tangling the legs of the living, a man with a drawn sword, face blackened by powder and blood, leading the charge. The Dokra had pulled back suddenly from the lip, leaving dozens of their own casualties impaled on the barricade. Fifty men in blue, many wounded or bloody lunged forward in a howling mass at the Erhul Horse, shooting blindly, stabbing with their bayonets, some trying to rip the sharp blades free from the wooden barricade with their bare hands. One huge Legionnaire seemed to have got under the biggest cross timber and was lifting it with his back, shoving it aside with main strength to make room for his comrades to flood in. The huge, metal-spiked balk of wood was rising, rising . . .

And another blast of canister blew him and a dozen of his comrades to bloody rags. The Dokra returned, muskets reloaded, some now with sidearm pistols, and smashed a devastating volley into the dazed and bloodied men cowering on the rubble outside.

Then it was over. The Legionnaires were running, scrambling down the slope, tripping over the wounded and dead, stumbling but fleeing as fast as they could—and leaving a reeking, steaming, writhing mound of their own people on the lip of the breach.

K aterina felt cold and sick as she witnessed the slaughter of her soldiers. The long stair of broken rock was thick with corpses, hundreds of dead, the rubble at the top entirely carpeted with blue, and the 42nd Legion was now in full retreat; even the wounded were crawling down the slope to escape the murderous hail of missiles from the walls, which had neither slackened nor ceased with the retreat. A thin line of red-coated Dokra at the lip of the breach continued to flay the fleeing troops, the mercenaries firing muskets at will and dropping man after man, and leaving no one in any doubt who the victors of the contest had been.

The first survivors were at the base of the rubble slope, and noncommissioned Legion officers down in the dry ditch, whistles blowing, were directing them back up the other side and away to their trenches. Blinded men, or men missing parts of their limbs, men who were blood-drenched, powder-blackened and completely spent trickled back toward the start position. Some merely collapsed on the city road, sinking to their knees, toppling over, unable to force themselves to go a single step farther now that they were out of range of the killers on the walls. There were a few score among them who were not visibly injured, white-faced, shaking men, many without muskets, but men who were at least bodily whole.

"Well, that's that," said Major Sung, who was standing beside Katerina, his arms held rigidly behind his back, his face pale. "What are your orders, now, Highness?"

"Could we try one more time with the reserve. Could we send them in again?"

"Again?" He stared at her as if she were mad. "Did you not see what just took place up there? Were you not paying attention? You just slaughtered more than a third of my Legion, woman, in a scant quarter of an hour. And you want to send them in *again?*"

Katerina did not care for the way the major was speaking to her—but neither could she stem her sickening flood of guilt at the failure of the assault. It was, indeed, entirely her fault. Colonel Wang had tried to warn her—but she had insisted. One last throw of the dice. And she had lost. Now the Colonel was dead. And she had killed or wounded hundreds of her men, her fine, loyal men along with him. Looking out over the blood-rinsed slope, the human wreckage strewn along it, the shattered men limping back toward their trenches, she knew herself to be close to tears. But she knew if she wept now, it would open a floodgate.

"You had better run along and see to the wounded, Major Sung," she said curtly. "We shall hold our position here for the time being. Double rations and a double tot of marak to all the men tonight, I think. And please thank them all for their heroic efforts."

Major Sung glared at her, too angry to speak. He turned on his heel and stomped away.

Katerina slumped into the canvas folding chair at the rear of the dugout. She could have done with a double tot of marak herself; a whole bottle would be nicer. But she resisted the urge to call for alcohol. She must be clearheaded. She must organize her thoughts.

She could not send the Legion up against the walls again. That was obvious—quite apart from the unbearably horrific slaughter in the breach—if she lost too many more men, she would not have enough muskets to hold Istana Kush when the Federation came. That is, if she ever did fully capture it. So what to do now? What to do? Think! Maybe if they all withdrew to the Green and Red Forts, with sufficient powder and shot, enough food . . .

She found something was digging uncomfortably into her side. It was a stiff, folded piece of paper in her breeches pocket. She pulled it out and noted the bloody finger marks on the white. She opened the folds. It was the list that the unfortunate Dokra prisoner taken at the Red Fort had provided of the Federation officers inside the Governor's Palace. She had half forgotten about it. Now she scanned the list again and a tiny flicker of hope burst into life in her breast. There was one more thing she could try. Just one more. Then it was truly over.

"Ari," she said, and the knight was immediately beside her, looming over her menacingly in his black armor. "Ari Yoritomo, I must ask you to do something for me. A service. A mission. It is, I am afraid to say, a very dangerous and difficult task."

CHAPTER 45

"Ah yes, the money," said Mamaji. "I thought you might bring that up, Farhan dear."

The newest colonel of the Amrit Shakti, exhausted, his left hand newly bandaged but his body still filthy, stinking of blood, burned powder and mangrove swamp stood before her in the Round House, and wished he were almost anywhere else. He and three other men had escaped from the Green Fort, made their way through the jungle to the rendezvous point with Captain Hawill. They had taken his ship farther upstream, along the twisting, stinking waterway and hidden it under a huge, drooping banyan tree. Captain Hawill did not wish to attempt the journey back to Istana Kush in broad daylight now that the ire of the enemy ships had been raised—he was Singarasam bound, he told them, and no longer cared to risk his precious vessel in the middle of a full-scale war—and Farhan did not have the strength to argue with him. He had half a mind to seek passage with the Frankish captain himself, even to Singarasam, but first he had to get his promised money from Mamaji.

All day long they sat under the banyan and listened to the crack, crack, crack of the *Egil*'s cannon as it pounded the walls of the palace, and sipped raw marak from a filthy leather bottle and nibbled dry ship's biscuits. In the afternoon, for a quarter of an hour, they thought they could hear the roar of men and the popping of muskets, and then there was quiet. As the shadows lengthened and the mosquitoes began to whine about them, Hawill guided the ship back down the river and into the Strait without incident. They gave the lone warship in the center of the channel a wide berth—it was now brightly lit and with a certain amount of mournful singing coming from the decks—and staying on the far side of the Strait, they headed round the lighthouse point to be dropped off at the Small Harbor.

There had evidently been a great battle that day—ending in a victory for Mamaji, and she was clearly in a jubilant mood. The Round House had lost the glass from two of the big windows, the two brass cannon had disappeared from the prow, and the room was filled with wounded officers, sleeping or moaning on pallets everywhere. *At least I managed to avoid that bloodbath*, Farhan told himself. *Least I'm not dead, too.*

"I have thought long and hard about this," said Mamaji, "and I am not sure that General Vakul would ever agree to granting such a huge sum to a serving officer of the Amrit Shakti. I'm sure you understand, Farhan dear. We would be setting a dangerous precedent. The brave men and women of the Shakti serve the Federation out of loyalty and a sense of duty, not for grubby financial gain. That is not to say that I, and the whole of the Federation are not profoundly grateful for all you have achieved. One ship sunk, another badly damaged. You've done absolute wonders, Farhan dear."

"I just want you to keep your word, Mamaji. You promised me the money, indeed, you twice promised it. I have done all that you asked. Colonel Bandi is dead and so are most of the men you sent with me. I only survived by a miracle."

"Can't do it, dear. I'm so sorry. Every officer in the service would be angling for a payout on every difficult mission if we were to allow this huge transaction to proceed. However, I have decided to pay you a bonus of five hundred ringgu, for service above and beyond the call of duty—here, I have a draft of the money, drawn on the Bank of Dhilika but good anywhere in the world, for that amount, signed by the General himself. It comes, of course, with our grateful thanks for your extraordinary courage and resourcefulness both at the Green Fort and in Yawa, too. You've done very well, dear!"

In his dismay, Farhan did not pause to wonder how the General's signature might happen to be on the oblong of thick cream paper, embossed with gold, that he now found himself clutching. He felt as if a huge stone was sitting on his heart. All his fine plans, the settlement of his debts, everything he had hoped for had been swept away.

"But you promised . . ." He knew his tone was that of a child denied a treat but he found he could not change it. "You gave me your word, Mamaji. I risked my life for you . . . I need that money and my discharge from the Shakti. I must have them. I've had enough, Mamaji. I cannot go on like this anymore. I cannot . . ."

"Now, Farhan dear, get a grip on yourself. You have the thanks and praise of the General himself, a fine promotion, and the Order of the Elephant to wear on your breast. And as you can see"—she gestured vaguely at the window at the black zigzagging line of Legionnaires' trenches and the shattered town below—"the Federation is in dire need of your services. We may have held our ground today but we are not out of the woods yet. I cannot give you a huge fortune and release you from our service just yet."

"I—Want—My—Money." Farhan's bandaged left hand was bunched in the material of the garish sari, the draft crumpled in his right; his nose was inches from Mamaji's. He was shouting madly, drops of spittle spattering her. "Give—Me—My—Fucking—Money!"

"Control yourself, Colonel Madani. This is the way it must be. Surely you can see it." Mamaji's normally light and girlish tone had changed, dropping almost to a growl. Farhan felt something poke hard against his ribs, looked down and saw the diminutive maid, Lila, at his side, a long pistol pressed tightly into his waist. The maid pulled back the cock on the gun with a loud double click.

He let go of Mamaji, and stepped back, panting.

"Farhan dear," said Mamaji, once more in her usual tone, "I can see you're overwrought. Given the circumstances, your heroic work at the Green Fort, I can quite understand how you might feel a little frayed. I suggest that you return to your quarters and rest for a while. Think about your promotion, think about the honor of the Order of the Elephant. And when you are fit for duty again, come back to my side refreshed and ready. We will need good men like you in the coming days. And fear not. Istana is not lost. Help is coming. All we have to do is hold fast and all will be well."

Farhan turned and began to walk across the Round House toward the door.

"One more thing, Farhan dear."

Without meaning to, in fact without any of his own volition, Farhan turned his head. He caught a glimpse of several Dokra officers and members of the former Governor's staff gaping at him. He looked directly at Mamaji and the small dark servant with the large pistol standing beside her.

"We had several reports in Dhilika last year that cast doubt upon your trustworthiness as an agent of the Shakti. Some were saying that you had been compromised during a foreign posting—a grubby little liaison with some slip of a girl that might put you and us at risk. I am telling you this for your own good, although I am breaching a strict directive in doing so. General Vakul sent me here to keep an eye on you. And I have done so. Some men within the Shakti were suggesting that you might have the potential to be disloyal. I think they were wrong. I think you are a true and faithful Federation officer—and your actions in the Green Fort have confirmed that fact to me. But I do hope you won't make me look a fool in the General's eyes."

Farhan said nothing. He turned again and walked out the door.

CHAPTER 46

Extract from *Ethnographic Travels* by
Professor Tolmund K. Parehki of the University of Dhilika

*The myth of Vharkash the Rain-Bringer is still popular to this day
in the islands of the Laut Besar—despite the lush nature of the land
and the absolute dependability of the monsoon rains. It clearly dem-
onstrates that the New People of the region have not forgotten their
millennia-old roots as immigrants from the parched plains of the
Indujah Peninsula. I was told this version by a shadow-puppet
master in the city of Sukatan who seemed to think it was still relevant in the modern age.*

Once, long ago, during a terrible drought on the north Indujah
plain, Vharkash, then in the incarnation of a young man, had
watched the crops die all around Him, and then the animals, and
then the people. The God sat meditating on the people's suffering
beneath a towering banyan tree. Then, summoning His strength,
He sent His spirit up the roots, into the branches and leaves of the
tree and He caused them to shake and thrash as if they were in a
storm. And by simulating a storm in the branches of the banyan
tree, a real storm was created through Vharkash's power, and tor-
rential rain came to the dry Indujah plain and saved all the people,
their crops and animals. Thereafter the God was known as Vharkash Rain-Bringer by the local people. He had a staff cut from
one of the branches of the banyan tree, and it was given to the headman of the village, who was told that if ever the rains failed in the
future, they should plant the staff into the ground and a spring of
sweet water would immediately bubble up from the earth.

"Well, this *is* a jolly gathering," said Hiero Mangku, hopping over the bloody bodies of the Jath guards with the help of his staff and approaching the four travelers.

Jun stared at him. He couldn't resist the shiver of fear at the sight of the sorcerer. The tall, skeletally thin man who had haunted his dreams. He was dressed exactly the same as when he had first encountered him in the burning Watergarden: a black-and-white-checkered sarong and green silk jacket under a gauzy gray cloak. He seemed to be moving a little awkwardly, as if his back or shoulder was stiff. His left hand was heavily bandaged. And his narrow, dark-skinned face was disfigured by a deep, half-healed cut. But his eyes spoke to the true evil within: gray as dusk, the iris cracked and veined with black.

"Shall I make the introductions?" said Mangku. "Very well. Great Ongkara, Lord of the Islands, may I introduce the erstwhile High Priest of the Mother Temple in Yawa, once the greatest religious house in the Laut Besar—although these days with rather disgusting humility he prefers to call himself plain Semar. The Patriarch of the Temple here in Singarasam, a very old and valued teacher of mine, I believe you already know."

Ongkara, still held in silence by Semar's mental grip, merely gazed at the sorcerer from wide, pleading eyes.

"And this young sprig is none other than Prince Arjun Wukarta, the future Son of Heaven of Taman, or so he believes. These two other persons here are . . ." Mangku frowned briefly at Ketut and Tenga . . . "some of his friends or servants or something."

He was now ten paces from Semar, who was watching him with narrowed eyes.

"I regret to inform you, Your Royal Highness, that this overbred puppy"—he flapped a hand at Jun—"and that delusional old pantaloon"—that was Semar—"have been following me—chasing me, even—across the watery wastes of the Laut Besar these past few weeks. They were hoping to recover the Kris of Wukarta Khodam, to which this princeling thinks he's rightful heir. They also tried unsuccessfully to prevent me acquiring the Dragon's Eye in Sukatan. And that futile quest has led them all the way here and into your presence today. So, now, here we all are, at last. What joy!"

Mangku closed his unbandaged right hand over the metal blade at the head of his staff. He squeezed tightly and the green crystal beneath his palm began to glow and pulse.

Nobody else seemed inclined to speak. Nobody moved. But the sorcerer was the focus of all eyes in the Audience Hall.

"So," said Mangku, "it has been a fine chase. Most exhilarating for you, I would imagine. I expect you have enjoyed some, ah, escapades. The Konda Pali mines must have been an eye-opener, eh, Prince Arjun? But now, I am afraid, your adventures are done. It is the end of the road for you all. Have any of you anything to say before I consign you all to the Seven Hells? Anything? No? No pious comments, Semar? No threats, Prince Arjun? No? I *am* disappointed."

"It is not too late for you, Hiero," said Semar slowly. "You were once a good man—and perhaps somewhere inside you part of that goodness remains. If you were to renounce the darkness, forswear blood magic and retake your vows, make reparations for the evil you have done, you could be washed clean of your sins. Vharkash is a forgiving God . . ."

Mangku sighed heavily.

"Is that the best you can do? Offer me your God's forgiveness? I'm far beyond forgiveness; I'm far, far beyond the petty morals of your parochial little *religion*."

Tenga turned to Ketut, who was standing beside her: "This long streak of green shit is your wizard, yes? The one who killed Jun's daddy and stole his sword?"

Ketut nodded.

Tenga moved. Faster almost than sight could follow, she bent, scooped up her boarding ax, and rushed straight at Mangku.

Semar shouted, "No, wait . . ."

But the blood-smeared ax blade was swinging, back, up, and it chopped down hard toward the sorcerer's bare head in a smooth, deadly arc.

Mangku pivoted the long staff in his hands, the tip rose and caught Tenga in the fork of her legs, just as the ax was descending. There was a flash of green and a crack like the snapping of a palm tree in a high wind. Tenga was blown fully across the room, smashing into the far wall. She burned, emerald fire consuming her flesh. She screamed horribly, thrashed against the wall, arms and legs smearing gore and lymph against the lime-washed walls until her blackened corpse slumped to the floor. Ketut rushed to her side, shouting her name. She knelt beside the blackened, bloody remains of her friend, cradling the sticky, charred head between her two hands, her tears falling like rain. She sobbed, wailed once, a cry torn from her heart, then grew silent.

Not another person in the Audience Hall moved a muscle. Ongkara and the Jath guards were all staring in shocked awe at the weeping girl holding the smoking body of her lover. Jun took a small, swift, sideways step toward the Obat Bale.

Semar was staring at Mangku, "You will be punished for that," he said in an odd, calm tone. His eyes were black as death. "There can be no forgiveness for you now."

"Don't be ridiculous. I do not seek your forgiveness." Mangku pointed the staff at Semar, as a teacher might indicate a word on a blackboard. "I merely seek your death!" He said a word and a streak of green shot out from the staff's tip, heading toward Semar.

The old man moved a fraction to the right and the bolt of ichor cracked into the wood of the staff he always carried, ricocheted off to the left and incinerated a hideous golden lion on a blood-red pillar in a pungent cloud of viridescent smoke.

"What?" said Mangku. "Can it really be? No . . . Have you really brought me a gift to make up for all my travels and trouble? That old stick in your hands can only be the Staff of Vharkash the Rain-Bringer. The Key of Wood. The real one—nothing else would have that kind of power. So it was *you* who found it in Dhilika. I thought it lost but all the time *you* had it. And now you have brought it here for me?"

"Not for you, forsworn and murderous priest. It will never be for you. Yes, it is a Key of Power and, yes, I took it from right under your nose in Dhilika. But you will never have it, magic-maker, blood-spiller, demon-caller, you will never have it while I draw breath."

Mangku smiled. "Never while you draw breath? Hmm, well, I can think of an easy remedy for that."

The sorcerer pointed his pulsing staff at Semar once more, taking a firm grip with both hands. He braced his feet, uttered a word, and again a lightning bolt of ichor shot out. Once again it cracked into the gnarled staff in Semar's hands and immediately bounced off. The blast of magic leaped across the room and hit Ratna Setiawan full in the chest. The Patriarch exploded in a huge ball of aquamarine fire.

"Ratna," cried Semar, suddenly appalled. "Oh, Ratna, I'm sorry . . ." He took a step toward the burning pile of bloody-emerald jelly that had once been his deputy.

Mangku said, "Spill no human blood! Ha! Spill no blood . . . and you've just killed a man. You killed him—you fool—you've finally done it. You've finally broken your vow to Vharkash. Now you know what utter nonsense that was: spill no blood, pah! How absurd! Blood is *everything*. Blood is magic. Blood is power. Blood is life. Blood is who we are—and who we can never be. Blood makes one man a Wukarta prince and another a Dewa slave. And without the generous spilling of human blood *nothing* can ever be changed!"

"I . . . I did not mean to. I did not mean to spill blood. It was an accident."

Jun had never seen Semar so distraught. He crumpled over his ancient staff, weeping, seemingly broken. Jun took another step toward the Obat Bale.

"Thank you," said Mangku. "I truly thank you. First you bring me the Key of Wood—now this. A wonderful irony to end our relationship. Thank you, Your Holiness . . . and good-bye."

Mangku turned to the surviving Jath guards. There were more than a dozen of them still standing, perhaps even a score of the burly, bearded men. He raised his bandaged left hand, fingers splayed. Jun could feel the force coming off the old sorcerer like forge heat.

Mangku said, "Listen only to me now, men of the Jath tribe. You will forget any cunning words that Semar the priest has spoken, forget them entirely, and go and kill that old worm now. Kill him. Do not harm the Rain-Bringer's Staff but kill the old man. Go."

Whatever control Semar had exerted over the Jath was gone in an instant. Blown away like smoke in a storm. The black-clad guards seemed to awake from a trance. They shook their heads, hefted their scimitars and began to move toward Semar.

Jun leaped for the Obat Bale.

Ongkara saw him coming and lunged protectively for the Kris. Jun landed with both feet on the Bale and lashed out at the King of Singarasam. A solid, two-knuckle punch with his left fist, all his weight behind it, which struck Ongkara full in his froggy little face and tumbled him off the back of the throne. Jun seized the Kris, pulled it from its sheath in one movement, and placed the pitted blade against his left palm. The blood flowed; the blade bloomed into life. A tongue of rippling red flame.

And the Prince of the Wukarta, Khodam in hand, turned to face his enemies.

He saw Ketut, still crouched beside her dead lover, and Semar backed up against a pillar trying to fend off the Jath with his old wooden staff. Mangku looked on with arms folded comfortably round his own staff and a complacent smile adorning his dark face.

Jun attacked. He leaped off the Obat Bale and brought the Khodam down on his foes. He sliced through the back of the first Jath, dividing him into two parts in a shower of red, and slashed straight through two others in the same heartbeat. He hurled himself at a group of three guards, who were just turning toward him. Cut left, cut right. Lunge. He punched the burning blade easily through a man's skull, the tip bursting out the back of his head in a sizzle of frying blood. He took one man's leg clean off, and another's arm. He was moving smoothly, unthinkingly following the patterns that War-Master Hardan had instilled in him over many years of arduous training. He employed the figure of eight that destroyed two men, one on each side of a pillar; the difficult roll and thrust that brought him up under another man's guard. The blade cut like a straight razor through stretched silk, smooth, deadly, untroubled by sinew, spine or even steel. The Jath were all aware of him now and, abandoning their mission to destroy Semar, they all converged on the slim youth with the whirling red blade. A dozen trained professional killers. A dozen deadly slicing scimitars.

Jun killed them all.

He slashed and hacked the Jath to bloody ruin, dodging their blows, swiping off limbs and splitting skulls. He felt the splashes of their hot blood on his chest and face and arms, but his heart was singing, his soul was filled with a burning joy; the blade of flame leaving beautiful red trails in the air, and nourishing his Wukarta soul. He stabbed and sliced: he danced through the lumbering bodies and the blood fell like rain in the Audience Hall. Suddenly there was Ongkara himself, borrowed scimitar in hand, slashing up at him awkwardly. Jun sucked in his stomach and the steel hissed past; then he chopped through Ongkara's thick blade as if it were a slender reed, and with a twist of his wrist, he cut once laterally with the Khodam and sent the Lord of the Islands' head rolling across the floor.

Jun stopped. The blood mist cleared before his eyes and he saw that he was surrounded by the dead and fallen wounded. Semar was still by his pillar, unharmed, still clutching his staff in front of him. Mangku was staring at him awestruck from the far side of the room.

He was aware that there was a foul stench in the air, the stink of rotting, corrupted flesh—and yet the dark bodies he had made were fresh; some were even still feebly moving.

Mangku said, "Wukarta blood. Like father, like son."

Jun took a step toward him, lifting the Khodam high, small scarlet flames still flickering along its wavy, blood-clogged edge.

"And the son shall die, in the same manner that his father did," said Mangku. He gave a high, harsh cry, a word of timeless power; there was a creaking-cracking noise and the sorcerer's body disappeared; the long, steel-and-jewel-topped staff clattered to the marble floor. And where the tall man had stood was a large buzzing, pulsating, amorphous mass, glinting black and green. A swarm of tiny, angry flies.

The flies formed into a sphere bigger than a bull buffalo, rose in the air high above Jun's head, brushing the high ceiling of the Audience Hall, filling the whole vast chamber with their angry, sawing whine. The mass of flies hovered above Jun, who raised the Khodam, pointing it at the center of the swarm, yet knowing it would be useless against these thousands of tiny green-and-black bodies.

Then, out of the corner of his eye, on the very edge of vision, he saw something move. Something huge. Something horrible. Something utterly terrifying.

From the spot by the wall where the cooling remains of Tenga lay, Dargan the Witch Goddess, consort of Vharkash, Queen of Fire, rose up to her full height.

She was a gigantic figure, twice as tall as a man, with huge bulging red-and-black-ringed eyes, with curled, protruding fangs and claws of an enormous tiger. The rotting smell grew stronger and Jun saw the glistening pink necklace of human entrails around her neck, and at her waist a belt of skulls knotted together with flaps of rotting skin. Dargan took one huge stride toward Jun and he instantly forgot the looming cloud of death above his head and could do nothing but stare mesmerized as the she-monster advanced on him. He dropped the Khodam with a clatter and felt the hot, shameful spurt of urine down his thigh.

Dargan roared, louder than a thousand lions, a noise to break the sky. The fat, blood-red pillars of the Audience Hall shook like saplings under its power. And with that mighty roar came flame: a great, searing, belching tongue of fire, red, orange, yellow, which surged out of her opened jaws and licked deep into the mass of flies.

The insects exploded, popping in bursts of iridescent green and scarlet, indigo and coal black, like the burst of a Han firework high in the heavens. Dargan breathed again and another blast of fire rippled through the depleted swarm. The noise of the tiny, exploding bodies continued for a time, a string of distant firecrackers now, growing fainter. And with a thump, the body of Mangku the sorcerer fell out of the air on top of his abandoned staff.

It was clear that the sorcerer had been mauled. His skin was blackened by the flames almost as badly as poor dead Tenga's, and his body was diminished, too, smaller in form as if a quarter of his flesh, bone and fat had been burned away by the blast of Dargan's breath.

The Witch Goddess stood over the body of Mangku, stooped and slashed once with her tiger-clawed hand, the strike lacerating the crusted, blackened flesh of the sorcerer's back, cutting four bloody channels through the living meat. For Mangku still lived despite the fiery punishment he had endured. He turned one red-raw blistered cheek up toward the she-monster above him, and mumbled a single ancient word.

There was another loud crack. And Mangku's mangled body transformed once more—a chittering horde of cockroaches, shiny brown with grease, appeared where his prone body had been, and they scuttled in every direction, slipping under the corpses of the Jath, scrabbling through holes in the skirting boards and out of the wide-open doors on each side of the Hall. Dargan gave one last gigantic roar and her flame-breath blasted the marble floor, catching a single slow-moving cockroach and vaporizing it in an instant.

But the rest of Mangku was gone.

CHAPTER 47

———————◦❍◦———————

He was woken by a soft knocking on the door. It was full dark and for a moment Farhan was frightened by the sound. His whole body was aching, his hand was throbbing and he felt shaky and weak as he climbed out of the cot in the tiny bedroom he had been allocated in the rear of the Governor's Palace and made his way to the door. He peered out into the courtyard outside. A dark, slim shape slipped through the crack as he opened it, brushing past him. And Farhan found himself staring in the light of the crescent moon that gleamed through the narrow window into an intense pair of dark eyes. The man was dressed in soft black cloth and only the upper part of his face was uncovered. A long, curved sword in a black-lacquer sheath was strapped to his back and protruded above his black-cloth-covered head. Far too late, Farhan thought: *Assassin!* And fumbled on the desktop for the unsheathed sailor's knife he had been using the day before to open his correspondence. The moment his groping hand touched the handle, the man's palm slapped down on top of his, snake fast, pinning it to the table.

He said, "You don't need a weapon, lord. I come as a friend."

Farhan gaped at him. The man pulled down the mask that covered the lower part of his face with his left hand and Farhan saw that he had the features of a Celestial or someone from those northern regions. But it was not that which shocked him. The man had spoken to him in the Khevan tongue. He understood the words perfectly—he had painstakingly learned the language during his stint in the Imperial city of Khev.

"Who are you?" he said, his voice unreasonably, girlishly high.

The man frowned. "I am a friend. I told you. But I have a message for you. Are you listening? This is the message, 'It is cold tonight. Cold enough to make an ice-bear shiver. Come to me and warm my bones.'"

The night was balmy, warm even. Farhan gaped at him.

Then all the memories came tumbling back.

"She is here? She is in the palace?"

"The Lady is outside the walls."

"Katerina is with the Celestial Legion?"

"The Lady commands the Legion."

Farhan stared at him. It did not make any sense: why would a Khevan princess be thousands of leagues from her home—in Istana Kush, of all places, and attacking the city with a Celestial Legion that she commanded? Was he still asleep? Was he dreaming?

"Let us have a little light at least while we talk," said Farhan. His brain was racing.

The exchange about the ice-bear had been an old signal between them. Back in Khev, she would send a messenger with those words to invite him to come to her bed. Oh, how he remembered those magical words, the joy they used to bring when he heard them. He fumbled for flint and tinder. Clumsily, he struck a spark from iron and flint, coaxed the glowing tinder into flame and encouraged the lamp to produce a flickering yellow light.

As the man in black began to talk, his voice soothing, his Khevan impeccable, Farhan struggled to follow the extraordinary twisting turns of events that had brought his princess-lover from the snow-lands of Khev to this war-torn citadel at the gateway of the Laut Besar.

He realized that part of his comprehension problem stemmed from the fact that he was badly hungover. A little before midnight Mamaji had sent her terrifying little servant Lila to his room with two bottles of Rhonos wine from the palace cellars, as well as a small, velvet case that contained a large gold coin on a black-and-red stripy ribbon: the Order of the Elephant. The wine was a gift, Lila mumbled, from the Federation. A reward for his loyal service. Much more likely, Farhan knew, Mamaji wished to check that he had not escaped from the palace, or killed himself, or anybody else, for that matter. It was a routine check on him, that was all. He had drunk both bottles of wine as swiftly as possible in an attempt to quench his rage and disappointment, and now, an hour or so before dawn, his much-battered body and wine-shrunken brain were taking their revenge on him for his excesses.

"She gave away the Principality of Ashjavat to the Celestial Empire? Just gave it away? A gift? How on Earth did she expect to get away with that?"

"The Lady is an extraordinary person, as I think you know," said the man—who had told him that his name was Ari Yoritomo, and that he was a Niho knight in her service.

"Oh, she is, she is," said Farhan. "But, please, continue with your story . . ."

He went over to his dresser, where his gun case was, and opened the long box. He fumbled inside and found a screw of paper containing a white powder, poured a little of it into an empty water cup, refilled the cup from the jug, stirred it with his finger, and drank it down. It was an obat-based preparation made from the crumbled dried leaves of the young trees and a salt made from clarified resin. He could feel it fizzing in his belly and had to grip the desk to stop himself from immediately vomiting.

Some moments later, though, he did begin to feel a little more human. The aching in his body, his sore head and cut hand ceased to trouble him and he listened spellbound as the knight told him the tale of the long voyage from Ostraka, the Martyrite assassination attempt and the brutal march along the Barat Cordillera.

A few moments later, he said again, "And she is here now, outside these walls."

"She is, lord. And she requires your help."

"I find that hard to believe. She seems to be almost superhuman. Capable of any task that she sets herself to." He could feel the obat glowing in his veins.

"Nevertheless, she asks for your help. She told me to tell you that she asks for it in the name of the love that you once shared."

"What does she want from me?"

Ari Yoritomo told him.

When he had finished, Farhan goggled at the black-clad man with his mouth open. He was not, perhaps, as shocked as he pretended. But he needed a little time to think.

Farhan was not a fool. He knew that Katerina was seeking to use him. He was nearly forty and plump and his hair was not as thick as it had once been—and most significantly he was also very poor. All he had to his name was the promissory note signed by General Vakul for five hundred ringgu in his pocket. And she did not promise her love to him, she did not promise him anything, only asked him to do this deed in the name of what they had once shared. But whatever they had shared in the past: she could not want him now, could she? Old, fat, and penniless? He realized then, in a blinding moment of clarity, that whether she wanted him or not, whether she loved him or not, it made no difference at all to his calculations. He loved *her*. That was the point. She was still his angel; his light in the darkness. During all the rackety traveling he had done, all the dangers faced, all the difficult tasks accomplished, she had always been there in his dreams. A shining vision of future happiness. And if it was a delusion, so what? He loved her. To the voyager in him, the man ever among strangers, sometimes lost and always homeless, she was his home.

Farhan thought about the Federation. It had once been his homeland, his cause, the repository of his first loyalties—but was that still the case? Had it ever truly been the case? He thought about the Amrit Shakti—and what vengeance they would take if they knew he had betrayed them. What rage he would spark in Mamaji. He thought about the way he had been cheated and tricked by her—not once but twice. He thought of Katerina, pictured her face smiling up at him, grateful. Fuck Mamaji. Fuck the Amrit Shakti. Fuck the Federation.

"I'll do it," he said.

Colonel Farhan Madani strode into the wheelhouse, a long, narrow, dusty room directly above the main gate. He wore his best black uniform, sponged and pressed as well as he could manage in his cramped apartment, his black peaked cap with the golden badge of the Amrit Shakti on the front. The medal of the Order of the Elephant was pinned to his double-buttoned breast and highly polished, knee-length riding boots adorned his feet. Behind him came his servant, or bodyguard, or whatever he was, a Celestial-looking fellow all in black, too, with a long sword strapped to his back. "Who is in command here?" Farhan snapped.

A sleepy Dokra roused himself from the pile of old sacks where he had been resting, took in this vision of martial splendor, jumped to his feet and made a crisp salute.

"Me, sir, Corporal Ranjan, sir."

"And these are your brave men?" Farhan indicated four soldiers who had swiftly formed a small line, muskets held at port, standing between a pair of the huge wooden spoked wheels that controlled the massive iron-and-oak drawbridge and portcullis below.

"Yes, sir, this is Trooper Dengu, this is Trooper Banjit . . ."

"I don't need to know all their names, Corporal."

"No, sir."

"Where is your officer?" Farhan said.

"Lieutenant Tush, sir? He's resting, sir, upstairs in his quarters."

"Right, yes, Tush. So he is resting, is he? Hmm. Well, you will send three of your best men to arrest Lieutenant Tush immediately. He is not to be unnecessarily harmed but he is to be confined to his quarters until further notice. By order of the Amrit Shakti."

The corporal looked doubtful. "We have orders, sir, not to leave the wheelhouse during our shift, under any circumstances."

"I am countermanding your orders, as of now. I am Colonel Farhan Madani of the Amrit Shakti, you may well have heard of me, and I order you to send three of your men to arrest Lieutenant Tush and confine him to his quarters. Do it, Corporal, immediately."

"Sir?"

"Do you know, Corporal Ranjan, what the Amrit Shakti does to people who do not obey their orders?"

"Yes, sir."

"Well, then, hop to it."

The corporal gave him one last searching look and then nodded at three of his men. As they filed out, Farhan noticed that the wheelhouse door had a locking bar, which allowed it to be sealed from the inside. He looked out of the greasy oblong window at the town of Istana Kush below the main gate. It was a landscape of shattered houses, shops, burned-out taverns bisected by a cobbled road, now much potholed, that led all the way to the Red Fort on the other side of the bay. There were piles of rubble everywhere, mounds of broken timbers, too, from the bombardment two days ago. He could see the line of trenches a few hundred paces away and the shiny helmets of a handful of Legionnaire sentries just showing above the parapet. There was no sign of *her*, no sign of any assault troops. Gods, he hoped this was going to work! The timing was crucial. Dawn was breaking and Farhan could hear the distant sound of a cockerel pointing out that fact to the world.

He turned to the corporal. "Well, since I am here, you had better tell me how it all works. Call it a snap inspection."

"Sir, it is simplicity itself. This lever here controls the chain on the drawbridge. You pull that and the wheel turns and lowers the bridge. This other wheel, over here, is for the portcullis. You turn it and . . ."

Corporal Ranjan got no further. There was a flash of steel and his head jumped from his shoulders and hit Farhan in the center of his chest, thumping gorily against the Order of the Elephant. He closed his eyes, mumbling an apology to the victims, and a prayer to Vharkash to forgive him for this necessary bloodshed. He heard a scream and thud of steel striking flesh and the clatter of a musket hitting the wooden floor.

He opened his eyes and saw Yoritomo, bloody katana in hand, sliding the bar across to lock the wheelhouse door from inside.

Farhan peered out of the window again, trying to ignore the fresh-blood-and-shit stink, the two half-dismembered bodies and the gummy red pools forming beside his shiny black boots. He stared through the glass and could see nothing out of the ordinary out there.

"Dawn, she said; today, she said. You are quite sure, man?"

Yoritomo did not deign to reply. He was at the right-hand wheel, looking at the long, iron lever. He glanced once with eyebrows raised at Farhan, who gave a small shrug.

Ari pulled the lever, there was a terrifying clanking noise, and the drawbridge slowly began to lower itself jerkily. Down, pause, down. The noise got louder and louder. Until the bridge crashed against the far side of the dry ditch, a crunch that must surely alert everyone even half-awake in the palace as to what they were doing.

He looked out of the window again: still nothing. If they did not come . . . it didn't bear thinking about. He would shoot himself with one of the Dokra's loaded muskets, if it came to it, or get this strange Niho knight to end him swiftly with his long sword.

"Help me with this, lord," said Ari, now at the other wheel on the far side of the room. Farhan hurried over and between them they began to turn the wheel, lifting the portcullis, wrestling the spokes round, the iron chains creaking, groaning, protesting. The spiked-and-barred gate rose slowly, and it took all of their combined strength to force the wheel round. Once again the clanking noise was appalling. How could any defender sleep through this?

They secured the wheel with a lever and stout pin, and Farhan darted back to the window and looked out.

Nothing. Nobody there. He was a dead man. And if Mamaji got hold of him, and if she found out what he had done . . . O Gods, it would mean unimaginable pain, the kind of pain that makes you beg for . . .

And there she was. She appeared as if by magic. He felt as if a cold hand had seized his heart. A slight figure in a dirty linen shirt and fawn-colored breeches, her white-blond hair tied back, a long, shining saber in her right hand: Katerina. The woman he loved.

She was running along the road toward the dropped drawbridge, coming toward him, seemingly alone. No! Now there was a crowd of half a dozen figures all around her, masked men clad in black-lacquered armor. And behind them yet more folk. A mob of hundreds of blue-coated soldiers. They were all roaring something as they ran forward. A war cry.

"Kat-er-rina! Kat-er-rina!" Hundreds of charging men shouting out her beloved name.

A wash of relief swept through him. She was coming; she was coming to him!

He could clearly hear the cries of the Legionnaires, now, as the column passed under the wheelhouse—"Kat-er-rina! Kat-er-rina!"—

and more shouts and shots, screams and confused yelling, coming from below his shiny-booted feet.

There were noises from outside the locked wheelhouse door, too, someone, a Dokra officer, battering at it and angrily demanding admittance. But the door was solid. He listened for a while to the furious cursing, watched the thick timber shake as musket butts pounded it. But it held. It would hold.

He went over to the pile of sacks in the corner of the room and slumped down, listening to the sounds from below; awful screams, the popping of muskets, roars of rage, the clashing of steel on steel, the smashing of wood. Suddenly the noise, the chaos seemed to be coming from all around, even from above the wheelhouse. He closed his eyes again. It was the sound of a citadel that had been breached; it was the sounds of a sack, of pillage, of men who had been defied, and badly mauled by the defenses of a city, unleashed and eagerly seeking revenge. The sound of rape and murder. The sound of terror. The sounds of hundreds of people awakened to disaster, fighting for their very lives.

The battering at the door suddenly ceased.

Ari Yoritomo crouched beside him, and looked into his face. Farhan saw then that the man's eyes were a deep blue color, not black as he had imagined.

"You have done well, lord," he said. "The Lady will be pleased."

CHAPTER 48

———— ⚬❦⚬ ————

Mamaji bustled down the dark staircase behind the small figure of Lila, who was carrying a mound of luggage, and two other palace servants, who were also heavily laden. They were making for the rear of the palace for the sally port on that flat-walled side.

She had watched with incredulity from up in the Round House as, without any warning at all, in the first light of dawn, the ancient drawbridge had thumped down across the dry ditch. Instantly, a knot of half a dozen black-clad figures concealed on the far side of the moat behind a mound of timber had popped out and rushed forward across the ancient wood with long steel in their hands that reflected the weak rays of the rising sun. In their midst was a girl not yet seventeen, by Mamaji's reckoning, with a drawn saber in her hand.

Niho, she thought. What in the name of the Seven Hells are Niho knights doing in this part of the world? And who is *she*?

Behind them she could see at least three companies of Legionnaires, bayonets fixed, charging out of their hiding places and sprinting forward toward the open main gate. They were shouting something, three syllables that she could not quite make out. Now they were on the drawbridge, boots thundering on the wood, and now surging inside the palace. The noise of battle erupted below her: screams and shots. Her Dokra were fighting down there—and dying. The realization of disaster crashed over her. The enemy had broken her defenses. It was all over; it was truly all over. It was too late to hope for help. Istana Kush was lost.

Time to go. And she would have to go fast.

The secret door that opened at the base of the rear wall of the palace was painted the exact same streaked gray-stone color as the surrounding grimy walls. Mamaji poked her big head out. There was no one within fifty paces of the door.

Mamaji beckoned her three servants to follow her out of the palace. As she closed the door behind her she could hear the musket shots, the banging of blades, roars of rage and dying yelps as the Legionnaires took revenge for the slaughter at the breach the day before.

"Come along, dears," she said. "We must hurry on a little. No time to dillydally."

The little party stumbled down the rocky slope that led down to the Small Harbor. There were few people about on land but all the watercraft were by now alerted to the disaster of the fall of the palace; the sounds of the battle were clear even down here. There was fevered activity on the larger vessels, most making ready to leave as soon as possible and the lighter boats whizzing around conveying messages, rumors, requests, between them. At the water's edge, she produced a pair of gold coins; their glint summoned a woman in a conical hat in a one-oared dragonfly-craft, splish-splashing swiftly and efficiently through the weak morning light toward them.

"The *Mongoose*," she said. "Take us out to the *Mongoose*."

Captain Lodi was adamant. "No, Mamaji, with the greatest respect, I will not take you to Singarasam. The *Mongoose* would be instantly seized if she were to show her nose in that foul port. Do you think Ongkara has forgotten what we did in his name, under his flag?"

They were in the large cabin of the ship where Mamaji had installed herself and, once the Istana servants were dismissed, Lila was unpacking her mistress's belongings.

"Cyrus dear, we do not have very much time. You are aware, surely, that the Governor's Palace is under attack. The enemy are, in fact, inside the citadel. We must go, and go now, and go straight to Singarasam, where we can find shelter and friends.

"No, Mamaji, I will wait for Farhan. *He's* my friend and at times like this you need your friends. Furthermore, when he arrives, and I'm sure he'll be along very shortly indeed, we will not be going anywhere near Singarasam. I can positively assure you of that."

"He may already be dead, you do know that?"

Lodi shrugged. "I will wait for him anyway."

"Cyrus Lodi, I would hate to have to report your stubbornness to General Vakul. I am afraid it might look very much like insubordination to him. I really don't think you want that sort of permanent black mark against your name. Do you, dear?"

"It cannot be insubordination—I do not work for you, nor the General, nor even for Farhan, except on a contractual basis."

Captain Lodi was trying very hard to hold on to his temper. But he had had enough of this insufferable woman and her bullying ways. "Our mission is over," he said slowly and carefully, as if speaking to a child. "I have been paid, plus a very mean, and I must say grudging bonus considering the dangers faced, so my obligation to you is now at an end. I am not an employee of the Amrit Shakti—and I hope never to have the misfortune to be one."

"Oh, don't be such a timid mouse, Cyrus—that's not like you at all. We will make a fine new contract—with a handsome bonus written into it. Besides, Ongkara and the captains of his pirate swarm will now be heading east to confront the Grand Fleet of the Celestial Republic that is even now bearing down upon Singarasam. I have had reports that Ongkara has, in fact, already left. He won't be there. And we could change the ship's name, disguise her somehow, if you are truly concerned for your safety. Anyway, I would only ask that you drop Lila and me at the harbor. You could touch the quay and go—with your payment, plus a substantial bonus in your hand. Shall we say ten thousand ringgu in all?"

"I am not going to say this again. I will not take you to Singarasam."

"I would hate to have to report to General Vakul that you, a formerly loyal citizen of the Federation, were being difficult about this," said Mamaji. "What would our good General think of you then?"

Captain Lodi lost his patience. He shouted, "I could not give a ten-kupang arse-fuck what General Gods-damned Vakul thinks of me."

"I wonder if you would use the same intemperate language if you were in the presence of General Vakul himself," said Mamaji, frowning at him.

"Well, I'm not."

"Are you sure? Before you answer, let me ask you one question. Have you ever seen General Hamil Vakul?"

Lodi shook his head.

"Have you ever met anyone who has met him—face-to-face?"

Lodi just stared at her.

"I thought not. Only a handful of people have. Well, then, I will let you into a rather special secret of state. There is no General Hamil Vakul. He doesn't exist. He is a phantom of *my* imagination—and everybody else's, of course. Or, if you prefer to think of it another way, *I am General Vakul*. For I am the one who truly controls the Amrit Shakti."

The sailor just shook his head at her. He closed his eyes. "No," he said, "no."

"Captain Lodi—I hereby commandeer your ship the *Mongoose*

in the name of the High Council of the Indujah Federation," said Mamaji formally. "I will issue you with the correct paperwork in due course but for now you are to waste no more time and set a course to the city of Singarasam. We must leave here without further delay."

"No! No—it cannot be true!"

Mamaji sighed. "Must I do this? It appears so. Very well, Captain Lodi, I will say only this to you: Compound 44, Upper Jasmine Avenue, South Sector, Dhilika."

"What? That is my parents' house. That is their address."

"I know that. I also know that you have a wife and two young sons living in the compound with your parents—is that not correct?"

"Uh, yes. What of it?"

"Do I really need to spell it out for you? If you disobey me, you will be declared a traitor to the Federation. Do you know what happens to the families of traitors?"

"Yes. I've heard . . . things." Captain Lodi's tanned face had gone white as milk.

"Very good—now there has been more than enough delay," said Mamaji. "You will set a course for Singarasam immediately."

"You are a monster," said Lodi, slowly. "You are a vile creature beyond . . ."

"I have been told all that many times before. Now, will you obey me or will you make your whole family suffer for your stubbornness?"

"Yes," Lodi whispered.

"Yes what?"

"Yes, Mamaji," said the captain.

CHAPTER 49

The servant in the absurd golden coat was standing in the slid-back door in the side wall of the Audience Hall and looking inside, awestruck at the carnage. The bodies of more than twoscore Jath guards—some still alive and moaning, weeping—covered the marble like a bloody, black, moving carpet. The charred bodies of two human forms lay in still-gently-smoking, slightly greenish heaps, one by each wall. One pace from the servant's slippered feet was the decapitated head of Ongkara.

Semar took charge. "You there, the golden fellow! Summon the rest of the palace servants and get this dreadful mess cleared up quick as you can. And send for the healers of the Temple of Vharkash. Some of these men's lives may still be saved. Quick now!"

"Who *are* you?" said the servant.

"We are the ones who have justly executed the Lord of the Islands, the corrupt and foul tyrant Ongkara, and massacred his elite bodyguard. I might also mention that we have bested his evil sorcerer in a contest of magic. We are the new occupiers of the First House—therefore, we are your new masters, that is, if you wish to keep your employment. So, off you go, quick, summon your servant friends and send for the temple healers."

The golden man turned on his heel and disappeared without another word.

"Why did you not just seize his mind and compel him to do that?" said Jun sourly.

"That takes a good deal of mental energy and I am . . . I am very tired just now. The fellow will do as he is told, my prince, never fear."

Jun felt the wave of tiredness hit him, too, just then. Wielding the awesome power of the Khodam had left him completely drained. He longed for somewhere to sit down but the Audience Hall was bereft of chairs. Finally, his knees sagging, he climbed up onto the Obat Bale, lifted the upended gilded throne, positioned it in the center of the white mass and sank down in its surprisingly comfortable seat.

"A throne suits you," said Ketut. It was the first time she'd spoken since transforming back into her usual shape. She stood at the base of the Obat Bale and looked up. "I didn't think it would, rich-boy, but it does. You look—well . . . quite regal."

Jun saw that her eyes were red from weeping but she seemed otherwise unaffected by her possession. He glanced at the heap against the wall that was all that remained of Tenga.

"My deepest condolences for the loss of your . . ." Jun had no idea how to express his sadness for the death of their comrade. "I'm so sorry about Tenga."

Ketut looked down at the floor. She sniffed. "She is with the Queen of Fire now. I know that. I saw her go there into her keeping when I was in that . . . other place."

"How do you do that, Ketut?" Jun asked. "I mean, how do you summon the Goddess without, you know, without the temple, the smoke, the music . . ."

"I don't know. Semar has been teaching me some things. But it mostly comes from anger. Anger is the trigger, I think. And my scar, too. And when Tenga was . . ." She stopped suddenly. "I truly don't know," she said, and bent down and picked up the Kris of Wukarta Khodam that was lying at her feet, where Jun had dropped it. The flames were all now extinguished, the fresh blood, too, had been completely burned away and it once again merely resembled an ordinary dull gray, pitted blade.

"So this is what the fuss was about," she said, examining the sword carefully.

She touched the ball of her thumb to the blade and swore.

"It's a sharp old thing, isn't it?"

Nobody answered her. Every eye in the Audience Hall was on the ancient blade, which, at the touch of her drawn blood, had begun to pulse and glow. Ketut stared at the Kris; hungry flames were now licking along its wavy edges.

"How do you turn it off?" she said, shaking the blade as if it were a burning stick removed from the fire that she wished to extinguish.

Semar came and took the Kris from her hand. The flames disappeared but the blade glowed for a few moments before returning to its gray-metallic form.

The servants had returned and were beginning to carry away the dead and wounded. Very carefully, Semar handed the Kris up to Jun, who slotted it back in its wooden scabbard and placed it in its stand. He did all this while barely looking at the Kris. For his eyes were fixed on Ketut, an expression of questioning wonder illuminating his face.

"Oh yes, did I not mention that before?" said Semar, looking just a little smug. "Ketut is the illegitimate daughter of your father, Jun, the late Son of Heaven, who had a very brief though extremely passionate liaison with her mother some sixteen years ago. I thought I'd made this quite clear already. I certainly dropped you enough hints."

"She's my sister?" Jun could not believe he was saying these words.

"Half sister, yes. But she has the blood of the star princess in her veins, as you do, which is why the Khodam can be wielded by her just as well as you. I brought her along, in case you . . . Well, as a spare. No, not that, ah, what I mean is, for a little extra assurance that we would achieve all our goals."

"You planned all . . . this." Jun gestured to the blood-streaked marble, to the pair of servants who were hauling away the last of the dead Jath by his heels. "From Taman, from the destruction of the Watergarden, from the death of my father—you had all this in your mind, the killing of Ongkara, the death of Tenga, the confrontation here with Mangku."

"Well, I wouldn't say I planned it. No, not planned exactly, but I had suspected that Ratna was in league with Mangku for some time and I confess that I had hoped that we might have a confrontation. We followed Mangku from Taman hoping to take back the Khodam: that was the plan we all agreed to. And I was confident that, tonight, if you could manage to summon your power, Ketut, and Jun could wield the Kris, then, well, between us all we could handle Ongkara, the Jath, and the sorcerer. Seems to have worked out, too."

"Did you know Tenga would die?" Ketut said. She suddenly looked extremely angry, extremely dangerous. Her eyes, still red from her tears, now glittered with an unholy fire.

"No, no, absolutely not. And I am heartily sorry for it. But let us remember that it was not me who killed her; it was the sorcerer. It was Hiero Mangku. He is your enemy. Not me. I never wished your friend, our comrade Tenga to come to any harm. I swear it."

"But you told me that my destiny was to find love. And you saw richboy here on the Obat Bale. What did you see for Tenga?"

"She *was* a great warrior, Ketut; she was never going to enjoy a comfortable old age, knitting by the fire with a cup of warm milk, her grandchildren gathered at her feet."

Ketut said nothing. She was looking at the corpse of her lover, which was now being gathered up into a silk sheet by the golden servant and one of his fellows. The tears were once more running freely down Ketut's thin cheeks.

Jun said, "So what now? A ship back to Taman for all of us? You would both be most welcome to make a home with me in the Watergarden—when it's been completely rebuilt."

"Jun, Ketut, I want both of you to listen to me," said Semar. "Please give me your full attention. Mangku is badly hurt, but he escaped tonight and will surely recover in time. He has two of the Keys of Power. And he will not rest until he has all seven of them. He will come for the Khodam again, my prince. And next time he will not come bursting through the door with fire and sword. He will come in stealth; he will attack your mind or the minds of those around you. He will seek to destroy you in order to possess the Kris. This struggle is far from over."

Jun moved uneasily on the throne. "So what do you suggest?"

"I shall do what I vowed to do all those years ago. I shall track him again, I shall find him and I shall cause his end. And, Jun, believe me, if you want to keep possession of the Khodam, not to mention your life and lands, you will help me do this as soon as possible."

"How can I do that?"

There was the sound of a cough from the doorway. Jun was astonished to see a small, dumpy figure in a long, green silk gown, a little too tight around the middle.

"I hope you will forgive me for interrupting," said Xi Gung. "But I may be able to offer some little advice and assistance on this matter."

Jun was too surprised to see the little Han merchant to answer but Semar said, "Yes, that would be most helpful. If you please, Lord Xi, would you be so good as to tell my friends what we discussed last night?"

"Certainly, Your Holiness. What my venerable friend and I discussed after the temple ceremony was the, um, succession of the Lordship of the Islands."

Everyone in the room, except Semar, who now had his eyes shut, stared at Xi Gung.

"Ongkara was an admirable man in some respects," the merchant continued, "very good at keeping the pirate chieftains in line, for example. He threw some excellent parties, as well. Can't take that away from him. But he was also, in other ways, a very difficult man to do business with, not an ideal ruler at all, in fact. His notions on the payment of tribute were rather old-fashioned, hidebound, even; his tax system, and the methods he used to collect his grossly swollen revenues, was thought to be a little on the harsh side by many leading citizens of Singarasam, myself included. In short, I and a number of other figures of influence in this city felt that it was time for him to step down and for a younger, fresher and, how shall I put this delicately, less *greedy* man to take up the reins of power."

"What my friend is saying, Jun, is that you should accept the title of Lord of the Islands." Semar smiled up at him. "As the position is now so obviously vacant."

Jun was conscious that he was sitting on the actual throne, on the Obat Bale of the Lord of the Islands. But the idea Semar and Xi Gung were proposing was absurd.

He laughed. "And I—what?—just declare myself to be Lord of the Islands? I sit here on this overstuffed sack of crumbling leaves and expect everyone to bow down and grovel nicely at my feet. You've gone completely mad, Semar; you are moon-crazed."

"Is that so hard to imagine?" said Semar. "Who was Ongkara but an adventurer, a successful pirate before he seized the Obat Bale? You are a prince of the Wukarta; the blood of the star princess runs in your veins. You were born to rule Taman, trained to it from birth—why not seek to rule more than one tiny island? You are the rightful wielder of the Kris of Wukarta Khodam. You have just slain the tyrant; you will bring peace and prosperity to the whole of the Laut Besar: Arjun the Great, men will call you."

"All right, Semar, enough. I like flattery as much as any man but this is plain silly."

"You would have the full financial backing of the House of Xi," said the merchant, "and most of the other lesser trading houses in Singarasam would support you, too."

"There is also, sadly, a vacancy in the position of Patriarch of the Temple of Vharkash," said Semar. "I thought I might humbly propose myself for the role, as long as they were prepared to accept my choice of deputy: I have someone very special in mind—a young woman of spiritual power and authority, a *Vessel*, they will whisper, who can conjure Dargan, the consort of Vharkash the Harvester, at her will."

"Eh?" said Ketut, wiping her snotty nose on her bare forearm.

"The Vharkashta would, I'm sure, be honored to have you as Patriarch," said Xi Gung. "And the lady Ketut as your deputy. After the ceremony last night, the faithful of Singarasam now hold her in the highest respect. I think I can guarantee that you would be unanimously voted into the position by the temple electors. And one reason for this is that I happen to be their chairman." The merchant simpered a little and tried to look modest.

"Listen to me, Jun," said Semar. "You would have the backing of the wealthiest men in Singarasam and all their ships, and also the support of all the faithful Vharkashta. Money, ships and spiritual influence. A powerful combination. You have impeccable royal blood, too; you have the Kris of Wukarta Khodam, and your charm and looks would, I am sure, make you very popular with the masses. Look! You are even now sitting in the throne of the Lord of the Islands, on the Obat Bale itself. It well becomes you. You must accept this honor, my prince. For the good of us all."

"I don't know." Jun could feel himself wavering. In truth, all he wanted was to go home. To return to Taman, to his old, luxurious, lazy life in the Watergarden. But here he was being offered more than just a throne—he was being offered an empire. He was being offered the chance to rule much of the world.

"Trust me, Jun. This is also the best way to protect yourself.

Little Taman is weak—if you were to return, Mangku would surely come there again, in greater strength than last time. What then would you do? What would *he* do to you—he would not ignore you this time—and what would he do to your poor people? But if you were Lord of the Islands, you would command thousands of men and hundreds of ships across the whole of the Laut Besar. As King of Singarasam, Lord of the Islands, Dragon of the High Seas, Lion of the Southern Lands, you could help me to destroy this evil once and for all. Only when the sorcerer is gone will you, and the rest of the world, be truly safe. It is only by accepting this honor that you can help me destroy him. I am asking you, quite simply, to save humanity."

Jun looked at Ketut, a question in his eyes. Ketut merely shrugged.

"If you are worried about the heavy burdens of office," said Xi Gung, "I am prepared to offer myself as your Grand Vizier— I shall not require any payment, naturally. I would do it purely out of a sense of duty to the city of Singarasam. But I also assure you that I could certainly ease any financial pressures that might trouble the new Lord of the Islands."

"Excuse me, my lords," said a voice. The three of them looked over at the golden-clad servant, his brilliant coat now stained here and there with fresh speckles of Jath blood. He was standing diffidently in the doorway, looking very unhappy, and wringing his hands.

"Yes?" said Semar. "What is it?"

"There is a Han gentleman here, sir, who begs for an audience with the Lord of the Islands. He demanded admittance, insisted on it, despite the late hour, and says he is a High Envoy from the Celestial Republic. He says their Grand Fleet is only twenty leagues away and he wishes to discuss reparations for the outrages that the forces of the Lord of the Islands have perpetrated against the Celestial Republic, its people and its property. He says that if full restitution is not made immediately, then most regrettably a state of war will exist between the Celestial Republic and the King of Singarasam. What shall I say to him?"

Jun looked at Xi Gung, who bowed low. "Allow me to deal with this trifling matter, Highness," the merchant said. "Let it be my first task as your loyal Grand Vizier."

"Forgive me, lords," said the servant, "but the High Envoy— what shall I say to him?"

"Show him in," said Semar.

"But he wishes to speak to the Lord of the Islands."

"The Lord of the Islands is in his rightful place, as ever, enthroned on the Obat Bale. Show the High Envoy in and allow him to make his obeisance to the King of Singarasam."

Jun said nothing at all. He leaned back in the gilded throne and placed his right hand comfortably on the worn handle of the Kris of Wukarta Khodam.

CHAPTER 50

Three days after the capture of the Governor's Palace by the men of the 42nd Legion, Katerina stood in the Round House at the top of the palace and looked out of the tall, wide, curving windows. The thick glass was cracked here and there in long jagged lines, from the bombardment by her own ship of war, *Egil*, and a section was missing, allowing a cool breeze to flow around the chamber.

The two brass cannon had been returned to their mountings on the tip of the structure, its "prow," and two longer iron cannon had been added beside them. Now all four pieces looked out over the gray-green waters of the Sumbu Strait. It was a beautiful, cloudless day, the sky a deep, joyful blue, and Katerina herself was feeling no small measure of satisfaction: as she watched, down in the Grand Harbor, her ship *Yotun*, now repaired and refitted, was being slid down the slips and back into the sea. She could faintly hear the cheer from the dock as the huge vessel splashed into the water, and she felt like giving voice to her own pleasure at the sight, too.

The *Yotun* would join the *Egil* on patrol at the southeastern end of the Sumbu Strait—and could well be heading shortly into action. Two days ago, a fast Federation frigate had been sighted a league or two out from the Istana lighthouse. The *Egil* had immediately headed out to confront it but when the guns were run out, the Federation vessel had immediately turned tail and retreated over the horizon. A scout, then. There were certainly more Federation ships out there over the horizon and it was only a matter of time before they came to Istana in all their massed might.

Katerina, however, was not as perturbed as she might have been. Istana Kush had been created as an impregnable sea fortress—and now with all its parts in her hands, Katerina felt she could give the Federation fleet a very uncomfortable time if they chose to attack her.

On the far side of the city, the Red Fort was manned by a company of Legionnaires under Lu Sung—now Colonel Sung, since as ranking major, he had succeeded to Colonel Wang's position. He had posted a strong picket to the south on the slopes of the Barat Cordillera, in case any enemy should attempt to copy Katerina's feat. He also had more than a score of Ostrakan gunners with him and the cannon and munitions to dominate the Strait. Across the water in the Green Fort, the depleted Stormer Company under a newly promoted Captain Chang was busy rebuilding the shattered walls and remounting the cannon there. They too had been amply supplied with food, powder and shot from the full magazine deep inside the Governor's Palace. No ship could enter from the west without being destroyed by these two forts, and no ship coming in from the southeast could avoid their fire either.

Down in the city, the denizens of Istana Kush had returned, in a trickle at first and then a flood, when it became clear that the fighting was over. And Katerina could see rubble being cleared, broken timbers being stacked and even new buildings rising from the former chaos. In the Grand Harbor, she had two companies of Legionnaires restoring the defenses, five batteries of two long guns each that could make the Strait a hell of fire and shot for any enemy. Istana Kush was back to its old strength. *Let the Federation ships come,* she thought. *Let them come under my guns anytime they like.*

Katerina turned away from the window and looked at the small group of people gathered in the Round House. There was

Farhan Madani, her new Minister, looking pale and tired, much older now, a little fatter, and gazing at her with barely disguised longing in his eyes. She had thanked him prettily for his actions in the wheelhouse, and asked him to serve her as her right-hand man, her adviser and confidante—but no more than that—and he had accepted. But she wondered sometimes whether he would truly be able to master his deep feelings for her. She hoped so, otherwise she would have to remove him from her company, and he was a man with many talents and too valuable to waste.

And there was Captain Tesso, the new commander of the eight surviving knights of her Niho guard, his face impassive under his black-lacquered mask.

And there was Ari, bare-faced, smiling, her knight first grade. Soon, perhaps very soon, she must send him away. That would be a hard parting. But it must be done.

And there was Major Xi Chan—also soon to be a colonel.

"How goes the recruiting for the Istana Volunteers?" she asked Chan.

"Well, Highness, surprisingly well. I now have more than four hundred recruits who have taken the oath of loyalty and I have taken the liberty of clothing them in spare Dokra uniforms and of equipping and arming them from the palace's magazines."

"Very good—you will liaise with Minister Madani about pay and rations."

"Yes, Highness."

Katerina was less surprised than her Legion officer at the uptake in the Volunteers. Any Dokra mercenary who had survived and surrendered after the fall of the palace—and there were scores who had managed to do so—had been offered a place in the ranks of the Istana Volunteers and a generous signing bonus. And there were many citizens of Istana Kush, too, their businesses ruined by the fighting in the city, who were desperate to join up to provide a steady income for their hungry families.

"I have called you all here today," Katerina said loudly, "because I wish to discuss our long-term strategy. I am confident that we can face down the threat of the Federation fleet when it arrives in the next day or so. But we must acknowledge that we now have a powerful enemy in these waters. And I should be grateful for your advice—particularly yours, Minister Madani—about how we should best proceed."

"I suspect that, if they do their reconnaissance, and you can be sure that they will, they will not attempt to attack us immediately," said Farhan. "They will recognize that the potential damage inflicted on them by our gun batteries would be too great. The Federation fleet will not be commanded by fools. Never has been. Moreover, it is important to remember what the Federation is—a group of disparate nations united by a desire to trade. Trade is the lifeblood of the Federation, the reason for its existence. And so, ultimately, we must come to an accommodation with them that allows them to trade in the Laut Besar."

"You are as wise as you ever were, Farhan," said Katerina.

And Farhan had to shy away from her gaze. *Wise? Wise like a venerable old grandfather? Was that how she thought of him now?*

"We should seek allies as soon as possible," said Major Chan.

Katerina looked at him, considering. "Go on, Major . . ."

"I should not like to trust in the good sense of the Federation and therefore assume that they will not attack us. Their pride has been hurt. One should never disregard hurt pride when it comes to war. So we must seek support from potential friends and allies. And, it occurs to me, Highness, that the Federation is not the only power in the Laut Besar. There is the Celestial Republic, of course, but it is too far away to provide any immediate military help. And then there is Singarasam, only a day or two's sail from here, and the considerable fleet of the Lord of the Islands."

"Your thinking has matched mine exactly, Major Chan," said Katerina. "An alliance with the Lord of the Islands—and cemented in the traditional way. What do you know about the King of Singarasam, Farhan?"

"His name is Ongkara, and he is a hideous little frog of a man, cunning, brutal, greedy, ruthless . . ."

"I beg your pardon, Minister," said Chan. "But I received news just this morning from a close relative of mine in Singarasam—my uncle, in fact, who wrote to tell me that there has been something of a coup in the city. Ongkara has been killed . . ."

"The traditional way for a Lord of the Islands' rule to end," murmured Farhan.

". . . and a new Lord of the Islands has taken his place. A young fellow from Taman—I believe you know him, Minister. I believe you traveled with him here from Yawa."

Farhan was taken aback. "Are you sure of this, Chan?" he said.

"Yes, indeed, Minister. My uncle who sent me this news has himself been named Grand Vizier to the new King of Singarasam—who is one Prince Arjun Wukarta."

A horrible thought was forming in Farhan's mind. "What is . . . What is your uncle's name, Major, if you don't mind me asking?"

Xi Chan smiled happily at Farhan. "His name is Xi Gung," he said. "He's a man of some stature in Singarasam. I think you are acquainted with him, Minister. In fact, I'm sure you are. He particularly asked me to send you his warmest regards."

"Enough chitchat," snapped Katerina. "We have more important matters at hand. Tell me what you know of this new Lord of the Islands, Farhan."

It took her Minister a moment to gather his thoughts. "Jun is young, handsome and athletic," he said, and then added a little sourly, "but also spoiled, lazy and not terribly bright. By that I mean I think he would be rather easy to manipulate."

"He sounds absolutely perfect," said Katerina. "No wife or longtime lover?"

"No, there were two women on the ship with him but they had

eyes only for each other. He has a brotherly kind of bond with the younger Tamani woman, nothing more."

"Excellent! Well, your next task, Farhan, is to arrange the marriage."

"Marriage?"

"Yes, marriage. We will seal an alliance between myself and the Lord of the Islands with a royal wedding. That should please the Singarasam mob. We offer the King of Singarasam control once again over the Gates of Stone—and a piece of all the wealth that flows into and out of the Laut Besar and, in return, I shall require from the Lord of the Islands cash, ships, men and protection from the vengeance of the Federation."

Katerina's tone was deliberately brisk and businesslike. There was no room now for sentimentality. "You'll be my marriage broker, Farhan. You'll work out the details. Get as much as you can from this good-looking simpleton. Best get to work on this right away."

"As you command, Highness," Farhan said. But he felt his eyes burn with tears and he turned away quickly to keep his composure. *He had what he wanted, didn't he? He was at Katerina's side—he was her closest adviser and confidante, her friend. What more could he realistically expect from her? Love,* whispered a tiny voice. *Love is but a delusion,* he told himself. And, as the door to the Round House closed behind him, he roughly cuffed the tears from his cheeks, straightened his spine and went off to do his duty.

A few moments later, Katerina dismissed her advisers and, when they had gone, she turned once again to stare out of the cracked window. It was done. She had achieved all that she had set out to do. And soon, very soon, when she was married to this easily manipulated Taman princeling, she would be joint ruler of the whole of the Laut Besar. The first stage of her plan was almost complete. She wondered, idly, if this handsome new Lord of the Islands sometimes enjoyed a pipe of obat before he slept. That would be useful. If not, there would be other methods of achieving her ultimate goal . . .

On the roof of the Red Fort, a mile away, she could see that someone was hauling a flag up the pole. As the wind caught the material, and spread it wide, she saw that it was a black flag with a huge white bear, roaring red-mouthed from the center of the dark field—her own flag, designed by her, now planted by her own men, flying over the city she had taken with her own two hands. She felt a wild soaring of her spirits, a fierce joy greater than any she had ever felt before. What would her dead father, the Emperor of Khev, have to say about her now? Would he still sneer at her sex? Maybe. But she no longer cared.

She had marched, she had fought, she had conquered—as well, perhaps even better, than any man. And the proof of it was right outside this big, half-broken window.

For the Gates of Stone were finally hers.

Photo by James Clarke

Angus Macallan is a pseudonym for Angus Donald, a British fiction writer and former journalist who is now based just outside London. He was born in China and lived, worked and studied in Asia for much of his early adult life. He was awarded a master's degree with honors in social anthropology by the University of Edinburgh, partly based on his fieldwork in Indonesia, which led to a dissertation: "Magic, Sorcery and Society." He also worked as a journalist in Hong Kong, India, Pakistan and Afghanistan. The author can be reached via e-mail at angusmacallan@icloud.com.

CONNECT ONLINE

angusmacallanbooks.com
twitter.com/angusmacallan1

Ready to find
your next great read?

Let us help.

Visit prh.com/nextread

Penguin
Random
House